ANTHOLOGIES BY THE EDITORS

Christopher Hawthorne Moss

Time's Rainbow:
Writing Ourselves Back into American History

Lori L. Lake

The Milk of Human Kindness:
Lesbian Authors Write about Mothers and Daughters

Lesbians on the Loose:
Crime Writers on the Lam

Romance for Life

Time's Rainbow:
Writing Ourselves Back into American History

Time's Rainbow

Writing Ourselves Back into American History

Edited and with an Introduction

By

Lori L. Lake

and

Christopher Hawthorne Moss

LAUNCHPOINT PRESS

2017

A Launch Point Press Trade Paperback Original

Copyright © 2017 by Lori L. Lake
Individual copyright permissions in end notes

ISBN 978-1-63304-032-8

FIRST EDITION
First Printing, 2017

Editing: Lori L. Lake and Christopher Hawthorne Moss
Copyediting/proofreading: Nann Dunne, Luca Hart, Judy M. Kerr
Book typeset: Sandy Knowles
eBook formatting: Patty Schramm
Cover design: Ann McMan of TreeHouse Studio

Published by:

Launch Point Press

Portland, Oregon
www.LaunchPointPress.com
Printed in the United States of America

From Christopher

For Jim, who has made my life,
both as a woman and as a man, complete
as a true lover always does.

From Lori

For all the firebrands, trailblazers, rabble-rousers,
and radicals, many whose names have been lost
from history, but who were passionate and committed
to being seen, heard, understood, and treated fairly.
So many unnamed brave people put their reputations,
their jobs, even their lives on the line to forge paths
that make the lives of their queer "descendants" better.
This collection is dedicated to you.

ACKNOWLEDGMENTS

We'd first like to thank the talented authors who imagined the joys and sorrows in queer lives from the American past: Victor, Jane, Nann, Jess, Sue, Judy, EJ, Lee, Kate, Jon, Patty, and Ethan. The richness of your visions and the careful execution of each story make this volume breathtaking and alive.

We couldn't have done this without artful cover creativity by Ann McMan, typesetting, and design by Sandy Knowles, editing and proofing by Nann Dunne, Luca Hart, and Judy M. Kerr, advice and eBook formatting from Patty Schramm.

Christopher says: I am so thankful to Britta Adams for telling me about New Orleans, Stephen Foster for his evocative song lyrics, and Anel Viz and Gabbo De La Parra for their guidance, particularly for my use of French and Spanish. I don't know who programmed the Amazon Kindle text-to-speech feature, but whoever it is deserves praise and adulation. That simple app allows me, a legally blind author, to read literally hundreds of books I could not read before. Thanks also to Lori for helping me through my first experience of editing an anthology. I couldn't have asked for a better guide dog.

Lori says: I want to express appreciation to my co-editor, Christopher, who came up with the initial idea for this project and who is one of the most entertaining people I know when it comes to brainstorming. In addition, he has been a light in the darkness regarding transgender and queer issues. He's regularly inspired me with his courage and steadfastness in the face of bigotry and ignorance. My admiration is never-ending.

I'm also grateful for the love and support of my partner, Luca, who makes all things seem possible and is ever so much more than arm candy. Without her efforts and support, this anthology would never have seen the light of day.

From both of us: Much appreciation to all the readers and writers of historical fiction. Never forget that LGBTQ contributions to society have been and are significant. Let's keep writing ourselves back into our place in history!

Lori L. Lake and Christopher Hawthorne Moss
The Pacific Northwest
May 2017

TABLE OF CONTENTS

FOREWORD

"Those in power write the history,
while those who suffer write the songs."
~Frank Harte, traditional Irish
singer and song collector

Up through much of the Twentieth Century, it is clear that nearly all published fiction and nonfiction suffered from a tremendous lack of representation of "queer" people. From the time of the first recorded history, those who wrote about the Western world were privileged, usually wealthy, white, male, and well-practiced at excluding the importance of many roles played by women, people of color, poor folks, or, really, anyone who wasn't flush with power.

All the contributors in this collection spent a significant portion of their younger days denied a voice to publish their stories and without stories to encourage their voices. As writers in this anthology, we all seek to rectify that. Even today, in the supposedly accessible and liberated new millennium, the experiences of non-heterosexual people are still regularly disregarded and refused entrance into the mainstream of publishing. I would guestimate that *at least* twenty-five percent of the U.S. population falls outside the "norms" so heavily represented in most literature (i.e. a male head of household, a female partner, 2.2 children, and a chicken in every pot). And yet, the majority continues to prevail.

When Christopher and I began discussing this collection, we saw it as a kind of Reclamation Project, an effort to imagine who our queer ancestors were and how they lived so that we could write them—and thus ourselves—back into history. Some of the stories are playful; some hopeful; some tragedies, but all of them create characters who are authentic to their time. Many characters face the burden of not being able to fully express or reveal themselves, thus perpetuating that the next queer person who desperately needed support and recognition would also lack affirmation, a community, and a sense of Self. We aim to show that queer people are indeed a part of history and must be acknowledged and written back in—even if that requires imagination more than archaeology or research.

The stories here are not in the date of historical order, but are instead arranged for variety of tone and theme. At the end you will find biographical information and lists of selected works from the anthology's talented authors along with ways to contact or learn more about each of them.

The great Greek poet, teacher, and out lesbian, Sappho, recognized that the male-dominated history writers left her and others like her out of the historical narrative. In a fragment of her work, she wrote:

> *"I tell you, someone will remember*
> *us, even in another time."*
> ~Sappho, Greek poet, teacher, and lesbian in 630 BCE

It's now time to remember, time to right historical wrongs, and time to write ourselves back into history.

Lori L. Lake
Portland, Oregon
April 2017

INTRODUCTION

Everybody knows the story of Paul Revere's ride in April, 1775, immortalized in Longfellow's poem, and published decades later in 1861. But how many people have ever heard of Sybil Ludington, a heroine of the American Revolutionary War, who rode forty miles through the night on her horse, Star, to alert four hundred militia men of the approach of the British regular forces? She rode over double the distance that Revere did, and she was only sixteen at the time.

What would LGBTQ readers have given to have heard Sybil's story? How many young girls, queer and not queer, would appreciate reading about a brave girl in history books? How many boys would have found such a story inspiring and perhaps had more respect for girls and women?

Not until the late twentieth century did queer people begin to appear in literature published by smaller presses; and occasionally a mainstream press has published fiction or nonfiction that isn't completely exclusionary. Nevertheless, most historical records don't include queer people. Because of that, it's necessary for LGBTQ historical novelists to imagine lives for those left out of the official history. Using creative imagination and knowledge of past times allows writers to construct plausible historical lives for queer people, including those who want to be known as the gender opposite of what they were assigned at birth.

All of the stories in this anthology exemplify more than one of the themes typical of historical fiction, and reading these pieces with those themes in mind may give hope about how far American society has come. These themes include: evolving values and beliefs in a community; morality or "right" behavior; interactions between different cultures; the effects of oppression, war and class in society; the critical nature of human connection in times of trouble; and the quest for freedom.

In the stories in this anthology featuring real historical figures—or in which such figures provide role modeling—consider how they either represent or break off from the social norms of their times. For instance, in Judy M. Kerr's "Stamped Unnatural," Mary Katharine Goddard, who lived before, during, and after the American Revolution, was the real-life printer of one of the first copies of the Declaration of Independence. As a publisher and the first female postmaster general, she drew around her some of the most progressive thinkers and writers of her time. The young fictional protagonist of this story, Addie, would have had an immediate role model in Goddard because of her non-traditional activities as a printer, book publisher, postmaster, and influential woman about town.

In E.J. Kindred's "The Other Marie," the historical figure of Marie Equi, a pioneering medical doctor who campaigned for women's health issues and other concerns, is held up for the protagonist, Celia, by her partner, Marty, to illustrate commitment to and social action on behalf of women through time.

Any historical figure used as an example doesn't need to be exemplary either. In Ethan Stone's, "Hijacked Love," D. B. Cooper, the notorious hijacker, is imagined as a gay man. Cooper provides the FBI protagonist, Zack, with an example of gay independence and self-determination that Zack could not afford to reveal in the 1970s and 1980s. He pursues Cooper, clearly admiring the way the hijacker lives his life despite the fact that he's a fugitive on the run.

Not every story in this book is upbeat. In "Mercy's Eyes," by Kate MacLachlan, Mercy is a young woman in Salem Village during the infamous witch trials. She lives during a time of sexual and female repression from which there is no escape. When her case is considered, she makes a choice that takes integrity and real bravery.

In Jon Michaelsen's "Eyes for You," Winston tells the story of the swashbuckling actor, Dash, and his reckless life, but Dash also offers a lesson in *joie de vivre* that is not lost on Winston or the two married gay men with whom he shares the story.

Many of the stories in this anthology describe the environment of loneliness that LGBTQ people find in a hostile society. In "Coming Home," Sue Hardesty illustrates the difficult lives of displaced Native American girls at the Indian School. Their circumstances are contrasted with the boy, Ira Hayes, a real-life American hero. Together, the two girls are able to avoid loneliness, and their love gives them companionship, but Ira is isolated even among the other seemingly heroic "code talkers" in the army. He has to deal with the fallout from the objectification and fame that society puts on him.

In Christopher's story, "Hear the Gentle Voices Calling," the reader meets Captain Michael "Mick" Murphy, a wounded veteran who is lonely in the permissive city of New Orleans during the Civil War. Together with his client, he must face the grisly death of that young man's brother, but through the mercy of love he also finds solace. Friendship and companionship do indeed provide comfort and support to carry on.

In a pre-Civil War story called "Abigail's Freedom," Patty Schramm writes about a slave and the terrible abuses she suffers in her attempt to become a free woman. She undertakes a journey that no one should have to make, and Abigail's arduous path reminds the contemporary reader that summoning the courage to seek freedom may be dangerous, but it's a timeless and recurring call.

In an except from Victor J. Banis's novel, *Longhorns,* the lonely ranch boss, Les, realizes that his biracial Indian ranch hand, Buck, is more settled and confident than he is, despite facing racism in their Western society. This prompts Les to let down his guard and make connections with others that he hasn't allowed before.

Yet again, the theme of loneliness and the need to find community runs through the 1880s story "Deadfall" by Jess Faraday. In the creepy but well-populated tunnels beneath Oregon's biggest city, the main character, young Bailey, wanders the maze, trying to survive. She observes unscrupulous slavers capturing unsuspecting people through deadfall traps that lead down into the Portland tunnels. It's not until Bailey makes a stand that she finds caring and support from someone else in similar circumstances.

Lee Lynch's story, "The Time of Year that Really Got to Frenchy," is set in 1960s New York City, where Frenchy is struggling with her place in the world, especially after her young girlfriend is forced into a mental ward for her lesbianism.

In "Stepping Toward Freedom" by Nann Dunne, the protagonist's suffrage-seeking lover receives barbaric treatment in prison where she is force-fed, a torture that could destroy a prisoner physically or otherwise impair her mental health. Though separated by the imprisonment, the characters draw on one another's companionship to face the evils of the oppressive society.

"Ghostly Crossing" is Jane Cuthbertson's story in which a bereaved modern woman, Diane, meets a late 1800s woman, Sarah Hayes. The two women, both separated from the women they love, find hope and salvation in a conversation that spans more than one hundred years.

In Lori's story, "Fighters," a young woman who wants to be part of the Black Civil Rights movement faces homophobia and sexism as well as compulsory heterosexuality, but by meeting the gay, historical personage, Bayard Reston, she learns that LGBTQ people have just as much passion for freedom as people of color do, and she is given hope that the Civil Rights movement will eventually succeed.

As historical novelists ourselves, we hope that fiction writers, both queer and otherwise, will want to include lesbian, gay, bisexual, transgender, and other gender-variant people in their work in plausible ways. The lives of queer people in history may have been short, insignificant, or misunderstood, but it's possible to construct stories and create characters to at least give them a chance at a literary life, even if the records of the past have failed to preserve their contributions and their existence.

Perhaps these stories, taken as a whole, will illustrate how these queer "ancestors" found their own way, which can serve as an inspiration for moving forward with power and intent, and helping others to understand that writing ourselves back into history is a fair and necessary action.

Christopher Hawthorne Moss
Lori L. Lake
The Pacific Northwest
May 2017

Time's Rainbow

Writing Ourselves Back into American History

LAUNCHPOINT PRESS

Deadfall

By
Jess Faraday

Portland, Oregon
1885

BENEATH THE UNHEAVENLY CITY, tunnels coil and twist like dragons, north and south along the waterfront. There's an unseen underground life in these tunnels—a sweaty, torch-lit shadow-Portland that the fine folks above pretend doesn't exist. But I grew up down here, with the crimps and whores, the steam of the laundries, and the sickly-sweet smoke of the opium dens. I know its heartbeat and I know its secrets.

I know the special knock on the floor of the barroom upstairs, when it's time for my uncle to pull the lever. I know the creak of his trap door, and the leaden *thunk* when some opium-addled wharf-rat hits the bottom of the cell that will be his home until my uncle sells him to some crusty sea captain for fifty dollars. If the wharf-rat is smart, he'll make himself useful in that year-and-a-half between Portland and Shanghai. The useful ones are the last to be tossed overboard when the food runs out, and the least likely to be left to fend for themselves on some faraway, foreign shore.

I know the *clank-rattle* of the tin cans the Chinese string along the walls. They keep to their business, the Chinese, and we keep to ours. But underground business is shadow-business, and a visit from the surface means trouble for everyone. So when a stranger comes down from above, the first one to notice it rattles the cans so everyone can put themselves in order.

The darkest sounds come from the Closet. These sounds that make every woman, white and Chinese, laundress and whore and crimper's mate like me pause and shudder. The men who come down the deadfall end up in a little brick room until it's time to be reborn as some sea captain's slave. As for the women who find themselves dragged down into this alien world, One-eyed George trains them for their new, short, brutal lives in the Closet.

The Closet holds no danger for me. Even if I wasn't too mannish-looking to earn my keep as a whore, my uncle looks out for me. George glanced my way once, and it cost him an eye. Now we more or less ignore each other, though if George had his druthers, he'd slit my throat before tossing me into the river.

Thunk! goes the trapdoor—not ours, under the Valhalla Saloon. A different one. A new one. I follow the sound in my mind, through the billowing steam of the Chang family's laundry vats, past the little opium den underneath the tavern, past the little room tucked away in a little-traveled corner—the room Uncle Samuel and I call home. Structures go up and come down all the time underground, but when had someone put in a new trap door? I glance over my shoulder. No one's looking my way, so I put down the bucket of boots I'm carrying. That's one of my jobs—to sell the boots my uncle takes off the men who come down the deadfall. It's never completely safe to wander through the dark tunnels alone, even when Uncle Samuel is keeping an eye out. But this time I do. I run.

And arrive near the new deadfall just in time to see a flash of silk dress and polished shoes before the door slams shut.

Then I hear George's heavy tread and I press myself as small as I can into a corner while still looking at the trap door. The door is made from old wood and stolen springs, but the beams holding it in place are clean and new. And the cell below it—I'm very sure that wasn't there the last time I was in this part of the tunnels.

My stomach goes heavy at the thought of the woman. Expensive silk, new shoes. Not your garden variety woman of the streets. For a woman like this, the police would open their cash-blinded eyes. A woman like this will bring trouble.

But I don't have time to think about it much, because at just that moment someone rattles the cans.

JOSEPHINE BOWMAN IS THE most beautiful woman above or below ground. She's also growing into one of the most Bible-bangingist missionaries in the old North End, so there's no way anything will ever be 'twixt her and me. But a gal can dream—and I do—of my rough, callused fingers in her smooth brown hair; of her clean white skin, and what her fine features would look like in the flickering underground torchlight just before I press my lips to hers. That's what I'm thinking when the whispers shake me back into reality.

Silently, stealthily rising from the pallet where I sleep, I push back the curtain that separates the little room I share with my uncle. It's just a few hours before dawn, and most of the lights are out. Two figures—a man and a woman—are making their way carefully through the tunnel. The man moves hesitantly, unsteadily, shuffling his feet. Opium? Concussion? The woman, I don't recognize. I think about the lady who came through the deadfall. I'd heard nothing from her since her descent. Don't know if she's even still there. Right or wrong, it's none of my business. Leastways there's nothing I can do about it without bringing a heap of trouble onto myself.

"Bailey?" My uncle's voice is scratchy with smoke and grit and whiskey. "What are you doing creeping around?"

"Does One-eye have a deadfall now?" I ask.

"What? No."

"There's a new one over on the other side, behind Chang's laundry. Whose is it?"

The heavy pause tells me Uncle knows exactly what I'm talking about. The way the air gets all tense tells me he's not going to tell me a thing.

"It's none of our business. Now go back to sleep."

THE NEXT MORNING I creep through the dark, narrow tunnels to the new deadfall. The tunnels are crowded with people going about their business—pressing and folding laundry, moving crates between the warehouses and docks—and the unspoken movement of people, both of their own free will and against it. I say nothing, look busy, and keep my eyes to the floor, and no one bothers me.

I find the other deadfall—not so different from my uncle's: trap door, lever, cell below, basket outside for shoes. I press my ear to the splintering cell door, but all is quiet. No weeping, no stirring, no pushing at the slapped-together boards that make up the rickety walls. The rich woman's shoes are in the basket next to the door. I frown. They take the men's shoes after they come down the deadfall, while they're still snoring away in lotus-land. That way the men can't kick the door down when they wake up. But I can't understand taking a woman's shoes. No woman is going to make a dent, even in that wall, and once One-eye teaches them their new business, they'll need their shoes for walking the streets.

There's only one reason a woman wouldn't need her shoes. Something cold twists in my stomach, and I wonder why no one has stolen them yet.

I look over my shoulders once, twice, then snatch up the shoes. Too small and dainty for me, but the owner isn't coming back, and I know someone who could use them.

"I BRUNG THESE SHOES," I say to the matron at the front desk of the mission where Josephine Bowman leads a Bible meeting on Saturdays. "Thought someone here could use 'em."

I'm blinking in the daylight streaming through clean windows, and I stand in one place trying to make myself small, feared to death of getting the dirt of the tunnels on the freshly scrubbed floorboards. Where the tunnels are dark, filthy and cramped, the mission is open and bright. Sort of like I think Heaven might be if I ever get to see it.

I hold the fine, shiny shoes out to her and glance around hoping to catch sight of Josephine. She's not here, though. Probably on a street corner somewhere preaching the Word. The matron is just what you'd expect—a sour-looking old bag in a pressed cotton dress, hair like steel wool and a stomach like a flour sack, and heavy hands made for whuppin' unruly children.

But don't she look nervous when I hold out the shoes?

"Or you could sell 'em," I go on, "They're too small for me."

Women live at the mission, I know. Women trying to get off the streets and into a better life. Not sure what that meant. No rich man's going to marry someone like that, and emptying rich men's chamber pots ain't much better than what they were doing before, if you ask me.

"Stole them, I presume?" the matron asks.

"I did not! I…." It's on my tongue to tell her exactly where they come from, but something in the back of my head tells me to hold my peace. "I… found 'em."

The matron raises her chin and looks at me long and hard. Her face is tired, like she knows what she's been missing being good all her life and isn't sure anymore if it's worth it. She looks at me like it's my fault—me with my trousers, heavy boots, and manly swagger. I'm not feeling manly anymore, though. More like a tiny bug on a soot-grimed window.

"Look, if you don't want 'em, just say it. I'm sure I could sell 'em somewhere."

I'm about to say something more, something less polite, when there's a thump from above, somewhere on the stairs toward the back of the mission. Footsteps stop on the landing, then cautiously continue down. I turn to see Josephine Bowman, in a drab mission dress, her brown eyes as wide as teacups, her hair pulled back all prim.

"Where did you get those?" she demands, nodding at the shoes. She's looking at me like I'm something horrible come up from the deep. "You're the crimp's assistant. I've seen you!"

And it all becomes clear. She despises me. Could never want me. And I'm a cursed fool for ever entertaining the idea, even in the darkest, most secret part of my mind.

"How dare you?" Josephine continues, to my horror. "Looking for more hapless souls to send off to Shanghai or out into the streets? You'll have to look somewhere else!"

Fury rises in me. I'm not there to hurt anyone, I came to help. And besides, for all the mission rails against the demon alcohol, you'd think they'd figure anyone who fell through the deadfall was only getting what's coming. But my face is on fire and my eyes are burning and it's all I can do not to fling the horrible shoes in her face.

"Just take 'em then! I was only trying to help!" I cry. I drop the damned shoes on the floor and run.

"Wait!" Josephine calls after me, but she's taken too long. I'm running, running, back through the door of Valhalla, past the day-drinkers, through the door at the back and down the stairs. I rabbit through the dark tunnels like something's after me, and maybe it is. I'm running so fast, the little Chinese gal looks up from Chang's steaming laundry vat and rattles the cans.

And only then do I put two twos together and realize the new trap door is right under the mission.

SOMETHING ROTTEN IS HAPPENING at the mission. I'm not surprised or shocked. Church people ain't any better than the rest of us, and the way the mission is always after donations, they clearly need the money. The mission spends most of its time trying to save 'lost' women. The idea that they might 'lose' one or two on purpose to fund their work is nothing new.

But the idea that Josephine Bowman might be involved—well, that's like a kick to the gut. I'm going to find out what's happening and put a stop to it, if I have to die trying.

"I KNOW YOU SPEAK English, I've heard you," I say the next day, to the girl folding shirts on the Changs' laundry table. She's about my age—seventeen or so, and we know each other by face, though we've never spoken.

She doesn't say anything, but looks at me like she wants me to go on. I swallow. I'm powerful nervous. Something bad is happening—worse than the usual kind of bad—and I probably won't know what I've stepped in until it springs shut around my leg like a steel trap.

"A woman came through the new deadfall yesterday. Did you see her? She was a little older than us, I think, though she came down so quick it was hard to tell. A white woman with brown hair. Real high class—silk dress and shiny shoes. They didn't take her to the Closet, and she ain't there now. And she left her shoes behind."

The Chinese girl keeps up her steady stare. I'm babbling like an idiot, and I don't even know why I decided to talk to her. Probably because she kept to herself and wasn't likely to box my ears for sticking my nose into men's business.

"That new trap door leads up to the mission," I say.

This gets her attention. The missionaries make no bones that they think the Chinese a wayward and hellbound people. The idea of a missionary deadfall probably surprises her as much as it does me—which is to say not a whit, once I think about it.

"My name's Bailey," I say. "I intend to put a stop to it, and I could use your help."

She gives a nod. "Chang Meifeng."

CHANG MEIFENG IS THE kind of person who can blend in and out of the shadows of the tunnels, invisible in plain sight. She's a skinny thing, and silent. While she goes about her business washing, wringing, ironing, folding, no one gives her a second glance. When I'm with her, I'm invisible, too.

I lead her to the new deadfall, and she follows a good few paces behind me, on the other side of the tunnel, like a ghost hidden behind a stack of trousers.

I show her the trap door, and how the ceiling around it was cut out recently. The cell beneath the door was put up in a hurry—probably overnight.

"Why did they even bother?" Chang Meifeng asks, nudging the cell door with her foot. "My granny could kick down this wall."

"What do missionaries know about flesh peddling?" I scoff. But something dark stirs in the pit of my stomach. Flimsy as it is, the cell wasn't built to hold men.

Just then footsteps slap the packed earth behind us. A voice cries, "What do you think you're doing there?"

"It's One-eye!" cries Chang Meifeng.

And my blood turns to ice.

"Run!" she says. Chang Meifeng turns and throws her carefully folded laundry into the tunnel behind us. One-eye curses, and I hear him slap and flap through the sudden cloud of clean shirts and trousers.

We race through the tunnels, through a knot of people by the laundry, past the opium den, turning over a table or two, shouts and cries ringing in our ears along with the rattling cans. You can't say everyone down there knows everyone—it's a big place, and a lot of people come and go in the course of business where knowing too much don't do anyone any good. But a lot of people know George, and a lot of people know me, and they know not to come between us.

Chang Meifeng screams somewhere behind me. I whip around to see George dragging her into the shadows by her long braid. I turn and run toward them. When I get to him, I jump on his back and lock my elbow around his neck.

"You let her go, you whoremongering bastard!"

George spins around, trying to dislodge me, pulling Chang Meifeng after him. When he slams backward into one of the packed earth walls, something cracks. I think it's me. A crowd has gathered by then, and my uncle pushes to the front of it.

"Bailey! You get off him this minute!"

"What?" In my surprise I loosen my grip and slide to the ground, landing in a heap behind George's legs. I stand up and brush myself off. "But—"

"And you," Uncle says to George, "let that girl go."

George drops Chang Meifeng's braid. Anyone would have, considering the rifle my uncle is leveling at George's head.

"We had a deal, Samuel," George growls.

"And the deal still stands, but if I hear of you bothering either of these girls again, I'll shoot first and let the Good Lord handle the details."

With the rifle, Uncle Samuel gestures George away from us. Slowly, and with enough grumbling to save a scrap of face, One-eye George slinks away.

As for me, I'm still reeling from hearing the words 'the Good Lord' spring from my sailor-crimping uncle's mouth.

"As for you, Bailey," Uncle Samuel says, "You keep your nose to the grindstone and out of places it don't belong."

"But Uncle—"

"Not now."

"But Uncle, what deal? What did One-eye mean?"

He stops and turns. I can see in his expression, as the torchlight flickers over his craggy features, that he's considering telling me *something*. But then his face slams shut like an iron door.

"Uncle, *what deal*?"

He turns on his heel.

"Not your business, and best you don't know. Now, there's a chamber pot needs emptying in our room, girl," he calls over his shoulder. "You'd best get to it."

"I DON'T KNOW WHICH is stranger," I say to Chang Meifeng later, after we'd both finished our work. "My uncle making a deal with One-eye, or going on about the Good Lord."

"You said the new deadfall goes up to the mission," Chang Meifeng says.

I frown. There are only three things I know for sure about my uncle: he don't deal in women, he hates One-eye George, and he can't abide churchfolk. But now he seems to be in the middle of some unholy mess involving all three. Never mind that the high class women coming down that deadfall are putting the whole underground at risk.

"I don't like this," I say. "It ain't like Uncle Samuel to take up with George, nor with religion, neither. It's one thing sending a young man to Shanghai. We pay the police a good piece to keep off our backs. But you should've seen the woman who come down the deadfall the other day. That was some rich man's daughter, you mark my words. Ain't no amount of money can keep the police out of here once they get a whiff of that."

Chang Meifeng looks serious. "What can we do?"

I think about it. What *can* we do? Nothing until we at least find out more.

I slowly nod. "I'm going to camp out near that deadfall tonight, see if anything else comes down. Then I'll make my decision."

IT'S HARDER THAN YOU think to hide out at night underground. Deadfall business is night business—the miners and farmers and laborers coming to the Old North End for their last drink as a free man, little do they suspect. It's the damndest thing. They know they're taking their life in their hands every time they step inside one of those bars. Look away for a second, and the bartender's tipping laudanum into your beer and leading you over to the bench in the corner before pounding on the floor to signal some crimp to pull the lever. But a man needs distraction, I guess, and cheap beer and cheaper women are the only distraction most of 'em can afford.

The door of the cell under the mission deadfall is open. While Chang Meifeng keeps watch, I duck inside and find a dark corner. It really is a pitiful little cell, cobbled together from old wood and bent nails. Can't imagine why they'd think they could hold anyone in here.

Footsteps clunk on the mission floor above the trap door. Chang Meifeng douses her lantern.

"Just walking around, I think," I whisper.

"This time of night?"

More footsteps. More than one person. Some hushed lady voices.

"Maybe it's a Bible meetin'," I say.

Footsteps scrape by in the corridor outside the cell. Thin, strong fingers tighten around mine. Chang Meifeng's breath is hot against my neck. I'm about to say something, when someone knocks out a pattern on the mission floor just over our heads. Just outside the cell comes the sound of the lever, then the deadfall door sweeps down.

There's just enough time to pull Chang Meifeng to the wall before a heavy, perfumed, mass of silk and leather slides down the door, onto the cotton pallet below. Before I can say anything, the entire room is lit up by a torch. I glanced from the woman sitting on the pallet to One-eye standing in the doorway, apparently as surprised to see me as I am to see him.

THE WOMAN ON THE pallet looks from George to Chang Meifeng to me. She's surprised, but her eyes are clear, and as she stands and brushes herself off, I can see that she's neither drugged nor trussed up.

"Don't worry, ma'am," I say. "There's been some kind of mistake. Come with me, I'll get you home safe."

I'm not sure how I'm going to do that, but I'll die before I send her off with George.

"Home?" the woman asks. "But I—"

"This way," George says gruffly.

I step in front of her. "You don't have to do this, ma'am," I say.

"But—"

George pushes me to the side. "Runt, you don't know what you've stepped into. For your uncle's sake, I'm going to give you to five to step right out of it. After that..." He cracks his knuckles and leers like he's going to enjoy it.

"Over my dead body!" I cry.

Bad enough he was dealing in women. Bad enough he'd got my uncle into it somehow. But now he was snatching high-class ladies off the streets—the kind who were going to bring every last policeman down to the tunnels, and probably the army as well. It couldn't stand.

I launch myself at him.

"Stop!" a voice cries. The voice of an angel. And stop we did.

There, in the flickering torchlight, Josephine Bowman looks down through the deadfall, the gaslight in the upstairs room making a golden halo around her.

"Mr. Mason, let that young woman go."

SHE DESCENDS THE DEADFALL like she was born to it—sliding down through the door with grace, and landing on her feet in her sensible flat boots. Even down here the shadows and torches can't take her beauty away. She brushes herself off and accepts my hand. Her hand is small and warm and I could swear when our fingers touch, a spark runs between us like lightning. But when I look into her eyes all I see is the light of her righteous conviction.

"There's been a misunderstanding," Josephine says. One-eye takes off his hat in her presence. He loosens his grip on my arm, and out of deference to her presence, I resist giving him a shove. Chang Meifeng is standing there, looking between One-eye and Josephine, while the young woman on the pallet straightens her skirts.

The young woman turns to me and says, "You misunderstand. These people are helping me."

"Helping *you*?" I demand. "What can the likes of George do for you, but get you the last place any woman wants to be? Now come with me," I say, extending an elbow, "and I'll take you home."

"What if home is the last place I want to be?"

I frown at Chang Meifeng. She looks at me and frowns back. She has everything money can buy, this lady—silk dresses, fine shoes, probably servants at home and a carriage. What else could she be wanting, and where did she think she was going to find it?

"But you have everything you'd ever need—"

"Money doesn't solve every problem," Josephine says softly. "In fact, sometimes it's what allows problems to continue."

As the woman on the pallet turns into the torch-light, I see that what I'd taken to be shadow on her neck and collarbone is actually a series of ugly bruises. As she steps off the pallet, she moves like it hurts, and suddenly I understand. My uncle pays the police a right big cut to turn a blind eye to our crimes. Someone in this woman's life was doing the same.

There's a scraping sound, and out of the corner of my eye I see George scuffing the dirt with the toe of his boot like a little boy called onto the carpet.

"Mr. Mason and Mr. Burton"—my uncle, though I ain't never heard no one call him 'Mr.'—"are paid well for their assistance," Josephine continues. "It's an uneasy alliance, but a necessary one. One hopes that one day, they may see the error of their ways and repent."

I glance at old George again. He's looking away, but I don't trust this new face of his for a minute. I refrain from telling Josephine Bowman what I think about the chances of George's reform. I also hope she don't see that I'm squirming in my boots at the thought of how my uncle and I make our living. Ain't never considered it before now, but I get the feeling it might be keeping me awake tonight. My face is feeling hot, and I can't even look at Josephine right now, though I can see out the corner of my eye that she's staring straight at me. How had I ever thought I was good enough for her? I can't meet her eyes. I turn toward the woman with the bruises instead.

"Where you going to go?" I ask her.

The woman looks at me, then at Josephine. Then she says, "Away. Far away. I can't say exactly where, but I have a place waiting."

"That's good," I say.

George clears his throat. "Ma'am, I'll step out now, so's you can get dressed." He nods toward a pile of men's clothes neatly folded in a corner. Beside them is a pair of boots. Too large for a lady's feet. Hope she'll be able to walk in 'em.

"Thank you." She turns to me. "Even if my husband has set the police on my trail, they won't be looking for a young man." To Josephine, she says, "I'll leave my clothes. After a few months, you'll be able to sell them for quite a bit, I should think. And my shoes."

And then something completely unexpected happens. Josephine Bowman meets my eye, a smile teasing at the edges of her mouth.

"Leave the shoes for Miss Burton," she says. "I'm confident she'll find a good buyer. Besides, she and her little friend are part of the operation, now. Aren't you?"

Shame starts to drain away, and I stand up a bit straighter. A new feeling fills me, and I wonder if it's some of that righteous sense of purpose that makes Josephine Bowman glow from inside.

I reach back for Meifeng's hand, meet Josephine's eyes, and nod. "Yes, ma'am, we are."

Eyes For You

By

Jon Michaelsen

Present Day

GEOFF MARKS-GREENE'S RESEARCH into architecturally signif-icant structures of the early twentieth century had brought him to Atlanta to write a feature for *Architectural Digest*. He wanted to recount the con-ception and design of the once exquisite hotel, the Biltmore. Now he stood in the lobby of the once-thriving hotel, gazing around and marveling at the neo-Georgian design and craftsmanship.

"May I help you?"

Geoff started and turned to the cheery face peering at him from behind the check-in counter. "Oh...yes, yes of course. The reservation is under Marks-Greene."

"Mark Greene? "The clerk clicked the keyboard using her long fingernails. "One moment while I access your information."

"No, that's Marks *dash* Greene. It's hyphenated." Geoff smiled wide. "I'm married."

Puzzled, the clerk typed the information as instructed to retrieve his reservation. "Ah, yes, here we go. Geoff and Alan Marks-Greene." She peered over her glasses, narrowed her eyes at the computer screen. "Room 1009 on the tenth floor. It's a corner King Suite that overlooks Fifth Street and West Peachtree. Should I check to see if we have any doubles available?"

"Not necessary," Geoff said. He handed over his driver's license and credit card, signed the required documents, collected two heavy brass keys, and inquired about meals.

"We provide guests a continental breakfast each morning served in the library across the hall. All other meals are off property." She handed him a colorful placard listing nearby eateries. "There are numerous restaurants and taverns within walking distance from here, several open until late at night. Let me know if you'd like a recommendation."

Geoff thanked the clerk then walked back to the car to wake Alan, get their luggage and go to their room.

SHORTLY AFTER SETTLING INTO their room, Geoff and Alan stood silently before a spectacular oil canvas encased in a gilded frame and stared long and hard at a giant portrait of a young soldier in military dress. Neither knew the time period depicted in the painting, though Geoff insisted the garments were mid-nineteenth century. The soldier's jacket appeared to be a single-breasted, nine-button front affair in cadet gray, piped and trimmed, appearing much like a prewar militia ensemble, Geoff surmised. The trimmings were robin's-egg blue and lined the piped collar, cuffs, and front lapel edges.

"I see you two have come upon Dash?"

Startled, Geoff and Alan swiveled their heads in time to see an old man with a walking cane heading toward them.

"Excuse me?" asked Geoff.

"The portrait you are surveying there."

"Oh, yes, he's very striking. Do you know who the soldier was?"

"Of course. His name was William Gabriel Daschle. I called him Dash. He called me Charlie. The uniform was one worn by the Confederate cavalry in the War Between the States."

"He looks so young," Alan said.

"He was." The old man beamed as he reached them. "When I commissioned this portrait, Dash had just turned twenty-one and was on the precipice of achieving great stardom. He was a thespian of the Hollywood Golden Years." He chuckled and revealed a set of perfect dentures. "Though by today's standards, I suppose, he was simply an up-and-coming actor whose major claim to fame was as a supporting cast member in a multi-Oscar-winning film."

"He wasn't a soldier in the Civil War?" Alan appeared dumbfounded.

"Heavens no! He was in costume for the sitting. I can assure you, however, that Dash most certainly could scrap with the best of them, and often did, but fight in a war? Hardly." The genteel man glanced up at the portrait, his eyes reflective and misty. "He was a fine actor in his day, but he was certainly no killer."

"What movie?" Geoff asked.

"Pardon?"

"What movie is the uniform from?"

"Why the greatest film ever made of course, *Gone With the Wind*. It premiered here, in Atlanta, I mean. December 1939."

"Wow," Alan said. "I must've seen that movie a dozen times. What role did he play?"

"One of the Hamilton brothers. His largest screen credit was attending the barbeque at Twelve Oaks Plantation. He wore a dashing suit with tails."

"What became of him?"

Ford lowered his eyes. His features twisted in agony as he mumbled. "I killed him."

THE OLD GENT SHUFFLED across the ballroom. Geoff looked at Alan and shrugged his shoulders. Whether invited or not, they hustled after him.

Exiting the ballroom, they entered the hallway. The thick carpet looked faded and aged, but at one time had gleamed luxuriously in a deep forest green. The stranger turned to them with a slight smile.

"Might I have you boys up for a nightcap? I will tell all you wish to know." He shuffled off again, saying over his shoulder, "I have been meaning to confess such ill-fated deeds for quite some time."

Alan pleaded with his eyes not to accept the offer, but Geoff jumped at the chance to satisfy his curiosity. "We'd love to."

"I'm Charles," the man said, and pressed the button for the elevator. Geoff and Alan introduced themselves and all shook hands.

They rode in silence to the uppermost floors, each level highlighted on the old brass panel as the elevator ascended. The car didn't halt at the highest numbered floor, instead continuing on to an additional level and coming to an abrupt stop with a loud clang. The doors slid open and Charles ushered them out into a narrow, darkened hallway.

"Sherry fine with you boys?"

"I don't think…" Alan began, but Geoff cut him off.

"Sure, we'd love some."

Charles jiggled his keys and worked the stubborn lock on an unmarked arched door. They entered a room awash in shadowy light thrown from small lamps scattered about, the shades draped in sheer fabric. Their guest pointed them to a seat before disappearing to the rear of the room. They settled themselves onto one of the twin Victorian settees facing each other.

The cramped room showcased a bevy of vintage antiques, with aged wood and worn fabric. Geoff had the distinct impression he'd stepped onto a movie set from the 1940s. He admired the portraits set in ornate frames scattered about the washed-out wallpapered walls. The space felt claustrophobic with all the stacks and stacks of books and magazines everywhere.

Charles returned, pushing an iron and gilt rope glass tea cart that held a crystal decanter filled with burgundy liquid and a set of matching glasses. Positioning his cane at an angle against the arm of the settee across from the boys, he plucked two half-filled goblets from the cart and offered one to each of them, then picked up his own. He sat and drew the goblet to his mouth, pursed his thin, cracked lips, and took a sip. He closed his eyes and swallowed, savoring the wine like a fine connoisseur.

Geoff glanced at his watch, surprised at the time. He needed to get in bed soon. The hotel's representative had offered to give him a tour of The Biltmore and its two famed ballrooms early in the morning before staff set up for the day's scheduled functions.

"It's getting late," Geoff said, glancing at Alan. "We shouldn't keep you long."

Close up, Charles looked disheveled, his clothes rumpled and fraying at the collar and cuffs. His blue eyes appeared rheumy, the lids bloated. His hands, blotched with dark spots, twitched incessantly.

"Nonsense," he said in a manner that suggested something weighed heavy on his mind.

Judging by the deep crevices in Charles's forehead, Geoff figured his concerns must be burdensome.

The old man said, "I have wanted to share my tale for quite some time now."

Geoff wasn't sure, but he thought he saw the old man's expression alter, enrapt with guilt.

"I remember like it was yesterday," Charles said with his eyes closed to them, and he told his story.

November 1939

ON THURSDAY, NOVEMBER 9, 1939, I met the one and only love of my life. The day ended up like every other day of the week in a year of cruelty and uncertainty. Two months earlier the Nazis invaded Poland and the Channel Islands of the United Kingdom, and her allies had declared war on Hitler's armies. American politicians had shown their spineless reticence by reaffirming neutrality. They wanted no part of the war in Europe. So at that point, we Americans had no part in the war.

On that day in November, my two buddies Dugle and Griff and I desired a beer, so we went to a private club for drinks and to listen to some Billie Holiday and Count Basie records played on their ancient Victrola. The place we chose was a gentleman's parlor of sorts that served a particular clientele. Back in the day, we had to be very secretive. Degenerates and perverts; those were words we were called by society. Discovery meant instant shame put upon our families and jail time, perhaps even worse.

That night at the Blue Rat lounge, distinguished men, both young and old, participated in easy conversation with the company of others in relaxed splendor, a safe atmosphere not unlike a fancy parlor in an old antebellum mansion. Never were there guarantees of course, as the threat of a police raid always held true. The right folk must have had their palms greased because a shake-down had never happened in this particular establishment far as we knew. Rooms were available upstairs should any parties wish to partake in private time together, for a charge of course.

We sat long enough to finish a single beer when the door opened, and in walked a wildly good-looking, smartly dressed young man with dark brilliantine hair and eyes so blue you could see them across the room. The fellow seemed to suck the air right out of the place as he breezed through, quite taking my breath away. All chatter ceased until the man placed himself at the counter before the barman and asked for some booze.

Nothing effeminate about this fella, mind you, and certainly no cause to assume as much. He looked distinguished and well refined, no more a nance than President Roosevelt himself.

Conscious of the eyes flicking back at me, I took a quick sip of beer and chuckled at my friends. "Can a man not enjoy his beverage in peace?"

Dugle, a hillbilly from Coweta and the oldest chum at the table, grinned like a chisel. "Whatcha waitin' fer, Charles?"

"Hogwash," I said. "He might be a G-man for all we know."

My buddies continued to urge me forth, eventually getting me to step up to the counter and order us another round. I was to strike up a conversation and invite the stranger to join our group.

Image meant everything to these boys, so being seen with such a fine gentleman would have them bursting with pride for weeks. The request was innocent enough so I agreed. No sooner had I ordered did the stranger turn to me and ask for a light.

Reaching into my lapel pocket, I withdrew a silver engraved lighter my father had given me on my eighteenth birthday. The man smacked his pack of Camel's against the inside of his palm to extract a cigarette and offered up one to me.

"Care for a smoke?"

"Don't mind if I do."

He leaned into the flame, took a couple of deep puffs until the tip of his cigarette caught, then pulled back. "Thank you."

I lit up as well and offered a hand. "Charles Xavier Ford. Pleased to meet you." Lordy, I thought my hand might crush in the fellow's powerful grip.

"Gabriel Daschle," the gentleman said in a deep, western accent.

Feeling rather cheery, I said, "I'll call you Dash. It sounds noble with a hint of mystery, like you." Whether the fella knew I was flirting or not, he didn't seem to mind.

"Why, then, I'll call you Charlie."

I grinned and said, "Tell me, why have I not seen you here before?"

"I'm from out of town, new here."

"I see." I glanced back at my buddies and mustered the courage to ask him over. "Care to join me and my friends, Dash?"

"I would be delighted, thank you. I am most eager to meet new acquaintances since I plan to vacation here for several weeks."

Dash assisted in carrying the pilsners of beer over to the table. After smiles and handshakes all around, Dash sat down and proceeded to offer the gentlemen cigarettes, which they declined. Soon, we were all in jolly conversation, with Dash explaining the reason for his vacationing.

"Once filming with the actors wrapped and with no work for several months, I boarded a train headed east to enjoy this great city of yours. I intend to partake in its theatre, music and divine southern culture while here."

"An actor in pictures," said Griffin Trotter, my best buddy since the fourth grade. He seemed genuinely impressed. His pockmarked face blushed each time Dash regaled us with one of his many stories of working in Hollywood.

"Name some of the movies you've been in," I asked.

"Well let's see, I was a midshipmen in *Mutiny on the Bounty* in '35, an extra in *Camille* in '36, a boy in *Wee Willie Winkie* with Shirley Temple in '37, and in *Boystown* last year. I just finished my latest role in *Gone With the Wind*, premiering here next month."

"Yer an actor in *Gone With the Wind*?" Dugle was beside himself, pea-green with envy.

I didn't know whether to believe the young gent or not. He could have been pulling our legs for all we knew, but no one seemed ready to question his sincerity. He was a real smooth talker, that Dash. And those eyes: blue as a bright sky and confident, looked right at you when he spoke. The man had more confidence than a mongoose on a cobra.

"How come I ain't never hearda ya b'fore," Dugle asked, before sucking down the last of his sixth pint, twice the balance of the rest of us.

I was horrified and set about to admonish my good friend, but Dash took everything in stride, always the cool chap. He told us his parts until now had been small, but the Civil War epic would make him a movie star. I had no reason not to believe him. The evening wore on, and my buddies became boisterous and sloppy, embarrassments of the highest order. I conspired to get Dash away from them before they sullied their good names any further. The hour was late, so I was able to convince Griff to help Dugle to the "Y" so the farm boy could sleep off his drunk.

Left alone with Dash, I graciously offered to shuttle him around to the sights of the city since I didn't have to work until four o'clock the next day. We made plans for me to collect him after breakfast at his apartment on Fourteenth Street across from Piedmont Park.

THE FOLLOWING WEEKS SPENT with Dash were wondrous as we took in the town. The entire city was decorated for the holidays. Shuttling him around to some of the most spectacular landmarks brought forth a kind of rebirth in me that I never would have anticipated. My father had moved us to Atlanta from New York in '24 to take the job of hotel manager upon the opening of the Biltmore. I was ten at the time and spent my formative years growing up here, but never got to enjoy the city as a tourist since I'd begun working as a bellhop in the hotel at sixteen.

Touring the fascinating sights wouldn't have been as pleasurable, though, without the constant companionship of Dash. Everyday we set about as wide-eyed tourists taking in the operas, symphonies, stage plays and movies at theaters along Peachtree: the Grand, the Paramount, the Fox, the Capitol and the Roxy to name a few. We were, in a word, inseparable.

We visited Grant Park to see the new diorama at the Cyclorama War Museum, enjoyed afternoon tea at the Henry Grady and Capital City Club, paddled around in the lake at Piedmont Park, toured the historic Confederate Soldiers Cemetery in Marietta, and attended wondrous concerts at Ansley Hotel's Rainbow Roof and The Samoan Room of the Georgian Terrace. We even capped off our fourth week together by boarding a steam engine out of Terminal station to Dahlonega to pan for gold at the old abandoned mine.

Everything had been going so well that I was not prepared for the news Dash would impart the afternoon he returned from his daily run. I'd taken to spending a great deal of time at Dash's apartment and was lounging across the couch when he came in. Our friendship had grown much closer that first week, and when Dash suggested I consider staying at his place during my off hours to maximize our touring time, I jumped at the opportunity to escape the confines of the Biltmore. By the end of the second week, we'd shared more than his bed together.

Dash spotted the old tattered paperback I was reading, *Better Angel* by Richard Meeker. "Nose in a book again, I see." He was forever teasing me for losing myself in books. He was no doubt attempting to elevate my mood.

"What of it," I said. "You of all people should appreciate such artistry."

"You're confusin' me with one of your other fellas. A silly waste of time if you ask me."

"Ah, but there *are* no others, Dash. I only have eyes for you."

I explained the novel was about a coming-of-age love affair between two boys and their close relationship with another boy. He snatched the book from my hands and flipped to the first page.

"A debut of its kind when published eight years ago," I said. "It's the first homosexual-themed novel with a happy ending."

Dash blanched and tossed the tattered binding to me. "A couple of inverts fraternizing with a degenerate? That's impossible."

"You don't even read, so what do you know?" I said heatedly.

He gave me an odd look, so I apologized and admitted the reason behind my poor temperament. "Father and I had words again. He's forever pestering me to enter college. So my reading frees the mind of the trouble that taunts."

Dash sat beside me on the couch, playfully poking my chest with his fingers and nuzzling my chin. I didn't understand his need, but soon the reason became very clear.

"By and by," he said, "I received a telegram from the studio holding my contract. MGM is insisting I get engaged on the night before the premier to a girl who I've been linked with. Terrific publicity they say, and it'll clean up my image. Fans seem to frown upon a confirmed bachelor in this day and age."

"They want you to agree to a *lavender* marriage? How can they demand such foolishness?" My shoulders tightened and my stomach clenched. I thought I might be sick. "What did you tell them?"

"What could I say? I agreed, of course. What would you have me do?"

I felt punched in the gut, the wind knocked out of me. How could I have been so foolish to think we could possibly be together? Our relationship wasn't "natural," and certainly not allowed in society.

I'd been lying to myself all this time.

"Charlie, please don't be upset." Dash further enlightened me as to the name of the actress he'd been introduced to last year who was awaiting him back in Los Angeles. "It's not my wish, I can assure you."

He went on, but I tuned him out. As usual, Dash spoke in his ever-charming voice, his soft mumbling blabber. I was unable to speak, wishing on a thousand stars this was not happening.

"Charlie! It's an arrangement coordinated by the studio to promote a proper image. Nothing more. Surely, you can appreciate my dilemma, can't you? It doesn't mean anything to us." He took me into his arms. "You and I shall continue to see one another, I promise."

In spite of my confusion, I felt angry with him, jealous even. I pulled back, brushed away his advances. "Why have you never mentioned this broad before?"

The twisted emotion in Dash's face revealed his revulsion. "She's not *really* my girlfriend, Charles. She happens to like women. We're not intimate in the least. The studio asserts it's vital to my career to project a certain image, one the public expects. You understand, don't you?"

I didn't speak. I felt sick at heart, wanting to run from the room, but my feet remained rooted to the floor. Dash stared at me wide-eyed, stunned by my silence. What I wanted to say—what felt impossible to keep from saying—was how fond of him I had grown these past weeks. Perhaps our parting was due to happen for some time, I don't know. I truly believed I could never have confessed, not in a million years, how much I cared for him. Alas, it had taken Dash to bring out this unexpected depth of feeling in me.

"Dash, I care for you a great deal, more than you realize."

"As do I for you, my love. This is a temporary arrangement, I promise." He took my hands, kissed the backs of my knuckles, and smiled lovingly at me. "A few months beyond the premiere, I'll break the engagement. Regardless, I'm to remain in Atlanta with you, at least until I'm required to be on set for my next motion picture."

"Do you mean it, Dash? Truly?"

"Of course I do. Why else become engaged?"

We kissed as if for the first time, passionately, longingly, and made love right there on the couch. I swear I never thought it possible to care for a man as much as I did for Dash. Ours was an unnatural relationship of the time. We would forever be haunted by the fear of discovery, exposure, even jail. Still, I remained hopeful, ignorant to the path he was asking me to choose.

Afterward, we showered together. I dressed and readied to take the streetcar to the hotel for my shift when Dash confessed he had more to say.

"I will be attending the Junior League Ball and the premiere with Ethel. I'll propose to her at the dance with the cameras and bursting flashbulbs. We can get together later in the evening, once Ethel retires to bed."

"How? I fear your every move will be subject to witness. We can't possibly be alone together without roving eyes. We might be exposed!"

"Listen to me, I've got a plan. The studio is to put me up in a hotel for a few days before the premiere. I've selected the Biltmore."

"What? Why ever would you suggest such a thing?"

"To be close to you, of course."

"Dash, it makes me splendidly happy that you wish to be near, but we must be careful. We can't risk discovery, ever. We can use one of the underground passages and sneak through the ice plant and laundry to a service elevator that rises to the roof. We will be safe in my apartment."

Dash held out his hand. "Well then, I look forward to our engagement, Mr. Ford. Now off to work you go."

December 13-15, 1939

FOR THREE EXCITING DAYS, the citizens celebrated before the cinematic premiere of *Gone With the Wind* Friday evening. Atlanta reigned in revelry, a celebratory mood unlike anything ever seen. There were parades, receptions, dances, evening parties and other gatherings of the sort all around town. Dash and I hardly saw one another the entire time, what with all of his cavorting around with the beautiful bride to be, flashbulbs popping continually in their wake. I admit to being wracked silly with jealousy, but what should one expect? Dash made a promise to make it up to me after the required events and festivities were complete.

We were to meet up at midnight after the premiere near a passageway leading from the hotel to the apartments. Dash had assured me it was unlikely any photographer worth his price would miss the chance to catch the happy couple or other Hollywood elites. All top stars of the film were guests of the Georgian Terrace closer into town, but a few of their family members and studio staff were spread between the Henry Grady and the Biltmore. Dash held true to his word and proposed to Ethel at the Junior League Ball Thursday evening, so he was being hounded by newsreel photographers by Friday.

I'd initially refused to attend the premiere at the Lowe's Grand, but as the day drew near, I got caught up in the swell and chose to attend at the last moment with Dugle and Griff who somehow came up with an extra ticket. For ten cents we rode the trolley downtown, but when the car became ensnarled in traffic, we were forced to disembark and walk several blocks along Peachtree Street to the Grand Theater. Crowds of folks stood ten deep along the sidewalk surrounding the theater, ladies in their finest dresses and furs while their men wore double-breasted overcoats and slacks, many sporting fedoras. We eventually made our way through the throngs to the front as politely as possible in hopes of seeing the movie star Clark Gable and, of course, the lovely English girl, Vivian Leigh.

The evening was cold so I had worn my father's bomber jacket, but the heat of the crowd and the searchlights blasting giant white beams into the sky made it almost impossible to breathe. Sickly sweet perfume and smart aftershave filled the air, but I could still smell the fresh paint on the newly erected replica of the O'Hara plantation home, the facade covering the entryway to the theater. Dugle and Griff climbed on a nearby street lamp and were hanging by one arm shielding their eyes, gleefully alerting all to the motorcade coming down Peachtree.

The first to emerge along the rose-lined catwalk were elderly veterans of the Civil War helped along by aides. Soon Atlanta's favorite author, Margaret Mitchell, and her husband emerged. They waved to the crowd and entered the theater along with the stars of the film. The crowd went wild, the women screaming and the men whistling as the elite made their way past the news microphones to a display of bursting flashbulbs. Once all the special guests entered the theater, male ushers tore tickets for the general public. We all rushed and jostled to get in.

THE MOTION PICTURE DISPLAYED in Technicolor, the most sweeping, spectacular Civil War epic ever filmed, and by far longer than any movie I'd ever attended. The one saving grace was the much welcomed intermission halfway through the film when it seemed like everyone rushed to the washrooms.

After the multiple eruptions of cheering and clapping, the theater emptied and crowds of people poured into the streets to head for their motor cars or the trolleys. The lines were long to board, so my friends and I decided to walk several blocks to catch a different trolley. It began to drizzle, a most dismal prospect, and the trolley failed to appear. We continued to walk in the rain. I feared Dash had waited too long, and I worried that he'd think me not coming and would leave. At last, I accepted that I wouldn't show in time. It pained me to think of how he must feel, thinking I had abandoned him on such a joyous occasion.

Well beyond midnight, I returned to the Biltmore and rushed to our predetermined rendezvous location, but Dash wasn't to be found. My heart crushed, I went to my apartment, disrobed from the wet clothing and dressed for bed. I was dreadfully tired and fell instantly into slumber, only to be jolted awake from the pounding on my door a few hours later. I hastened to open the door so the neighbors wouldn't be awakened.

Dash stood there, drunk and disheveled, smelling of stale cigarettes and booze.

"Dash! My goodness, look at you. Are you all right?"

He tried to embrace me in the open doorway. I was horrified with the prospect of discovery and yanked him indoors.

"Whatever are you thinking?" I closed the door, sat him at the kitchen table and rushed to put on a kettle of water.

"I've made a serious mistake, Charlie. I can't marry Ethel. I don't love her! You are the one who has my heart."

I sat at the table and held his hands. "I'm sorry I was late getting back. It was total madness leaving the Fox. When I got here, you were gone."

"I didn't show. We had harsh words, Ethel and I, during intermission at the theater. I found it necessary to advise her of my plans to remain in Atlanta for the foreseeable future. I had arranged for her to be driven to Candler Field to board a flight the very next day, but she wouldn't hear of it."

The kettle let out a loud whistle. I rushed to grab the pot and pour hot water over Nescafe in two mugs. Dash's hands trembled as he sipped. His eyes were red and bloodshot. I stared at him and my heart sank, wondering what he had done. I was less concerned for myself than I was for him.

He looked up from his coffee. The pain in his eyes was heavier than any I've ever seen in a man.

He said, "I'm sorry, my love. I didn't mean to lose my temper with her, but you know how women can be most difficult. She would have none of it, and I raised my voice, called her a spoiled, sniveling woman."

"Dash!"

"It's not proper, I know, but she provoked me. What's a man to do? We left the premiere early claiming her ill and came back to the Biltmore. She shut herself in the room, so I went to the gentleman's parlor downstairs."

"And closed it down, I see."

"I've really loused things up, haven't I?"

Dash begged me to leave with him, to go to New York, away from prying and disapproving eyes, but I refused. His emotions were raw and confused. He wasn't himself. I continued to fill him with coffee until he finally calmed and grew silent. I helped him remove the stained trousers and sweat-covered shirt he had worn to the premiere and got him into the bath. He said little, a man defeated, as I washed him with a sponge.

After dressing him in a pair of my trousers, a clean white shirt, and my Atlanta Crackers baseball cap, we rode the service elevator to the sub-basement, two floors below the lobby, praying few employees had arrived for work. I planned to sneak Dash past the ice-house plant and through the laundry, trekking through a labyrinth of passages to get to the rear stairs, which was the best way possible to avoid seeing a member of the hotel staff. We'd then climb to the lobby and exit near the apartments. From there, Dash could casually cross the lobby to the guest elevators and make his way to his room.

Dash continued in earnest trying to convince me to leave with him as we slipped past the low-ceilinged rectangular room where the iceboxes stored giant blocks of ice for the hotel's daily needs. We entered the laundry room, a cold space since the machines had not been fired up for the day's flat work. The huge room contained two giant washers, extractors, a flat work ironer, and a drying tumbler, which we slipped past to reach the opposite side, beyond a separate guest apparel laundry.

"Charlie, please listen to me. We can leave all this behind with nary a care in the world."

I tried to hush him, mortified someone might hear his nonsense. I couldn't very well up and leave my responsibilities at the hotel. What would folks think?

Worse even, what would my father think? What was it I wanted anyhow? Did I even know at this stage of my life: A true friendship or the will o' the wisp I had pined for the moment I laid eyes on him? I knew others wanted to have such relations with Dash as I had, but he assured me none were successful.

I kept Dash a step behind me should we come upon anyone. No light blazed through the tiny windows in the doors of the carpentry and paint shops, so we eased against the wall past them. The door to the chief engineer's office opened with such swiftness that I had scant time to shove Dash into the baggage storage room opposite and order him to hide. I glanced over as Mr. Silvertone turned to lock the door to his office, ignorant of my antics.

"Why Mr. Ford, my good man. How are you this early morning? Is everything all right? You look as if you've come upon a ghost."

"Fine, fine, sir. I was just down to drop off some personal apparel for cleaning."

Mr. Silvertone began to walk off then turned back with a query. "Say, Mr. Ford, have you searched for our missing guest? Your father is beside himself with worry. No one ever has gone missing in the Biltmore."

"Missing guest?" I felt faint, wondering how the cold concrete floor might feel against my face should I collapse. "Excuse me, sir, but I attended the motion picture premiere last evening and wasn't here. To what missing guest are you referring?"

"One of the male actors staying here." The man pulled at his gray-sprinkled beard. "Mr. Gabriel Daschle. Not been seen for quite some time. His fiancée is worried sick. Your father ordered all security personnel to search every floor of the hotel."

"I'll keep an eye open."

Mr. Silvertone nodded, and I waited until he disappeared down the corridor before fetching Dash.

"Did you hear the chief?" I whispered. "People are looking for you!"

"Do you know how to operate a vehicle?" Dash asked.

"What? Of course. I've driven father's Ford a time or two. Why?"

Dash frowned and reached into his pocket to withdraw some keys. "I can't very well pop into the lobby now, can I? Take these. My motor car is parked at the rear of the gardens. It's a light yellow DeSoto. Drive around and meet me at the corner outside the entrance to the apartments."

"Are you crazy? Someone will see you."

"What else do you suggest? That I've been in your quarters for the past few hours? I need to get away from the hotel to think, to devise a story about where I've been all night."

I snatched the keys, and we made our way up two flights where I instructed Dash to remain while I went to retrieve the vehicle. "If anyone enters the stairwell, go back to the baggage storeroom until all is clear. I'll honk the horn once when I arrive on Fifth Street, but

I'll need to keep circling the block to avoid suspicion if you don't exit right away."

Dash agreed. I kissed him quickly, then made haste to exit the stairwell. I skittered through the southern edge of the building, past the head porter's office and the cigar and news departments, beyond the twin broad marble staircases leading down to the West Peachtree lobby. Several guests milled about or sat in easy chairs facing inward around an expansive area covered in thick rugs with a giant Christmas tree dressed in sparkling tinsel in the center. I noticed cameras hanging around the necks of a few men. They appeared to be reporters. Darting into the marble foyer, my stomach clenched, and I almost turned around as I walked toward the garden entrance. Father stood speaking with two men in trench coats in the multi-columned portico.

Ducking my head and looking away from my father, I walked as fast as possible without raising suspicion across the inner circular drive, across the terrace and down the steps to the garden. I turned to ensure no one had followed before continuing along. The air was cooler and mist hovered in the first traces of early morning light. I followed a narrow pathway through the northern edge of the gardens. Crossing the outer portion of the circular drive, I saw Dash's DeSoto and took off running in a full stride.

I climbed into the automobile and cranked the engine, giving her a little gas to choke to life. I popped the clutch and immediately stalled. Cranking the engine again, I grinded into gear about the time a black sedan with blazing spotlights and siren wailing cut the corner sharp at Sixth Street and headed my way. A police officer was standing on the passenger side runner of the vehicle, his arms looped inside the open window to hold on.

Panicked, I shifted into second gear and sped down Cypress Street. Steering hard right, I cut the corner at Sixth Street too tight, and the vehicle's right wheels jumped onto the sidewalk. I raced past the point where Dash should have been waiting and rounded the next corner onto West Peachtree practically on two wheels. The police were close, but they would have had to turn around, and the DeSoto was a newer automobile and much faster. I eventually lost them on the magnolia-lined streets of a well-to-do neighborhood just east of the hotel. I'd no idea if Dash saw the police were trailing me or what he must be thinking.

Knowing the authorities would continue to look for the speeding yellow automobile, I killed the headlights and made my way back to the hotel using side streets, again circling the back corner of the hotel at Cypress and

Fifth. About the time I reached the portico of The Biltmore Apartments, Dash bolted out of a service door in front of me. I planted both feet on the brake pedal and jerked to a stop. He jumped in looking as dazed and as frazzled as I felt.

I didn't have time to explain. The policemen were coming up behind us fast. Shifting into gear, I pressed the gas pedal to the floor. The sedan shot out onto West Peachtree too fast and too wide. I tried to swerve the vehicle back into my lane but must have overcorrected. The automobile slid sideways. I lost control and a big delivery truck rammed into the passenger side of the DeSoto.

Present Day

BOTH GEOFF AND ALAN were stunned by the old man's story. Neither knew what to say, whether to console or remain quiet. Charles looked more tired and frail than when they first met him in the grand ballroom. He sipped the last of his sherry and sat back against the frayed pillows of the settee, exhausted, the energy gone out of him. Heavy tears flowed from his downcast eyes.

After a few moments Charles spoke again. "I awoke in Grady Hospital three weeks hence. Nurses informed me that I'd been in a terrifying motor vehicle accident and in a coma the entire time. They also told me about Dash. He'd been killed upon impact."

Charles cleared his throat. "I never had to invent a story about why I was driving Mr. Daschle's DeSoto with him inside and us running from the police. A reasonable tale was created by my father, and folks assumed as much. Why else would the famous young Hollywood actor be wearing my clothing after all? Father discovered Dash's soiled apparel in my apartment and had believed I'd lent him my clothes. My father knew I had befriended the fellow, so it made sense that Dash had sought me out and needed a place to sleep after he got sauced that night following the disagreement with his girl. People also assumed the reason we ran from the authorities was due to the young man's shame of getting tanked the night of the premiere."

Charles set his glass on the table between them. "I never bothered to correct the story, or to explain that we were in love and were just terrified of being discovered and possibly jailed." He glanced up, his eyes moist and bloodshot. "I lived my entire life with the secret. Dash was my one and only love."

Geoff glanced at his watch. His curiosity was satisfied and at this late hour, he was bone tired. He said, "Thank you for sharing your story with us. It's clear Dash was a very special man indeed."

Charles pointed toward their hands, and Geoff realized he was looking at their matching bands.

"You're married?"

"Yes," Alan said, reaching out to take his husband's hand.

"To each other?" A note of awe crept into his voice.

"Last summer in Seattle."

"Newlyweds," Charles said, smiling. "My, my, have the times changed."

THE NEXT DAY, GEOFF and Alan toured the mostly abandoned hotel with a perky saleswoman, starting with the lower floors of the structure. Geoff seemed to know his way around in the former laundry room and ice-house plant, often leading the way and drawing a comment from the representative.

"Are you sure you've never toured here before, Mr. Marks-Greene? You seem to know an awful lot about the interior."

"No, never. Lucky, I guess." He smiled at Alan. "I've researched and toured many grand hotels built in the early twentieth century, so I feel at home here."

She smiled and continued ushering them along. At last they reached the spacious Georgian Ballroom, one of the two grand ballrooms still in use for hosting wedding receptions, bar mitzvahs and other elaborate functions. The dignified expanse looked radiantly different in the daylight, featuring exalted arched windows framed in luxurious draperies and portieres, crystal chandeliers, elegant hardwood floors, and a soaring ceiling with hand-sculpted plaster designs. Massive rows of double columns flanked the sides of the hall.

Geoff and Alan moved away and walked straight to the portrait of William Gabriel Daschle.

"Well, hello, Dash," Geoff said, gazing up at the life-sized portrait of the young man with a renewed sense of familiarity.

"How did you know the man's nickname?" asked the representative, coming up behind them. "Most people don't even know who he is."

"Charles Ford told us. He's a very nice man," Geoff said.

"You've met the former hotel manager? How long ago was that? He was long gone when I arrived, but I know from reading old newspaper accounts and the hotel's history that "Dash" was the nickname Mr. Ford gave the young actor when he stayed in the hotel for the *Gone With the Wind* premiere. Sadly, Mr. Daschle died early that next morning."

"We met the old fellow last night actually," Geoff said. "We got in late and walked up the street to get a bite to eat. On the way back, we saw the lights on in the ballroom and decided to take a peek before the tour. We were admiring the portrait when Mr. Ford entered the hall. He shared the story behind the painting and of Dash before inviting us up to his apartment for some sherry."

The sales rep seemed nonplussed. "Oh, you must be mistaken. Mr. Ford has been dead for a quarter century or more. You must have met someone else, a steward of the apartments perhaps."

Geoff glanced at Alan, ready to challenge her. "Isn't there a small apartment on the roof of the hotel? That's where he lives."

"There was. It was abandoned years ago. Once upon a time they used it for storage, but not since the hotel closed in '82. I'm not aware it was ever used for anything other than storage."

Geoff thanked her for the tour and walked away with Alan feeling more confused than ever.

"I don't understand," Alan said. "If the man we met wasn't Charles Ford, then who was he?"

"I'm as surprised as you," Geoff said. "Let's go to our room and change so we can have some lunch. I'm starving."

"You, my good man, have a deal."

As they headed for the elevator, something caused Geoff to glance toward the darkened recesses of the long narrow hallway. He tugged Alan's arm to get his attention. At the end of the long corridor, shimmering within shadows, stood the nearly opaque images of two very handsome young men holding hands. They were dressed in fashionable clothing of the late 30s.

Charles and Dash smiled and nodded at them, but before Geoff and Alan could advance, the shadowy images evaporated like a wandering mist.

Geoff was so surprised he didn't breathe for several moments.

"Did you see that?" Alan asked in a whisper.

Geoff let out a breath. "Only if you did."

"What the hell. I don't know what to think."

Geoff took his hand. "You know, I think we're a lot like them."

"Oh yeah? How so?"

"Well, for one thing, I only have eyes for you."

"The feeling is mutual." Alan squeezed his hand as they moved away from the dark corridor.

Glancing back down the hallway, Geoff said, "Alan, my love, I think I've found the perfect angle for the feature I'm going to write."

Stamped Unnatural

By
Judy M. Kerr

Part I – June, 1773

ADDIE TRIPPED OVER THE long skirt of her flower-patterned cotton gown as she approached her favorite shop. She righted herself and grabbed hold of the gown to lift it clear of her leather-booted feet. The Baltimore Street Goddard & Hadley Book and Stationery was her favorite part of visiting stores in Baltimore, and she happily accompanied her much older cousin, Hester Worley, on each visit.

Hester cuffed Addie on the back of her head. "Young lady! Why can't you comport yourself properly in public? You are such an embarrassment." She pinched the back of Addie's upper arm for further emphasis. "Move along. You're blocking the door and I would like to get inside out of the hot sun." Hester fanned herself as she shoved past Addie.

"Forgive me, cousin. If you didn't force me to dress this way I'm certain I would not cause such distress." In these modern times and in this year of 1773, why couldn't she wear breeches anyway? Addie preferred men's clothes as opposed to the yards of linen, silk, and wool formed into the dresses that women were required to wear. What would it hurt to dress more simply?

Hester's face scrunched up like she'd bitten into something sour. They'd had this discussion before, and Hester had not budged at all. "Breeches are for men, not ladies. You should be grateful that Horace and I provide for you." She marched across the store to a shelf of poetry books.

While she tried to control her temper, Addie rubbed at her sore arm and nodded at Rebekah Hadley who stood behind the counter. "Good morning, Miss Hadley." Addie moved toward Rebekah.

"Good day, Addie." Rebekah's forehead creased in a frown as she watched Hester peering at a volume of poetry across the store.

"Do not pay her any mind." Addie sent a final glare toward Hester's back. "Is Miss Goddard working the press?"

Rebekah said, "Yes, MK has been hard at work all day."

Mary Katherine Goddard and Rebekah Hadley were the owners of the book and stationery store, and they also printed the Maryland Journal, Baltimore's only newspaper, as well as books and almanacs. Addie longed to learn the printing trade and yearned to be strong and independent like these two women.

Hester approached the counter, rubbing her left temple with a white-gloved hand. "What is that awful noise?"

"Dear cousin, 'tis the printing press, I'm certain." Addie could not contain the excitement in her tone. "Miss Goddard is printing the next edition of the Maryland Journal or perhaps a book. Which is it?" As Addie turned to Rebekah for an answer Hester struck like a snake and slapped Addie hard enough she stumbled backward, tripped over a stool, and fell to the floor.

"Dear God, Mrs. Worley, the child is bleeding!" Rebekah ran from behind the counter, a white cloth clutched in one hand.

"No less than she deserves for talking back to me." Hester sniffed. "Come, Addie. The noise in here is too much. I'm developing a headache and need to get home to take my powders." Hester marched toward the door.

"And wash it down with a late morning whiskey, no doubt," Addie mumbled as she held the cloth to her swelling bottom lip.

"What did you say?" Hester whirled around and strode back to where Addie stood and slapped her again. She bellowed, "Disrespectful child!" then backhanded Addie's other cheek. "Ungrateful young woman."

"Mrs. Worley, stop this minute!" Rebekah practically dove between Hester and Addie.

"This is not your concern, Miss Hadley." Hester's back was as stiff as the cover of a new book, and her cheeks bloomed with red blotches.

The press stopped running in the back half of the store. Sudden silence filled the shop.

"This is my place of business, so it is my concern," Rebekah said, hands fisted on her hips, her voice raised.

Mary Katharine Goddard appeared suddenly. She wore a long printer's apron, nearly to her mid-calf, but Addie could see that her legs were clad with a dark brown cloth that tucked into her high boots. Breeches. The woman wore breeches. She said, "My goodness, what's going on? Rebekah?"

"MK, Mrs. Worley hit Addie so hard she's split her lip." Rebekah addressed MK, but did not alter her position between Addie and Hester.

"I am fine," Addie mumbled through the cloth. "Just a bit of blood."

"Dear Lord. The child's face is dark as a plum." MK came forward and examined Addie. "Hmm. Looks like you'll have quite a shiner on that eye, and I see a red handprint on your cheek."

"Please. Pay me no mind. I am fine." Addie blinked hard, trying to stanch tears that had welled. She drew strength from the simple presence and obvious concern of Rebekah and MK, and she would stand strong in the face of Hester's wrath. She sniffed and attempted a smile, which quickly turned into a grimace. "Ow." She probed at her bottom lip with a finger.

Hester moved to grab Addie's arm. "Let us take our leave, Addie." She towered over Addie's five-foot-three-inch frame. "I will deal with you further at home. No wonder your parents sent you away. You being an unnatural heathen is bad enough, but you are ungrateful and horrible as well. You best mind me or we will send you off to the hospital for those sick in the mind. You can be sure I will talk at length with Horace about this when he returns from his travels." Addie's fiery blue eyes caught Rebekah's. "Pardon me, Miss Hadley." She moved to step around Rebekah.

"Wait one moment, Mrs. Worley." Rebekah reached for Addie's arm and pulled her out of Hester's reach and behind her again. MK stepped alongside Rebekah, creating a wall of safety between Hester and Addie.

"Pardon me?" Hester's brows drew together. She impatiently folded her hands in front of her. "Please step aside so that this child and I may take our leave."

"I will not," Rebekah said. "You do not appear to like this girl. And you are causing her harm. This is not right."

"'Tis none of your concern," Hester said.

"It is our concern when you bring it to our place of business." MK's voice was firm and her tone direct.

"She is my ward and you will not stand in my way." Hester took a step toward the two women.

Addie couldn't stop the rush of words that fell from her mouth. "She does not like me. She beats me for every little misstep. And she drinks alcohol when her husband is away, which is most of the time. I fear if I stay in her house she will kill me."

Hester's right hand flew to her chest and she waved a fan at her face with her left. "Oh, my. I feel faint from the lies and insults visited upon me."

MK and Rebekah looked at each other and then at Hester.

Rebekah said, "I'm certain you will be fine, Mrs. Worley. Perhaps Addie would be better off with us. We can teach her a trade and provide a room for her in our home. This will relieve you of responsibility and the headache of dealing with her." She placed an arm around Addie's shoulders.

Addie let her shoulders relax under the comfort of Rebekah's hold. She looked up at her flustered cousin. "Cousin Hester?"

Hester sagged. "Perhaps it would be best for all. I am not good with children. Of any age." She huffed and fanned herself again. "This early June heat is dreadful. I must get home and lie down." Hester looked at Addie over her fan. "I will have your belongings, meager as they are, sent here immediately." She turned on her heel and walked out of the store appearing as prideful and ridiculous as Addie had ever seen her.

Part II

ADDIE'S CARRIAGE RIDE FROM the store to MK and Rebekah's home was filled with enlightening news and conversation. Addie admired the ease with which MK and Rebekah comported themselves. The two were intelligent, steadfast businesswomen, and yet they both had a sense of humor and a special closeness that she'd not witnessed in her many visits to the store.

Addie sat between MK and Rebekah, listening to MK speak of raids occurring throughout the colonies, as Rebekah handled the reins.

MK said, "According to the latest newspaper report, British loyalists are breaking into businesses owned by patriots seeking freedom from Britain. There is talk that war is on the horizon."

"Will you print these stories?" Rebekah clicked her tongue at the horse pulling the carriage. She held the reins confidently, and Addie realized these two were like none she'd ever met.

MK sighed heavily. "Yes. We all have the right to know what's happening."

"But what if your stories anger these loyalists?" Addie asked. "What if they raid your newspaper?"

MK glanced at Addie, her hazel eyes warm and intent. "That's a chance I'm willing to take, my dear. I believe in freedom of the press. And I'll do whatever it takes to spread the news as far and wide as possible."

Rebekah said, "I've heard rumors that the Crown Post will not deliver newspapers that speak poorly of Britain. I overheard several of the townsmen talking when I picked up a tin of tea at the dry goods store yesterday.

They spoke of ways the British are trying to control the colonies. High taxation puts some newspapers out of business. The Crown Post refuses to deliver the papers of those who pay the outrageous taxes anyway."

"We shall persevere," MK said. "No fear."

"You are so brave, Miss Goddard," Addie said.

"Ah, not brave, dear. To break from the ties that constrict us, Americans must break free of British rule. I intend to publish these truths in order to inform and educate as many Americans as we can reach." MK smiled at Addie and reached across and gently squeezed Rebekah's hand. "Am I right, my dear?"

Rebekah nodded. "As always, dear MK."

MK's conviction stirred unfamiliar, yet not unwelcome feelings within Addie. "I could only hope to be like you. To be brave enough to speak out. To broadcast the truth. On a personal and political level."

Perseverance. Honesty. Strength. Addie noted these qualities, as well as a deeper intuitive connection these two women shared. And with that, she felt something take shape inside her. Something that no one could touch or take away from her. A kinship she shared with MK and Rebekah? Maybe so.

ADDIE FOLLOWED REBEKAH OFF the carriage and stood, valise in hand, staring at the red brick house in front of her. They were on East Avenue at the opposite end of Baltimore from where the store and newspaper were located. Beautiful rolling hills surrounded the house, and as evening draped shadows around them, a peace of mind she'd not known in her sixteen years descended upon her. This felt like home.

"Welcome." MK rested her hands on Addie's shoulders. "Here you will never be called 'unnatural.'" She paused, and Rebekah gave her an encouraging nod. "We, too, have been labeled 'unnatural,' so we understand how that feels. That was the very reason we left Providence. We did not allow gossipmongers to ruin our lives. Here, in Baltimore, we have earned the status of businesswomen and we live in the same house. However, we do not tempt fate and thus choose carefully our social engagements."

"This is beginning to sound like a lecture," Rebekah said. "Come. We shall have Ella prepare a room for you." MK stepped back and Rebekah guided Addie toward the front door.

"Is Ella your slave woman?" Addie asked.

Rebekah said, "In Charleston did you always refer to people as slave woman or slave man?

Addie wasn't sure what the right answer was, so she didn't say anything.

"Ella is a black woman, but she is not a slave."

MK said, "I gave Ella her papers documenting her freedom when we arrived here from Providence. I do not believe in slavery. Ella is a person. A free person. She chose to stay with us and we pay her to run our household."

The front door swung open as the threesome approached. A short, round black woman with a smile as wide as the Potomac stood on the threshold. "Miss Mary, Miss Rebekah, welcome home." Then her gaze zeroed in on the girl walking between them. "And who might you be?"

With a hand resting lightly on Addie's shoulder, Rebekah said, "Ella, this is Adelaide Smith who has come to stay with us. Let's put her in the blue room."

Ella nodded. "Welcome, Miss Adelaide."

"You can call me Addie." She glanced over at MK. "Should I call you Mary or MK or Miss Goddard?"

"My given name is Mary Katherine, however, I use MK for business purposes. I actually prefer MK and either is fine, my dear. How old are you, again?"

"I will be seventeen at summer's end. In August."

"I do believe that is plenty old enough to address me as MK, if you are comfortable with it. Ella will show you to your room. Please unpack and then join us in the dining room for supper." MK nodded toward the stairs where Ella waited.

At the table, Ella served them a savory stew and fresh crusty bread and tea. The dining room was larger and brighter than cousin Hester's.

Rebekah laid her spoon aside. "Now, Addie. Share your story. How did you come to be with Hester Worley? She's your cousin?"

Addie was famished, and told her tale between bites of food. "My father owns a rice plantation in Charleston. He sent me away." She paused and chewed thoughtfully. Did she dare tell the rest of the story? What if she were misunderstanding the relationship between MK and Rebekah?

Rebekah touched Addie's forearm lightly and smiled. "You can tell us anything. We will not brand you unnatural for your honesty."

Addie looked back and forth between the two women, then let out a sigh. "One day my father caught me kissing a girl in the barn. He sent Bethany home and told my mother to 'get rid of this filthy unnatural.' He—" Addie stopped abruptly as tears came to her eyes. She blinked to clear her vision, then dabbed at the corner of her mouth with a napkin and set it aside. "His last words to me were that I was dead to him."

Rebekah let out a sympathetic "Oh," but said no more.

Addie didn't meet either woman's gaze. She took a sip of tea and continued. "My mother was horrified at my behavior. Her look of distaste was almost worse than my father's words. She did my father's bidding without question. She said a distant Cousin Horace in Baltimore and his wife would take me in, for a price. So, she packed me off with one valise and an envelope of cash."

MK said, "That's a great deal of anguish and dislocation to manage for such a young person as yourself."

Addie nodded. She took the last bite of her stew and let her gaze wander to the parts of the house she could see from the dining room. She wondered if Rebekah and MK would send her packing as her parents had.

"And how long have you been in Baltimore then?" Rebekah asked.

"I arrived two months ago. And from the first day I laid eyes on Cousin Hester I knew my life would be hard. I spent every waking minute of every day trying to figure out how I could get away."

MK said, "I had no idea that Mrs. Worley was so horrific a person. She's been a customer since the day we opened the store. And she and her husband pay for a subscription to the newspaper. By now I should know better than to be surprised."

"I have never seen her in such a temper," Rebekah said, "but then again, I've only ever seen her alone. Maybe once or twice with Mr. Worley."

Addie sopped up her plate with a crust of bread. "I learned quickly that Horace travels almost nonstop, something to do with shipping. I believe that he does so to get away from Hester and her love of whiskey. She loses her temper more with each sip." Addie grimaced. "I must tell you that the only bright spot for me has been the trips to Goddard and Hadley Books and Stationery."

Rebekah patted her hand. "You needn't go on, dear, if it is too troubling for you. I think we have an understanding, do we not, MK?"

"Indeed," MK said. "Let's look forward, shall we? A new life for Addie. Starting tomorrow we'll bring you along and you can help Rebekah at the store."

"Yes, but for now, I think a little dessert is in order." Rebekah stood and headed toward the kitchen. "I'll help Ella bring in the strawberries and cream."

ADDIE FOLLOWED REBEKAH AROUND the store. She learned to assist customers and tidy up. When she cleaned and tidied the back room, she wore an apron over breeches. When she served customers out front, she slipped a gown over her head so that the customers would not think of her as mannish.

She loved working in the store, and she felt more real, of more substance and matter, than she ever had in her short life. Though she missed Bethany, she felt as if she had found hope. Maybe there were others like her. Others like MK and Rebekah. Strong women without fear of expressing their strength.

"Addie, I need to step out to the dry goods shop. Will you mind the store for me?" Rebekah set a straw hat atop her blondish tresses and tied it under her chin. "MK is in back with the press should you need assistance. I won't be long."

"I'm happy to be of service." Addie returned to straightening a shelf of books as Rebekah exited the store. Humming to herself, Addie dreamed of what it might be like to own her own business. She reflected on how close she had come to a life of servitude to Cousin Hester, or worse yet, being hired out to some other evil old devil woman, as Hester had threatened on several occasions.

"Addie?" MK called across the store from her place behind the press.

"Goodness, Miss…ah, MK…" Addie held a hand over her chest. "You frightened me." She had been so lost in thought she hadn't heard the press stop.

"Where is Rebekah?" MK asked.

"She went to the dry goods shop. Is there something I can help you with? The press?" Hope filled her for a moment, because truth be told, she loved the books and stationery, but the real draw was the hulking printing press that churned out fact- and fun-filled reading material for colonists far and wide.

"Ah, do I detect a hint of interest in learning the trade?" MK asked, a twinkle in her hazel eyes. She pocketed an envelope she'd been holding. "Perhaps soon, dear girl. For now, however, I shall take my leave, as I need to search out Rebekah. I've a matter that needs to be discussed immediately." MK wiped her hands on a cloth she dug out from under the counter. "We shall not be long, I'm certain."

"I'll mind the store, happily."

"I trust that you shall do so. Should you require assistance you know the dry goods is only across the street."

Addie noted that MK did not don a hat and was constantly poking the hairpins back into her light brown hair. Addie wondered if MK ever wore her hair down. And then she thought what an odd thing for her to think about.

"Addie?" MK clapped her hands in front of Addie's face. "Are you feeling unwell?" MK bent slightly and peered closely at the girl. "Your eyes appeared a bit glazed. Perhaps you are still feeling effects of the slaps? I see discoloration has formed about the cut on your lower lip." MK's brow creased with concern.

"Oh my, no!" Addie felt her cheeks color with embarrassment. "I am quite fine, I assure you. I was lost in a bit of daydreaming is all." She felt foolish for drawing unnecessary attention upon herself. "Please, miss, I am fit as a fiddle. Please go and take care of your pressing business." Addie returned to the shelf of books to prove she was focused on the task at hand.

"Very well, then. I'll be off. We shall return shortly."

"MY DEAR MK, ARE you certain 'tis not too much strain upon you to take on such an arduous position?" Rebekah pushed open the door to the store, allowing a light breeze to color the interior.

Addie sat on a stool behind the counter reading a book. She popped up and moved to reshelve the volume, but neither of the women seemed aware of her, so she kept hold of the volume and reclaimed her seat.

"I assure you, Rebekah, that I'm quite able to handle the position. My father was a postmaster when I was a child. And William wouldn't have recommended me had he not faith that I could muster the fortitude necessary."

Postmaster, Addie thought, intrigued.

"Of course, I don't doubt your ability. I simply fear for you overtaxing yourself with the newspaper, the almanac, and the book printing. How ever will you find time?"

MK didn't answer, and Addie wondered if she was irritated at Rebekah.

Rebekah untied her hat and hung it on a hook on a side wall before turning her attention to Addie. "I trust all went well in our absence?"

"Yes. A Mr. Bartholomew stopped in, and I assisted him in choosing and purchasing a set of stationery for his wife's birthday gift. He seemed quite pleased by the selection." Addie was proud of having accomplished this task without assistance and happy that the interaction had been pleasant.

"Very good, then." Rebekah looked at MK. "I do not trust your brother, my dear. There. I have spoken the truth out loud. Since his hand in forcing us to leave Providence, I have no assurance that he will not turn on us yet again."

"William is so entrenched in the politics of the impending revolution and in devising a new postal system he can convince Mr. Benjamin Franklin will work better than the Crown Post, that I doubt he has two seconds to plot against us." MK's tone sounded soothing. "And if I take the postmaster position, I can assure our newspaper is delivered quickly and to the far corners of America." MK waved her arms expansively and paced the length of the store from front door to back wall. Back and forth, she paced. "Think of it." Her voice rose, excitement evident in the glow on her face. "We can inform, educate and entertain America, not just Baltimore. We can be the best newspaper of this land, and I would be in the position of ensuring it is dispatched properly."

Rebekah smiled, despite her obvious misgivings. "And so it shall be, then. You shall be the first woman postmaster in the Americas. We will be quite busy then, shan't we? Perhaps we do not need sleep. We can work round the clock, the two of us." A tinge of weary acceptance filled her voice.

"Ah, but my dear, have you forgotten?" MK lifted an eyebrow and tilted her head in Addie's direction.

"Forgotten?" Rebekah sounded confused, but then her eyes widened as she grasped MK's meaning. "Addie!"

Addie jumped off the stool, heart pounding. "Have I done something wrong?" She set the book on the stool and folded her hands in front of her.

"On the contrary," Rebekah said as she moved behind the counter and grabbed Addie's hand to draw her toward MK. "I think we have a proposition that will benefit all of us. Am I right, MK?"

"Indeed, Rebekah, you are correct." MK met Addie and Rebekah in the middle of the store. "We shall teach you how to run the printing press, if you desire to do so, that is."

Addie looked from one to the other and back. "Truly?" she asked, stunned. Could this be happening? She felt like she'd fallen asleep and woken in a dream world where her life finally had meaning and good things happened. "Oh, my, but of course! Yes, please! And thank you." She hugged first Rebekah and then MK. Then she stepped awkwardly away, wondering if she'd gone too far.

"Yes," MK said. "It truly is happening. So much change is in the air. I can feel it."

"And we need you to be part of it," Rebekah added. "Addie, with you helping us we can do this."

Addie gazed at the worn planks of the wood floor. Then she looked up and noticed the dust motes spinning in the sunlight. Her body felt light, her head felt lighter. "Miss Rebekah. Miss MK. I am honored. I feel…" She swallowed hard, working to keep tears from spilling forth. "Why me? Why have you both taken me in and offered me so much so quickly?" Addie feared to believe what was happening was real. If she believed then would it be taken away as quickly as it was given?

Rebekah's gaze locked with MK's and then returned to Addie. "My dear child. I think it best put to say that we see a bit of ourselves in you. And though, in the year of our Lord, seventeen hundred and seventy-three, we are seeing changes and pushing for more changes, we must be cautious."

"But not too cautious." MK picked up the thread of Rebekah's reasoning. "Freedom, Addie. We are living in a time where we're all fighting for our freedom from British rule in hopes of a better life here. And that fight is not limited to the political, but includes the personal, as well. I think it safe to say that though men are making the decisions at every turn, women, too, have ideas and voices. Wherever we can make our voices heard, we should."

"Not all women's voices should be heard. Your Hester is a good example of a voice that should be silenced." Rebekah brought a hand up to her mouth. "Perhaps I've said too much." A giggle escaped her lips.

"'Tis true," Addie agreed solemnly. "The only ideas Hester has are whiskey-induced. And you have both witnessed the outcome. For that I both apologize and thank you."

Their conversation was interrupted by a couple of customers opening the door. The chatter of the two women's voices drove away Addie's evil whiskey-spirited memories of Hester. The taller of the two women, dressed in a fine pale yellow linen gown with matching yellow hat touched a white-gloved hand to her chest. "Goodness, Abigail, I could hardly believe it. Poor Mr. Ingram. He'll be closed at least a week to clean up the mess, and the Lord only knows how much longer to replenish the stock that was destroyed. I simply don't understand why this is happening."

The other woman said, "Dear, me, Sarah, but my Thomas has told me this is just the beginning. Things will get worse before they improve." Abigail was about four inches shorter than Sarah, with dark curly hair tucked under a plain white cotton mobcap. "That Samuel Thorpe and his club are dreadful. It's his lot that drove us out of Britain in the first place. Now they want to reign over us here, as well. Hmmmph." She crossed her arms over an ample bosom. "I think not."

"Good morning…or is it afternoon already?" Rebekah said to the newcomers. "May I inquire what happened with Mr. Ingram?"

"Oh, dear, hadn't you heard?" Abigail straightened to her full five-foot-one inches and whispered, "His apothecary was raided last night, or early this morning. Bottles broken. Glass and elixirs everywhere but where they should be." She pulled a fan from the deep pocket of her dress and furiously fanned her face.

"What's this I hear?" MK strode toward the threesome and stood next to Rebekah. "Did you say raided?"

"Oh, my, yes," Abigail whispered.

"For Lord's sake, Abigail, speak up so we can all hear you," Sarah said. "There's no secret. Ingram's Apothecary was raided, I'm certain, by Samuel Thorpe and his no-good club. The lot of them should be jailed."

"The raids are becoming more frequent, then," MK said. "We heard just today that Thomas's Dry Goods was raided three nights ago. The tension is rising."

Overlooked and outside the circle of women, Addie spoke up in order to get their attention. "What club? Who is Samuel Thorpe?"

"And who do we have here?" Abigail insinuated herself between MK and Rebekah to get a closer look at Addie.

"Abigail, Sarah, this is Addie Smith," Rebekah said. "Addie, this is Abigail Wentworth and Sarah Jeffers.

"Pleased to meet you Madam Wentworth. Madam Jeffers." Addie gave them each a nod.

"Hmmm." Sarah said. "Say, aren't you Hester Worley's charge?"

"Right you are, Sarah." Abigail narrowed her eyes at Addie. "I remember seeing this young lady about town with Hester. So, why are you here with Miss Goddard and Miss Hadley?" She looked from Addie to MK and Rebekah and back to Addie. "Where is Hester?"

"I—" Addie began.

Rebekah laid a gentle hand on Addie's arm. "Hester felt it best for Addie to learn a trade, so she is with us now." She will be working here at the store and learning how to run the printing press. Poor Hester was worried about how Addie would support herself, so we offered to take her on. Addie, I'll help Mrs. Wentworth and Mrs. Jeffers. You go on to the back with MK, and she'll give you a lesson on the printing press."

"Come along, Addie. Rebekah has this under control. We can get the press prepared for the next edition of the newspaper. Good day, ladies." MK guided Addie by the elbow to the back of the store and closed the double doors behind them.

"Who is this Samuel Thorpe?" Addie whirled around to face MK. "And what did they mean about a club? What kind of club?"

"Samuel Thorpe is a local merchant. He and several other merchants and tradesmen formed a club called The Loyalists."

"The Loyalists?" Addie's brows drew together. "Who are they? What do they do?"

"They are loyal to the British crown. They are against the patriots whose voices cry for freedom from Britain. And so those who show affiliation with the patriots are labeled traitors to the crown, and Mr. Thorpe and his crowd raid their businesses and cause harm. They break, tear, and destroy whatever they can lay their hands upon." MK fisted her hands. "The closer we get to a revolution, the angrier these men become. I'm not sure what it will take to stop them, but they must be stopped."

"Have they ever raided here? The newspaper or the store?"

"Not so far. And, God willing, they won't." MK clapped her hands together. "Now, let's get you acquainted with this press." She laid a hand lovingly on the mahogany frame. "This press was built in New Haven, Connecticut, by Mr. Isaac Doolittle. He was a watch- and clock-maker. My brother William commissioned him to build the press when he started his newspaper in Philadelphia."

"How did it come to be here, then?"

"William and his partners were notorious for printing stories sympathetic to the revolutionary messages, and the Crown Post taxed them heavily to deliver their paper. When they refused to stop printing patriotic stories, the Crown Post simply refused to deliver the paper at all. This finally drove them out of business. William is now working on devising a mail system that is independent of the Crown Post."

"Now you have taken up where your brother left off?"

"In a manner of speaking, I suppose. I, however, have never been jailed, and I feel I'm much better at maintaining a business than my brother. But we can talk more about that another time. We should get to work."

Part III

OVER THE NEXT TWO years Addie worked diligently running the printing press and helping to decide which stories to print. That gave MK time to write for the paper and to administer her duties as Postmaster of Baltimore.

But the revolution was nigh. In April 1775, the Battle of Lexington and Concord tipped the scales.

One rain-drenched morning, MK said, "We shall run the story of the Battle in Saturday's edition. No other newspaper will have the detailed account. We shall achieve freedom, I'm certain." MK's face was flushed a pale pink with excitement. "The truth will be told!"

"Dare we?" Rebekah asked, trepidation clear on her face. "The situation is becoming more dangerous with each passing day."

"I feel no fear. And the people deserve to hear the truth."

"I agree with MK," Addie said. "Reporting about the war will be exhilarating. If we don't print it, another patriotic newspaper will, and we'll have missed the chance to be first."

"It's as if you've contracted a fever, the two of you." Rebekah shook her head. "And how will you pay the Post riders? Did you not tell me only yesterday that the monies for paying the riders had dwindled and you've not received more funds?"

"'Tis true," MK said, "the funds are low. But they've been low in the past. I shall pay the riders from my own pocket. I believe it to be that important that the news be shared across as many cities and towns as possible."

"As you wish, dear MK. I only hope it's worth it in the end." At the sound of the front door opening, Rebekah hurried away from the back room to wait on the customer.

"Quickly now, Addie. We must finish this edition. The riders will be ready to depart tomorrow."

"Is your editorial completed?" Addie busied herself in setting up the press.

"Yes, 'tis. Read my final quote and tell me what you think."

Addie read the words from the paper MK handed her. "The ever memorable Nineteenth of April gave a conclusive answer to the questions of American freedom. What think ye of Congress now? That day…evidenced that Americans would rather die than live as slaves to the Crown!"

Addie was in awe of MK, yet she feared MK might lose the newspaper at the hands of the British, not to mention the Loyalists. "This brings shivers up and down my spine. You are so open with your expression of freedom and independence. Hopefully the message is well received by the readers and you won't be run out of a job."

"As editor and publisher, it is my job to bring the truth to people. I will fight for my right, for every woman's right, to own a business. To have a career. Have no fear."

Hours later they finished the printing. MK counted out money to pay the Post riders when they arrived in the morning and locked it in a drawer. "We'll come in early tomorrow and hand off the papers to the riders, and I'll pay them at the same time."

Addie straightened a towering stack of newspapers. "All the papers are prepared for dispatch."

"Very good. Now, let's see if Rebekah needs assistance in closing the store. Then we can go home and enjoy a nice supper."

ADDIE, MK AND REBEKAH arrived bright and early on Monday morning to find the door to the store hanging askew.

"What is this?" MK pushed the door open. "Dear God."

Rebekah gasped and brought a hand to her mouth. "What happened?" Tears welled in her eyes.

"I'll tell you what happened." MK stopped amidst the torn, ink-stained sheets of paper and broken-spined books, hands fisted on her hips. "Samuel Thorpe and The Loyalist Club is what happened."

"They did this?" Addie turned in slow circles taking in the devastation. The stool that normally sat behind the counter was splintered and tossed into the middle of the shop. She kicked at a pointed shard of wood and then kicked it again, harder, sending it flying into the base of the wooden counter. "They cannot get away with this. We cannot allow them to go unpunished."

"I agree, my dear," MK said. "But the best we can do is go to the governor and plead for him to censure Thorpe and his followers."

"That hardly seems effective." Addie felt the steam of her anger coming to a low boil. She had no idea how to release her pent up feelings. "Is there nothing more? No actual punishment? No jail? Just censure?"

"Come. Let's clean up this mess and see what we can salvage." Rebekah's voice of reason cut through the tense air. "We need to see if any of the books can be repaired and how much of the stationery can be saved. The rest we will dispose of and replace. They will not win." Rebekah picked up torn pages from several different books and placed them gingerly on one end of the counter.

MK stood shaking her head, a look of resignation on her face. "Rebekah is right. We need to move on."

"Do you think they did this because of what we printed in the paper? The editorial?" Addie picked up the pieces of the shattered stool and leaned them against the wall near the door. Suddenly the door was thrown open. She jumped aside before it could hit her.

"Good morning, ladies." Samuel Thorpe stuck his pumpkin-shaped head into the store. "Oh, my. What have we here?" He scratched at his powdered wig and hoisted up his breeches as he stepped in and peered around. Then he strutted through the shop like a rooster, a finger on his chin as he surveyed the mess.

"Seems like you would know what we have here." Addie bit off her words, but couldn't resist continuing. "Why? Why would you do this?"

"My dear child, why would you think I had anything to do with this?" He smirked. "But let us assume that I did have a hand in the event that caused this disruption. You had been warned. Those who go against the Crown—you bunch of patriotic ne'er-do-wells—people like you need to be taught a lesson. And so, perhaps, that is what this is." He turned on his heel and marched toward the door. "Good luck with your clean up." He laughed and left the door open upon his exit.

"That man is a no good scoundrel," Addie said. "And he has a tear in the back of his stocking. He's not only no good, but a poor dresser. No gentleman in his right mind would be seen in public looking like that." She shook her head. "This calls for action." Addie's veins throbbed with the pulsing need for revenge.

"The first action we must accomplish is to finish cleaning up," Rebekah reminded Addie.

"Yes, of course. But, I mean, after that. I cannot stand to let this be. I need to do something. I need to…to fight!" Her body trembled and she clenched her hands into fists.

MK and Rebekah stopped picking up and stared at Addie.

"What, exactly, do you intend to do?" Rebekah asked. "Are you talking about joining the men on the battlefield? Certainly, you cannot be serious?" Her green eyes widened, fear darkening them.

MK placed an arm across Addie's shoulders. "Explain to us what it is you wish to do."

MK's calm voice did naught to still the demons raging inside Addie's head. "I want to go to Philadelphia. I want to be involved in the fight—politically. Not shooting at people. But fighting with—"

"Fighting with words!" MK finished Addie's train of thought.

"Yes! Precisely that." Addie pounded her fists into her thighs. "And Mr. Thorpe made me realize that I need to do more than I'm doing here. I want to make a difference, too. Like you." She faced MK. "You've taught me that women can be strong, and we can have a career and make a difference. You show it to everyone in this town every day. Women are naturally made of much tougher stuff than we are given credit for. If we dare to take the chance. And I dare." She blew out a huge breath.

"And so you shall." Rebekah clapped her hands. "I had no idea you felt so strongly."

"I've learned from the two of you. You're both brilliant businesswomen. You live truthful lives. You treat people with dignity and respect and you fight for what you believe in."

"I had no idea we were so influential," MK said, a smile creasing her face. "What say ye, Rebekah? Shall we help Miss Addie see her plans to fruition?"

"Yes, indeed," Rebekah said as she drew them into a big hug. "But first—"

"We clean up this mess," MK and Addie said together.

"Exactly." Rebekah replied.

Epilogue

My dearest Rebekah and MK,

I cannot thank you enough for helping me. The monies you loaned me have sufficed to get me to Philadelphia and to rent a room from a rather nice woman who reminds me so much of the two of you. I'm excited to share with you some great news. I kept in mind MK's adage that because I cannot fight with a weapon, I shall fight with words. I secured a job with a man named Thomas Paine and am assisting him in preparing for print a pamphlet entitled, "Common Sense." Those are fighting words if ever I've heard any. Thank you both, for all you've given me. I'm forever indebted to you.

Yours in Freedom,
Addie Smith

Fighters

By
Lori L. Lake

August 1966

Ruby Robinson stood waiting outside Olivet Baptist Church, sixth in line behind a group of young black men who were horsing around and seemed anxious to prove their physical prowess. They nudged and poked and challenged one another, occasionally glancing at her for any reaction. She chose to ignore them.

Behind her, a long string of people straggled down the block, mostly teenage boys. A lot of bragging and name-calling and tomfoolery was going on, though just behind her three young men, Afros combed high, were having a philosophical conversation about nonviolence and whether it was effective or not. She gazed at the line serpentining down the sidewalk and didn't see a single woman, then she homed in on a middle-aged matron in an olive green skirt set and matching pillbox hat. She squinted. Some kind of brooch was attached to the high side of the hat. The woman looked like something out of the Forties. Ruby gazed down at her own outfit. She wore sneakers, pegged jeans with the material tight at the calf and ankle, a long-sleeved, collared white blouse, and a hair tie to pull her long, naturally straight black hair into a ponytail. She was sure the older woman wouldn't approve.

Suppressing a sigh, she turned when she heard the sound of the church's side door opening. The blackest man she had ever seen leaned out and said, "Next." He glanced past her at the long line and shook his head slowly as he let the next volunteer in.

Now there were only four ahead of her.

Ruby pulled a dainty handkerchief out of her jeans pocket and wiped her forehead. The Chicago summer sun was brutal today. She glanced at her Timex and saw that it was just after noon. She'd been in line for two hours. She'd wasted the better part of half an hour walking from her

South Side home to the church, and it was critical she get back before four o'clock when her father returned home from his job at the police station. James Robinson opposed the Chicago Freedom Movement. Though he abhorred segregation, he was also a lawman, and lately he'd repeatedly said, "Protests and marches turn into riots that only serve to turn the whites against us. It needs to stop."

Heeding her father's warnings, Ruby had watched from a distance when the Reverend Martin Luther King and hundreds of followers had marched for open housing the week before. A white crowd gathered and threw bottles and rocks and screamed horrible epithets. She didn't see when Dr. King was hit in the back of the head with a rock, but she read a description in the local paper and at once felt the need to be a part of the campaign for better housing, fairer treatment, and an end to segregation.

The boy ahead of her turned and looked her up and down. He wore brown slacks and a yellow, black, and orange shirt tucked in at his scrawny waist. The end of a dark blue comb stuck out of his Afro. He wasn't much taller than she, and since her height topped out at five-four unless she wore high heels, she figured he couldn't be more than five-six. In contrast, the three guys at the head of the line loomed over him. She silently named him Shorty.

"Whatchu doing here?" he asked.

She gave him a quizzical look, hoping he'd back off.

But he didn't. "You the oddest lookin' black girl I seen in a long while."

A flush of heat surged up her neck and into her face. She marshaled her emotions in an attempt to stay calm. "You aren't so fancy yourself," she said softly. She didn't want to attract attention, but the men at the front of the line turned to stare at her.

Ruby knew she didn't look like a typical South Sider. While she'd inherited her father's darker skin and broad nose, she'd gotten her Japanese mother's pitch-black hair and angular near-black eyes. Afros were in, and her thick hair was never going to cooperate. Sometimes she wore a do-rag or a scarf to cover her head, but it was too hot today. She curled her hands into fists and tried to breathe regularly. All through high school she'd had to deal with people making remarks about her hair, and she was sick of it.

The boy said, "Why you wearin' jeans on a hot day? A skirt be better." He gave her a look she could only describe as leering.

"Hey, man." A fellow in a black suit, white shirt, and narrow tie said, "She can wear what she wants to."

"Yeah, it's her biz." The second man who spoke wore white bucks chalked and brushed to perfection, lightweight linen slacks, and a tight, short-sleeved navy blue shirt that showed off well-formed biceps. He had a terrific physique and was gazing at her appraisingly, but she had no interest in him.

The fourth man was chubby and light-skinned, with some natural red highlights in his Afro. His eyes were an odd color—perhaps green? Hazel? He met her gaze and said, "Whatchu doing here anyway? You little. You a girl. You don't belong in this kinda dangerous situation."

"Stop buggin' her," Buck Shoes said. "She can do what she likes."

"Red's right," Shorty said. "This is too dangerous for girls. We all get into some brawl and she gets hurt, why then we gotta stop what we doing and take care of her. Sorry to say, and I don't mean offense, miss, but girls don't belong in this risky business."

Ruby tightened her fists even more and glared at him. "I suppose you would have sent Miss Rosa Parks to the back of the bus."

"That was different," Shorty said. "This is 1966, a whole different time from back then. That was, what, 1950?"

Black Suit said, "Your ignorance does not become you. Miss Parks's famed bus ride took place in 1955. If I remember correctly, it was December the First."

"Yeah, yeah." Shorty sneered and his voice went up an octave. "You think you so smart, Mr. Vale-DIC-torian." He stared daggers at the other men. When he turned back to Ruby, he was even more emphatic. He shook his index finger near her face. "You mark my words. You gonna go and get yourself hurt, and I be standing there sayin' I told ya so while you bleed in the street."

She bristled. She'd like to knock his lights out. She had three older brothers, and they knew full well that when she got mad, they better stay out of her way. She could be a vicious wildcat when they baited her. Her brother Alvin was an amateur boxer who styled himself after Muhammad Ali, and she'd learned a lot about defending herself from him. He called her "Fighting Harada," after the Japanese boxer, Masahiko Harada, who had just defended his world Bantamweight title in June. He also called her Mighty Mouse, after her favorite Saturday morning cartoon character.

The opening of the church door interrupted the conversation, and the same man waved the next person in.

Red said, "I'm up!" He waddled toward the stairs, tucking his shirt tail into the back of his pants.

The line moved forward one step. Ruby tried to ignore the three remaining guys, but Black Suit said, "You in high school?"

She shook her head. "Graduated in June. Were you really valedictorian?"

"I was. I'm going to Roosevelt University in the fall. I'll be studying social justice."

Shorty rolled his eyes. "Try living up to that expectation."

Black Suit said, "Try exceeding it for once."

"Studying's a drag. I wanna have fun."

"You can't earn a living being a cool cat."

Shorty didn't seem to know how to respond to that.

Ruby looked back and forth between the two. She hadn't seen the resemblance at first, but their heads were shaped similarly and their mouths frowned in the same way. "Are you two related?"

Shorty said, "Brothers."

"I see. Your brother just graduated, so what grade are you in?"

"I got two more lousy years left, but I'm gonna get me some scratch, buy a race car, and lay rubber escaping this rotten place."

"You do that," his brother said, "and I'll tan your backside 'til ever sitting again is a pipe dream."

Buck Shoes said, "And I'll help him."

"Easy for you to say," Shorty whined, "when you got an athletic scholarship. Both of you are like made men."

Black Suit said, "You work a little harder, Melvin, and you'll succeed, too."

"Don't call me that!"

"It's your name, isn't it, brother?" Black Suit laughed.

Shorty nearly snarled, "You know I go by Ace now." He looked down at the ground and muttered.

Ace? Ruby stifled a laugh that she was glad Shorty/Melvin didn't notice. She thought he said a few curse words, but she wasn't sure.

A ripple of sound went through the crowd as a shiny black Cadillac came down the street and pulled to the curb right in front of Ruby. She shaded her eyes against the sun and watched two men get out. The one from the passenger seat nodded as he emerged and surveyed the long line. He was dressed impeccably in a dark gray suit and black tie and wore heavy black glasses. Lines creased his dark brown forehead, but the smile under his clipped mustache was merry. As he and the driver moved toward the church, he caught her eye and winked.

The church door opened, and the man called out, "Next," but then he caught sight of the two newcomers and his bored expression changed to one of delight. "Mr. Rustin! Why, we didn't know you were coming in today. Welcome!"

Buck Shoes made a motion toward the organizer, but the man shook his head. "Wait a moment, son. I'll be back as soon as I get Mr. Rustin settled."

The door shut behind them, leaving people in line chattering with excitement.

"Who was that?" Ruby asked.

"Bayard Rustin," Black Suit said in wonder. "How hip is *that*."

Buck Shoes squared his shoulders and looked uncomfortable. "I know he's one of Dr. King's staunchest supporters, but I heard he's made problems for us in advancing, umm, due to his, you know, his ways."

"Come on, William," Black Suit said. "Who cares about his personal life?"

Shorty shuffled his feet. "Just say it out loud. He's a damn homo."

"Lower your voice!" His brother looked around nervously at others in the line. "Besides, that's plain rude, Melvin."

"Stop—calling—me—that! And I don't care what you say. He's a pervert who went to jail for fornicating in California. I heard about it from Jarvis at the protest last week. Jarvis said the creep was too chickenshit to go to war, so he's a convict on account of that, too."

"Sometimes I can't believe I'm related to you. I've heard him speak about our Freedom Movement, and he was eloquent and smart. Bayard Rustin engineered the March on Washington three years ago. He was in on the Freedom Rides and put his body on the line marching all over the south. He's *sacrificed* his whole life for the movement."

Shorty smirked at him. "But he's a homo. Too bad Malcolm X bought it. He could've whipped that guy's ass."

The church door opened and Buck Shoes was beckoned in. Ruby hoped the conversation was at an end, but the two brothers stood arguing for some time. She tuned them out and thought about Mr. Rustin. Was he really homosexual?

As best as she could tell, she'd never met a homosexual, other than when she looked in the mirror every morning since the age of fifteen. She'd thought she was a rarity, like the Siberian Blue Robin she'd learned about in the ornithology section of her science class. Then she'd met Tamara Harris, who rode the motorcycle her now-dead brother had left behind when he went to fight in Vietnam. Tamara was big and blustery and unapologetic. She was a black woman with a mouth on her, and Ruby loved that about her. She'd kept her relationship with Tamara a secret from her family. Her proper, petite mother would have a cow. Her father would probably put her on restriction for life. Who knows what her brothers would do.

Somehow, some way, she and Tamara would figure out how to be together. Three years older than Ruby, Tamara worked the meat counter at the Jewel grocery store, which is where they'd met a year earlier. Ruby's head still went a little woozy when she thought back to the four-month-long courtship they'd carried on, neither quite able to admit their feelings for the other until late one October night when they'd put a blanket down on the roof of Tamara's five-story apartment building and lain close together to look at the stars. Somehow Ruby's hand found its way into Tamara's, and when she didn't pull back, Ruby leaned over and kissed her. She had no idea what had come over her, but she'd read Tamara right. The two of them decided to be bonded for life.

Ruby shook herself back to reality, her breath coming a little faster. The sun beat down on her dark hair, and she felt a rivulet of moisture run down her neck. She wiped it away and glanced around to make sure nobody was watching her. The two brothers were still arguing, and she was relieved to see that no one seemed to have noticed her momentary flight of fancy.

When she finally reached the front of the line, she had a moment of misgiving. What if Shorty was right? What if she'd waited in line for nearly three hours for nothing? She couldn't think that way. She was determined to be a part of this fight, so by sheer dint of will, it had to happen.

The door opened and she was ushered in. As she followed the organizer down a series of hallways, she relished the blessed cool inside. The man stopped at a doorway and gestured for her to enter.

A tired-looking man in a rumpled suit sat behind a desk in a room bookended by shelves crammed full of hundreds of books. Venetian blinds blocked the one window behind the desk but let in slivers of blinding sunlight. The maroon carpet was well-worn, and she followed its bare track over to a chair in front of the desk.

"Have a seat, miss," the man said.

Ruby relaxed in the chair and noticed a tiny woman in the corner to the right, seated at a table no more than two-by-two-feet wide. Her blouse was an amazing shade of deep blue. With deft hands, she picked up her steno pad and turned the page.

The woman looked up. "I'm Mrs. Adley," she said in a voice surprisingly deep and resonant for one so small. Even Shorty would probably tower over her. "Your name?"

"Ruby Robinson." She gave her address, date of birth, and phone number, and Mrs. Adley wrote them down.

"All right, child, Mr. Evanston has some questions for you."

"Thank you for your patience, Miss Robinson," he said. "I know it's been a long wait."

"Yes, sir."

"You're eighteen and a high school graduate?"

"I am."

"Are you going to college in the fall?"

She gazed at the worn carpet. "I'd like to, but I'll have to work a year or two and save more money for it."

"Can you type?"

She looked up. "I sure can."

"Have you done any office work?"

"Not really. Mostly school work. I have an old typewriter that I've typed my class papers on. That's why I'm pretty good at it. I'm self-taught, though."

"Would you like to learn office work? It's a useful skill to have."

Ruby looked over at Mrs. Adley who was busily making notes. Ruby's stomach plummeted. She had come to volunteer to be part of the movement, to organize marchers, to learn nonviolence skills so she could teach others how to best protect themselves. No disrespect intended, but I don't want to sit it around typing membership cards. The training for that probably took about twenty minutes.

She sat tall in her chair and took a deep breath. "Sir, I came to learn how to be a freedom fighter."

"I understand, but after all the recent violence and the hatred spewed by those pitted against our movement, we have to consider how to responsibly deploy our manpower."

He ran a hand through his short silvery Afro, and Ruby was struck by his use of the word manpower. Wasn't it supposed to be Power to the People? And weren't women people? Shouldn't it be humanpower?

"I want to make a difference, sir. Being behind the scenes wouldn't suit me."

Mrs. Adley piped up from the corner. "You're just an itty-bitty little thing, Ruby. No one wants to see you get hurt. We'll send the men out to do battle, figuratively of course, and you and I can stay back and run the show from behind the scenes. I could use the help."

Ruby felt lightheaded. This was not how things were supposed to go. She took another deep breath. "Please don't shut me out of the movement.

Haven't you heard of Diane Nash? Fannie Lou Hamer? I want to be like them, to do something that matters. But on the front lines. Not sit around filing recipe cards."

Mr. Evanston scowled. Mrs. Adley sat up straight in her chair. Ruby gazed back and forth between them, and all she observed were disapproving looks. Mrs. Adley seemed particularly offended.

"I'm not sure we have a use for you at this time, Miss Robinson." Mr. Evanston gave Mrs. Adley a knowing look. "If you change your mind about the assignment we offered, please stop by the church. Otherwise, we need to move on to the next person."

Ruby got to her feet, so sorely disappointed that she wanted to cry. She headed for the door and stomped down the hallway, turned left down another hall, then right. Eyes blurry, she stopped, unsure of where she was. Thinking she'd gone the wrong way, she reversed course, turned the corner, and ran smack-dab into someone.

"Oh, miss, I'm so sorry."

She looked up into the kindly eyes of the man named Bayard Rustin. "My fault, sir."

"Now, now"—he put a hand on her shoulder—"you look upset. What's wrong?"

Tears threatened to fall, but she blinked them back. "I want to help with the movement, but Mr. Evanston sent me away."

"You don't say." He gently squeezed her shoulder, then let go.

"He wanted to assign me some boring office work."

"And what would you rather do?"

"March. Be a part of organizing the protests and teaching non-violence. Be active."

"I see." He put a hand to his chin and nodded. "Why don't you come this way. You like tea?"

In short order she was seated on a sofa in a room she thought might be used when the pastor conferred with families before a funeral. Rustin sat in a wingback chair across a coffee table from her and poured her a cup of tea from a porcelain pot.

"Do you like sugar or milk in your tea?" he asked.

"No, sir."

She accepted the cup from him. "Thank you."

"I know there's a whole ceremony for properly serving tea, but am I right that we black folk just pour it and drink it?"

That made her smile.

He raised the delicate teacup. "Cheers."

She lifted her cup in return, then took a sip of the hot liquid. "My mother does the entire ritual for serving tea at least once a day. You have to have tea bowls, a caddy, bamboo scoops, and a whisk. As a child I had no patience for it, but now that I'm older, I see that it's something that makes her feel calmer, less anxious."

"Does she prefer black or green tea?"

"Green. But I like this kind better. Black tea seems less bitter to me."

"So your mother is Japanese?"

She nodded.

"And your father is a Negro?"

"Yes. They met after the Battle of Okinawa at the end of the war. He'd been injured by flying shrapnel, and she nursed his wounds. Even though she hardly spoke any English, they fell in love, and she came back here with him."

"You must have some issues arise at times regarding your heritage."

"Sometimes. When I was younger and other children teased me, Mama always said, '*shikata ga nai.*' That basically means there's nothing that can be done. My mother taught me to turn the other cheek, as the Bible says. My father taught me to be cautious. My brothers taught me to box."

He gave her a surprised smile. "So you're a pugilist."

"I'm a fighter for our rights." She didn't know what else to say.

He set his cup down. "So tell me more about your meeting today."

"I know I'm keeping you from your duties. You must be very busy, sir—"

"Now, now, none of that. I've got all the time in the world. What shall I call you?"

Flustered, she set her teacup down. "I'm sorry. I should have introduced myself. I'm Ruby. Ruby Robinson."

"Pleased to meet you, Ruby."

His voice was clear and rich. She thought he sounded cultured. She bet that Black Suit had been right about his speech-making eloquence.

"How do you know who I am, Ruby?"

"The boys outside mentioned—uh, said who you were. Are." Her tongue seemed to have tied itself in knots, and heat suffused her face.

"I take it that those young men were less than complimentary?"

"Yes, sir. I'm really sorry. I didn't know what to do—"

Bayard laughed. "You need not have done anything, Ruby. I thought I heard a few stray comments. Young men these days get very nervous about that which is different from them. Prejudice knows few bounds. It's hard when others don't understand people like you and me."

Was he referring to her racial heritage? Or had he somehow puzzled out that she preferred women? She had no idea how to ask that question. She nervously drank some tea instead.

"So," he said, "Mr. Evanston wasn't impressed with your ability to box."

"I didn't mention it, but I'm sure he wouldn't have been," she said with a smile.

"Sometimes fighting is an inside job. We often admire the man in the boxing ring for his ability to punch another man into submission, but this world requires more from us than brute strength. Wouldn't you agree?"

"I've never had brute strength, so I've had to resort to other methods." She didn't mention the tactics she used with her brothers, most of which they called "dirty" tricks because it involved "kicking where it counts."

"Other methods, yes, that's it exactly. I think people like us have to walk a fine line to survive, and one way to do so is to be slow to anger and quick to try to understand. We must use our minds and our wills. We want peace, but we can't achieve it through violence. We want a society without discrimination, but we ourselves must not discriminate against anyone in the process of building a just society. We must also be ourselves. We must not be afraid to stand tall and strong in the face of adversity."

"I'm only just beginning to understand that, Mr. Rustin. I know I'm not turning out the way my parents wanted."

"Few children turn out exactly as expected. For parents to have such weighty expectations is unfair. We are each as God made us, and we all have specific skills to offer to one another and to humanity. My activism doesn't spring from my being homosexual, or for that matter, from my having black skin. I believe I've been shaped in fundamental ways by my Quaker upbringing and by the values my grandparents instilled in me."

Ruby was rather shocked that he'd used the H word. She hardly knew what to say. When she went to drink her tea, it went down in a gulp and she coughed. He handed her a napkin and waited with an amused expression while she composed herself.

"Ruby, before I committed my life to activism, I dearly loved to sing. I acted in musicals and recorded some records with other blues singers. I even recorded an LP of old Negro spirituals and other tunes. I loved the night life and met so many interesting people. Did you ever hear the music of Bessie Smith, the Empress of the Blues?"

"I've heard of her, but I don't know her music."

"Such a shame. She had so much joy of life, and it comes out in her music. You might want to scare up some of her old records. How about Lorraine Hansberry, who died recently?"

"Of course I know her. She's from right here in Chicago, and I read her play, 'A Raisin in the Sun,' in school."

"Another talented black woman, full of vim and vigor, who wanted to make a difference in the world. How about Josephine Baker? You know of her?"

"Wasn't she the first black woman to star in a movie?"

"Yes, and she's been working in the civil rights movement for years. When she first came to the States from France, where she'd been living, she was denied hotel accommodations repeatedly. She wrote outraged letters to politicians and articles that were widely published, and she's given quite a number of talks around the country. I was honored to spend a little time with her at the March on Washington."

Ruby said, "All those men spoke—she was the only woman. Well, Mahalia and Ella sang."

"Yes, they did, but you're right. The men overshadowed the women that day."

She mumbled, "Men overshadow women nearly every day."

"Unfortunately, that's often the truth."

He refilled his teacup and pointed toward her cup.

"No, thank you. I've had enough."

He set down the teapot. "Do you know what Bessie and Josephine and Lorraine have in common?"

"They're all talented?"

"And they were all lovers of women."

Ruby's heart plummeted somewhere—or maybe it was her lungs. All she knew was that for a moment, she felt like she wouldn't be able to draw breath ever again.

He went on. "Bessie didn't even keep it a secret. She had big appetites, and she fed them. Josephine was married at least four times, but she had relationships with women on the side. And Lorraine—poor Lorraine didn't live long enough to proclaim herself lesbian, but I met her and I can attest to her belief that homosexuals should have rights and be left alone to live their lives. She was a member of the first lesbian organization, the Daughters of Bilitis. Do you know of it?"

Ruby shook her head slowly. How did this man figure her out? How did he know about her sexuality?

"You're an intelligent woman, Ruby, and you have sixty, seventy, maybe even eighty years ahead of you. Do you know how much you could accomplish if you set your mind to it—how much you could do to move forward civil rights, human rights, women's rights, and the rights of homosexuals? You see, it's not merely matters of race for us to focus upon. Add to that list poverty and war and the environment, all of which need keen minds and strong hearts to lead us forward as a society. We must also protest people's intolerance and society's refusal to acknowledge our dignity as human beings, in all the ways we're disparaged and undervalued. Every act of protest we make confers dignity on each of us and moves us ahead. Do you agree?"

"Yes." She did agree, but she couldn't see how any of this applied to her. How could she protest bigotry and intolerance if she wasn't allowed to be part of the movement?

"Let me say something else about heritage. You come from two lines of ancestry filled with strong, determined, and persistent fighters. I think of Yuri Kochiyama, the Japanese activist from New York City. Did you see her photo in *Life* magazine?"

"No, sir, I didn't."

"Yuri is the Japanese woman cradling Malcolm X's head in her hands after he was betrayed and shot in Harlem. The course of her life that brought her to that moment in time is quite telling. She was born in California, so she's a United States citizen. She got her first job as a schoolteacher at a nearby church.

"When the Japanese bombed Pearl Harbor, the FBI came and took her father away and put him in a federal prison. He'd already been ill, and when they finally released him a year or so later, he died. Shortly thereafter, she and her family were interned in a concentration camp in Arkansas."

"This was during the Forties?"

"Yes."

"And now here on the South Side of Chicago it sometimes seems like an internment."

"At least you can get out and about," he said. "You can travel some places in the world."

"If you can afford it," Ruby said.

"Yuri and her mother and brother stayed in the camp until war's end. She married someone she met there and moved to New York City, where she lived in a neighborhood that was primarily black. She made friends, including Malcolm X. She became a champion for the rights of all. She's a small Asian woman with a big voice and substantial influence. You, too, can emulate that."

"So what are you saying? What do you want me to do?"

"You're a fighter, right?"

She nodded.

"Fighters train. Fighters learn the history of their opponents, of their sport. Fighters prepare."

"That's what I want to do," she burst out, frustration coursing through her. "That's why I came here, to see how I can help."

"The Chicago Freedom Movement is important, but it's only one small wedge of an enormous pie. There's work to do that will last past my lifetime, past your lifetime. Your eagerness to enter into the fray is honorable, Ruby, and I commend you for it. But you have more to offer than laying your body on the line at the next march."

"You sound like the boys in line today. One of them mocked me to no end."

"I'm not mocking you at all. Please don't misunderstand. As one old, worn fighter to a blossoming contender, I'm suggesting that you study and prepare for the coming battles. You want to last in the ring for a very long time, and in order to do so, you'll need mental, emotional, and intellectual training."

"But, sir, didn't you learn out in the streets?"

"To a certain degree, but I'd gotten an education first to teach me how to think, how to plan, how to influence other people."

"One of the guys in line is going to Roosevelt U to study social justice."

"Aha! An excellent school."

"I did get a small scholarship for books based on my grades, but I don't have enough money yet to attend college."

"Then let's acquire it for you."

"Acquire?"

"A number of philanthropists I know offer funds for young people like you. Hmm...I'm thinking in particular of a Jewish financier who might be very interested in helping you. You could stay right here in Chicago and attend any one of several colleges."

"A Jewish man?"

Rustin nodded. "You might be surprised at how many Jews and white people are sympathetic to civil rights being extended to all people. Many influential people are eager to assist."

Ruby was dumbfounded. She opened her mouth to speak, but no words emerged. She swallowed, then choked out, "Why would someone I don't even know want to help me?"

"Justice isn't just for one race or one religion or one social group. As Dr. King has often said over the years, the arc of the moral universe is long, but it bends towards justice. If you feel a passion toward work for justice, then why shouldn't your path be blazed by others who share your desire?"

She thought Rustin looked rather pleased with himself. He placed his teacup and hers on the tray next to the teapot and slid it to the side. He reached into the inside pocket of his jacket and pulled out a small notebook, whipped through a few pages, then leaned forward and set the notebook on the coffee table in front of him, a pen poised to write.

"Give me your address and telephone number, and I'll put you in touch with one of my best friends. As they say, he's 'queer as a three-dollar bill,' but his fortune is made up of real money."

After he took down her information, he rose. "Miss Ruby Robinson, when your studies are complete, you and I will work together. Once we succeed with the Civil Rights Movement, there are all manner of Human Rights you can help me to secure. Do we have a deal?"

"Yes. Yes, sir. A thousand times yes." She rose, her head filled with wonder. He offered his hand and she shook it.

"Always have faith," Bayard Rustin said. "Someone will always be in your corner, Ruby. That's the way the world works when you're a fighter."

The Other Marie

By
E.J. Kindred

"YOU KEEP THIS UP, Celia, and you're going to be the Marie Equi of the twenty-first century."

"Who?" I looked at her, bleary-eyed. I couldn't remember the last time I was so exhausted, not even during my internship, but seeing Marty's spiky red hair and blue eyes was comforting. Her concerned expression didn't lessen my relief at being with her again.

She gave me a quick hug and said, "Never mind. Let's go home."

She took my hand, I suspect more to steady me than to show affection, and led me away from the Multnomah County Justice Center, where I'd been an overnight guest.

"You probably need a good meal," she said. "And trust me, you definitely need a shower."

An hour later, I emerged from the shower, grateful for its restorative powers. I opened the bathroom door to let the steam out and was greeted with the heady aromas of frying bacon and toasting bagels. That's all it took for me to run a comb through my hair, slip on my favorite baggy sweats, and head up to the kitchen.

Marty was at the stove, keeping a close eye on a pan of sizzling eggs. She didn't object when I snitched a piece of bacon. It tasted so good I practically swallowed it whole.

"Have I thanked you yet for bailing me out?" I wrapped my arms around her waist and rested my chin on her shoulder.

"Again." She tended those eggs as if they were the most important ones she'd ever cooked.

"Yes, again." I released her and, grabbing a mug, poured myself some coffee. "And thank you."

Without speaking, she put two perfectly cooked eggs, a toasted bagel, and several slices of crisp bacon on a plate and handed it to me. I took it and my coffee and sat at our kitchen table.

The kitchen was the main reason that we'd bought the house a decade ago. The corner breakfast nook had large windows on both sides, affording unobstructed views of a backyard that was much larger than most properties in Portland's northeast neighborhoods. Trees that lined the lot gave us plenty of privacy and also provided habitat for the birds and butterflies that we enticed into the yard with feeders and flowers. The rest of the house was an uninspired mid-century assembly of square rooms with no character when we bought it, but we'd both loved the kitchen from the start.

"Looks like we have goldfinches again," I said. I dunked a bit of bagel into the creamy egg yolk and took a bite.

"Which you could see every day if you'd quit getting yourself arrested."

I should have known.

"Look, baby, you know how important this is. As a nation, we can't go to war unless there's no other option. We've already sent our people to Afghanistan, and I'll bet you my retirement fund that we'll be there for years."

She finally looked at me.

"I know," she said.

"I hate war," I continued. "I saw what it did to my father." His time in Vietnam destroyed him and wrecked our family. Mom said that before he left, he was a soft-spoken caring man and after he came home, he was not the same person. He was withdrawn and angry, and he killed himself when I was ten. That so-called police action ruined lives and tore families apart. "We simply can't continue to treat more generations of young men and women as if they're disposable."

"Yes, but—"

"And this push to invade Iraq is bullshit."

Marty pulled a chair up next to me and sat down. She took my hand.

"Celia, one of the things I love about you is your passion for doing the right thing. I'm sure it's one of the reasons you went to medical school, so you could help people. And you're a wonderful doctor."

I looked away from her beautiful blue eyes. Taking a compliment gracefully was not one of my strong suits.

"Thanks," I mumbled.

"But," she continued, "you're not helping anyone by getting arrested every other week, and to be honest, I don't like that you don't seem to be considering how I feel knowing that you're in jail again. If that moron in the White House wants to use the power of his office to try to convince everyone that's he some kind of macho bad-ass, all the protests in the world won't stop him."

"We can't just roll over," I said.

"I agree with you, but can't we just once try to be practical about it? I need you to think of me sometimes, too." She released my hand and stood. "I have to go to work. There are forty antsy seventh graders just waiting for me to make them run around the track. You get some rest and we can talk more about this later."

I stood and stretched my back. "I have to go in, too," I said. "I'm sure that Jose's got my day booked up."

Coffee mug in hand, I followed her into the living room and watched her pull a jacket on. "Tonight, I'll want to hear why you said I was this century's Marie Somebody. Antoinette?"

She opened the front door and grinned at me. "I hope not," she said. "She lost her head."

AS I EXPECTED, JOSE had indeed scheduled a full day of appointments. I was still tired from days of protests on Portland's downtown streets and a night in a cramped cell with half a dozen other women who were also outraged by the country's imminent invasion of a sovereign nation. Fortunately, tending to my patients' concerns restored some of my energy.

My office was in a small single story building in one of Portland's poorer neighborhoods. I had two small exam rooms, constantly occupied by the patients that my nurse, Terry, rotated in and out as the day progressed. The tiny waiting area was overseen by Jose, who could have been a model but instead chose to keep my practice running smoothly, answering phones, scheduling appointments, all the while soothing crying children and their worried parents. I'd never get rich serving the neighborhood's lower middle class residents and the homeless people who seemed to migrate through, but I loved helping them as much as I could.

The constant stream of kids with runny noses and ear infections and parents with no money or insurance didn't dispel my concerns about Marty. My persistent involvement with anti-war and anti-government protests was causing a rift between us. She said that she understood, and we did agree on most political issues, but she was getting tired of playing second fiddle to issues that I knew I couldn't influence, even if I wouldn't admit it out loud. And who was this Marie person she'd mentioned?

The last appointment of the day was a new patient, a small boy of four who had cut his hand on a broken window.

"Mrs. Velazquez," I said in Spanish. "Reynaldo needs stitches in his hand."

She shook her head. "No money, Doctor Celia," she said in halting English. Tears ran down her face and she hugged her son, mindless of the blood staining her thin blouse.

"It's all right," I said, enunciating carefully. "I'll take care of him."

"SO HOW WAS YOUR day, dear?"

It was a game that Marty and I played, taking the roles of characters from old television shows. This time, I was the wife keeping the home fires burning and Marty was the husband arriving home to find that the little woman had dinner on the table.

"Fine, sweetheart," she said with a smile. "I'll get that gold retirement watch yet."

We laughed together for a moment, unable to maintain the charade. We both knew that I couldn't cook anything more complex than toast, and even then the outcome was questionable. I was relieved that she seemed happier than she had in the morning.

"Seriously, how was your day? Did you keep the brats in line?"

Marty was a middle school track coach who taught history part-time. Even after our years together, she frequently surprised me with the depth of her knowledge about the past, especially Oregon history.

"Yes," she said. "They were okay today. Good thing we're getting close to spring break." She scanned the kitchen and took a deep breath. "You got pizza," she said with a little happy dance. "Pepperoni?"

"Of course, pepperoni. And olives and other good stuff. It'll be done in about ten minutes, so you have time to change."

Half an hour later, we each sat back in our chairs with satisfied expressions. We'd devoured half of the large pizza, and I was already anticipating leftovers. We both started to get up to clear the table, but Marty waved me back.

"I'll get it," she said. "You look beat."

"Thanks, hon."

Grateful for her thoughtfulness, I watched her clear the table and wrap the cooling pizza and put it away. While she worked, I remembered what she'd said.

"Hey, professor," I said, calling her one of the pet names I had for her. "Who's Marie What's-her-name? That you mentioned this morning? Was it Marie Curie?"

She looked at me for a moment, puzzled, and then she remembered and smiled.

"No, not Madame Curie. The *other* Marie. Marie Equi," she said, her smile fading. "I think you might be her reincarnation. At the very least, you're her sister from another generation."

"I've never heard of her."

Marty brought us both cold drinks and sat opposite me at the table. "I'm not surprised. I mean, how many women are in the history books? Marie was an extraordinary woman, but few people know who she was." She paused for a moment. "She was one of Oregon's first woman doctors. She was a lesbian, about as out as a lesbian could be in the late eighteen hundreds. She was born in Massachusetts, but came to Oregon in 1892 with a woman named Bessie Holcomb. They lived together in the Columbia Gorge somewhere."

"Boston marriage," I said.

Marty nodded. "I've read that the term was used mostly for upper class women in lesbian relationships, and Marie had a working class background, but it still works. If I remember right, her father was an Italian immigrant."

"I don't understand why you think I'm like her. Lesbian doctors can't be so uncommon."

"Not today," she said. "But in Marie's day, she was definitely unusual."

I nodded, waiting for the rest.

"She was also involved in politics. She campaigned for a woman's right to vote and for the rights of workers to join unions and receive a fair wage. She was part of getting women the right to vote here in Oregon in 1912, years earlier than most of the rest of the country. And she wasn't shy about standing up for those who couldn't help themselves. She supported women cannery workers who were paid pennies an hour." She reached out and grasped my wrist for a moment. "And get this. When a man in The Dalles refused to pay Bessie for work she'd done, Marie took a horsewhip to him."

"Wow."

"Yeah, and she did it in public, too," Marty said with a smile. "Apparently the people in town didn't like the guy, either, so they held a raffle for the whip and gave the money to Marie and Bessie. How cool is that?"

"And interesting, since it sounds as if there was some local recognition of their relationship."

Marty nodded her agreement.

"After Marie became a doctor, she treated poor people who couldn't pay her, and she made up for it by charging her richer clients higher fees. She also provided contraception information and did abortions, which was damn ballsy since both were illegal then. She was arrested at least once for giving out advice on contraception."

"How could that have been illegal? I mean, sure, abortions were illegal, but telling people how to avoid pregnancy?"

"Actually," Marty said, "giving out information about contraception was illegal in some parts of the country until the nineteen sixties, which seems unimaginable now." She took a sip of her drink. "She didn't let being arrested stop her from taking care of her patients. She also went to San Francisco to help the people there after the 1906 earthquake. She was about as fearless a woman as I've ever heard of."

I tried to absorb this for a moment. Of course there were people who did remarkable things, people that we'd never learn about, but this woman sounded like a force of nature. How could her story have become so obscure?

"I would have liked to meet her," I said.

"You'd have had to be born earlier. She died here in Portland in 1952." Marty smiled. "But you ain't heard nothin' yet."

I raised an eyebrow. "Better than horsewhipping someone?"

"The good doctor got involved in anti-war demonstrations prior to World War One. For one thing, she said that all of the war preparations were meant only to make rich people richer."

I shook my head in mock disbelief. "Imagine that."

"She was arrested under what was called the Sedition Act, which prohibited speech against the government. She spent nearly a year in San Quentin for something that we'd consider free speech today."

"And Bessie?" I asked, starting to see the bigger picture.

"They didn't stay together, but Marie did have a ten-year relationship with a woman named Harriet Speckart. She and Harriett even adopted a little girl."

I sat back in my chair and took a long drink of my soda.

"So," I said slowly, "when you said yesterday that I'm this century's Marie Equi?"

"Hon, you're just like her in so many ways and—" Marty took a deep breath and blew it out. "And not all of them are good."

"But—"

"Wait, let me finish." She paused for a moment. "Surely, you see the surface resemblance. Two lesbian doctors who care for the poor and displaced and who want nothing more than to see that the right thing is done. That's wonderful, and I love that about you, that you care so much."

I waited for the other shoe.

"But Marie Equi's intense focus landed her in prison. It also ruined her health. And—" She stopped and looked down at her hands. She wiped a tear away.

"And?"

"And it damaged her relationship with the woman she loved most. When Marie was in San Quentin, Harriett moved to Seaside with their daughter and even though they stayed in touch, they were never together after that." She dabbed the corners of her eyes with a tissue.

I looked past Marty and out into the yard. I didn't know what to say. I knew that she was unhappy with my involvement in the anti-war protests, but even I got the message: she was feeling pushed aside, as Harriett must have felt when Marie's activities led to her imprisonment.

"Hey," Marty said in a gentle tone. "Don't get me wrong. I love your passion and commitment. You know that I agree with you on the political stuff. I think that fool in the White House is damaging the country, and if—*when*—he orders our troops to invade Iraq, hundreds, maybe thousands of our young people will be killed and maimed, and for what? I wish the protests could change that, but they won't."

I nodded, unable to speak, trying to hold back my own tears.

"So," I said, wishing that my voice didn't waver. "What do you want me to do?"

Marty sat back in her chair. "I don't know. I would never ask you to change who you are. I love you and I like that you're such a firebrand sometimes. Your enthusiasm can be contagious, and I like that, too." She paused and then nodded her head, as if she'd made a decision. "You know what, I'm tired and I know you are." She stood and stretched, and then grabbed my hand to pull me up from my chair. "What do you say that we continue this conversation another time?"

TWO DAYS LATER, I came home, weary after another long day seeing patients and trying to remember the Spanish word for "scabies." I showered and changed into my pajamas with every intention of going to bed early.

Marty had dinner ready. I should have known that she was up to something. She'd made fried chicken, mashed potatoes and gravy, and macaroni and cheese. If any woman knew her way into my heart, Marty did.

"If you tell me that there's pumpkin pie in this house, I'm going to suspect that you're having an affair." I gave her my best look of suspicion.

She laughed, a happy sound that had been absent from our house for the past few weeks. "No such luck, doc. You're stuck with me."

I enveloped her in a hug. "I'm glad to hear it, but you've made my favorite meal, so you're not as innocent as you're trying to make it seem. What's going on?"

"Wait and see," was all she would say.

After we'd eaten dinner, but before she cut the pumpkin pie that, sure enough, was hiding in the fridge, Marty got up from the table. When I started to rise, she waved me back to my chair.

"Stay put," she said. "I have something for you."

She went around the corner and returned with a parcel wrapped in rainbow striped paper and tied with rainbow-colored ribbons. She put it down before me with a wide smile on her face.

"Remember when we were talking a couple of days ago and you asked me what I wanted you to do?"

"Sure." I was starting to worry.

"Well, I want you to open your present and do what it says."

I raised an inquiring eyebrow, but she waved toward the wrappings.

"Go on."

I untied the multi-colored ribbon and coiled it up and set it aside. Whatever was inside the package was soft. I ran my fingers along the edge of the paper to loosen the tape. When the paper fell open, I laughed out loud.

On the table before me was a bright red t-shirt emblazoned with the words "Do What Marie Equi Would Do" and in smaller print below "mostly."

Longhorns

(An Excerpt from the novel, *Longhorns*,
where Buck, Red, and Les go to a hoedown)

By
Victor J. Banis

THE HANSEN FARM WAS the next property over from the Double H, so they were the nearest of neighbors, but this was Texas, and neighbors did not mean close. It was a twenty-mile ride from house to house, and that was going directly across the prairie instead of by road.

The three of them set out in the gloaming, but it was night by the time they arrived there and hitched up their horses. There were other horses by the score, and buggies and wagons from around the county, and some had even ridden out from San Antonio in fancy carriages. Texans mostly lived a hard life, and they took their fun where and when they could find it.

The Hansen's enormous barn had been cleaned out for the occasion, bales of hay put around for the men to sit on, and chairs brought from the house for the ladies. The dirt floor was watered and packed down for dancing, and the glow of scores of lanterns made the inside of the barn as light as day.

The boys had dressed in their best, and Buck had washed and scrubbed until his hands were red and raw and his face just about glowed. He put some bear grease on his hair to try to hold it in place—with only modest success, since one or two shiny curls insisted on spilling across his brow, grease or no grease—and he picked his teeth clean with a sprig of wintergreen from the garden, to be sure that his breath was sweet.

One of the hands who was close to his size loaned him a fancy shirt that had come all the way from down Mexico way, embroidered across the front with red and white roses. Buck was rightly proud of the dungarees he had bought while he was in Galveston, which were the height of fashion just then, and he had gotten the attention of one or two of the hands earlier in the day while he knelt bare assed by the horse trough for the better part of an hour to scrub his trousers to a fare thee well, so that they were spotless now and nearly as good as the day he bought them. He had purchased a new bandana at the Mercado when he was in San Antone the week before, yellow as the eyes of a wildcat, and he wore that tied at his throat, and his white snakeskin boots were cleaned and polished, to where you could just about see your reflection in them.

Only his Stetson was old and shabby. He would like to have replaced that, but there hadn't been the time, and he hadn't wanted to ask any of the boys about borrowing one, since a cowboy's hat was a personal thing and something he was hardly ever without. Buck wore his own, old one instead, and though he felt somehow half naked without it, he hung it over the horn on his saddle and strode hatless with Les and Red toward the light that spilled out the barn door.

Glancing at him as they went in, Les thought that the boy looked right fine. It appeared to him, surveying the room, as if Buck was the handsomest young fellow in the place, in fact. For some reason, it made him feel downright proud to have the boy alongside him like this, and his chest kind of puffed out, like. If there were any unattached girls present, he felt sure they would sit up and take notice.

Red looked at Buck, too, as they went into the barn, and found himself wishing after all that him and Buck were back at the ranch. Damned if the boy didn't look like he was good enough to eat. Well, it was hard to imagine that any little girl here wouldn't feel the same, seeing him, so maybe this idea of Les's had been a good one after all.

There was a moment of stillness as the three stopped in the barn doorway, and even the musicians at the far end of the barn let their music trail off as everyone turned to look. Old man Hansen himself, though, came quickly across to welcome them, his wife at his side, and after a moment, the hum of conversation started up again, and the fiddlers picked up their tune and began to scrape and saw again.

"Mighty glad you could come," Miz Hansen greeted the cowboys. She was near as tall as her husband, a big boned woman with a sun-dried face like a prune, but her smile was friendly and her eyes shone warmly.

"Mighty good of you to have us," Les said, and introduced the two with him.

"There is some punch over there where the ladies are standing at that long table, if you are thirsty from your ride," she said, waving a hand in that direction, "And I expect that one or two of the fellows might have something stronger, if you were to ask around, but of course, I know nothing at all about that." She smiled and her husband gave the boys a wink as if to say they would get to that later.

"Reckon you should meet the rest of my family," Hansen said. He led the way across the open floor, where a few couples had begun to dance together. His three sons stood with their friends off to one corner, all of them wearing the farmer kind of overalls that cowboys disdained.

"You know my oldest boy, Ron," Hansen said, "And this here is Brett, and the youngest, Tom." His oldest boy, Ron, ignored the hands that were offered, but the other two shook with the cowboys, although they did not look too enthusiastic about it, particularly when it came Buck's turn.

Buck did not much mind for himself. He was a half-breed, and he was used to the idea that some people didn't care to shake his hand, but he took offense at seeing Les and Red rebuffed, since he felt certain that they were the better of any man present. If either of them minded, though, it did not show on their faces. You might almost have thought they had not even noticed when Ron turned his back on them.

"And these are our daughters," Miz Hansen said, and led the cowboys to a pair of young ladies seated on wooden chairs nearby. "Emma is our oldest. She will be getting married in the fall." Emma was tall and willowy, plain of face, although she might have been pretty if her lips had not been set in such an icy line. She only nodded at them without saying a word, and quickly averted her eyes.

"And this is our baby, Margaret," Miz Hansen said, indicating the other girl.

"Maggie," the young lady corrected her. "Margaret makes me sound like an old maid, Mama."

"I don't reckon anybody would mistake you for that," Buck said, grinning, and she responded with a little giggle and bowed her head, blushing shyly, but not before she had favored him with a friendly smile. "Not as pretty as you are."

She was pretty, too, Les thought, with hair the color of corn silk, and cheeks that needed no rouge to paint flowers on them. He began to feel that maybe this had been the right idea, after all, to invite Buck to come along with them. If that little girl couldn't run the idea of butt fucking out of that Indian's head, he reckoned nothing could. After which, maybe he could have some peace back at his ranch, which was greatly to be desired.

The fiddlers launched into an energetic polka, and more couples joined the enthusiastic movement on the dance floor.

"Say," Buck said, "that music has my toes to tapping, Miz Maggie. What do you say, the two of us take a whirl?"

Maggie giggled again, but she held out her hand to him and got up from her chair. "If it's all right with Mama?" she said, and gave her mother a quick glance.

The pause in her mother's reply was no more than a heartbeat long. "No sense in wasting the music," she said, and turned to Les. "Would you care to try your luck with an old farm woman?" she asked.

"Thank you most kindly, ma'am," Les said, "but you'd be lucky to have the use of your feet by the time I got done stomping on them. I never did learn how it was done. Now, Red, here, he knows his way around a barn dance."

"If you would do me the honor, ma'am," Red said, taking his cue, and led her onto the floor.

Les and Hansen stood together and watched the couples twirling and jouncing energetically. The polka ended and was followed by a reel, the dancers lining up in facing rows. Les saw that several of them were looking sideways at Buck, like they were not quite sure that they ought to be on the floor with him, but he was with their host's daughter, and while one or two couples retired to the sidelines, most chose to wait and see.

If Buck noticed their reluctance, though, he paid it no mind. He gave a tap of his foot, and seemed to fly across the floor with his partner, dashing at the line of dancers before him as if he would run right into them, then spinning his partner about with graceful abandon, her skirt billowing in a cloud about her legs, and a swift promenade while the others clapped time. There was the rippling sensuality of a gamboling colt in the easy swing of Buck's hips and thighs, and the other dancers on the floor with him forgot entirely their reservations, and found themselves instead sharing his boyish delight, and threw themselves into the dance with renewed vigor, the men determined not to be out-danced, and the ladies thrilled to be whirled about with such manly enthusiasm.

It came as no surprise to Les to see that Buck was as light as a feather on his feet, and it seemed as if he and the girl were enjoying themselves mightily. She laughed at something he said, smiling up at him, and it was clear enough that she found him pleasing to look at.

Well, shit, who wouldn't, Les asked himself? The boy was truly a treat for the eyes, all fancied up the way he was tonight, as sweet looking as an angel, if he *was* full of the devil inside, with them dark curls of his and that big grin, and built as lean and hard as an Indian pony—and he had a pretty impressive bulge himself in the front of them dungarees, now that Les's eyes happened to look down there by the merest chance.

Les was immediately embarrassed by that thought, though. A man wasn't supposed to notice that about another man, was he? Let alone think of a man being pretty. Hell's bells. What was happening to him? It seemed any more like he didn't hardly even know himself.

He dragged his eyes away from the dancers and turned to Hansen. "I guess I could use something to wet my whistle," he said, "if there was anything a little more interesting than that punch your wife mentioned."

"I think we can find the right thing," Hansen said, with a friendly smile. "Let's us stop over to the house for a minute."

RED ESCORTED MIZ HANSEN back to her chair after their one dance and thanked her for it, and was relieved that she did not expect another one. He thought his dancing was about the same thing as watching a dog walk on his hind legs. You were so surprised to see him doing it at all, you just about didn't notice that he was doing it so badly.

He watched Buck and the girl, gliding about the floor now in a two-step, as elegant as his reel had been spirited, and he was happy to see how well Buck danced. He kind of wondered where and how he had learned it. However it had been, though, it was clear that the girl was enjoying herself, and the looks she was flashing up into Buck's face were plenty pleased.

For some odd reason, that gave Red a pang. But that was the way of it, wasn't it, he told himself quickly. A boy and a girl met, and fancied one another, and generally they did something about it, and maybe they even got hitched in time. That was not likely to happen in this case—he had seen the quick glances that Miz Hansen had given her daughter and Buck while they danced, and it was certain she would not welcome a half-breed Indian into her family, if she did let her daughter dance with one.

More than likely, though, Buck would get himself hitched in time, if not with this filly, then with another one day. It saddened him to think that what he and Buck had going between them would mostly likely come to an end when that time came.

"Well, it ain't come yet, not over one little dance or two," he told himself. He took his tobacco pouch out of his pocket, and made to roll himself a cigarette, but then he looked around at all those bales of hay, and decided to do it outside after all.

Wouldn't do neighborly relations any good to burn the barn down in the middle of a dance.

BUCK SAW HIM GO, and when he had escorted Maggie, laughing and with her yellow hair falling across her face, back to her chair, he excused himself and went in search of Red. He found him by the glow of his cigarette, in the shade of a live oak at the far edge of the farmyard. Red passed the cigarette to him as he walked up.

"Looks like you are enjoying yourself some," Red said.

"Been a while since I done any dancing," Buck said, laughing softly in the darkness. He took a puff off the cigarette and passed it back.

"She is a pretty little thing," Red said.

"That she is."

"You getting any ideas?"

"What kind of ideas?" Buck said, and looked at him in the darkness, just able to make out his face, and laughed again. "Well, I ain't no farmer, exactly, but I have never minded doing a little plowing now and again, when the opportunity presented itself."

He reached to put a hand on Red's shoulder and gave it a friendly squeeze. "Don't you be worrying none about that, though. Girls like that, they don't get themselves tangled up with half-breeds, except for some wrestling out behind the barn, which I got no objections to, but I can take it or leave it. I told you before, I like what I like, and I ain't forgetting who my friend is."

"That never even crossed my mind," Red said, but he felt better for hearing that said.

WHEN THEY CAME BACK inside, Buck saw that Maggie's oldest brother, Ron, was engaged in some serious sort of conversation with her. They appeared to be having an argument. She tossed her head at something he said and gave him a fierce glower.

Buck walked over to them and, giving Ron a nod, he said to Maggie, "I was hoping you would favor me with another dance, Miz Hansen."

"The dancing is over," Ron said.

Buck glanced at the dance floor, where other couples were two stepping to the beat of the music. "Looks like some are still at it," he said.

"Let me make it plainer, then," Ron said, "we are done dancing with you."

"Ron," Maggie said, "I told you to leave it be."

"Well, now," Buck said, smiling at the young man, "I had in mind dancing with your sister, but I guess I could accommodate you, if you are wanting it badly enough. The thing is, I only know the man's part, by which I mean to say, you would have to be the girl of it."

"You come outside with me, half breed," Ron said, looking nasty, "and I will give you a dance all right."

Buck took a moment to consider this in silence. Over Ron's shoulder, he saw Red hurry out the barn door—going, he supposed, to find Les. He knew exactly how Les would feel about his making any trouble. The last thing he wanted was to cause Les any aggravation—of that sort, anyway.

"I ain't of no mind to fight with you," he said.

Ron sneered. "I might've knowed you would be a chicken," he said.

Buck looked around. Others had begun to notice them and to listen to their exchange. Still seated in her chair, Maggie was red with mortification.

"Oh, Ron," she said. Beside her, her sister Emma smirked and looked hopefully from one to the other of the two young men.

"I guess I could teach you a step or two," Buck said with a sigh. "Whyn't you lead the way, then, seeing as this is your dance?"

"Come on, then," Ron said, and began to shoulder his way through the crowd that had gathered. They went out into the barnyard, a distance from the barn, so that they were mostly in shadows. Buck stripped off his shirt as he went, since it was borrowed and he would not want to give it back with no blood on it. His bandana went too, and he tossed them to the ground, and unlaced his holster, and the sheath for his Bowie, and put his weapons aside with his shirt.

Ron began to do the same, but seeing his opponent like this, he couldn't help having some second thoughts. Parading around on the dance floor the way he had been, Buck had looked more like a frolicsome boy than a man to be concerned about, but now that he was shirtless, flexing his muscles as he waited, he looked like someone to be reckoned with.

Ron looked at some of the boys crowding around the open door of the barn. "Someone go find Brett and Tom," he yelled, "tell my brothers to get their asses out here."

One of the boys in the throng turned toward the barn and yelled, "Brett, Tom, Ron is fixing to kick the shit out of this half breed."

A minute later, the two younger Hansens, neither as tall as their brother but both of them thickly built, rushed out and pushed their way through the crowd.

"Hang on, there, brother," Tom called, and Brett said, "I'm wanting to carve me a piece of that Indian's ass while you are at it." Tom already had a Bowie in his hand and Brett pulled his from the sheath strapped to his legs as he ran.

They stopped abruptly. A six foot three inch cowboy had stepped directly into their path, his feet planted wide, his hands resting on the handles of his six shooters. While the brothers blinked, trying to take this in, the big red headed fellow came up to stand alongside him, hand on his gun as well.

"What you cowboys got on your mind?" Brett asked, making a show of bravado.

"We got on our mind that those two over yonder will have themselves a fair fight, one on one," Les said. "Without no help from you two and without no knives."

"Well, who says you got any right to say how things will be, here on our farm?" Tom asked, but he took a step back so that he was half behind his bigger brother.

"It ain't me saying it," Les said, running his fingers over the butts of his guns. "It is Mister Colt's idea."

"Maybe we could just tell you and Mister Colt to go somewhere and mind your own fucking business," Brett said.

"You could," Red said, speaking calmly, like a man without a care in the world, "but you wouldn't want to if you had good sense. Some people don't take kindly to being smart mouthed."

Tom took another step behind his brother, and Brett swallowed hard and slipped the knife back into its sheath, but he put his hand on his gun instead.

"You ain't scaring me none with them damned guns," he said. "Hell, I got me a gun of my own, if you are looking for a shooting match, and I know how to use it, too," and he started to draw it, but it hadn't begun to clear its holster, before he saw that there were two six shooters aimed right at his middle section. Damn, he hadn't even seen the fucking cowboy's hands move. The other one, the redhead, his gun was still holstered, but he was grinning from ear to ear like he had just heard a good story.

"Shit," Brett said, shoving his gun back down into his holster, "ain't got nothing to do with us anyway, that's between the two of them, seems like to me. Say, Tom, I hear some of the boys have got them some Pensacola rye down back of the house, and I reckon I am feeling a mite thirsty. Whyn't you and me go get ourselves some?"

"I could use a snort myself," Tom said. They began to move in the direction of the corner of the house, backing up at first, and then turning and moving quickly.

"Hey, where you guys going?" Ron called after his brothers, but they didn't answer, they just kept going, not quite running but not exactly walking either, until they reached the corner of the house and had disappeared around it.

"You come back here, Brett, Tom," Ron called after them, and got no reply. "Damn chicken shits," he said, and spit at his feet.

He turned back to the half-breed and took stock of his situation. Damn, what worried him the most was that the guy didn't look like he was scared at all, even though he stood a head shorter than Ron himself. Didn't even look nervous, in fact. What it was, actually, was he looked like he was fucking crazy, now that Ron took a good look at him. Shirtless, the half breed stood kind of in a crouch, like a cougar getting ready to spring, his muscles still shiny with sweat from the dancing he had done earlier. His eyes glittered in the moonlight, it almost seemed like there were sparks coming out of them, and the way he grinned, his teeth showing, unnerved a fellow. There was something else too, that he did just then, that Ron had never seen nobody do before. His nostrils flared as he stood there waiting, like he was sniffing the air, or something—like an animal, looking for a scent.

Ron suddenly thought of when he was a boy, and older fellows had scared him with stories of Apaches, the things they did when they were in hand fights. He had heard of one, sprang on a man and ripped the fellow's throat wide open with nothing but his teeth. There was another tale, too, about a fellow, got into a hand fight with an Apache and had his balls clawed right off him while they was wrestling on the ground, the Apache just reached down and grabbed a hold of them fast as lightning and tore them loose before the other man knew what was happening.

Remembering, Ron felt a little shiver of fear zigzag its way up and down his spine, and all at once it felt like he was about to take a shit in his britches. Sure thing, this fucking Indian looked plenty crazy enough to have something like that in his mind. He did not much care for the idea of losing his balls, let alone having his throat ripped open.

"Shit, I ain't of a mind to fight with no half-breed Indian trash," he said, buttoning his shirt up again. "I got me more important things to do."

He turned his back and began to walk away, but you could see that he was listening for any movement behind him. Buck was motionless though, until Ron had disappeared after his brothers, walking a bit faster as he got further away.

Buck looked at Les and Red then. "I didn't start it, Les," he said. "Don't be sore at me."

"I know you didn't," Les said, holstering his guns.

"And I appreciate your help, boys, really, I mean it," Buck said, donning his shirt and his bandana, and strapping his weapons on, "but I wasn't worried about that peckerhead. I could've took him on with one hand tied behind my back, him and his pissant brothers too."

"Sound mighty sure of yourself," Les said with a grin. "He is a pretty good sized dude, appears to me."

"Reckon so, but he was scared shitless," Buck said. "I could smell it on him."

"Like them Indian horses do?" Les asked.

Buck grinned back at him. "Guess it just runs in the blood," he said. "Anyway, once you got a fellow scared, you got him half beat already."

"Reckon you could have whipped him, at that," Les said. "Didn't mean to say that you couldn't. Imagine you could have easy enough, as long as a fight stayed fair. We was just providing knife insurance. Ain't got no mind to see any of my cowhands carved up by a couple of polecats."

"I am much obliged to you for that." Buck stepped forward and the three of them shook hands all around, in a strangely formal sort of acknowledgment of their comradeship.

"You planning on any more dancing?" Les asked.

Buck glanced at him, and toward the barn, and thought of little Maggie, but there wasn't much likelihood now of any trips behind the barn, and he knew well enough that nothing more than that was ever going to come of it.

He looked back at Les and shook his head. "I reckon it would just cause trouble for her with her brothers," he said. "They won't forget they was humiliated, and others to see it happen. And by a half breed, that will make it worse."

"Then I expect we might as well be heading for home," Les said.

Red said, "Unless you want to wait and dance with old Ron there and his brothers when they come back, looked to me like they was pretty light on their feet," and they all three laughed.

WHEN THEY WERE ON the trail for home, Buck looked from one of his companions to the other. The night smelled of sage and dust, and the faint scent of something dead and decaying that came downwind at them, a stray steer, maybe, that the coyotes had brought down, but a long ways off. The air was warm and dry, and fine for riding.

He thought about the two of them backing him up the way they had, and he felt like his chest was about to bust with happiness. There wasn't anything in the world better, the way he saw it, than to have a couple of true friends, cowboy friends. He began to sing at the top of his lungs: "Oh, bury me not, on the lone prairie...."

"If I had known you was going to howl like a wounded coyote," Les said, "reckon I would have let them boys cut you up back there."

He larruped his palomino up to a gallop, and after a moment Red and Buck spurred their horses and galloped alongside him, Buck between the other two, the three of them pounding across the plains, feeling free in the way that only a cowboy can feel free, on his horse, out on the range.

Out of nowhere Les, who was not as a rule a man to show excitement, yelled at the top of his lungs, "Yippee-i-o, cowboys."

Buck answered him by throwing back his head and giving a coyote howl, and they all three laughed, for the sheer joy of being cowboys and being alive, and riding through the summer night together, the hooves of their horses beating a steady thrumedy-thrumedy-thrum on the iron hard ground.

The Time of Year
that Really Got to Frenchy

By
Lee Lynch

THE TIME OF YEAR that really got to Frenchy was the fall. You wouldn't think you'd get to see it much in the Bronx, but in their park hundreds of trees wore headdresses of red or orange, brown and green and yellow. The earliest fallen leaves sounded crispy underfoot. Purply asters and giant shaggy white mums nodded in chilly breezes. This showy display choked her up with both eagerness and dread because of what happened when she turned fourteen a year ago, in 1953.

Frenchy and Terry pretty much spent their lives in the park near where they lived, and it was a whole huge world of its own. They rode their bikes around the pond and explored the worn trails by foot. Maman hated to throw good clothes away, so after school and on weekends Frenchy dressed in her brother's hand-me-downs.

Summers, they swam at the crowded pool. Maman wouldn't let Frenchy out of the house without a sandwich wrapped in waxed paper. Sometimes she'd get a peach or an orange. Terry knew how to peel an orange so the skin came off all in one curlicue. Then she did something to make the orange look like a flower. Terry was always doing one magic trick or another. A real magician gave a show near the pool. Terry saved Frenchy a spot up front. Afterward, Terry could do some of the tricks right away. When Frenchy asked how she did them, Terry told her you had to be a magician to learn.

Were they tricks or were they honest to God magic? Magic was only one of the wonders of Terry. It was Terry who gave her the names Frenchfry and Frenchy, because of her mother being from France, and her father, too, except he left a few years ago. Sometimes Maman said he was dead and sometimes she complained that Frenchy asked about him, *encore et encore*. The truth was, Frenchy and her big brother Serge learned French first, then, when they started school, learned to use English more and more. Now and then she caught herself thinking in French. The A's she got were in French class.

Terry, short, crazy high-spirited, with tight wavy hair and brown, challenging eyes, was known for taking on bullies with her small fists. She told Frenchy she had a hard time sitting still so school was torture. Gym was her best class, despite ballroom dance and undressing in the locker room.

They could hear the boys play basketball on the other side of the gym's folding partition. As soon as the teacher wasn't looking, Terry rounded her hand like she had a basketball, dribbled it in a circle around herself, and jumped to get the ball in the baskets only the boys were allowed to use. If the teacher left the gym, Terry bounced the imaginary basketball to Frenchy, or passed it two-handed from her chest. If a court in the park was empty, they'd play a long game of invisible basketball, fingers gripping the rough rubber.

One day that fall, the teacher called the roll and no one answered to the name Theresa LoPresto. Worry distracted Frenchy to the point that she answered late to her own name, Genevieve Tonneau. At Terry's apartment, Mrs. LoPresto said Terry wasn't home. Mrs. LoPresto, not all that tall herself, looked down at Frenchy and teased, "Maybe she's sorry you can't be on the new girls' basketball team, too?" While it was true that Frenchy was shorter than Terry—and a lot shorter than anyone on a team should be—it wasn't true that there was a girls' basketball team. Terry lied to her mother, and Frenchy didn't see her in school again.

A couple of Saturdays later, they rode their bikes to the park. Terry carried a football under her arm. They found a strip of grass, crunchy with dried leaves, and for a while tackled and tickled each other, then settled into throwing the ball, making it spiral over the sidewalk and nearly conking the head of a woman pushing a stroller. They got scolded, which kind of took the fun out of their game.

They sat together on a bench. Terry stretched her legs out to the sidewalk. Frenchy swung hers back and forth. She loved these times best. Warmth rose in her when she was with Terry. She felt like a lightly toasted marshmallow.

"Where'd you get the ball, Terror?" she asked because it was new—and because she was afraid to ask why Terry wasn't in school. Terry usually cracked wise non-stop, but sometimes she had silences that made Frenchy uneasy.

"I lifted it, Frenchfry," Terry said.

"You stole it? When?"

"You know," said Terry, "when I was in the city this week."

"Where?"

"Where did I steal it? This store I was in. I get stuff from a lot of stores," said Terry, as if shoplifting was the most natural thing in the world. She was bragging.

Frenchy drummed her heels against the bottom of the bench, worried someone would know the football was contraband.

Terry pulled a pack of Lucky Strike cigarettes from one jacket pocket and a Zippo lighter from another. She was wearing a New York Giants baseball jacket which looked hot for the weather, but a lot hipper than Frenchy's faded cotton windbreaker. The Giants' lettering matched the orange of the trees. Was it stolen, too?

"You want a smoke?" Terry asked.

"Sure," she answered. She'd never seen Terry smoke before. "Do your parents know?"

"Would that stop me?"

Frenchy held the cigarette between her index and middle fingers and tried to balance it the way she'd seen grownups do, but she pinched it too hard, bent it and ripped the paper. This was like trying to learn one of Terry's magic tricks.

"Hey," said Terry. "You have to put it in your mouth to light it, dummy."

"I know, I know." She wouldn't hack out her first drag like she'd seen other kids do.

Terry tilted back the Giants cap, big enough that her ears supported it.

Nothing came out of the lit cigarette. She sucked in harder. A raspberry sound escaped her lips, and Terry quickly looked the other way.

"When did you start smoking?" Frenchy blew her nose to cover her cough. Maman also wouldn't let her out of the house without a girly home-sewn handkerchief. This one was embroidered with her initials and had lace edges.

"I get to smoke when I see my cousin Janice." Terry exhaled. "The one who's not my blood cousin, but my family has known hers since her mother and father were kids so I call them aunt and uncle. Janice books off school all the time. She works taking tickets at the movies."

What was going on? Was Janice Terry's new best friend?

"Are you coming back to school next week?" she asked.

"I don't see why I should. I'm applying for a job to be the movie projectionist."

"But, Terror, you're 14! You can't get your working papers yet."

"What they don't know won't hurt them. I'll be 15 next month. And I look older, don't I?" Terry hunched over. She didn't look older at all.

Without warning, Terry dropped to the sidewalk, legs crossed. She threw two pennies to the ground, picked them up and placed one on each palm. She flipped her hands palms down on the pavement. When she turned them over, both coins were in her right palm.

Terry grinned at her, the cigarette shifted to the corner of her mouth.

"How in heck do you do that?"

"I'll never tell." Terry moved back up to the bench. "You want to know something?"

"I want to know a lot of things, Ter." She took tiny sips of the cigarette and looked through the trees at the apartments that surrounded the park. "What's the matter with you today anyway?"

"You ready for this, Frenchfry?"

"Tell me already, Ter."

Terry looked like she'd swallowed a gulp of air and gagged on it. Her face got red and she took another Lucky from the pack. "I turned gay," Terry said, flicking flame from the Zippo.

"What's that supposed to mean?"

"Geeze, do I have to explain everything?"

Frenchy didn't want to hear what she thought she was hearing. Gay was a word the other kids used to make fun of her and Terry: gay, dyke, queer, butch. She didn't exactly understand what their taunts were all about, but they said them to be mean and she understood it had to do with sex, like if Doris Day made out with another actress, say, Debbie Reynolds, instead of, say, Rock Hudson, which was crazy. And now Terry was like that? She couldn't think fast enough. If it was true about Terry, her best friend, was it true about her?

"Don't look at me like that," Terry said. "We know I'm going to hell anyway."

Terry's family was Catholic. Being gay was probably the worst sin.

"How do you know?" Frenchy asked. She'd wondered about herself because of the name-calling. It was true she couldn't see growing up to be like Maman, in long dark skirts and dresses, marrying some guy who'd disappear on her. But to buck the whole world? To be something that got you nothing but put down?

She exhaled smoke toward the sky, her arm on the back of the bench. She was a natural at smoking, couldn't be easier. Terry was still puffing on hers, all hunched over.

Finally, Terry said, "I just know." She dropped the butt and mashed it into the sidewalk. "I tried it."

"With your cousin?" Ugh, she thought. They played with Terry's cousin on holidays when the families got together. The girl was bigger than the two of them combined, which might not be nice to say, but Janice was such a spaz and was always borrowing money when the Good Humor man came around.

"I told you she's not my real cousin."

Frenchy ground out her cigarette the way Terry did.

"But we got caught."

"Caught being gay together?"

"Bare-ass naked. You know how my dad worked on that house in Corona? They finished it this morning. He had a few with the guys and came home early."

"What did he do to you?"

Terry met her eyes for the first time since her announcement and tossed the football along the bench to her.

"He frigging picked Janice up and pushed her out the front door into the hallway."

"Holy cow," she said, not sure if she was more shocked by the push or the curse word. "What did you do?"

"Like I said, he'd downed a few."

"So?"

"I grabbed her clothes and mine and played dodge with him. He tripped over a throw rug, landed on his knees—you know how he hurt his knee on a job? That stopped him. I got out the door, him bellowing, 'Not in my house! Not in my house you don't!'"

"Man, am I glad I don't have a father."

"Wait. Here we were out in the hallway, Janice and me, scared to death to take the time to put our clothes on. We get in the stairwell and run up, carrying our clothes. I mean, he was like King Kong after the plane shot at him, but I knew he'd never have the wind to chase us all the way to the roof."

"Geeze, Ter."

"I know my building inside out. We make it outside and get dressed, then cross the roof to the front and take that elevator to the basement."

"I can't believe this."

"Remember I told you how my building and the one across the street connect basement to basement? I know how to get through. You go to the end of the storage room and there's these crisscrossed boards.

I was exploring one day—call me Christopher Columbus. He was Italian, too."

"How come you never showed me this secret passage?"

"I knew I might need a place to hide from Pop some day. He might get it out of you." Two gray squirrels skittered by, chasing each other, tails twitching. "So anyways, I led Janice through where you can pull out a board."

"Why didn't you call me?"

"I did call you, from a pay booth. Your mother answered. I hung up."

"Why?"

"I didn't know if you'd still want to be my friend once I told you why I needed a little help. I had a shortcut through other buildings that put us two blocks away, right at the subway. Janice wouldn't stop crying. She begged the only money I had off me and ran for the train." Terry shook her head and pulled another Lucky from her pack, then lit it with a shaking hand. "What am I going to do, Frenchy?"

"Couldn't you go home with Janice?"

"Oh, sure," said Terry, "and have her dad run me off. You know mine called hers by now."

Frenchy took her first full breath since Terry started the story. This was like some adult thing. She didn't know zilch about fixing it. "Maybe you could come home with me till it blows over? You could call your mother?"

Terry sucked in her lips, squeaking. She looked at Frenchy. "I wouldn't want to get you in hot water."

She wanted to fix it so bad for Terry she'd take the chance. "Maman will only know you fought with your dad."

"You think I could stay over?"

"We can tell her it's safer."

"She won't call my father?"

"Are you nuts? Maman never wants to get involved in trouble."

"What if she asks what the fight is about?"

As she thought about Terry's question she became aware of that marshmallow warmth inside. It spread until she was hot all over. Steamy hot. She needed to hide her face so she got up and went behind the bench to pace.

"We'll tell her you got bad grades."

Terry nodded. "And I told Dad I was dropping out of school."

"She'll get on you about that."

"I'll say I need to get a job so I don't have to live with my dad because he hits me. "

"She's not big on sob stories."

Frenchy couldn't figure out if the heat that came up inside her was good or bad. It reminded her of autumn itself, where she was kind of excited about the smell of fallen leaves and kind of nervous about the new school year, this last year of junior high and so aware that life was coming at her down the widest street in the Bronx, the Grand Concourse, like she was a bowling pin and the ball was doing this ferocious roll right at her.

"You can't call Janice, though," Frenchy said and wondered where that came from. What did she care if Terry called Janice?

Terry looked at her with her eyes all squinty.

"I mean," Frenchy said, "if you don't want Maman to figure it out."

"Your mom will be okay with it if I show her this." Terry turned and lifted her jacket and blouse to the bottom of her little bra. A bruise covered most of the left side of her back. "He caught me with his fist."

"Your own father did that?"

"Sweet guy, right? It hurt bad."

For a second she thought how Terry asked for it being with Janice like that. Were her thoughts disloyal? She kind of thought, was it anybody's business? Well, yeah, she decided, if Terry brought it home. Brought that creepy Janice home. But to hit your own little girl like he did?

"He knows where you live," said Terry, zipping her jacket.

"Who? Your father?"

"Well, my mother, but she leaves the address on the telephone table in case she has to find me."

FOR ALL THEIR GUESSWORK and planning, they never expected the police to show up at Frenchy's door that night.

They were playing Rummy with Frenchy's mother and brother at the kitchen table. The doorbell rang and a man called out, "Police. Open up."

"Dad sent them," hissed Terry, skidding in socks to Frenchy's room.

Frenchy's brother Serge was older. As Terry scooted across the floor and disappeared from sight, Serge looked at Frenchy. Maman signalled not to let them in.

Serge said, "The war is over. They're not the French Militia, the *Milice*."

In French, Maman said, "The little girl is our guest."

Serge closed the door behind him when he stepped outside. Frenchy couldn't make out what was being said on the landing, but the police stomped in and slapped formal looking papers on the table in front of Maman.

Frenchy followed and watched in shock as the officers dragged Terry face down from under Frenchy's bed, one of them pulling her out by the ankles while the other pounded her on the back of her calves with his night stick to make her let go of the bed frame. They trooped through the kitchen, Terry dragging her feet and grasping at anything that might help her loosen their grips. One cop's face was bloody with scratches, the other's hand bled from what looked to be a deep bite. Maman collapsed on the couch screaming and sobbing that Theresa was an innocent child. The bloodiest cop cuffed Terry and yelled, "Innocent? Then what's all this about raping another girl?"

Serge explained that he'd tried to put the police off, but they threatened to charge him with kidnapping. He'd never been involved with the law— any resistance would kill Maman and he'd lose the good job he got after his hitch in the Army.

"What do you know about this?" he asked Frenchy.

She was still shaken at seeing her best friend roughed up, at Terry's revelation earlier in the day and at the accusation of rape by ratfink Janice.

"Nothing!" she cried out. "Janice is making things up."

"But why?" Serge asked. "Why would any girl say something like that?"

She was mortified by the tears that wouldn't stop and the tremors she couldn't control.

"You will not see that nogoodnik again!" her mother screamed. "*Non! Non! Non!*"

Serge left Frenchy to soothe their mother, but Maman pulled away, went to the sink and ran the hot water. She scrubbed the dishes until her hands were red. By then Serge, who had left the apartment while Maman washed and Frenchy dried, pushed a huge box through the door. He was a saver, she knew, waiting to marry his fiancée until he got enough money. He must have emptied part of his hoard to rush to the appliance store down the block and buy this for the family: their first television.

What a Saturday night. The police had ripped away her best friend for being gay, and here Frenchy sat in the safety of her mother's apartment watching people laugh, fight and advertise watches on this small screen until it was time—time for what, she wondered. Her mother had gone to bed—probably to worry—long ago. Frenchy left Serge with a horror movie. She'd had enough horror for one day. It was time to sleep.

FRENCHY COULD NOT STOP being scared. She didn't know at first what had happened to Terry, and she wondered and hoped and fretted. Mrs. LoPresto finally called with details five days after the bad scene. She told Frenchy Terry was now allowed visitors. Scared or not, of course Frenchy went. Terry always said Frenchy was her *goombah*, her sidekick, co-conspirator, and lookout. Frenchy didn't get how one day they're kids playing in the park and the next day they're supposed to be grownups in a real world they never knew existed.

The hospital where they put Terry was no rinky-dink place. It seemed like she had to walk a mile from the subway, and she stopped an old lady with a net bag hanging from her wrist to ask if she was headed the right way. The woman turned and pointed up—to the tallest building in sight. Frenchy hiked past small stores and apartment buildings. Why couldn't she be over at Terry's, drinking soda at the kitchen table with her best friend, Mrs. LoPresto pouring and gabbing, instead of on this scary, dreary trek?

She was embarrassed when she asked for Terry at the desk in the huge cold lobby. She was on a mental ward, Terry said when she called Frenchy last night. She also talked big about fighting the cops. She said she'd hurt two more at the police station. Wouldn't Frenchy fight, too, Terry had asked.

No, she wouldn't. If she wasn't a girl, she would have wanted to go out for the cops after graduation. She'd been thinking that or the Army, but she heard the Army stuck you in nursing or secretarial. If the cops wouldn't accept her and she couldn't fight for her country, then nothing doing, she'd stay put.

She stood before a heavy, locked door waiting to see Terry. A guy with a crew cut checked her out through the small wire-reinforced window. He led her to the dayroom where a few girls stared at a television. One girl twirled her long hair around a finger and then tugged hard at it, like she was honest to God trying to pull it out, one hank at a time.

Terry was in pajamas and a bathrobe. If she'd combed her hair, you couldn't tell. Her smile was really faint so Frenchy wasn't sure if she was glad to see her. She'd brought Terry two packs of Lucky Strikes from a machine, but the guard—orderly, she learned—zoomed in when she tried to give Terry matches. He lit a smoke for Terry, muttering to Frenchy, "No matches, no scissors, nothing they can use to hurt themselves or each other." He slid the matches under a window to an office.

When the guard was out of earshot, Frenchy asked, "What are you, in jail?"

"Might as well be," Terry said, her voice stifled. She hadn't looked at Frenchy once since the guy led her in. "Only," Terry said, her voice loud now, like she wanted the guard to hear, "in jail they don't force you to take pills."

"What kind of pills?"

"Crazy pills," Terry shouted.

Where was her pal? Who was this Terry? Her face was all broken out and bruised yellow.

"How long do you have to stay?" she whispered.

"Too goddamn long!" Terry's voice was angry as well as loud.

Terry was scaring her. Did she really go crazy? Frenchy made a bad mistake then and asked if Terry had heard from Janice.

Terry looked like the kid in third grade who fell from the top of the monkey bars and landed with his arm bent backwards under him. He'd roared like a lion at the Bronx Zoo. Now so did Terry. She rose up from her chair, stumbled, and yelled at Frenchy, "Never say that bitch's name in front of me. If she loved me so much, why did she put me in here!"

Two orderlies rushed to Terry. One told Frenchy, "You have to leave."

Frenchy was in tears. They yanked the stubborn weight of Terry back down the hall.

Were the pills making Terry crazy? Frenchy had never heard her so mad before, even at the kids who called them names. She wanted to ask what was going on, but a nurse just about pushed her out the heavy door. Maybe she better not ask any questions. They might think she was a rapist, too, and she'd end up in here. She didn't wait for the elevator, but hurtled down the stairs and didn't stop running, crying all the time, until she was out of sight of the hospital.

How could she leave Terry there? Not even Terry LoPresto's magic would open those doors.

TERRY'S MOTHER CALLED FRENCHY the next week. Thank goodness Maman was doing the Friday night shopping with Serge.

"You have to go see her," Mrs. LoPresto said.

"I did. Didn't she tell you?

"Again, I mean. Go see her again and talk some sense into her. She listens to you."

Frenchy asked, "Can't you get her out?"

"She's got to cooperate with the hospital if she wants to come home before ninety days," Mrs. LoPresto explained. "Maybe you can persuade her."

Why should she? "Maybe she doesn't want to go home," Frenchy suggested instead, because she'd been thinking how, at least for now, Terry's father couldn't hit her. Frenchy was getting up courage to tell Mrs. LoPresto that Terry's father showed his love in a weird way when Mrs. LoPresto interrupted, begging, and Frenchy agreed to visit Terry again Saturday.

"But Maman can't know," she warned Mrs. LoPresto. "She thinks I'm biking around the neighborhood when I go out."

Frenchy hoped Terry would be back to her old self, but she was wrong. Boy, was she wrong.

THIS TIME TERRY WAS already in the day room, sitting on the couch, twitchy, watching TV, seeming as out of it as the others. Two new girls sat beside her, and one, with peroxided long hair and eyebrows plucked to skinny lines, played with Terry's hair. It looked as if Terry had lopped off most of it, but she remembered the orderly saying, "No matches, no scissors, nothing they can use to hurt themselves or each other." She wondered who had cut Terry's hair.

Once this was over, once Terry was out of here, Frenchy swore she'd make sure Terry never went back.

By the window were two older girls doing a puzzle, probably seventeen because Mrs. LoPresto had told her that once they hit eighteen they got housed with the adults. Frenchy, shook up, tried not to look at a raunchy white girl, more like fifteen, reading a book in a corner chair, one hand moving fast under her skirt.

Terry seemed unaware of it all. When she saw Frenchy, she stood and motioned her toward her room. "I'm being a good girl now. I can have a guest in my room," Terry said in a dry, slurred, sarcastic voice. She kept clearing her throat. On their way they stopped to get a light for Terry's cigarette.

"Leave your hair alone," said the nurse. "We'll check on you." She turned to Frenchy, a scowl on her face. "Don't you give her a fit, or we'll put you on the Deny Access List."

Frenchy could only nod and stare at the uneven ends of her friend's hair. She felt sick to her stomach. When they got into Terry's room, she said, "Oh, Terry, you burnt off your hair with lit cigarettes?"

"I have to do *something*. This medicine they give you, I don't know, I do all kinds of crazy shit over and over. Everybody has their thing, like Skinny Minnie out there in the dayroom who can't keep her hand off herself, and Heidi who can't keep her hands off me." Terry lowered her slurred voice. "We've got one girl here, from somewhere down in South America, who never moves. Lies there with her eyes open, still as a rock.

The orderlies turn her over twice a day. Nobody visits her. When she turns eighteen, she's in for life." Terry met her eyes and Frenchy saw her friend in there again, all fired up for adventure, her magic on hold. The rage seemed to be gone.

"I can't take it, Frenchy. I never forced anybody to do anything. Janice—*she* was teaching *me* all about it, but the shrink here says doing it with another girl makes me a juvenile delinquent. They said I have to act right or they'll put me in the slammer for real."

Frenchy nodded. What was there to say?

They went to the barred window and looked down at the street. People did Saturday shopping, kids played outside old six-story apartment buildings.

Terry went on. "I don't need their pills. I'm not nuts like some of these. The girls always playing cards? One of them taught me how to catch pills between my lip and gum so I can spit them out once the nurse is gone, but usually they catch me and make me swallow."

"I haven't been back to the park," Frenchy said. "It's not the same."

"What I wouldn't give to be at the park or on my bike anywhere." Terry didn't stop talking. She'd always been a big talker but today she sped up. Was it the medicine? Frenchy thought that maybe it was a good time to ask the questions that had been keeping her awake.

"What's with this gay deal anyway, Ter? Why do they call it gay?"

"Beats me. Queer, gay, lezzie, all I know is I really go for it. Never wanted to do it with boys. Did you know boys can do it together? I won't go with just any girl. Not with any of them in here. Maybe, when I get out, I'll show you the life, we'll find you a girlfriend. What do you think?"

Frenchy didn't get a chance to answer the question. Terry kept motor-mouthing along. "Janice says there's lots of queers in Greenwich Village. What do you say we go down there, you and me when I get out of here, and check out the scene. I ought to get out soon, maybe tomorrow. They have to let me go sometime, right? It's making me crazy being in here. As if I wasn't crazy enough to start with, right?" Terry's laugh sounded like Woody Woodpecker's. That was new, too.

Frenchy asked, "Can't your mom get you out?"

"Mom? What mom? She'll do whatever Daddy wants. You're lucky your dad's out of the picture. I never want to live with a man again. Get this. That book I took out of the library to learn magic tricks? He saw it and tossed it. Threw out a library book. Anything to keep me from having fun at all. I should report him, tell a librarian he did it. I'm the one to catch hell from the library plus Dad, for telling. I'll have to borrow books on your card."

Frenchy was horrified. She returned library books on time, never cut school, did homework. She was more like Serge than Terry. She stayed out of trouble and took care of Maman when she was sick. She saw herself as sort of a little Serge and expected to lead her life like his except for getting married and having kids. If she kept to the straight and narrow and graduated high school, she'd be okay.

"Do you think I'm like you, Ter?" she asked. She believed Terry knew all the answers and always would, magically. She thought of herself as such a little kid next to tough, adventurous Terry.

"Oh, yeah, Frenchfry. No question. And you're butch like me."

"What's that, butch?"

"You'll be the guy when you fall in love."

This was way over her head, but Frenchy was fascinated. It was like she was meeting a stranger, but the stranger was herself.

Terry finished her cigarette and went out to the office for another light. When she came back they sat on the narrow bed. Frenchy bummed one of the smokes, lit it off of Terry's, and they puffed for a while, Frenchy getting ready for whatever came out of Terry's mouth next. Her palms were sweaty and inside she felt like a snow globe, tiny bits of herself stirred up and falling into a mixed up, but shiny new sparkly pile. She waited for Terry to tell her the secrets to the magic tricks that would be their lives.

"It's like this, Frenchfry," Terry started. She tapped ashes into her ashtray. She swung her crossed knee in circles. She frowned at the floor, then at Frenchy once, twice, a third time. Finally, she said, "They call it coming out—coming out of the closet where gay people hide. I don't know all the words. I'd have to show you." Terry stretched a hand toward her.

Frenchy was shaken by a jolt to her heart, which was already beating as fast as when she'd run down the stairs last week.

"I never thought about you, doing anything with you," Terry said, eyes meeting hers, then surveying the cinderblock wall little more than an arm's length away. "Do you ever touch yourself? Down there?"

Frenchy tried not to show her panic about being found out. She'd never done it without fear that her mother could tell. In the two-bedroom apartment, Serge had the smaller bedroom, so Frenchy had slept in her mother's room ever since she was in a crib.

Fear and touch, they went together now. Did Terry do it, too? Did anyone else? Maybe that kind of good feeling was another magical thing Terry would know about.

Her face was hot, and she didn't want Terry to laugh at her for being a know-nothing so she didn't ask. Terry looked away as if to give her some privacy.

"One minute we're kids," Terry said, "riding our bikes and the next— but you're my goombah. I think it's against the rules, two butches, but what the hell. Why not?"

She saw Terry swallow hard, like she was trying to take in all that happened to her in the past few weeks and get it down it in one big gulp. She guessed it choked her because Terry started coughing and coughing and seemed unable to catch her breath. Frenchy jumped up to get help, but the nurse rushed in, a stern-looking, sickly pale woman with a weird accent who'd looked at her with suspicion when she signed in. "What's she doing?" the nurse asked. "Some of them try suicide by plugging themselves up and strangling."

Frenchy started backing out the door, keeping an eye on Terry, trying to come up with a way to help, when one of the football player orderlies rushed through the door and ran into her. She started to pitch forward. With one arm, the orderly pulled Frenchy upright against him, both steadying and turning her out of the room. He nudged her down the hallway.

"She upset the patient!" the nurse barked. "We can't have that!"

"I didn't!" Frenchy cried.

"Don't come back," the orderly commanded in a low voice. "You're going on the DA List."

She stood there, wretched with helplessness. She wanted to prove she hadn't made Terry worse. *They* were the ones making her worse. Who did Terry have on her team but Frenchy?

The orderly went back into Terry's room. She could hear Terry still coughing, sputtering. Another nurse rushed by, hypodermic at the ready. What were they doing, knocking Terry out? What should she do? She was fourteen years old, what could she do?

Frenchy took the elevator this time. A tall gray-haired woman in a gray uniform, her skin ashen brown, wheeled a cart in next to her. "Why so glum?" the woman asked, in an accent like her own.

From the way the woman studied her, Frenchy could tell she looked the way she felt, like a dying creature.

"Life is tough," the woman told her. "Do like me. Go for a long walk. Tire yourself out, sleep till you can take it again."

Frenchy nodded.

"Here," said the woman, pulling a chain over her head and pressing it into Frenchy's hand. "I've got more at home. Some give them to me when they leave the hospital. That's St. Christopher. He'll walk with you to keep you safe."

Frenchy closed her fist around the medal and stuttered a thank you. She'd get off the train early, walk through the fall dusk, past yellow streetlamps, and let the autumn-colored leaves light her way.

IN THE WEEK AND a half before Terry got out of the hospital, Frenchy had a lot of time to think, but she didn't. She could have gone to the school library and used the encyclopedia, but someone might see her look up the word "homosexual." Everybody said her gym teacher was gay, but they said that about all the women gym teachers, and she knew for a fact that some of them were married to men.

So she explored in ways she already knew. The first thing she did was sneak down to Terry's basement and find that tunnel. As she pushed her way through the gap, she tried to push aside her fears. The passage was spooky, but clean and dry, although it smelled like fresh mixed cement. Her flashlight shone on concrete walls shored up with lumber; no sign of rats or people. Still, she sprinted under the sidewalks and street, then eased open the door at the other side. Terry was right, there was a crack to squeeze through—although Janice was so big, she couldn't work out how Terry got her through there.

In the alley, she panted. She'd practically held her breath all the way through. What kept her exploring was the thought that Terry was brave enough to find her way. Frenchy wasn't sure she was gay, but it would explain how come she got marshmallowy when they were together. Maybe that was why she needed to do this, like she couldn't resist the urge any more than Terry could stop burning her hair. Did she belong in the hospital with the crazy girls?

She found the rest of Terry's route, which turned out to be a good one—she didn't meet a soul. She remembered her history class about the Underground Railroad. If this was back then, she could help a slave escape. Did they use horse-drawn wagons? Were any of them gay? Would Terry need escape routes forever?

She told her mother she had to do a paper about the Museum of Natural History. Instead of waiting on the corner for the bus—she knew her mother sometimes watched her from their window—she took the underground passageway in Terry's building and ducked into the subway.

In Greenwich Village she went looking for the queers, but on a Sunday all she saw were regular people. What was the big deal? Everyone looked normal. Wait, she told herself as she headed back to the train: maybe they were all gay people in disguise. She stood on the pavement, wishing for x-ray vision so she could see inside the women and men who were wearing church clothes or beatnik clothes or old people's clothes. She supposed gay people were still gay when they were old. She walked past a place with a small sign that read "55 Bar." You had to go down steps into the shadows. Terry had once told her something about a club with a number name where men dressed up like women—was this it? Was there a gay code number? Going gay was like getting let into a secret society, she thought, grinning like she'd won a million bucks. She'd never been in on a secret anything.

The day Terry went home, Frenchy went to see her after school, but they didn't have much to say. Terry still wasn't feisty like she used to be and didn't want to go out to play. It was pretty clear those days were over, not just because of Terry's condition. The condition of Frenchy's own heart both alarmed and excited her, especially because the sight of Terry really stirred her up.

Frenchy went away that day glowing like a fall flower in the sunshine, about to bloom into the color of a turning leaf, dipping and swinging on a musical breeze. She could have danced like Gregory Peck in *Roman Holiday*, a movie she'd seen with Terry.

The drugs took a while to leave Terry's system. Frenchy wished doctors weren't allowed to give drugs to kids. The hospital doctor and social worker held a big powwow with Terry's parents. Terry told them she was through hiding, that she was gay and she wasn't going to change. The hell with protecting Janice. They at last believed her about Janice's rape story. She promised to go back to school and to see a shrink. Janice was off limits, but she could hang out with Frenchy, who they thought was safe.

That *Roman Holiday* mood returned every time she saw Terry now. In truth, Frenchy realized the mood was nothing new—she'd never given it a green light before. The light had been red. When they went to the park they strolled the paths now, or sat on a bench and talked while Frenchy's light flickered yellow. They took to roaming Greenwich Village, hunting queers, they told each other. Terry started shoplifting again and wore guys' clothes.

After a heavy kissing session in the tunnel under Terry's street, Frenchy got scared. They stayed away from each other for two weeks while she thought and thought about what they'd done. It was against her religion, for one thing, but she didn't think God was a bad guy, he'd probably understand. She didn't want Maman and Serge to be ashamed of her. Terry said it was against the law.

She awoke one morning with her decision crystal clear. The first snow had fallen overnight, breaking the news that fall was over. She didn't need anybody telling her right from wrong and wasn't about to wait for the elation of spring. She went over to Terry's.

"I got you something," Terry whispered when they were in her room. They were getting ready to go downtown as usual.

Terry's hair was shorter than ever. She kind of strutted around the small space, like roosters they'd seen in the kid part of the zoo. Terry had always been self-confident, but now she acted proud of herself and hid whatever she'd gotten Frenchy behind her back.

"You look more like the gay girls in the Village than ever," Frenchy said.

Then Terry sat on the bed watching every move as Frenchy put on a dress shirt of Serge's which Maman didn't know she had and the shiny cufflinks that went with it. They didn't speak.

After Frenchy buttoned up the dress shirt, Terry held up a tie and thrust it toward her, saying, "I bought this for you."

"Bought it?" said Frenchy, stepping back. Terry never paid for anything she could steal anymore.

Terry put the tie around Frenchy's neck and straightened her collar. Her fingertips were soft, like melting snowflakes. All the little hairs on Frenchy's neck stood up at Terry's closeness. Terry went in even closer and kissed her. They fell on the bed and didn't get off it until they heard Mrs. LoPresto come home late in the afternoon. Terry snatched their ties from the floor and hid them.

WINTER COULD NOT HAVE been kinder to them. They got snow days off, and Terry's parents were at work. When snow melted during a warm spell, the temperature rose enough that they could walk in the empty park, holding hands, making out behind trees. Frenchy begged bread crusts from Maman and spread crumbs for the birds. In an Army-Navy Surplus store, Terry stole two pair of small combat boots left over from the Korean war so they no longer had to wear the rubber boots issued by their mothers.

"I can't get enough of this new you, Frenchfry," Terry said time and again.

"I'm happy with you, Ter."

Terry looked surprised. "You're taking to this like a fish to water like I did, aren't you?"

Falling in love was supposed to be a spring thing, but winter was better. Everything got quieter. Snow subdued traffic sounds deep in the park. Tourists stayed away from the Village. They told their families they were going bowling so they had hours for their roaming feet, roaming hands, roaming lips. They planned the apartment they'd share after Frenchy graduated high school and the car they'd drive, the places they'd go.

They leaned against a tree, holding each other, protected from the wet, cold bark by their heavy jackets. Frenchy wanted for them what Serge would have with his girl.

Terry pulled a bouquet of leftover leaves, red, orange, brown, green and yellow, from behind her back.

Frenchy took it, laughing. " I never saw you pick those up. I still don't know how you do your magic."

Terry was working with a professional magician now, a gay guy they met downtown. Frenchy was a part-time cashier at the neighborhood grocery store with the help of fake papers Terry got her. She felt less guilty about being gay because she could hand her paycheck over to Maman.

Frenchy examined the loose bouquet.

Fall had not been all pretty colors. She'd never forget what could happen and was still scared about her family finding out, of the police catching her and Terry, of getting locked up and drugged for the rest of her life. She heard stories about kids who killed themselves. Women in the bars got jealous and fought with their fists. No one they'd met had been together long, boys or girls.

Twilight was coming on. The temperature was dropping. While she stood in the park with Terry, snowflakes drifted down, like the leaves of fall.

Abigail's Freedom

By
Patty Schramm

*"I looked at my hands to see if I was the same person
now that I was free. There was such a glory
over everything. I felt like I was in Heaven."*
~Harriet Tubman

November 24, 1851
Jenkins Plantation, Atlanta, Georgia

THE DRIVING RAIN STUNG the wounds on her back. Her naked body shivered, and Abigail prayed the Almighty would end her suffering, even if that meant death. She would never see Cynthia again. Her lover's bruised, bloodied, and swollen face was seared into Abigail's mind. Master Jenkins had beat his only daughter to death. He'd ignored the screams of Missus Jenkins and pounded on Cynthia with brute strength until she no longer moved.

He turned to Abigail, his face flushed and his eyes crazy. He struck her face.

Abigail went numb. The world caved in around her, and in what seemed an instant, she was dragged outside and thrown to the hard ground. Master Jenkins, his rage beyond control, ordered the overseer, Mister Drews, to bind her to the whipping post and flog her.

The overseer bound her so tightly she couldn't feel her hands. He followed orders and pain seared through Abigail. She closed her eyes as her mind left her body behind. She envisioned Cynthia's soft features, heard loving words whispered in the heat of passion. As her consciousness waned, she remembered Cynthia, not the first woman Abigail had been with, but the only one she'd ever dared to love . . .

SOFT KISSES STROKED THE tender area behind Abigail's ear. Light breath tickled her skin. In a voice thick with passion, Cynthia said, "We have time, my love."

Abigail turned so she was looking into Cynthia's pale face, illuminated by the orange glow from the flames. "Lord knows I wish that was true." She placed a sweet kiss upon Cynthia's lips. "You need to get in bed. I'll straighten up."

Cynthia stuck her lip out in an adorable pout. "You're mean."

"I'm sensible. That's what my mamma always said." Abigail stood and held out a hand to Cynthia. "C'mon."

Cynthia's alabaster skin made a stark contrast against Abigail's ebony hand. While she felt great affection for Cynthia, Abigail never once forgot the danger of what they were doing. Not that having sex with a white woman was the danger. Abigail had been with both men and women, none by choice. But she *wanted* to be with Cynthia. Though by law Cynthia could do what she wanted with Abigail, she never did. She took care that Abigail felt pleasure.

"I'm going to take a trip next week," Cynthia said, a sparkle in her eyes.

"Will I be going as well?"

"Of course, silly." Cynthia kissed the knuckles of Abigail's fingers. "We're going to Ohio."

"All right."

"Don't you want to know why?" There was a teasing tone to Cynthia's voice that matched the smile she gave.

"It's not my place."

"Because you're a slave?"

"Yes."

Cynthia released Abigail and paced in front of her bed. She worried her hands and Abigail sensed her frustration. But what else could she possibly say? Abigail was captive to every whim of her owner. Master Jenkins had specifically assigned her as Cynthia's personal slave five years earlier. Cynthia was a pleasant woman, and when she discovered that Abigail had rudimentary reading and writing skills, she made it her mission to improve upon them.

They'd been lovers for over a year now. Abigail didn't dare let herself fully love Cynthia, though part of her already did. She kept her gaze on the floor.

"I love you," Cynthia blurted out. She stopped in front of Abigail and lifted her chin so their gazes met. Her deep green eyes locked on

Abigail's. "I love you, Abby. It may not be right, but there it is. I love you and I want to spend the rest of my life with you."

"Cynthia, please—"

Love was not something Abigail expected in her life. She never planned to get married. She could never live with the constant fear of being torn from the family she desperately wanted to have. She'd seen women whose infants were taken from them. After the screaming and crying came the haunted looks. Abigail knew three woman who killed themselves not long after the children were sold. Four others ran away; only one was ever brought back. The slaves were told the other three had been killed. Red Jack, the biggest man among the slaves and Abigail's best friend since childhood, insisted that some ghostly railroad had scurried them to the Land of Canaan, a place where slaves could be free.

Abigail doubted such a place existed.

She believed with all her heart that with Cynthia, she was as free as she'd ever get.

"Let me finish." Cynthia eased the harshness of her words with a kiss on Abigail's lips. She ran her fingers through Abigail's thick, black curls. Her palm came to rest on Abigail's cheek. "I've already made arrangements with a local conductor that Red introduced me to. The conductor will meet us in Ohio. We'll have to keep up pretenses that we're not lovers, but at least in Ohio you'll be free. We'll share a house I found in Cincinnati. You'll be my head of household and get a regular wage. You can come and go as you please."

"And what about Master Jenkins? He going to let you just take me there?"

"He gives me whatever I want," Cynthia said matter-of-factly. "You know that. I've already been sending money to my cousin who lives there. He's part of a secret society called the Underground Railroad. They've been helping slaves get to places like New York, Ohio, even as far north as Canada for years now. I had him set up a bank account for me so that if Daddy ever decides to stop funding me, I'll have my own money."

Abigail didn't try to hide her shock. "You haven't thought this through. I'm still your father's property. He can come get me whenever he wants."

"You're not property." Cynthia spoke with a vehemence Abigail never heard before. "You're a human being. You have a soul just like the rest of us. I'm tired of seeing you treated like chattel. It's not right."

"The law says I belong to your father. Right or wrong, that's how it is."

"The law be damned. I've already worked it out. We're going."

Abigail's gaze met Cynthia's, and she saw complete confidence in her eyes. She also saw conviction. Cynthia believed she was doing right by Abigail. As much as Abigail returned her love, she knew full well there was no future for them as a couple. Cynthia's "offer" for Abigail to be her head of household told Abigail that Cynthia still didn't understand. Even if she was free, Abigail would never, could never, be her equal. They could never truly be together. Abigail opened her mouth to speak again but was silenced by the explosion of the door against the wall . . .

THE RAIN SLOWED AND Abigail floated up into consciousness. She heard Mister Drews call Red Jack to him. Abigail hadn't been aware he was there.

"You take over," Mister Drews said. "Mind you, if I don't see the bitch bleeding, you gonna be next."

She sensed Red Jack's hesitation and wished she could see her friend's face. The gentle giant must be sickened at what he was being told to do. He'd been forced to whip other slaves before, but this was different. She and Red were raised together. He stood heads over all the other boys and was put to work in the field long before anyone else was. His father was white—his previous master—and because of the mixed lineage, Red Jack's skin wasn't as dark as Abigail's. The sun always burned him at the start of summer, earning him the nickname of Red Jack.

His physical size belied the gentle man that he was. Abigail never saw him raise a hand, even when pushed to fight by other children. It was horrific for Red Jack when Mister Drews chose him to mete out punishment to other slaves. The overseer enjoyed inflicting pain on others. By contrast, Red Jack would bite his tongue to keep from crying.

His first strike wasn't as hard as Mister Drews's. Abigail winced at the fresh burn of the whip. She didn't want to show Red Jack the pain she was in, but he'd been in her position. He knew full well what it felt like.

"You take it slow, you hear? Master Jenkins wants her alive in the morning. You keep goin' 'til you hits a hundred. If you don't, I'll make sure you get twice as many."

As Mister Drews walked past Abigail, he spat in her face.

Once he was out of sight, Red Jack said, "I'm sorry, Abby."

"It's all right, Red. Just do as he says."

Red Jack continued her punishment. Fortunately for Abigail, she blacked out.

November 28, 1851
Slave Quarters, Jenkins Plantation, Atlanta, Georgia

ABIGAIL WOKE TO INTENSE pain. She lay on her stomach with something cool and wet pressed lightly against her back. She wanted to move, but didn't dare. Breathing turned difficult. She couldn't fill her lungs without excruciating pain.

"Lay still, child." The woman's voice was soft and kind. "Glad you awake now, but you gots a long ways to go."

"Why—why am I here?"

"Red Jack didn't have no place else to go. That boy of mine done took a shine to you a long time ago."

Letitia. She was in Letitia's quarters. Abigail said, "He—he shouldn't have—"

"Shh. He done the right thing. If he hadn't, you'd be dead. Lord knows he ain't the brightest, but that boy's got a good heart."

"Master Jenkins will kill him."

"Master Jenkins don't gots no idea where he is. Red Jack gots help from a couple of boys and made three different trails. Gonna take them a while to figure out he didn't follow any of 'em. You ought to be good enough to travel by then."

"She gonna be all right, Momma?"

Abigail heard Red Jack's voice and smiled. "I'm fine, Red."

"Good." There was an awkward silence, as if he didn't know what to say next. "I gots us a ride outta here, but we gots to go in four days."

"That's not a good idea," Letitia said. "I only just gots the wounds to close. Too much moving around'll tear 'em right open."

"We don't gots no choice, Momma," Red Jack said. The door closed quietly behind him.

Letitia draped another cool cloth on her back. "He's planning to take you all the way to Canaan."

Abigail tried to sit up, but Letitia stopped her. "He's crazy," Abigail said. "You have to talk him out of that. We'll never make it. He'll get caught and killed—or worse. He should have left me to die out there."

"He's brave and once he's done made up his mind, that's it. You know that. He gots it all worked out with one of them conductor fellas. It's gonna take 'bout two or three months, but they say they'll get you to Canaan. After that, Red Jack say he's coming back for me." Letitia sighed heavily.

"That's what you have to talk him out of. No sense coming back here once yous two are free. That's crazy."

"It's a nightmare."

"No, child. This life is a nightmare. You have the chance to be free. You take it. Get to Canaan and don't never look back."

January 5, 1852
Somewhere in Northern Kentucky

WIND BLEW THROUGH THE cracks of the wagon and stung Abigail's exposed arms. She was pressed against the sideboard and unable to move. One other body shared the minimal space, and she felt Red Jack's chest brush against her with every bump and jerk of the wagon. They'd been in the cramped area, in a hidden bottom of the wagon, for most of the day. Abigail had no idea how far they'd traveled, but she knew that night had fallen a while back as the light dimmed between the slats of the sideboard.

More than once Abigail heard the driver cursing the bad weather. Snow started falling yesterday and showed no sign of letting up. Everything was frozen, including the Ohio River, their current destination. Once across, they would set foot in the free state of Ohio and be halfway to Canada— Canaan.

It was more a frightening trek than a journey. Since they'd left the plantation, slave catchers were never far behind. While Red Jack had every step planned out with the conductors of the Underground Railroad, the hunters had nearly managed to catch up with them. Red Jack said one of the conductors must have told them. It happened sometimes. Even the Underground Railroad wasn't completely safe from traitors.

They'd traveled day and night with few moments of reprieve. However, not long after they left Letitia's quarters, they'd been forced to stop for a week to allow Abigail's wounds to heal after being torn open. A white doctor did his best to help her and sent them along with salve and bandages.

She was healed enough now that she no longer needed the bandages, though the pain still persisted, both physical and emotional. She missed Cynthia so fiercely that her heart hurt. Tears stung her eyes, and she brushed them aside. She was tired of crying. It seemed like that's all she'd done since that horrible night.

The wagon came to a stop. Whispers floated in the night air, and Abigail gasped when their hidden compartment opened. She saw the dim, orange glow of a lantern and the outline of two people. Her heart raced. Were they the next in the line of conductors? Or slave catchers to send her back to Hell?

"C'mon y'all. Everyone out," the man said in a harsh whisper. "We got to get to the river in a hour. Gotta move fast."

Gentle hands lifted Abigail's bare legs to help her from the cramped space. She stood and stretched, and it felt good until the biting cold struck her. When they left Georgia she'd only had a shawl. Along the way, someone gave her a tattered old coat, though it didn't do much for her as the temperatures dropped. Seemed to get colder after the wagon picked them up. Even with Red Jack being so close to her, Abigail couldn't get warm. Maybe because she hadn't eaten since the day before.

She wondered if Canada would be as cold as Kentucky.

Red Jack unfolded himself and wiggled out of the wagon, and she moved to the side. The two conductors exchanged a few words, and the wagon was turned around to head back south. She hoped the next load of travelers would make it at least as far as they had.

Red Jack stood next to Abigail. He was two heads taller than any man she'd ever seen and twice as wide. Red Jack could lift an entire wagon if he chose to do so. But he was the kindest man she'd ever met. He kept his eyes lowered as the conductor explained the next part of the journey.

"We're heading for the river. It's froze right now so we should get acrost without trouble. Got to be real quiet since I heard there was slave hunters in these parts. Those bastards can be slick so you never know where they are. Just follow me, keep quiet, and move fast."

Abigail was terrified. One misstep and they could freeze to death. Or be caught by the slave hunters, men she'd heard nightmarish stories about from Letitia. Those stories had kept her on the plantation with no thoughts of ever running away. Until Cynthia put thoughts of freedom into her head. But that wouldn't have been running, would it? Would she have been Cynthia's slave? Or her partner? A combination of both?

But it no longer mattered. Now she was a runaway. And so was Red Jack. No matter what they did, if they didn't go north, they'd certainly die. In the frozen river or by the hands of slave hunters, there was no other choice.

Red Jack's deep voice interrupted Abigail's thoughts. "C'mon, Abby." His big hand gave her a gentle push so she was walking ahead of him.

"We get to the river," the conductor said, "make sure you follow right behind me. It's getting warmer so the ice could be cracked some."

"This is warmer?" Abigail lurched forward, having to raise her short legs higher than normal as she trod through thick snow that was just above her knees. The wet and cold seeped through her skin. She had never seen or felt snow before. She didn't like it. Already her legs felt like ice.

Her shoes weren't any better for snow than her clothes, and twice she got herself stuck. The second time, Red Jack lifted her free, but one of her shoes had come off. After digging the shoe from the snow, Red Jack had to run with her in his arms to catch up to the conductor.

"We gots to git you shoes that fit," Red Jack muttered.

"When we get to Canada we'll get everything we need," Abigail said. "How long you figure 'til we get there?"

"Dunno. Last fella said we gots 'bout four weeks or so to go."

"Hope once we get across the river it won't be so cold."

"I heard tell it's always cold in da north."

"Better free and cold then. I'm sure we'll get used to it."

Red Jack didn't reply.

Apprehension filled Abigail the moment they reached the shore of the Ohio River. The other side was hard to see by the light of the moon. A lone, yellowish glow in the far distance twinkled like a star. Was that their destination?

"All right," the conductor said in his harsh whisper, "we're gonna cross here. There's a station on the other side. But you got to be careful. The river ain't fully froze and if ya hear cracking, move forward real slow like. No talkin' 'til we get acrost. Got it?"

The conductor started out on the ice. Red Jack went next and helped Abigail to follow. He kept hold of her arm as they made their way along the frozen waterway.

Abigail couldn't feel her feet and prayed she walked carefully enough.

The sound of ice cracking was a lot louder than Abigail imagined it'd be. She wasn't sure if she'd caused the noise or if someone else had. Red Jack reached for her a second too late. She slid down so fast she didn't even have a chance to gasp. Water surrounded her, suffocating her.

An unimaginable weight squeezed her chest.

Icy cold shocked her body.

Abigail couldn't move. Couldn't scream. She sank farther and farther. She was going to die.

Something pulled her.

She couldn't tell if she was going up or down. Her head broke free of the water, and she gulped in a lungful of crisp air. Strong arms cradled her, and she buried her face in Red Jack's chest. The coughing wouldn't stop, though she did her best to muffle the sound.

Moments later they were going up the river bank, Red Jack's breath coming in big gasps. He stopped when they reached level ground and gently set her on her feet.

"Will you be all right?" he asked.

"I th-th-think so." The wind struck her, and Abigail's teeth chattered. The wet cloth that clung to her began to freeze. She took a tentative step forward and couldn't feel most of her body.

"Hey, what happened?" the conductor asked. Though she couldn't see his face, Abigail heard the concern in his voice.

"She done fell through," Red Jack said. "Mister, we gots to get her inside and warm."

"Yeah. Don't want her to catch her death of cold out here. C'mon." He moved at a fast pace.

Abigail tried to keep up, but she could hardly make her feet point in the right direction. Red Jack wordlessly lifted her into his arms and carried her. Normally she'd have argued with him, but all she could do was rest her head on his shoulder. She didn't have the energy to muster a simple thank-you. Instead, she closed her eyes, and darkness claimed her.

January 8, 1852
Ripley, Ohio

ABIGAIL AWOKE TO THE warmth of a fire. Strong arms curled around her belly, and she snuggled into the embrace, half-dreaming she was with Cynthia. "I best get my night clothes on. Don't want your daddy to see us."

"He's already up and counting his money," Cynthia said. "It's all he cares about anyway."

"I'm sure he cares about you and your brothers."

"No. He cares about Alfred because he's the heir to all this." Cynthia waved a dismissive hand in the air. "I don't want any of it. I'd rather have my own place. Be my own person, not something for him to show off at every dance and cotillion he drags me to."

"I thought you enjoyed the dancing."

"I do. But I'm twenty now. Practically an old maid. Daddy's been trying to get me to marry this old coot from Mississippi. Says he's got over three-hundred slaves and thousands of dollars in cotton production each year. If I marry him, Daddy will benefit through some business connections the man has here in Atlanta."

"You should marry for love."

Cynthia scoffed. "Love has nothing to do with it. He'll do the same to my brothers. They'll all marry some socialite who will bring more money into the family. At least they'll be able to do what they want. I'll be tied to this old coot the rest of my life."

"I don't understand why your daddy is like that. I never knew mine, but I always imagined that he loved me more than anything else in the world. If he'd been here, he'd take care of me until I married."

"But my bastard father sold your father the day you were born."

"How do you know that? I never told you."

"I looked it up," Cynthia said. "He keeps meticulous records about such things. Sold him to the same old coot he wants me to marry now. I guess my father's been trying to get in with this man for years, since back when the coot was young and his parent's ran the plantation."

"Is he still alive? My father?"

"I don't know. I only know he was sold to someone in Mississippi. It's been so many years. He's probably been sold on to other owners since then." Cynthia's eyes held compassion as she spoke. "I tried to find out. I'm sorry, Abby."

Abigail's momentary joy was replaced by disappointment and sorrow. "I hoped I could meet him someday."

"I can't imagine what that's like. To never know your father—to see your entire family ripped apart at the whim of someone like my father. It's beyond unjust. It's inhumane."

"Do you mind if we don't talk about it?"

Cynthia held out her arms and pulled Abigail into her warm embrace. "Of course."

"Tell me more about the cotillion you went to last week. Other than the old coot, I know you had fun gossiping with the other ladies."

"You know me so well." Cynthia's laugh was delicate and sweet, like music to Abigail's ears. She rested her head against Cynthia's chest and enjoyed the latest tales of the local southern belles.

ABIGAIL OPENED HER EYES to darkness. Strong arms cradled her, but not Cynthia's arms. Her head rested against a wide, distinctly male chest. Red Jack. Though it was too dark to see him, Abigail knew he was asleep. His breathing was steady, and he made tiny snores with each inhale.

She was wrapped in wool blankets and completely naked. The wool itched her bare skin, but she didn't want to remove the warmth. Sweat trickled from her brow. Had she been feverish? How had they gotten here? Where were they?

Abigail wanted to ask all this, but kept quiet. They were obviously hidden, and she wasn't sure if their voices would be heard.

The last thing she remembered was falling through the ice. She felt a stab of horror in her chest. How had she even managed to survive?

She tried unsuccessfully to suppress a cough.

"You awake?" Red Jack asked, his mouth close to her ear. "Try ta be quiet. Slave catchers was here lookin' for us."

"All right," she said, her voice squeaky and rough. Speaking made her throat hurt. As if he sensed it, Red Jack held a flask to her lips. She took a few sips of water. "Thanks."

"I was worried. You been sleeping for three days."

"Oh, Lord. I'm sorry, Red."

"Just glad you awake now. We can git soon as it's dark."

Abigail looked around them, though it did no good as there was no light. "Where are we?"

"Cellar—" He stopped speaking.

Abigail heard the floorboards above them creak. Heavy footsteps passed over them. The person stopped almost on top of their heads. Abigail felt a cough coming on and held her breath. Her chest was tight. She needed to breathe. She buried her face in Red Jack's chest.

Light poured into the cellar. Abigail let her cough out, and Red Jack pulled her tighter against him.

"She awake?" a woman's voice asked.

"Yessum."

"Good." The woman held a lantern that cast an eerie glow in the tiny area. "I have some clothes for her." She descended the steps and handed a bundle to Red Jack.

"Thank you," Abigail said.

"You're welcome. Get dressed. The hunters will be back after they've supped. We have to get you out of here in an hour."

She left the lantern on the floor and exited the cellar. In the dim light Abigail made out that they were in a root cellar that held a pile of potatoes and apples. Despite the available space, clearly they didn't use it for much else than keeping food cool.

Red Jack gently helped Abigail to stand. "There ain't much room overhead here."

Abigail had to stoop a little, but the space was wide enough she could easily maneuver around. "It's all right. I can make do." She slipped out of the warmth of the blankets and shivered as cool air touched her skin. The bundle contained a dress, stockings, and a pair of boots. Everything fit well enough, though the boots were a little big. She tied the lacings tight in hopes they wouldn't fall off her feet.

"Red, there's something I need to talk to you about."

"What's that?"

She faced him and smiled. He had his eyes on the floor to provide her with some privacy as she dressed. Abigail sat next to him, her cramped legs complaining as she did. "First I need to thank you. I don't believe I did that yet."

He shrugged, his gaze still down. "It was the right thing to do."

"Maybe. It was brave, and I want you to know how glad I am that you did."

"Welcome," he muttered.

"Do you know what happened that day? Why Master Jenkins had me flogged?" Red Jack shook his head and she continued. "He caught me with Miss Cynthia."

"Caught you?" he asked, finally looking up at her.

"Yes. We were—lovers. I did love her, Red. That's probably a sin, and I might go to Hell because of it, but I can't help how I feel—felt. I saw Master Jenkins beat her to death right before he dragged me to the whipping post."

"He's the one going to Hell," Red Jack said. His voice held a conviction Abigail never heard before. "Not you. You a good woman, Abby. Don't matter who you love. You always a good woman."

"Thanks, Red. I really needed you to know the truth."

Red Jack surprised her by taking her hand in his. His grip was gentle as he examined her smaller hand. "I done knew what yous two done, Abby. Wasn't no secret. Not to me."

His gaze met hers, and she realized how right Letitia had been. Red Jack cared deeply for her. It made Abigail want to cry. "Oh, Red—"

"Don't matter. I's with you now, and you gonna be jus' fine. I promise."

The door above opened again and Abigail froze. The light outlined the frame of a man, and her heart hammered in her chest

"C'mon, you two," a friendly voice said. "We need to get moving." He held the door open.

Red Jack lifted the lantern from the floor. He went first and reached back to help Abigail climb the steps. Her body was stiff and sore. The boots fit better than she expected as she made her way out of the cellar.

In the room above, a single lantern was lit. Red Jack set the other lantern on a table.

Abigail stood beside Red Jack as the man closed the trap door. "Martha has coats for both of you, and Ellie's got some food. She's going to take you on the next leg."

"Thank you," Abigail said.

The man was young, fit, and muscular. The smile he gave her was kind. "Thank me when you get to Canaan."

A woman Abigail assumed was Martha joined them. "These should fit." As tall as Abigail, Martha had a figure that filled her dress better than Abigail's skinny body could. Golden brown hair trailed across her shoulders and down her back. Her full bosom fairly burst from her chest. She held a coat out to Abigail. "It's the best I could do on short notice."

Abigail accepted the gift and put it on. She felt warm already. "Thank you."

Martha gave one to Red Jack. His was a tight fit. Abigail doubted there were many men Red Jack's size. He mumbled his thanks, keeping his eyes averted from Martha's gaze.

Martha said, "Lowry, you better get them—"

Abigail started at the sound of hands pounding on the door. Martha and Lowry exchanged looks, and Abigail knew whoever was there wasn't welcome.

Lowry motioned Abigail and Red Jack to be quiet as he slowly opened the trap door. She and Red Jack scurried into the cellar. She held her breath as the door was closed and the sounds of male voices reached them.

"Where the hell is she? I want that damn nigra!"

"I told you to stay out of my house," Martha said.

"You don't have any right to be in here," Lowry said.

"The hell I don't." The man's voice was closer and very familiar. Abigail grabbed Red Jack's arm and felt him tremble. He recognized the voice, too.

The man was Mister Drews, Master Jenkins's overseer.

"Unless you have a warrant, you best get out of here right now." Martha sounded like she was standing on the trap door above them.

"I don't need a damn warrant. That nigra is in here. If you don't want to go to prison for harboring a fugitive, then you best get her out here now," Mister Drews said. "Me and my boys will do whatever it takes to get her back." She heard someone walk across the floor and stand beside Martha.

"Don't you dare touch her," Lowry said.

"Get me the nigra and we'll leave. You Rankins don't got no say in this."

"Lowry, don't." Martha looked to Drews. "We don't have anyone here you can't see."

"That so? Funny that me and my boys followed the trail right here. Man down the road says he seen you take two of them inside a couple days ago. You got Mister Jenkins's property in here, and that makes you a thief. I'll get the law if I have to."

"Guess you'll have to do that then," Martha said. "When you come back, you better have a warrant."

Abigail pressed against Red Jack as a pregnant silence fell over them. Moments passed before Mister Drews spoke. "Move."

"No."

"I said, move!"

Martha screamed. Lowry yelled something, and Abigail knew they were fighting. These people were risking their lives to help her and Red Jack to freedom. She uttered a silent prayer for them and started for the steps, but Red Jack held her back. It didn't matter. The trap door flung open and someone, she figured it was Mister Drews, pulled her from Red Jack and into the room. He shoved her to the floor while two men yanked Red Jack out of the cellar.

"See," Drews said. "I knew you was hiding our property. You Rankins think no one can touch you, but I got news for you. You're all going to prison."

Abigail swung her gaze from Mister Drews, who held a pistol in his hand, to Lowry and Martha. Neither of them showed any fear. Lowry spoke in a low, hushed voice. Abigail could hear enough to know he was praying.

Mister Drews said, "Get Red chained up. He's worth a thousand dollars if we bring him back healthy."

"Yessir," one of the men said. He dug a set of leg irons out of a satchel. Up until then, Red Jack had remained passive. He'd kept his gaze to the ground. But now his eyes met Abigail's, and she saw something change. As if he'd had enough. A light shone in his expression, and she realized he was no longer going to submit.

Red Jack laid a big hand on the man's shoulder. "No. I's standing in Ohio now. I's free. I ain't no man's property."

"Ignorant nigger," Mister Drew said, a laugh in his voice. "You're property no matter where you go. Law says we got the right to get you and take you back."

"No." He squeezed the shoulder he gripped until the man squealed in pain and dropped to his knees. Red Jack grasped the shackles in a tight fist. "I's free."

Mister Drew cocked his pistol. "It'd be a damn shame to waste a strong one like you, not to mention the money I'll lose, but I will shoot you if you don't put those chains down."

Two more men now flanked Red Jack. Abigail hadn't seen them before and worried about how many "boys" Mister Drews had with him. One of them had skin as black as night, but she didn't know him. Did Mister Drews bring slaves to help track down other slaves? Was this man one of the "traitors" Red Jack told her about? One of their own kind selling them back into slavery? It made no sense to her.

Red Jack stared straight at Mister Drews. "You the meanest man I ever met. Lord says I ought to forgive you for all the things you done to me and mine. But I doan know I can do that." He swung the shackles in a tight circle and connected with the jaw of the man on his left. The man fell to the ground like a heavy sack of potatoes.

The black man grabbed Red Jack's right arm, but Red Jack was twice his size and lifted him off his feet. He tossed him toward the cellar. The trap door was still open, and the man screamed as he fell into the darkness.

Mister Drews didn't move. His pistol remained pointed at Red Jack, and Abigail knew he was going to kill him. She got to her feet, ignored by everyone around her, and threw her body into Mister Drews's. The gun fired.

Martha screamed.

Abigail and Mister Drews landed on the floor in a tangle of arms and legs. She had no idea what to do, except to try to get the gun. Her hand flailed as she reached for it. Mister Drews shoved his elbow into her chest. A whoosh of breath left her body.

Mister Drews pushed to his feet. Blood dripped from his gut. The gun wavered in his grasp.

Lowry jumped forward and took the weapon from him. He kept it pointed at Mister Drews. "You had no right to break in here. Martha, go get the sheriff."

Martha helped Abigail stand and exchanged a look with Lowry. Something passed between them, and Martha left in a hurry.

"Sit down," Lowry ordered Mister Drews. "Martha will get Doctor Campbell to come and see to your wound—after she gets the sheriff."

"That bitch attacked me. She needs to hang for it!"

Lowry took Abigail by the hand, his kind eyes locked with hers. "You all right?"

"Yessir."

"Good." He glanced at Red Jack. "Be ready. Y'all be leaving soon."

"Where they goin'?" Mister Drews looked pale, but his face was still twisted in anger.

Lowry ignored him. "Go stand by the back door and wait. Ellie will be here any minute."

Abigail hesitated. So much had happened in a short time. Would the sheriff be waiting for them? Would they hang her for shooting Mister Drews? Even if she hadn't?

Lowry lowered his voice so only Abigail could hear him. "The Almighty will watch over you. Be quiet, be safe, and be quick."

Abigail, though never sure who she could trust, recognized the kindness for what it was. She took Red Jack's hand and led him to the back of the house. The door opened, and a woman dressed in dark clothing motioned them outside. Abigail squeezed Red Jack's hand as they passed over the threshold and into the dark night.

ABIGAIL AND RED JACK traveled from house to house, on foot, on horseback, in wagons, and made their way farther and farther north. After two weeks they came close to a city called Dayton. They were given instructions to go to a cabin at the end of Market Road. The sun was rising as Abigail knocked on the side door.

A dark-skinned man answered, his smile bright and cheerful as he ushered them inside. Abigail noticed the blinds were down on all the windows in the small space.

"Welcome, friends. I'm Richard Beckfield. My wife, Heather, is making something for you to eat. Warm yourselves by the fire." He took their coats, and Abigail and Red Jack settled onto chairs that winged the fireplace.

She was grateful for the blazing warmth. "Thank you, Mister Beckfield."

"Please, call me Richard."

"You free?" Red Jack asked. Abigail was surprised by his bluntness, but after the incident at Martha and Lowry Rankin's home, Red had changed. He was more suspicious of other black men, having seen firsthand that some helped the slave catchers. Richard was the first freed black man who offered them help.

Abigail chose to believe that men like the ones they'd encountered at the Rankin's place were far outnumbered by men like Richard. It wasn't clear to her why, but she felt she could trust him. There was something about the way he smiled, how it reached his eyes, that she believed in him. Red Jack would not be so easily convinced.

Richard said, "Yes. I was born free. My mother works as a domestic in the city, and my father works at the mill. I've got four brothers and sisters."

"Is it true the slave catchers kidnap free black men?" Red Jack asked.

"It is. Friend of mine was taken three years ago. We only got him back last week. Some white folks are trying to change the law, but unless you can prove in a court that you're free, you have the danger of being kidnapped."

A woman came in holding a tray on which a coffee carafe, cups, and sandwiches sat. "We live with that danger anyway. Every day is dangerous for us."

"This is my wife, Heather." Richard took the tray from her and placed it on a table between the chairs. Red Jack stood and offered her his seat.

Heather shook her head. "You rest. We'll have to get you moving, soon as it's dark again. Once you're warmed up, I'll get a bath going for you. I imagine you each could use one."

Abigail couldn't stop her grin. "That would be very nice, Heather. Thank you."

"You're welcome." She turned her chestnut eyes to Red Jack, who was still standing. "Please sit."

Red Jack lowered himself into the chair, and Abigail giggled, reminded of the many times Letitia had to repeat orders to make him listen. Heather was lucky she only had to say it twice.

"Why is you helping us?" Red Jack posed the question to Richard. "You folks is free. Law could come and put you in prison or sell you off to some plantation. Why you risk all that?"

"Because slavery is a crime against humanity," Richard said. "As a friend of mine once said, 'If there is no struggle, there is no progress.'"

"Who is your friend?" Abigail asked.

"Fella named Frederick Douglass. He was a slave once and fought his way to the north. Now he's a free man and uses his story to get others to join the cause. If enough of us stand up and fight for what we believe in, then eventually slavery will be a thing of the past."

Abigail said, "I'd like to meet him."

"Perhaps someday you will." Richard poured them each a cup of coffee. "I have to get some chores done. You two eat and rest up. I'll be taking you as far as Marysville tonight. By the end of next week you'll be in Cleveland. From there you'll catch a boat across Lake Erie and into Canada."

"Canaan. Freedom," Red Jack said with a hint of wistfulness in his voice.

"Yes, my brother." Richard smiled and Abigail returned the gesture. "Freedom."

January 10, 1853
Elgin Settlement of Buxton, Ontario, Canada

ABIGAIL SAT IN A chair on the porch of her tiny, three-room home and watched Red Jack chop wood. Unusually warm for January, the weather was a welcome relief from the constant snow.

Red Jack brought a cord of wood onto the porch and set it in a corner near the door.

"You outta be inside, Abby. Ain't good if you catch cold."

Abigail reached for his callused hand and squeezed it fondly. He'd rarely left her side once they crossed into Canada. He'd asked her to marry him, but she'd declined. While Red Jack never pressed her again, he clearly didn't understand why she wanted to be alone. "I'll be fine, Red. I just needed some fresh air."

"If you're sure."

"I am. You don't have to keep coming over here to cut my wood for me. It's enough that you helped me build this house."

Red Jack cast his gaze at his feet, which he often did when speaking to Abigail. "Ain't no bother, Abby. I likes the work."

"You work all day."

"So do you," he said.

"Why don't you go get cleaned up? I'll make us some supper."

"Yessum." He raced down the steps and across the dirt street to his own one-room cabin.

Abigail watched him with a bit of sadness. He was such a good man, and though she tried to convince him to look around at the other eligible women in the area, he refused to consider marrying someone else. Abigail wanted him to be happy, but the stubborn man wouldn't listen. At least she'd managed to follow her promise to his mother and talk him out of going back to Atlanta for Letitia. For now.

A pang of sadness reached her when her thoughts suddenly turned to Cynthia. They often did so these days. Abigail was safe and secure for the first time in her life. But no matter how good things were, a piece of her would always be missing.

She forced her thoughts away from such things. She had a home, a good and faithful friend a few feet away, and a community she could belong to. Best of all, she was free.

Abigail was free.

Coming Home

By

Sue Hardesty

1940

JACY CRUZ WATCHED IN amazement as her long black hair fell to the floor in thick graceful strands. She was so tiny her feet didn't even reach the footrest on the barber's chair, so she couldn't run, especially with the clunky ankle-high leather shoes much too big for her. She desperately missed her soft moccasins, but even more, she hated the heavy gray dress dragging on the floor. Not that she had any place to run to. Tears welled in her eyes.

"Next!"

When the tall, white barber pulled her out of the chair, he wrenched her arm, then dropped another girl in the seat. A small brown hand reached out to steady Jacy. She looked up to see an older girl wearing a dress just like hers. The girl's sweet, wide face reminded Jacy of her home far away. She felt a strange thrill as the girl took her hand, but holding her hand made her feel too nervous, so Jacy jerked free to shuffle behind. They passed trash cans filled with wet black hair. The room smelled like her old dog after he got out of the crick and shook on her.

Outside, Jacy took a chance and looked up. The girl was still smiling. She patted Jacy in a reassuring way and said, "Don't be afraid. It is not so bad here."

Jacy couldn't think of anything to say. She took one awkward step after another, the shoes flopping on her sore, blistered feet. The hot sun burned her nearly-bald head, and slimy sweat dripped down from her armpits. She stumbled forward, concentrating on the tight knots in the frayed shoelaces and the scuff marks of the other girl's ankle-high brown leather shoes.

The girl stopped, waiting for Jacy to catch up. "Your clothes are too big because the food here makes you grow fast. Do you understand?"

"That's what a skinny white lady said," Jacy reluctantly answered, "when she shoved these shoes on my feet." Jacy looked down at the dry ground.

"That was Teacher Watson. She teaches embroidery."

Jacy nodded. The girl took her hand, and Jacy felt the same thrill as before along with a feeling of safety for the first time since she had left her village. They walked across a parched brown grassy area toward a huge red-brick building with a tower on the top. It looked like a church, but the sign above the door at the top of the steps read *Phoenix Indian School*.

"I'm your go-to girl. You know what that is?" Staring up at the building, Jacy was too terrified to speak.

"If you need anything or have any questions, you go to me."

Jacy looked around at all the brick and wooden buildings surrounded by dead brown grass and a brick wall. She whispered, "I don't know where to find you."

"You'll get used to getting around." The girl's teeth sparkled as her smile broadened. "We're lucky. We aren't hungry. Or thirsty. And the beds have clean mats, pillows and blankets. No ticks or fleas."

Jacy wanted to tell her that she wouldn't like this place as much as her adobe house at home, but she stayed silent.

Because the girl had bronze skin and obsidian black eyes, Jacy decided she was a Pima like her. Her long black hair hung in pigtails down her back like Jacy's had until a few minutes ago. Jacy wondered how long it took for the girl's hair to grow out.

Suddenly realizing she was staring, Jacy got embarrassed about her strange feelings and turned away. The girl tugged at her hand, then put a candy cigarette in it and said, "My name's Lulu. What's yours?"

"Lulu means rabbit. You don't look like a rabbit."

"Mess with me and see how fast I can run." Lulu giggled. "Now what's your name?"

She ducked her head again and whispered, "Jacy."

"What?"

"Jacy."

"Really? It's a boy's name."

"My mom said my dad wanted a boy."

"Jacy means moon. I like your name." She rubbed Jacy's head. The touch felt good for a moment, but then Jacy jerked away, not knowing what else to do. Lulu grinned, "Just making sure they got all the lice."

"I don't have lice."

"I see that now. Jacy what?"

"Jacy Cruz."

"I knew some Cruzes over by Sells. Is all your family here in Arizona?"

Jacy shrugged. "Don't know. I'm from Bapchule."

"Got any brothers or sisters here?"

Jacy squirmed from all the questions. "No. Just my friend Ira Hayes."

"Really! How do you know him?"

"I was sitting on a bench in front of the store."

Lulu wouldn't quit. "And?"

"I was eating a licorice stick. He asked me if I was a Papago from Gila Bend because my teeth were all black."

Lulu laughed. "What'd you say?"

Jacy felt more at ease remembering Ira. "I cussed him out. The next day he helped me with my English at school. I asked him how come he knew English so good. He said he could read and write since he was four and asked why I couldn't."

"Ira never talks to me. Or anybody else." Lulu paused for a few seconds and looked thoughtful. "Don't feel bad if he won't talk to you here."

"What do you mean?"

"When we chase the boys and try to kiss and hug them, they like it. Not Ira. He always runs away."

"He won't need to run away from me. I'd never chase boys to kiss them." Jacy thought she'd rather kiss Lulu.

"Tell me about your mom."

Jacy was glad Lulu had changed the subject, but the new one made her even more uncomfortable. "She's gone."

"Where?"

Jacy shrugged.

"Your dad?"

Jacy shrugged again.

"Don't worry," Lulu said.

Jacy heard a sound like a banshee's shriek and fear gripped her heart. She grabbed Lulu.

"It's just the whistle for lunch," Lulu said calmly.

"Why don't you tell time with the sun?"

"Because this is what white people do. The whistle tells us when to get up, when to eat, when to do everything."

Jacy thought responding to a whistle was stupid, but she didn't want to tell Lulu that. Instead she looked at her surroundings and periodically gazed at Lula out of the corner of her eye. She tentatively tasted the candy cigarette. The sweetness on her tongue was heavenly. She broke the candy in half and stuck the whole thing in her mouth to suck on.

She strode with Lulu to the back of the brick building, and Lulu stopped.

"This is where we eat. The cafeteria." Lulu opened a door that led into a big room. The smell in the room called a cafeteria reminded Jacy that she hadn't eaten for a long time.

"How old are you?" Lulu looked quizzical.

"Fifteen."

"You're little for your age."

Jacy didn't respond.

Lulu smiled. "You're about as talkative as Ira."

Jacy nodded.

"Today I'm going to show you around. Okay?" Lulu reached for Jacy's hand, but she dodged away to survey the long room. More people than she could count sat at four rows of tables with white tablecloths. At the end of the room, up on the wall, was a sign, "There is no excellence without great labor." She crunched on the last bit of candy cigarette to the sound of bodies rustling and metal on glass. Nobody was talking.

Lulu handed her a tray and a plate and helped her ladle the food. "Spam," Lulu whispered. "Mixed with soda crackers. Sometimes we get horse meat. The yellow is called mac and cheese. I help in the kitchen sometimes. The food is strange, but you'll get used to it."

After Jacy filled her hungry belly, Lulu led her around the school, which was filled with noisy, staring children. With every step Jacy took, she felt a longing for the quiet of home. She wished she could find Ira. He seemed so safe.

The classrooms, dorm room, and bathhouses confused her, and the frowning faces frightened her. She knew the others were from different tribes because their faces were different from hers. She clung to Lulu's hand.

By the end of the day, Jacy was exhausted, but she still hadn't found Ira. Lulu promised her she would see him the next day.

The dorm was stuffy and hot. Girls sat on single cots strung throughout an overheated, windowless room with faded pale green walls the same color as tired, old, prickly pear pads. "Your bed is next to mine," Lulu said as she opened the drawer in the nightstand between their beds. "Here's your kit. Grab your nightgown and follow me." They went out to the bathhouse where Lulu took two towels and washcloths from the cabinet inside the door. The steamy room was even hotter than the dorm.

"Your soap and toothbrush are in your kit," Lulu said. "Brush your teeth before you shower."

"What?"

"Brush your teeth."

"How?" Jacy felt warmth suffusing her face. She had no idea what Lulu was talking about.

"With your toothbrush." Lulu demonstrated with her own.

"Why?"

"You see any charcoal around here? Brush your teeth so they don't fall out."

The nude girls in the shower embarrassed Jacy, but she squirmed even more as Lulu undressed. When she caught sight of Lulu's full breasts, Jacy turned to the wall and kept her gaze averted while she showered quickly in tepid water. She didn't use the washcloth and wasn't sure what it was for. She dried off with the towel and dressed with her back to the other girls.

Before Lulu could introduce her to the other girls, a woman hollered, "Lights out!" Lulu told her that any tomfoolery after the lights went down resulted in punishment, and the girls fell silent quickly.

Noises and dreams of monsters filled the long, pitch-black night and kept Jacy from getting much sleep. At one point, she awoke to feel tears silently rolling down her face. She was finally drowsing off into deeper sleep when the whistle shrieked and jerked her out of slumber. She sat up feeling exhausted.

Lulu pulled her out of bed and introduced the other girls. All Jacy could think about was that she wanted to hold Lulu's hand.

In the cafeteria, the giggles made Jacy feel more at home until an old white woman shushed them. Jacy finally spotted Ira sitting alone at a back corner table. Twisting through the tables and people, Jacy grabbed for him as he stood and gave her a one-arm hug. Close behind her, Lulu grabbed her arm and dragged her away.

"Why can't I eat with him?" Jacy cried.

"Because we have assigned seats, and you are next to me."

JACY LEARNED HOW TO properly clean and cook, and she attended classes, study group, and church. She longed for Lulu who was gone most days and some nights working at the tuberculosis sanatorium a mile from school. In her free time, while she waited for Lulu's return Jacy made needlepoint souvenirs that the school sold. The few pennies she earned she mostly spent on Abba-Zaba candy bars to share with Ira. She was delighted to learn that they shared the same birthday, January 23rd, though he was two years older. Once, in honor of their birthdays, she'd even gotten to go into town to the movies with him and some other students.

She didn't have much time with him, but sometimes they got to read under the cottonwood trees where she seemed to irritate him by asking too many questions.

"Read!" he would demand. Sometimes he let her watch him play Twenty-one pickup basketball. One time she asked him why he didn't play with the senior Apache boys.

"See those two Apache clowns over there pushing that Hopi kid back and forth? They hate each other. Even worse, they hate us. They can't even understand each other's language or ours, and you can't understand their English."

"Why don't you ask them in English?"

Ira stared her down. "What'd I just say? See those two clowns over there—"

"I saw you talk with them the other day and they didn't push you around."

"What'd I say?" he asked calmly. "They hate us. Don't push your luck."

"How come you never get mad?"

Ira turned away.

"The other day I heard them asking you where you from." Jacy poked Ira in the ribs to get his attention.

"Shut it!" Ira finally snapped.

Jacy reached to pull out some of the coarse grass surrounding the tree they sat under. "Sacaton, Sacaton, Sacaton," Jacy said. "I love the way that word for grass sounds. You can feel it right up in the roof of your mouth. Sacaton."

"Enough!"

Jacy grinned and sat quietly for a few minutes. "Hey, Ira. How come I'm the only girl you talk to?"

"Because I can't get away from you. Now will you shut it?"

Jacy knew Ira didn't really get mad at her because he always protected her and kept other kids from teasing her. Except for Lulu who only teased her about Ira's friendship. "Why you hanging out with Ira all the time. You in love? Oh, yes. Jacy's in love."

"You only say that because you want him to pay attention to you."

Ignoring Jacy, Lulu continued in a singsong voice. "Jacy loves Ira. Jacy loves Ira."

If only Jacy could explain how she really felt. Ira was just a friend, but Jacy knew her feelings for Lulu were wrong. She couldn't tell Lulu she wanted to hear her say, "Jacy loves Lulu." Even when she listened to the girls talk about wanting to kiss the boys, all she thought about was how she wanted to kiss Lulu.

EACH DAY JACY AND her schoolmates followed the whistles. The one at 6:00 a.m. got her out of bed, doing chores in the dorm, and going off to breakfast. Another one at 8:00 a.m. started school. Other whistle shrieks told them to go to lunch or quit work or go bed. Jacy eventually settled into a world that was whistle-driven and boringly routine.

After the Japanese bombed Pearl Harbor, they heard reports about battles in Japan and Europe. Every morning they sang the Army, Navy, and Marine anthems.

Ira had grown into a man, and Jacy saw him rarely now. Most days, he disappeared to work leather for the shoes the school children wore or to make cabinets and shelves. Jacy envied him while she washed the filthy clothes and dishes or floors. She hated the menial work. Even Lulu got to work with the doctor in the school hospital.

Every time Jacy saw Ira, he said he wanted to join the Marines to become an "Honorable Warrior." He seemed dissatisfied. Unhappy. She knew something was up when he nonchalantly gave her his jackknife. The day after, he told her he was joining the Civilian Conservation Corps, and the next morning he was gone, and Jacy was left behind. He wrote her an occasional, short letter, but she missed him terribly.

With more time to think, Jacy noticed Lulu had been right about growing. Her shoes fit, and her dress no longer dragged on the ground, although it flopped on her tall lanky body. Even Lulu noticed the change one day as they both lay on their cots in the hot dorm.

"Wow! You're definitely much bigger." Lulu frowned at Jacy. "Guess I can't whoop your ass no more."

"Since you never could anyway." Jacy snorted. Hoping Lulu would listen, Jacy tried to explain how lonely she was when Lulu went off to work at her second job in the tuberculosis sanatorium.

"Grow the hell up," Lula snapped. "You need to take care of yourself and leave me alone."

Jacy felt her heart had broken. She skipped class and packed her duffle bag with food, mostly hard biscuits and candy, and a few clothes she had taken from the clothing stock room. She added Lulu's comb to have something that Lulu had touched. Late in the evening, when Lulu was working at the sanatorium, Jacy left a note in Lulu's kit to tell her about going to find Ira because it was wrong for her to love Lulu the way she did.

Ira's last letter said he was in San Diego to join the Marines. Jacy's first stop before crossing the desert was at a service station bathroom. Deciding it was safer to travel as a boy, she took the switchblade Ira had given her and cut her hair. She bound her small breasts and changed into a shirt and Levis. The best feeling was trashing her heavy, ugly dress in a burn barrel out back.

Jacy headed south, moving in and out of the streetlights until only early dawn lit her way. Walking was too hot during the day, so Jacy slid under an old wrecked truck off the road to rest. Fighting her fears, she imagined wrapping Lulu's arms around her as she tried to sleep.

In the early evenings she filled up her canvas canteen at service stations and begged rides in the back of pickup trucks from people who stopped for gas.

One ride was in the front seat of a spiffy Cadillac LaSalle all the way to Wickenburg where the fat cheerful man dropped her off beside the Hassayampa river.

"You know what Hassayampa means?" He looked at Jacy. "It means if you drink the water you will never tell the truth again." He laughed as he drove away.

She didn't know if he was serious, but she walked along the riverbanks, drank the water, and slept under mesquite trees. Missing Lulu every step of the way and afraid she couldn't find Ira, Jacy trudged through long, lonely hours.

The night sounds frightened Jacy, and she was grateful for the bright full moon shining on the narrow animal trail that wove around mesquite trees and through catclaw brush. The catclaws caught her jeans and poked her. Worn out from extracting one needle claw at a time, she circled back to the road for rides.

Out of food and tired of chewing on hard, dried-up, sickly-sweet mesquite beans, Jacy entertained herself with the signs along the road outside Salome. "Crawl out and cool yourself," one read. Another was: "Old Rockefeller Made His Pile–And Maybe We Will – After a While." She laughed out loud at "Smile, Smile, Smile. You Don't Have to Stay Here But We Do." She wished Lulu had been with her to read them.

Jacy walked into Salome just as the morning heat danced in mirages on the road ahead of her. A Help Wanted sign led her into a long, dingy, white adobe building. Sheffler's Cafe & Soda Fountain, the only restaurant in town, was almost cool when she pushed open the back door. She smoothed back her shaggy boy's haircut and cleared her throat so she could use her deepest voice.

Cook seemed to be waiting for a boy to show up and help him. He started Jacy washing dishes and scrubbing down the stoves before he fed her, but her job turned out to be cleaning everything, restrooms, glass top counters in the gift shop, sidewalks, floors. She'd had so much practice at the school keeping everything clean so it was an easy job. Listening to the Jukebox playing Glenn Miller's "Chattanooga Choo Choo" helped the boredom as she dusted the toys behind the counter, carefully picking up each car on the miniature train. She loved the Slinky and saved to buy it for Lulu. She couldn't stop missing her.

The Indian relics, rugs, and paintings of famous Indians reminded her of home. Her favorite, *End of the Trail*, hung over a wood fireplace. It was so beautiful even though it reminded her of how sad she felt.

At night, she slept out back of the restaurant in a lean-to. The cot was hard, but Cook loaned her a blanket, and she never got cold.

Knowing how to be invisible made it easier for Jacy to be around people in the restaurant. She loved looking at their fancy clothes while she cleaned. Even in the heat, men wore suits and hats, and women had dresses with gloves and hats and high heels. And silk hose with crooked seams. Watching them sweat made Jacy even happier to be wearing her work shirt and Levis.

Jacy loved cleaning the bird aviary next door, which was supposed to have eight hundred tropical birds, but she couldn't count them because they kept hopping around. Sometimes she just sat and watched, even when it made her homesick for the desert birds back home: the smart red-winged blackbird, the roadrunner that raced cars, and the white-winged dove that cried "cooo" three times in the quiet of the darkening night.

Each morning before the aviary opened for business, she filled buckets of water and laughed at the antics of the brightly colored birds as they bathed. The bird she liked the most was the large, white cockatoo sitting high above on his swing, squawking and waiting for people to visit. He talked and danced to get their attention before he flew above, flicking his tail up and down several times, and let 'er rip. Jacy had learned what that behavior meant, but the big bald man looking up at the cockatoo didn't have the foggiest notion.

Jacy started to say, "You better...," but it was too late. Ira's lessons in stoicism paid off when she saw the look on the man's face after the bird pooped on his head. At least he was bald. Laughing inside, Jacy kept a straight face, but she suddenly sobered when Lulu's face appeared in her mind's eye, and she wished Lulu was there to share the moment.

Two weeks went by, and Jacy was paid with more money than she had seen in her life. Jacy could have been happy—if she didn't miss Lulu and Ira so much. The heat made her decide to stay a few months until the days cooled off. And then she'd have enough money to travel.

At night while she ate in the kitchen, Cook would tell Jacy about Dick Wick Hall's history. Hall was the first resident of Salome and quite the humorist, and he'd edited the *Salome Sun*. Cook recounted stories from the old, yellowed newspapers that he kept in a stack on the kitchen table. While he made tortillas with his favorite roller, a three-foot piece of broomstick, Cook rambled. "Did you know Charles Pratt, Dick Wick Hall, and his brother Earnest established this town in 1905?"

"No, Cookie. I didn't know that. Who's Charles Pratt?"

"He was Salome Pratt's husband. He named the town after her dance. 'Salome Where She Danced.'"

"Why'd she do that?"

"Well, they said she wanted to go barefoot, so she took off her shoes and ended up hopping on the hot desert sand trying to keep from burning her feet." Cook laughed so hard he had to sit down. He loved to laugh. It kept him young he said. Cook had been an Apache warrior at Fort McDowell Reservation until he learned how to cook in the army during World War I. Stringy except for a pot belly, he always held himself tall and proud.

"Did you know that the Yuma-Resque highway was laid out by a tipsy prospector fleeing from scalp-minded Indians?" Cook nearly fell down laughing when telling this one. "That crazy road out there is all your fault."

"Me? I wasn't even born yet. You're the one."

"Not me. Maybe my granddaddy. He loved to scalp white folks."

Jacy grinned and waited for Cook's next Dick Wick story. "Did you know it was so hot and dry here, they irrigated potatoes by planting onions between them and scratching the onions so that the potato eyes watered?" This one had Cook banging the table in howling laughter.

"My favorite is the frog," Jacy said. "Tell me about him."

"You know why that big, wood frog, cut-out by Dick's grave is sitting on the only green patch of grass?"

"No. Why, Cookie?"

"Cuz only brown grass grows here."

Jacy laughed with Cook. "I believe that one."

In the late evening Cook would say, "Read me about his story in the *Saturday Evening Post*. The serious one." Jacy would stop washing dishes and sit back at the table, picking up the tired and worn *Saturday Evening Post* magazine.

"This valley appealed to me strangely the first time I came to it; not only its abundant warmth but the wonderful peace and quiet of it, which only a dweller of the desert can understand and appreciate, where I can get acquainted with myself and maybe find the something which every man in his own soul is consciously or unconsciously searching for—Himself."

Wiping a tear, Cook would nod. "I know how that is."

"Is that why you say you'll never leave here?"

"It's home, Jacy. Like the poet says, home is where they have to take you in. These good folks took me in."

Jacy knew it wasn't her home, and she knew it was time to find Ira.

One evening she collected her pay and hugged Cook goodbye. Hanging on to her for a minute, Cook said, "You be careful out there. They find out you're a girl you could get hurt."

Jacy shook her head in amazement. "How'd you know?"

"There are always things men and women don't share growing up. Different ways talking about sex. About women." Cookie grinned. "How long your dick is. You never spoke as a young man would, but I sure could tell you love this Lulu." Cookie got serious again. "Those white folks find out you like girls you could get hurt worse."

She was still thunderstruck about his insight, but said, "I promise, Cookie. I'll be careful not to talk about Lulu anymore."

As she departed, Jacy pondered Cook's acceptance, wondering if what she felt for Lulu might not be so wrong after all.

Jacy walked across the cool desert through the bush along the Colorado River for five long days before she got to the Yuma sands. From there her journey got worse. The sand wormed its way into every opening of her body, and the long silent hours gave her too much time to think about Lulu. At first, Jacy walked the old original plank road, replaced long ago by the nearby asphalt where trucks roared by, but the planks kept disappearing into the sand.

Out of water and worn out from struggling across the hot desert, she retreated to the nearby highway. A pickup stopped, and the driver gave her a drink from a canvas bag hanging on the front of the radiator to keep the water cool. Jacy crawled into the bed of the pickup truck and didn't wake up until he let her off in El Cajon. Her next ride was with a Marine headed to Camp Pendleton. He told her he couldn't get her on the base, but he'd drop her off at the gate. The guard there finally relented enough to make a call and smirked when he said Private Hayes was no longer there and, no, he couldn't give her any more information.

Jacy wandered outside the camp fence to a tree and sat under it, crying, until her tears dried. Her only choice was to find out if she had a letter from Ira saying where he had gone, and Lulu was the only person she could call. She knew Lulu would hate her for the note she left, but at least she might tell Jacy if she had a letter. Misery drove her to a phone.

Lulu's flat tone made Jacy take a deep breath before she said, "I can't find Ira here in San Diego. Did he send me a letter?"

"Yes." Lulu's voice upset her, but Jacy also wanted to jump for joy because Ira had written her.

"Open it," she demanded.

"If I do, I won't tell you what he said because you'll keep looking for him."

Jacy begged, "Please."

"Jacy. The note you left me. Did you mean it?"

Not ready for Lulu's question, Jacy finally mumbled, "Yes."

"Jacy? You need to come home. I love you, too."

The sudden warmth in Lulu's voice made Jacy blush. She blurted. "Really? Truly really? Why didn't you say anything before?"

"You were too young, Jacy. They would have sent me away. I've been in nursing school since you been gone, training to be a midwife, and I want you to graduate high school with me so we can go back to the reservation together."

"Really?"

"I want to start a baby's health clinic."

"That's wonderful! Where?"

"Akimel, where else?" Lulu said in a matter-of-fact tone.

"But what about Ira?"

"The war has to end soon, and he'll come home."

"Okay."

"Okay?" Lulu sounded doubtful.

"Of course, okay. I've missed you so much."

"Okay! Find the nearest bus and come home. And Jacy? I've missed you, too."

Home. Jacy knew being with Lulu was home. She couldn't wait to see her.

BACK AT SCHOOL, IRA'S letter waited for her along with a relieved Lulu and an angry superintendent. After the superintendent yelled at her for an hour for being irresponsible, Lulu dragged the joyous Jacy into a bathroom and smothered her with kisses. Lulu's secret touches and smiles in the passing days almost made up for the school's restrictions, especially the long heavy dresses she had to wear once again. God, how she missed her Levis.

Back on kitchen duty, she read Ira's letters to the other workers. They weren't as lively or entertaining as Cook's banter, but that was okay. She had Lulu again.

Lulu's training kept them apart much of the time, but when they were together, they made plans for the clinic. And kissed and hugged. During her time alone outside of sewing and cooking classes and work, Jacy borrowed books from the small library and taught herself bookkeeping.

Ira's next letter talked about their mutual birthday:

> *Dear Jacy, we got another year older today. Would you believe it's not only January 12th today, it's also 1943? Happy birthday to us for another year. I got the bus to town and went to a movie called* Bambi. *Remember when we saw* Fantasia *at the Fox Theater in Phoenix? Where you got in trouble. Again?*

The kitchen busboy, Reddy, wanted to know why Jacy was laughing.

"Long time ago, Ira Hayes and I were in the balcony at the movie theater, and this kid beside us started making puking noises and dumped a sack of stinky mess on the audience below. They almost threw *me* out before Ira grabbed the kid and showed the manager the slimy bag he'd hid away in his pocket."

"I already heard about that," Reddy said. "Keep reading."

"Okay, okay." Jacy grinned at the chubby Chiricahua boy, picked up the letter, and kept reading.

> *I got through basic. Never been so tired or hurt so bad. Can't complain about the weather. It is beautiful here at Camp Gillespie. I know you won't believe it but I decided to be a paratrooper. They call me Chief Falling Cloud. Can you believe that? And I got my silver wings. Jacy, next time you see me, you can address me as Private First Class, Sir!*

Jacy stopped and wondered out loud. "I thought he was a Marine. Does that mean he joined the Air Force now?"

"Read!" Reddy said.

I miss all of you very much. Don't know where I'm going next but the war will be over and I'll be home soon now. Jacy, listen to Lulu and behave. Your friend, Ira.

Later she read the letter again to Lulu, who also did not know if Ira was a Marine or in the Air Force. She told Lulu that she worried about him jumping out of planes.

"See what I told you," Lulu reminded her. "Ira will be back soon now, and we'll all go home."

"It's been over two years since I saw him, and the war's never going to end," Jacy complained. She moved closer to Lulu.

Lulu smiled at Jacy and give her a long hug. "Maybe more later."

"A kiss?"

"Maybe two. Later."

IRA'S NEXT LETTER SAID he was still in training, but he couldn't tell her where. The envelope bore a New Caledonia stamp, though, and he talked about riding on amphibians. The old 1911 Encyclopedia Britannica in the library that claimed it had all the knowledge in the world didn't have anything about New Caledonia, and Jacy couldn't figure out why Ira was playing with frogs. And when did any frog grow large enough to ride? She smiled remembering the Salome frog and wondered how Cook was doing.

Jacy sputtered in amazement when Ira's next letter talked about their birthday again. "Is it already another year, Lulu? I swear every day around here stretches into a month. How could it be another year already?"

"At least he's still alive!" Lulu reassured her. "And it's your birthday."

Jace grinned. "Do I get chocolate cake?"

"Yes."

"Chocolate frosting?"

"Only if you share."

"Who with?"

"Save a piece for Ira."

"Spend the night with me?"

Lulu's smile was beautiful. "That's why I'm here."

"Hot damn!"

According to the stamp, Ira was in Hawaii. Jacy looked up in amazement. "He never said anything about going to Hawaii. Everything's crossed out in this one. He says he was home a weekend from training but not when." Jacy looked up. "Wonder if any of his brothers knew about this?"

"Leonard did, but I didn't want to say anything. Leonard went home for the weekend to visit with Ira who told him he was on his way to Iwo Jima."

Jacy felt outraged. "Why didn't you tell me?"

Lulu pulled Jacy close and smoothed her hair. "I knew you'd take off to go see him. We're almost done with school now and don't need any more trouble."

Absorbing the warmth of Lulu's body, Jacy felt herself melt. Before they got caught up in each other, Lulu moved away pointing at the letter. "Read."

"Well, shit!" Jacy sputtered. "Just about the only place they didn't black out is Guadalcanal. Bet they missed that one. Says he trained to be an automatic rifleman and has been in battles. He's not a paratrooper anymore." Jacy slammed the letter down. "How come he didn't call me or come visit?"

MONTHS LATER, LULU WAS waiting for Jacy in a thicket of oleander bushes growing along one of the fences in the corner of the school. Jacy ran toward her waving a letter in Lulu's face. "Look at this postmark! What the hell is Ira doing in Washington D.C.?"

"Open it and find out."

Tearing into the letter, Jacy couldn't believe what Ira had written.

> *"I'm selling war bonds now. We hop from town to town and I stand around praying no one will say anything stupid to me like calling me a hero and expect me to say something back. I'm no hero. Everybody shoves drinks at me. Sometimes I drink it just to get through the day. I hate every boring minute of it. One thing I liked. They made three of us raise the flag again at the Capitol and I got a chance to talk to my buddies and be with men who understood what it was like. And I met President Truman. That was nice."*

Jacy stopped snuggling into Lulu and shook her head. "Ira doesn't drink. This is bad."

"Yes, but think, Jacy. He got to meet the president!"

"I guess," Jacy reluctantly agreed.

JACY AND LULU FINALLY graduated, gathered their few belongings, and said their goodbyes. Lulu's brother drove them back home to their small adobe clinic. Lulu wiped a few tears from her eye as Jacy gleefully threw her heavy dress out the car window. Back in her Levis, she shouted to the wind hitting her face, "Glory be! Free at last!"

Lulu's brother shook his head at her. "People won't like it, Jacy."

Jacy smiled. "People get used to things. After a while, they won't even notice me."

Two months later Jacy got another letter from Ira. "Listen to this. He says he had to leave the tour early because he kept drinking too much. They're discharging him." Jacy shredded the letter in frustration. "Damn it! What did they do to him, Lulu? They're killing him!"

"I'm so sorry." Lulu held Jacy tight for a long time before she kissed her.

LULU HAD JUST SURPRISED Jacy with her first birthday cake in their new home when the front door flew open, and Ira walked in with the cold wind. "Look at this!" He turned in place and surveyed the room. "You've got a sign outside and everything. You wrote that you two were going to have a baby clinic, but I had to see for myself. I'm real proud."

Jacy was so shocked to see him that she stood glued in place as Lulu leaped on Ira with a big hug and a kiss on his a cheek. He blushed with embarrassment, but he hugged back. "Looking good, Lulu. You keeping Jacy behaving herself?"

"Mostly Ira, mostly. Now that you're home you can have the job back."

Ira let loose of Lulu and gave Jacy a long hug. "Where's your dress?"

"That all you got to say?"

Ira grinned and shrugged, watching Jacy dance up and down around him. "Not all. How come you're way out here? Population got to ten yet?"

"It's sort of central to most of the people in these parts," Jacy said. "What's it to you? How many times over the years you walk this far anyway?"

"That's why I'm complaining."

"Bullpucky. You just got used to people hauling your ass all over the country in fancy cars. I heard you're a war hero now."

"The riding around part seeing the country was nice. And so were the people."

Jacy could tell from the look in his eyes he didn't mean it. She watched him slump onto the couch and sigh.

"Everywhere I went, people shoved drinks in my hand and said 'You're a hero.' We knew we hadn't done that much, but you couldn't tell them. God, Jacy, I can't forget most of my buddies were dead and I'm not. It was bad, Jacy. I'm really glad you're a girl and didn't have to see it. Smelling it was even worse."

Once Ira got started, the words just poured out. "The nurses had the worst of it, Lulu. They worked so hard trying to keep us guys alive, and nobody looked out for them. Not ever. I'm just glad you stayed here. Jacy, you won't believe this one. Some guy took a picture of us raising the flag. That's why I had to go on that bond tour. Then this guy wanted my name, but I wouldn't tell him until the commander made me."

Lulu said, "Just the fact that you survived is a miracle, Ira."

"If this is survival, then I'm not sure I want it." He ran his hands through his hair. "I'm haunted by my friends who died. This one guy, Harlon Block, was one of us six who raised the flag at Iwo Jima, which those idiots had us do twice because the press wanted a picture. But command identified Block as this other guy, Hansen. I been trying to tell them it's not Hansen in the picture, and they won't listen."

"Why is that a big deal?" Jacy asked.

"Did you see the photo in the papers?"

Jacy looked away. "I heard about it, but I'm real sorry that I never have seen it. We've been so busy here at the clinic."

"Hansen died. Block died. So damn many guys died. But it's Block in the photo, and I felt his family had a right to know."

He looked so dejected that Jacy took his hand. "I'm sorry, Ira. What can I do?"

"I don't know. I can't get the quiet back. People keep driving by and following me around, asking me if I'm the Indian what raised the flag on Iwo Jima."

"Tell them to give you a dollar and you'll answer."

"I don't want their damn dollar. I don't want all those hundreds of letters I get every day either. And the next person calls me a hero... I just want to be left alone." Ira rubbed hard at his head. "I shouldn't have come home." His voice rose, and he began to shake. "I shouldn't have come."

Jacy had never seen him so upset. "Hey, Ira. Lulu's brought a Coke for you." She watched Ira try to regain control. He stood and stepped in front of a big fan. "You got electricity."

"Got a generator out back."

"Walls are smooth." Ira ran a hand down a wall. "Didn't know you could paint mud." He walked around and stared at the equipment they had collected and asked about everything. He pointed at one device. "What's that for?"

"It's for prenatal care. We try to help mother's have healthy babies."

"That right, Jacy? You help Lulu catch babies?"

Jacy laughed. "Women don't squat anymore, Ira. Mostly I pay the bills, order supplies, drive Lulu to the homes, and run errands. She keeps me busy."

"Looks good on you, Jacy."

"I love it here, Ira." Jacy smiled at Lulu. "It's the first real home I've ever had."

Rubbing Jacy's arm, Lulu turned to Ira. "Maybe you could go on rounds with us. Everybody would love to see you."

"Don't think so, Lulu. But would you have anything to stop nightmares? I can't sleep anymore."

"Let me look into it."

JACY'S DAYS WERE FILLED with playing with babies brought to the clinic, and her nights were spent entwined with Lulu. Sometimes, when they lost one of their babies, Jacy would comfort Lulu as they cried together in the night.

One day after a sweet girl too young to carry delivered her baby stillborn, Ira dragged into the clinic, flopped in a chair and groaned. It had been months since Jacy had seen him, and his loss of weight and unkempt appearance worried her. "Damn, Ira, where the hell you been?"

"I hitchhiked to Texas and back again. God, I'm beat."

Jacy handed Ira a Coke. "That's over a thousand miles."

"Closer to thirteen hundred."

"What for?"

"You remember I told you about the mix-up with my friend Harlon? How they told me it wasn't Harlon holding the flag with us?"

"Sure. I remember."

"I just wanted his folks to know it was him. I found Harlon's dad in a cotton field and told him it was Harlon in the picture with me."

"That's it? You were there two minutes before you turned around and walked thirteen hundred miles back home?"

"I got rides part of it."

Jacy shook her head and felt a load of worry rise up. Ira closed his eyes and quietly went to sleep.

ON THE CLINIC'S THIRD anniversary, Lulu had gained acceptance within the community as more and more families came to her for help. Jacy's life was perfect—except for her concerns for Ira. Every time she saw him, he was hiding in a bottle. One day he called, sounding more like the old Ira. "Guess what, Jacy, I'm in a movie about Iwo Jima. Guess what, Jacy, John Wayne hands the flag to me!"

"Guess what, Ira. How much they paying you?"

"Money all you think about?"

"Every dollar keeps a child alive."

Being in the movie didn't help Ira, and his drinking got worse. Jacy heard he got arrested over fifty times for being drunk. She wanted to cry for him. She couldn't figure out how to help. The war had destroyed him, and all she could do was listen if he wanted to talk. Over and over, he would say, "I'm going crazy thinking about my buddies and what happened to them. They were better than me, but they're not coming home. God, Jacy! Will I ever sleep again?"

"Remember when you went to the Marine Corps war dedication sober?" Jacy said to him. "You did good then. You even met President Eisenhower, and he called you a hero."

Ira frowned. "That was when this dumbass reporter asked why didn't I like all the pomp and circumstances I had to walk away to keep from hitting him."

"I really wish I could take your hurting away."

"No one can, Jacy. I'm just glad you and Lulu are happy together. You make a beautiful couple."

"You know we're together?"

"I always knew how you felt about Lulu. I'm just grateful she feels the same about you."

"How come you don't mind about our, uh, relationship?"

"Some of the soldiers I fought with loved men. I got along fine with them. But because I was respectful to everyone, sometimes people sneered at me and called *me* queer. I don't want that for anyone."

OVER THE YEARS THAT followed, Jacy kept celebrating her birthday with Ira even if she didn't always see him. One year, she took a cake to his house, but he wasn't there. Twelve days later, his brother Vernon came to the door of the clinic, hat in hand.

"Ira's dead. I thought you'd want to know. Froze to death on a cold night."

"Oh, God!" Jacy said. "How? What happened?" She sank into a chair, her legs too weak to hold her up.

"We were over in Bapchule playing cards when Ira and Henry Setoyant got into a fistfight. So Kenneth and I went home. Kenneth thinks Henry beat on him so bad Ira couldn't make it home. That's why he fell and froze to death." Vernon wiped his eyes. "I think Henry's to blame, too. I'm probably to blame. We should have stayed and helped Ira get home."

In coming days, it was Lulu's turn to comfort Jacy.

ON FEBRUARY 2, 1955, Ira Hamilton Hayes was buried in Section 34, Grave 479A, at Arlington National Cemetery. On a hill overlooking the gravesite, Lulu stood with Jacy as they said their tearful goodbyes.

Walking back down the hill, Jacy pulled Lulu close, grateful they were going home and, at the same time, sad that Ira never found his.

SIXTY-THREE YEARS AFTER Jacy and Lulu first met, they stood on the steps of the Phoenix Indian School, now called the Steele Indian School Park, and watched the rainbow flag dance above the sign: "2003 - Let Your Pride Be Your Guide." Holding hands, they walked among the booths at the first Pride Parade Festival held in the park. They stopped at the last booth, smiling as they looked at each other.

Jacy said, "Ira would have loved this."

Ghostly Crossing

By
Jane Cuthbertson

A CLIPPING WAS STUCK to Diane Spencer's refrigerator by a magnet, a list from the local newspaper, a roster of names of people dead, all killed at once, all killed suddenly when a 737 spiraled down into a hillside near Manassas. Over a hundred names on the list, but only one mattered to the woman who'd stuck the clipping up.

Carlisle, Blaine, 32. Systems analyst, Reston, VA.

The obituary mentioned two brothers, parents who'd predeceased her, and the ubiquitous "companion." The companion had thrown that away, though, and kept this list, stark and brief. More than the obituary, more than the memorial service or the sympathy of friends and family, the name on the list brought home all that was left of five years of love and laughter and happiness. All that was left was a name…Blaine….

Diane had gone more than a little crazy after the plane crash. Refusing to talk to anyone, ignoring friends and job, she let all her feelings but the grief bury themselves so deep in her soul that the grief, lonely by itself, finally joined them, leaving nothing.

She would cut herself accidentally and notice the blood only after it stained everything she was wearing. She drank herself into unconsciousness at night, and into awareness during the day. She talked to no one, leaving the house only to buy more liquor. The thought did occur to her once that she should be concerned; but concern was a feeling, too, and poof. Suddenly it just wasn't there.

One night Diane found a video she and Blaine had made the previous summer. Testing the numbness theory, she watched it. Filmed out in Wyoming at Independence Rock, it recorded when she and Blaine had gone there with their friends Amy and Deborah. It had been Blaine's idea.

She was fascinated with history, and Independence Rock was so isolated that the names of Oregon Trail immigrants carved on it long ago were still visible.

They all took turns with the camera; the next to last shot was Blaine on top of the rock, arms spread wide.

"Isn't this incredible?" she was saying. "Two hundred years after white people saw this place, and nothing has changed. It could be 1849, or 1920, or 1993."

Amy poked her face into the picture. "Except for the names."

People still carved their names into the granite. They'd found almost every year since 1847 represented.

Blaine smiled at Amy. "Yes, the names. Everybody's little shot at immortality."

The last scene on the video was Diane herself, standing alone on top of the rock, gazing out into the distance, looking like she was alone on the planet. The sun was setting behind her, and Blaine must have been holding the camera, because the shot went on for a long time. Diane had had no idea she was being "watched," and the thought of Blaine shooting the footage almost caused tears to well up in her eyes. Almost. As the video faded to black, Diane stared at the TV screen, remembering the rock and how it felt to stand there in the middle of nowhere. She actually did remember the feeling, and that stirred her to movement with a germ of an idea.

IT TAKES TWO DAYS to get to Casper, Wyoming, from Reston, Virginia, if one drives the speed limit. Diane did and reached the town nearest to Independence Rock late on a summer evening. She checked into a motel near the city limits and beside a package store. She bought enough booze to supply a softball team, and, thus reinforced, spent the next days out at the rock. Drive there in the morning, climb, explore, drink. Other people came and went, none staying long enough to realize that Diane essentially never left at all, until the sun went down or she ran out of alcohol. Nights she spent in the motel room, drinking with the TV on.

There was nowhere else to go, nowhere else to be. Nobody knew she was here, and nobody knew who she was. Early in the morning she had the place completely to herself, so she tried to get there just as the sun rose. This could be difficult if she'd stayed up late drinking, but she didn't let that stop her. Sleep wasn't necessary anymore. And the dawn's quiet gave Diane a strange sort of peace. Feelings didn't enter into it, and if she'd had some vague plan or hope of sensing Blaine's presence here, reality took another path. Blaine was dead. Her ghost was not in Wyoming.

But Diane was, and as long as she was under the limit on the MasterCard, she stayed. She didn't think about the five years of happiness with Blaine, the perversity of the life insurance settlement that had left her financially secure, or the empty future spread out before her. She didn't think at all, and she didn't feel. This was the middle of nowhere, after all, and the oblivion in her soul fit in perfectly.

One night the sun went down and caught Diane on top of the rock. She'd started the day with a full bottle of pretty decent gin. Now it was just about empty, and she didn't trust herself to climb down without breaking her neck. So she holed up in a little cave in the middle of the rock, killed the last of the alcohol, and settled in for the night. Diane wouldn't risk a fall, or a DUI, but part of her was half-hoping she'd freeze to death. It looked like drinking was going to be a problem for her now. Better to die here than deal with that in the real world. Better to die here than deal with *anything* in the real world.

Her lack of feeling, though, extended to the cold. Later on, she figured that was why she survived. That, and it was summer. Some people might compare this whole numbness thing to being dead, but she knew that wasn't true. Blaine was dead, and she wasn't with Blaine.

The rock was so isolated that no one knew Diane spent the night. A state trooper noticed the car parked at the rest stop, but never checked inside. He knew people slept there all the time. The Honda Accord looked like a thousand others, and he never realized it had been there every day for the last three weeks.

Diane woke up stiff, her head pounding with its now-constant hangover. She was still alive. The cold had not been cold enough. Unfolding her tall body, she crabbed her way out of the little cave. She couldn't feel her legs, and she knew better than to stand upright too quickly.

Sitting in the shadows watching the sky grow light, she flexed everything until, gradually, her limbs worked again. It was time to try the standing thing.

Before she could get to her feet, however, Diane heard a scuffling noise above her. She wasn't alone on the rock anymore. Whoever it was had sure gotten here damned early. Unless it was a coyote. That would be inconvenient, to say the least.

The noise was not repeated. To hell with it, Diane thought after a moment. If it was a coyote, she was bigger, and she wasn't in the mood to be scared. "Besides," she muttered sourly, "it's probably just a rabbit."

As Diane raised her head out of the shadows, she felt a gentle touch on her shoulder. This startled her and she banged her head on the rock above. The hangover hit nine on the Richter scale.

Turning slowly, she saw a young woman sitting on the higher ledge, a teenager with long, flaming red hair and a look of profound concentration.

Definitely not a rabbit.

The girl was listening intently for something, and she motioned for Diane to keep quiet.

No problem. Diane just stared, taking in the stranger's piercing blue eyes, very sunburned skin, and a dress right out of the 1905 Sears catalog. The things kids were wearing these days. It occurred to her that she herself must look like a corpse, or maybe a caveman, with her disheveled hair, hungover eyes, and dirty Levi's.

Finally, one of them found words.

"Are you all right?" the girl asked.

"That depends," Diane replied, "on which part you ask about. My head's full of concrete, and my heart's just gone." Ugh. "Where did you come from?"

"Our party arrived last evening, before sunset. I found this place last night, and I wanted to come here before anyone else woke. Mornings are the only time I have to myself." The girl straightened her skirt and smiled, open and friendly and apparently not at all upset to find her solitude interrupted. "What is your name?"

Something wasn't making sense here, but Diane was too tired and hungover to think what. So she stopped her brain and answered the question.

"Diane. Diane Spencer."

The girl nodded, a bit puzzled. "I am Sarah Hayes. I thought you were a woman. You have a woman's hair, but a man's clothes."

Diane didn't know what to make of that comment. "It's been a long time since anyone accused me of that. I'm sorry I'm not more presentable. It's—I've had a difficult summer."

Sarah smiled. "I understand. This journey is truly hard, but often beautiful as well." Her eyes grew distant at her next thought.

Diane nodded, totally clueless. "What are you listening for?"

"Coyotes. Can't you hear them?"

Diane made an effort, cocked her head up and tried to hear something. It didn't work, and she found herself again examining the other's old-fashioned dress, the skin that told of long exposure to the sun, the total lack of makeup. Her mind tried and failed to make sense of it. Sarah, for her part, seemed totally at ease with this wild-haired stranger in "a man's clothes."

"I don't hear anything," Diane admitted finally. Of course, no guarantee that her ears worked right now.

"You're sure you're all right? You do not look well."

"I did hear coyotes yesterday, right as the sun came up."

"Sometimes I think they follow us, but my father says it's a different pack every time."

Diane's brain finally caught up with one of Sarah's first comments. "Sarah, you said you got here last night?"

"Right before dinner." The girl thought a bit. "Perhaps two hours before sunset. My father carved our names into the rock, then we ate and slept. But I needed to see this place alone, before the others awoke."

"I'm sorry I interfered with that."

"But you didn't." She paused again, and Diane marveled at the girl's calm, and her own increasing disquiet. Sarah took in the stare. "What is it that troubles you so?"

Diane hung her head. "I've been here since yesterday afternoon. I would have heard you arrive—wouldn't I?"

"There are twenty wagons in our party. You should have."

Diane's eyes narrowed. "Wagons?"

The girl nodded. "Wagons, cows, horses. We make a lot of noise."

Wagons? "Sarah, what year is it?"

"1859."

Diane backed against the rock for balance and bumped her head again. She put her hands to her face, hiding behind them, trying to quell the fear that shot up inside her all of a sudden, trying to make some sense of this. It had to be the alcohol, right? If hallucinations this powerful were a side effect, maybe she could stop drinking. When her hands came down to chance a peek, Sarah still sat there, looking puzzled and a little bit peeved.

"What other year would it be, Diane?"

Diane looked the girl in the eyes and said very distinctly, "1994."

Sarah Hayes's eyes widened, then she laughed out loud.

It was Diane's turn to feel peeved. "It's 1994," she repeated firmly, hoping that would make the hallucination go away.

Sarah stopped and sobered. Diane glanced down at her clothing. No wonder the girl was staring so hard. Diane figured she must look like quite the troubled, disheveled figure.

She watched the expression on Sarah's face. Abruptly, Sarah looked up at the sky. And smiled.

"Danielle said things like this were possible," she observed with wonder in her voice. "I didn't believe her."

"Things?" Diane asked dully. "Who's Danielle?"

The girl folded her hands on her knees and smiled, as if the picture brought to mind was a particularly special one.

"Danielle is my best friend," she said simply, but even through the hangover Diane sensed something deeper under Sarah's words. "And Danielle says that on certain days, when the sun rises with the moon behind it, people from different times can meet each other."

"Danielle is nuts."

"But you're here," Sarah said with quiet faith.

Diane became a little more alert. "So you believe I'm real?"

"Yes. You believe I'm real, don't you?"

Well, the kid hadn't disappeared yet. She certainly seemed plenty real. Diane put one hand back on her forehead, for comfort, and nodded. "So which one of us is out of place?"

"Neither."

"That doesn't make sense, Sarah."

"Danielle says magic doesn't have to make sense."

"Your friend Danielle is either deranged or stuck in the wrong century."

"How can she be deranged? Here we are."

Diane tried again. "How can you accept that? Things like this don't just happen! Besides, there's no way the moon can be behind the sun."

"I can see both the moon and the sun right now."

"Well, then, I want to." Diane started to climb up the rock, but Sarah stopped her with another touch on the shoulder.

"No," the girl said firmly. "That would ruin it."

"How?"

"I don't know," Sarah said without releasing her grip. "But it would, and I don't want it to."

Diane, mentally grumbling that a teenage psycho was ordering her around, lifted a foot to climb right on up anyway, then stopped. She looked deeply into Sarah's widened eyes, felt the heat radiating from the girl's touch on her shoulder, felt the warmth of a living hand, *felt* the concern of a caring stranger—and suddenly she very much didn't want to ruin this moment. Diane reached up and placed her hand over Sarah's so she wouldn't let go. And decided to trust.

"Can you still see them? The sun and the moon?"

The girl nodded.

"All right. Please don't go until you can't anymore."

"I won't go until I hear the others. But that won't be long now."

Something started to come loose inside Diane. She fought it, tried to distract it. "Sarah, aren't you afraid?"

"No. Why?"

Diane shook her head. "I must look like I'm half-dead. Doesn't that scare you?"

The girl shook her head slowly. "You won't hurt me. I know that."

"But to meet someone like me, from another time?"

"Are you afraid, Diane?"

"No," she lied. "But I know where I am." Diane realized how stupid that sounded the second she said it. But Sarah let it slide.

"So do I." Sarah smiled again. "This is Wyoming territory."

Almost, almost did Diane let herself smile. "It's a state now."

"Do people live here?"

"Not really. Only near big cities. This place is still the middle of nowhere."

"Then it hasn't changed," the girl said thoughtfully. "That's why we're here."

"What?"

"This place is the same. That's why we could meet."

Diane's features softened a little. "You're so sure."

"Why not? I just wish Danielle was here. She'll be angry she missed you."

"Blaine would be jealous."

"Blaine?"

Without even thinking, Diane kept talking. "My lover," she said as her insides loosened a little more. "My life. We came here right before she died. She said you could feel the history here. She liked that a lot."

Sarah's expression grew puzzled. " 'She?' Your lover is a woman?"

"*Was* a woman," Diane confirmed, the bitterness returning. "She's dead now."

The teenager seemed to sense the pain below the bitter tone and squeezed Diane's shoulder tightly. "I'm sorry," she said softly.

Diane blinked. Tears? No way. "Not as sorry as I am." God, that touch felt good. Hallucination or no, it felt good. Still… "Your family will be up soon, I guess."

Sarah looked over at something, frowned. "Yes. You're right." Her tone was reluctant.

"Think of the story you can tell your best friend."

Still looking off into the distance, Sarah's smile deepened. Diane watched the young woman's face transform. She'd seen that look before, in the face of someone she'd never see again. Her tears made another attempt. To squelch her rising feelings, Diane said, "Danielle is very special to you, isn't she?"

Sarah nodded, her eyes turning back to Diane. "There's no one else like her in all the world."

Sarah suddenly seemed to hear what she'd said and looked scared for the first time all morning. "The moon is fading. The party will be awake soon." She started to rise, but this time it was Diane who held her grip.

"There's nothing to be frightened of, Sarah. There's nothing frightening about loving someone."

The girl said nothing.

"Sarah, don't go yet." Diane was speaking to the distance in the young woman's eyes. "Did you hear me? It's all right to love your best friend."

"It hurts," Sarah said softly.

Diane stood taller to hear. Her turn for silence now. Oh, did she know how things hurt. Now the tears burst out. She blinked them back.

"Yes," she started to say finally, but Sarah cut her off.

"Danielle's father is taking them to California. We are going to Oregon." She spoke quickly, like this was a burden she had carried for weeks. "And there's a man, Aloysius. He wants to marry her."

"Does she want to marry him?"

Sarah's eyes met Diane's again, burning with intensity. "She hates him."

Now the girl's eyes welled up, and Diane felt—really felt—what this young woman was going through. The dam broke, and emotions coursed through her for the first time in weeks, months, eons. And with the emotion came a clarity, a true seeing of Sarah's situation.

"No, Sarah," she said softly. "Danielle loves you." Diane was just tall enough to reach up and caress the other's cheek. "You love her, and Danielle loves you."

Sarah's eyes added wonder to the tears, as if she had never seen it that way before. Bringing her hand up to her cheek, she held both Diane's hands now, and their eyes met as well.

"Really?" she asked tentatively.

Diane smiled for the first time that morning, for the first time in months. She nodded. "Really. Sure sounds like it."

Sarah's smile suddenly faded, and a look of utter loss took its place. "But what can we do?"

Diane thought about what little she knew of the nineteenth century. Not a good time for women, not a good time for *young* women, particularly women who loved each other. What *could* they do?

Suddenly Sarah started. "I hear voices."

Diane didn't, but maybe sound didn't carry very far between centuries.

"Wait a minute." Diane loosed her grip, held out her left hand. "Take this ring I'm wearing. Then Danielle will know you met me."

Sarah hesitated. "She'll say I found it."

"No, it's engraved, see?" Diane slid the ring off, showed the girl what was written inside.

Blaine C loves Diane S
1989

"My best friend gave it to me," Diane said softly, "and now you can give it to yours." She gently put the ring in Sarah's palm. Sarah looked at it carefully.

"Are you sure?" she asked.

"It's the right thing to do," Diane said firmly. "I don't know how else to help you. All I can tell you is to keep a connection, even if you two are separated for a while. Try to talk Danielle's family into going to Oregon. Or your father to California. Don't let her marry that guy if she doesn't want to. I know it'll be hard. It's hard in my time, too. But the love I had was worth everything, Sarah. Every pain, every obstacle. We overcame all of them but one."

Diane reached up and took Sarah's hand, kissed the palm, then let go for the last time.

"Be careful of your friendship with Danielle. But don't let anyone take it away from you, ever."

Sarah nodded and stood. She seemed a little less certain of things now, a little scared of Diane's intensity. But she fingered the ring, then met Diane's eyes and smiled. Taking a breath to speak, she blinked—

—and shimmered suddenly, and faded out.

Sarah was gone. Diane was alone.

She looked at the empty air, wide-eyed, then scrambled up the ledge, ignoring the pain in her aching legs. She found nothing there, and she climbed higher, listening for the sound of voices, the crack of whips, or the creak of wagon wheels.

But all she heard were coyotes, only the coyotes, their lonely howls echoing from a distance. Reaching the top of Independence Rock, Diane turned to face the dawn, saw the sun blazing in the sky—and no moon in sight.

She knew she presented a disheveled, dejected figure as she made a slow circle, standing in place, eyes noting the hills in the distance, the river meandering along, the rest stop, the car. No wagons, no sign at all that anyone other than she was there, or ever had been.

But Blaine's ring was gone, and so, too, Diane realized, was her numbness. She yearned to see a wagon train, yearned to know that her gift to Sarah had strengthened her, sealed a bond, helped guide the life of a girl—two girls—one hundred and fifty years previous. She squatted down, then sat, wiping away tears as she tried to find her bearings again. Her head still beat like steel drums, but it was okay. Maybe it wasn't so bad to have something to feel.

The sun rose slowly, but the air stayed cold. She shivered in the morning coolness. Diane breathed in the clean, crisp morning air. Sarah's image danced before her once more, but only in memory this time, as she thought about what they'd said. Blaine, the hopeless romantic, would have approved.

Even as Diane cried, she smiled a little, and realized it was time to move on. Finally. With surprise, she realized she had no need to be here anymore.

Diane stood, stiffly, awkwardly, and promptly stumbled. She managed just enough balance to keep from falling into a pool of rainwater, but it was a near thing. She bounced around like a bad dancer, ending up on all fours. Looking down, she saw letters carved into the niche of the catch basin, peeking just above the water's surface.

Sarah H loves Danielle S
1859

Her breath left her, and she stayed on her knees as a flood of tears gushed out; tears of grief, and release, and wonder at something she would carry in her heart but never explain. Part of her knew that, like Blaine,

Danielle and Sarah were long dead now. But seeing those names still filled her with hope, hope that the two girls had grown into women whose love had kept them together, who had been able to live a life with as much happiness as challenge.

Diane got her legs under her and slowly straightened. She felt dizzy and woozy, but she also felt that hope, and for the first time in months, it outweighed everything else. She took a last look at the names.

"Thank you, Sarah," she murmured. When the wooziness passed, she made her way down from Independence Rock and back to the car, ready at last to go home.

Mercy's Eyes

By
Kate McLachlan

THE DUNGEONS FLOODED EACH time the tide came in. It was not much water, only an inch or two deep, but it was enough to soak shoes and freeze toes. As long as Mercy was awake when the first trickles crept in, she could remove her shoes and stockings and roll up her skirts so they didn't drag in the water. It made some difference, though everything remained damp anyway, all the time. Occasionally Mercy slept through the rising water and didn't wake until it soaked through the wool of her skirt and the layers of underclothes to stroke her skin with icy fingers. Those were bad days.

Mercy turned the water into a game. She learned how to make her bare feet slap it in such a way as to make an echoing crack against the stone walls, loud and enjoyable. The dance kept her feet from freezing and scared the rats away for a time. She called out to the women in the other cells to join her in the play, but the only replies she received were muffled groans and a shout of *sinful* from the woman in the cell on her left.

Mercy didn't know who the woman was, but she was certain she knew her. She knew everyone in Salem. But the woman had been brought in after Mercy was charged, and it was folly to try to guess who might have been imprisoned next. The accusations flew through the air like dandelion seeds, based on no reason anyone could fathom, so there was no way of knowing which widow or spinster or child was next accused.

At least Mercy had a real sin to her name, though they'd pegged the wrong one to her.

The door from the jail above opened and closed. Mercy felt it as much as she heard it. She'd been in the dungeon for weeks now, long enough to know how it breathed. It was too early for her basket, but she hoped anyway. Her belly was turned nearly inside out from hunger. She ceased her dance in the receding water and listened.

She heard two voices, a man's and a woman's, descend the stone stairs. The man was the guard, the woman a visitor, and Mercy's brief hope died. She did not have visitors. But it was at Mercy's cell door that the voices stopped. Before she had time to prepare herself, the door opened and light shone in, just a single candle, but it was a bright star compared to the blackness that was all she'd seen since the meal delivery of the day before. She couldn't see behind the light and was surprised when she heard the woman's voice

"She is tied to the wall?"

"Chained fast. Stay beside the door and she cannot reach you. 'Tis the eyes you must be wary of with this one."

"I know about her eyes. I'll not look at her. You may go."

The man set a basket down where the slope was high and the ground already dry. Mercy saw bread, and her mouth filled with water. The basket was fuller than normal. She was right in her suspicion, then, that the guard had been helping himself to a portion of the delivery each day. With the woman accompanying him this day, he dared not filch from her. The door closed, and Mercy was alone with the basket and the candle and Anna.

Mercy tore her eyes from the bread. It was not polite to reveal such hunger. "You did not send the basket today, but have come yourself."

"Yes," Anna said. Her white bonnet shone in the candle light. The brim hid Anna's face, which she kept turned away from Mercy. "I had to speak with you one last time."

"One last time?"

"Your trial is tomorrow. Did you not know it?"

"No." Mercy's heart dulled. A trial meant a reprieve from the dungeon, but she was not looking forward to hanging.

"Mercy, I came to tell you, you must declare innocence. They have not hanged the last two who pleaded innocence."

"You ask me this?" Mercy laughed and felt a trickle of blood as a crack in the corner of her mouth opened up again. She wiped the blood with her thumb. "It was you who accused me in the first place. If you have changed your mind, go tell the magistrate."

The bonnet drooped. "I cannot. I cannot change my words. They would know I lied. You did do what I accused you of."

"I heard the charge. I did do what you said I did, but you twisted the order about somewhat. Anna, look at me."

"I dare not." Anna turned to face the wall. "The last time I looked in your eyes, the devil was in them."

"That was no devil, Anna. There was no devil in that room with us."

"There was. You know there was. I never would have—" Anna's voice wavered. She took a breath and resumed speaking in a lower tone. "I never would have done those things if I had not been possessed. If *you* had not possessed me."

"Why do you tell me to plead innocence then?"

"Don't you understand? They will hang you for certain if you plead guilty."

"Why do you care if I hang?"

Anna did not move, nor did she answer.

Mercy felt a surge of hope again, unrelated to bread or hanging. "Anna, look at me."

"I dare not."

"Are you afraid, here? I cannot touch you. I'm chained by my ankle to this wall. Do you think I will smite you with my eyes and tongue and force you to writhe upon the ground and shake and cry out loud and tear your clothes? That is what you accuse me of, is it not? But I remember that you tore your clothes off first, Anna, before you lay on the ground. I did smite you with my tongue, I admit it, but you opened your thighs for me most willingly, and only then did you writhe upon the ground and tremble and cry out. There was no devil in that room, Anna. There was only you and me."

"The devil is in you, Mercy," Anna said, and her voice was thick with tears. "When you did kiss me and look at me, your eyes, they made me act not like myself. I did not lie. I am sorry for you, that you have the devil in you who makes you do these things. I do not want you to hang."

"It was not the devil," Mercy said again. "It was you and me creating pleasure with our bodies. It may have been a sin, but it was our own."

"No." Anna shook her head again. She turned and almost looked at Mercy but caught herself in time. "It was no sin of mine. It was a hideous and frightful thing. I am tormented still. You don't know. The devil tries every day to enter into my body. I—I fight him every day."

"The devil is not tormenting you, but the memory of our pleasures. Do you not remember the smiles we shared, and the looks? There was no devilry in that room. It was love, Anna, that's all it was. Love."

Anna looked up, and their eyes met as the word settled into the room, punctuated by the sounds of trickling water and their breathing, which grew louder the longer they stared. Anna took a step toward Mercy. The candle trembled in her hand.

Mercy stepped forward as well, as far as she could before the chain on her ankle stopped her. "Anna," she whispered.

NOT ONLY WAS ANNA possessed by Mercy in devilish ways, but the possession happened on the Sabbath. After the long sermons that morning, Anna had walked from the village to Mercy's house. Long before she reached the front step, she saw Mercy standing in the doorway watching her approach.

Anna stopped when she reached the stoop. "You did not attend church," she said. "I feared you were sick." Indeed, it was the only possible reason for her presence there. Visits were forbidden on the Sabbath unless to care for the ill.

Mercy did not smile, but her eyes made Anna welcome. "I did not think I would be missed."

"You were missed," Anna said. "This is the second time this spring you have not attended. There is talk among the congregation that you are becoming Quaker." She smiled to soften the words.

Mercy stepped back into the house and Anna followed. A pot steamed on the stove, and the smell of malt was unmistakable.

Anna felt a tremor of concern on her behalf. "On the Sabbath, Mercy?"

"Beer is a Godly drink." Mercy moved to the stove and stirred the brew to prevent it boiling over.

"It is indeed," Anna said, but she bit her lip.

"There is ready beer in that barrel. Fetch a mug for me and for yourself, and let us sit."

Anna filled the mugs and brought them to the table while Mercy moved the pot from the stove to let it cool, then joined her. Anna drank the thick beer and enjoyed the rich flavor. Many in the village favored Mercy's beer.

"'Tis your good fortune that 'twas I who came to see that you were well," Anna said. "Another would not overlook your breaking of the Sabbath with work."

Mercy placed her hand over Anna's and gave a slight squeeze. "I am too unwell to attend church. I am shaking and feverish and weak. You may report that to anyone who asks. Will you?"

With the warmth of Mercy's hand on hers, Anna could not say nay. "Yes." She met Mercy's fine eyes. Mercy wore no collar, and the green of her dress made her eyes glow like young leaves in the sun. "Yes, I will say whatever you want me to say."

For the first time since Anna arrived, Mercy smiled. She did not take back her hand, but she moved it to turn Anna's hand in hers. She stroked her fingers along the inside of Anna's wrist and slipped them inside the cuff of Anna's dress to reach the soft flesh of her arm.

Anna took a shaky breath and did not look away.

"I knew none but you would come today," Mercy said. "I am not much loved in the village of late, though they are happy enough to drink my beer."

"They are worried. You keep here alone. Until now you have come at least to church twice a sennight, but—"

"But now I am not pleased to enter the village every three days for sermons I find poorly thought or spoken."

Anna could not help but admire such forthright talk from Mercy, as if she were a man of stature who had a right to speak of such things. Still she warned her. "Don't say things like that. You could end up in the stocks for such talk, and whipped besides."

Mercy smiled again. "I am safe enough. You will not tell."

Anna was pleased at the trust Mercy placed in her. "They don't know what to think of you. You are five years now a widow and do not marry."

"I will not marry," Mercy said. "I own this land and this house. I cannot do so if I take a husband. But you are a married woman now. How find you the marital bed?"

Anna flushed, though it was not an unexpected question. It was Mercy, after all, who had warned her a few short weeks ago of what to expect from her husband that first night. "It is much as you said it would be," Anna said, "although not—"

"Not what?"

Anna hung her head. "I do not find it pleasurable in the way you described. I do it wrong, I am certain."

"What is it you feel, when you lie with your husband?"

"I feel cold and stiff when he kisses me and touches me with his hands. Later, when he presses himself upon me, I feel some stirrings, it is true, as if those pleasures you described were but a hairsbreadth away. But then he falls away, and I feel much uneasiness and despair."

"Tell me, Anna, what is it you feel now, from my fingers?"

Anna had been trying to ignore the feelings created by Mercy's fingers on her arm, but at the question she could ignore it no longer. "I feel heat, and yet I shiver."

"Does your husband stroke you so, like this, but elsewhere on your body?"

"He strokes me quick but his fingers are not like yours. They are hard and rough and bring me no pleasure like…like yours."

"Perhaps you can show him how to stroke you to bring you heat that makes you shiver." Mercy's thumb made slow circles on the flesh of Anna's inner elbow.

"I don't know how," Anna said, and her breath was strangely uneven. "I wish…"

"What is it that you wish, Anna?"

As if a devil had taken her tongue, Anna whispered, "I wish you would show me."

"ANNA," MERCY SAID AGAIN from her post in the dank dungeon. She stretched out her hand as far as she could reach.

Anna took another step forward, touched her fingers to Mercy's, and tears filled her eyes. "I am sorry, Mercy. I wish I had not confessed to my husband what we did. I know the devil used you that day, but I do not want you to hang for it."

Mercy tugged gently on Anna's fingers until she reached her wrist and let her fingers slip inside the sleeve. As she had done before, Anna shivered at her touch.

"Did you show your husband what I taught you?" Mercy asked.

Anna gave a harsh laugh. "I showed him but a bit of it before he whipped me and forbade me touch him in such a way again. He does not stroke me now but takes me quick and pays no heed to my discomfort."

"Oh, Anna." Mercy felt a twist inside that was not hunger, but regret. She was prepared to die, as all must, and hanging only brought it quicker, but she was sorry indeed to leave Anna more unhappy than she had been before her visit to Mercy that day. She tugged again at Anna's wrist.

A soft smile crossed Anna's face and she took another step toward Mercy. Her foot landed in water. She stopped, sucked in a breath, and her eyes grew wide. She wrenched her hand from Mercy's grasp and scurried back to the door, showing only her back.

"You do it again," Anna cried. "Don't look at me!" She pounded on the door. "Guard!" She kept her hand upon the door as if afraid of being pulled back, though Mercy could not reach her. "The devil is in your eyes, Mercy, and in your touch, I swear it. It tempts me so."

"It is not the devil," Mercy said. "It is only me."

The door above opened and the heavy steps came close.

"Plead innocent, Mercy," Anna said. "They'll banish you, but they won't hang you. That is all I came to say."

The cell door opened, and Anna slipped away, taking the light with her. The guard shoved the basket with his foot so that it tipped over onto the damp floor. He closed the door, and Mercy was alone. She fell upon the bread.

MERCY TOOK HER FINGERS from Anna's cuff and brought them up to Anna's cheek. "I could show you much, Anna, but—"

Anna turned her head so that her mouth rested in Mercy's palm. It smelled of malt and beer and sweat. "Show me," she said.

Mercy shifted her chair close and brought her other hand to Anna's chin. Anna looked again into Mercy's spring green eyes and brought her head forward so that their lips met in a kiss. The kiss was unlike those pressed upon her by her husband in the dark. Mercy's lips moved soft and gentle as Anna's did. When Anna opened her mouth and Mercy's tongue swept in, it did not probe or gag but was soft and rough at once. Anna moved her own tongue against it, and she shivered again with much heat.

The promise of the great pleasures denied her in her marriage bed made Anna wild. It was she who threw off her apron and tore open her bodice, pulled down her chemise and offered herself thus bared to Mercy. When Mercy pressed her mouth to Anna's bosom and caressed and suckled there a while, it was Anna who flung herself from the chair, tore off her skirt and petticoats and lay down on the floor with no stitch upon her.

"Show me pleasures, Mercy," she nearly sobbed. "Oh, please!"

Mercy dropped beside Anna and kissed her and used her fingers to stroke Anna most sweetly until Anna spread wide her legs. "'Tis strange," Anna gasped. "I do not like the touch of my husband's rough fingers, but I want your fingers rough upon me. There is more, I know there is. Show me, Mercy!"

Mercy knelt then between Anna's thighs and pressed inside her with her thumb and fingers, but withdrew at just the moment when Anna felt the start of pleasure spreading over her from within. She nearly wept from disappointment, but Mercy leaned forward and pressed her mouth to Anna's opening and suckled and stroked with her rough feather tongue. Anna felt the pleasure overcome her. She screamed and writhed upon the floor.

When she had calmed and lay covered in naught but sweat, she looked again into Mercy's eyes and saw therein a look so tender it made Anna weep. She sat up and kissed Mercy sweetly and put her hands under Mercy's skirt to feel the swollen flesh that dripped between her legs.

At Anna's touch Mercy moaned and fell back and raised her knees into the air and writhed as Anna had done, and then they kissed some more.

It was only after Anna dressed again and left the house, when the pull of Mercy's eyes was no longer upon her, that a blanket of black shame fell over her. Never had such a horrible fit befallen her as had come over her at Mercy's house. The sin was too terrible to confess, but confess it she must or perish in damnation for all eternity.

Unless…unless it was not Anna's sin at all. Would she ever have behaved in such a wanton manner if Mercy had not cast a devil's spell over her? The enchantment was not natural, after all, for eyes to glow with green embers as Mercy's eyes did. And she did not attend church.

Anna reached her husband's house, fell prostrate upon the doorstep, and wept most madly. She tore her clothes and hair and spoke strange words until the doctor was called, and the minister, and shortly thereafter, a posse of men went to Mercy's house to apprehend her and charge her with breaking the Sabbath and with being a witch.

THE BASKET CONTAINED FRESH clothes and soap, as well as food, so Mercy was nearly clean and barely hungry when she stood at the dock the next day and heard the charges read against her. The magistrate was a large and fleshy man with red cheeks and lips. He spoke in a loud voice.

"Upon deposition, Goodwife Sarah Williams did state she did observe the accused, Goody Mercy Spark, as she did stand upon a hillside near Goodman Williams' pasture and did wave about her arms and stamp her feet and did have a fit and cast obscene words upon the ground and air and so stopped the flow of milk from Goodwife Williams' cow. How do you plead, Goody Spark?"

Mercy stood at the dock, her eyes straight forward. "I am innocent," she said, and her voice was strong and clear. "I did not stop the flow of milk from Goody Williams' cow. I did wave my hands about at Goody Williams who was in the yard. I hailed her but cast no obscene words lest good morrow be obscene."

Titters from the crowd of onlookers in the courtroom caused the magistrate to frown.

"Upon examination Mistress Martha Frost did find upon you a witch's teat. How do you plead to this charge, Goody Spark?"

"I have no witch's teat nor devil's teat but only two large teats provided thus by God." She gestured to her breasts and more laughter came from the crowd.

The magistrate shouted for silence and glared red-faced at Mercy. "Goody Spark, how explain you then that Mistress Frost upon examination did find a third teat of such great proportion as to most certainly serve as a devil's teat?"

Mercy was too near the hangman's noose to feel shame. She felt only fury that Mistress Frost dared testify in such a way against her. She spoke sharply. "Mistress Frost did find betwixt my legs that sinew of women's flesh that grows and swells when stroked excessively, which Mistress Frost did do whilst on her knees before me peering closely."

At that the crowd erupted into gasps and laughter. Mistress Frost's shriek of fury could be heard above it all, which seemed to feed the laughter.

"Silence!" shouted the magistrate. "Goody Spark has cast her spell upon this crowd. Mark you, guard against this witch's humors, lest you be found a witch as well."

The crowd became still and quiet. Mercy lowered her head. The magistrate believed her guilty, that was clear. God willing the jury would not.

"Goody Spark," the magistrate said, his voice barely steady, "upon deposition Mistress Esther Jacobs did state that you did touch her hand and cause her to fall in fits upon the floor and fill her limbs with pain and agony and much screaming in her head, that Mistress Mary Jackson and young Jane Hutchens did observe you when you put your touch upon Mistress Jacobs. How plead you?"

Mercy raised her head again. She did not look into the crowd to see Esther Jacobs smirk at her, as surely she did, and Mary Jackson and Jane Hutchens too. All were girls who had at one time sought the attentions of Mercy in an unseemly way, which she denied them, and now they stood in triumph at seeing Mercy brought so low. She could still feel pride, and though she was brought low, she would not let Esther Jacobs or Mary Jackson or Jane Hutchens, jealous girls all, know of it. "I am innocent," she said.

The magistrate waited as if expecting Mercy to start the crowd with laughter again, but she had nothing more to say. He looked back down at his official papers and appeared disappointed.

"Goody Spark, upon deposition Goodwife Anna Emerson did state that you did smite her with your tongue, and with your eyes you threw the devil into her and did cause her to fling herself upon the floor and writhe in a horrible fit and tear her clothes and hair and moan most terribly. How plead you?"

Anna sat in the front row of the courtroom, demure and still beside her husband, Goodman Emerson. She would not look at Mercy throughout the trial, nor did she look up now. Her head remained bowed and only the top of her white bonnet could be seen. Mercy waited, but Anna did not look up.

"How do you plead, Goody Spark?"

Mercy's heart stilled as if preparing itself to beat its last. "I am guilty," she said, her voice still as clear and even as it had been at the start.

Many in the courtroom, and on the jury as well, had little belief up until then that Mercy was truly a witch, but all doubt was swept away at what happened next.

Anna looked up, met Mercy's eyes which were fixed upon her, and shrieked "No!" with the force of the devil. She leaped from her seat and writhed in her husband's grasp as if twisted by an unseen force, pinned by the devil in Mercy's eyes until she collapsed as if dead in the arms of her husband. The villagers shrieked and backed away from the dock as the guards rushed forward to pull Mercy away from the crowd and the unfortunate victim.

She was sentenced to be hanged in the morning.

Hear the Gentle Voices Calling

By
Christopher Hawthorne Moss

I'm coming, I'm coming, for my head is bending low:
I hear those gentle voices calling, "Old Black Joe..."
~Stephen Foster, in "Old Black Joe"

A RIVERBOAT GLIDED INTO the port of New Orleans in a fog that hugged its lowest deck. A man, handsome, debonair, with a pencil-thin black moustache and wearing nothing else, lay in a bed on the top deck. He smiled languidly and reached toward the dreamer. His lips moved. He said, "Mick, I am so sorry, but it is only Johnny now." The sun affixed above him, made of bronze, seemed to glow and grow larger until its sheer brightness seared into Mick's retinas.

Michael "Mick" Murphy opened his eyes. The dream faded and he found himself in the cottage, far from sea, far from riverboats and bronze suns.

"Oh, dear God in Heaven," he swore as light came through the uncurtained window onto his face. His head immediately erupted into a feeling as if pickaxes were randomly taking out chunks of his brain, and he shut his eyes tight. He was momentarily unable to respond to his surroundings or see where he was. He struggled to sit up and hit his hard head against something harder. "Jesus, Mary, and Joseph!" He reverted to an oath from his childhood, from his father, and promptly fell off the bed where he sat clutching his head and moaning.

He gingerly felt the lump starting on his forehead and slowly opened his eyes again to find himself staring directly at the indistinct shape of a dark-skinned man's face looking through the side window. He jerked away, then it all came back flooding into his brain.

The man's eyes looked worried. He clearly had tapped on the window, which is why Mick awoke. As he came to his senses, he gestured for the man to come around to the front of the little cottage. The smiling man, whose skin was a lovely coffee tone, shouldered a small knapsack, put on a cap, and went out of Mick's view.

"Wonder what *he* wants," Mick muttered to himself. He rubbed his forehead again, then noticed his disheveled state. He was in his uniform, but it was wrinkled and dirty. He managed to get himself onto his feet, tried to brush off his trousers, and looked around for where he had dropped his hat. He had to pee, but he had no time as he could hear the man knocking on his front door.

He limped his way out of the room and across the sitting room to the door. His leg hurt more than usual, but he attempted to ignore it. He opened the door and tried to smile as he examined the young black man standing on his threshold. He was dressed in a threadbare suit that was scrupulously clean and in good repair in spite of its age, and he was well-groomed. He bowed slightly in deference. Mick knew Lincoln's Emancipation Proclamation had become effective on the first of January, 1863, that it was the law in New Orleans, and that the man need not defer to him at all.

"Come in," Mick said. "I need to use the chamber pot. Will you wait in here?"

The man stepped through the door, but stood, cap in hand and waited.

When Mick came back, he found the man still standing where he'd left him. "Have a seat and tell me why you're here." The man looked about, went to a chair in the sitting room, and lowered himself tentatively into it.

"Yes, sir. Are you Captain Michael Murphy?"

"I am." Mick went into the alcove kitchen and checked the fire in the stove. It was long out. He shrugged and turned back to the sitting room. "You mind if we go over to the big house?"

"The big house, sir?"

"Just come with me," Mick said, then limped his way out of the cottage door and around the side of the Deramus house to the back door. "In here."

At the doorstep, Mick glanced back and saw the man looking all around him as he passed by expertly cared for bushes and flowers below clean windows furnished with elegant drapery.

"Whose house is this, beggin' your pardon, sir?"

"Frankie Deramus's house, but don't worry about that. "He reached to knock on the back door but saw it swing open, and a tall older black man stood in the doorway, grinning. Mick smiled back. "Hello, Charles William. Can I get a cup of coffee? And one for my guest as well?"

Charles William ushered them in. He was Mick's friend and Frankie Deramus's servant. He lived in the big house with his wife, Dominique, taking care of it until his Confederate officer owner, now employer, came home, *if* he came home from the war. It was 1863 and while the Union held New Orleans, farther north in Louisiana, the Civil War was still very much underway. That was where Frankie was, or so Mick and Charles William and everyone else assumed. News of Confederate officers was few and far between in New Orleans, unless someone in General Nathaniel Banks' office knew otherwise. For all anyone knew, Frankie Deramus was dead and gone. Mick held out hope that he was still alive, as did Charles William and Dominique, fond as they all were of the former riverboat owner and gambler.

"Take a seat," Mick told the man, whom Charles William was eyeing with speculation.

"Thank you, Captain Murphy," he said as he lowered himself into a plushly cushioned ladderback chair.

"I'm properly called Captain Michael Murphy, but you can call me Mick like everyone else does. Will you want sugar and milk?"

"Yes, thank you."

Charles William got the coffeepot and brought it and two cups over to the table. "Won't you have a cup with us?" Mick said as he poured.

"If your guest does not want privacy," Charles William said.

Mick looked at the man sitting in the kitchen chair across from him. "I'm sorry, I don't know your name."

The man glanced from Mick to the black man holding the coffeepot. "My name is Septime Archibault from Mound Bayou. I don't mind if he sits down with us. And you can call me Archie."

"Well, Archie, this is Charles William Albright. He lives here and is looking after the place with his wife, Dominique. Help yourself to sugar and milk," he said as he did the same. "What can I do for you, Archie?"

Archie cleared his throat. "It's my brother Quintus. He's in the federal army. No one's seen nor heard of him in weeks. I thought maybe you could help me since I heard you used to be a confidential investigator before the war began." He added a respectful "sir" to his sentence.

Mick stopped his coffee cup's progress to his mouth to take a sip and looked up at Archie. "You said you were from Mound Bayou. How did you know about my previous occupation?"

Adding a little milk to his own coffee, Archie said, "My cousin used to work on the *Beau Soleil*. He mentioned you."

Mick immediately thought of the burned-out hulk on the levy in the city. It had been his friend Frankie's pride and joy, his side-wheeler riverboat, and had been one of the dozens of craft torched by the residents of New Orleans as the Union ships came into the harbor in April 1862. "Oh," he said mournfully. "She was a beautiful boat. It is sad to—wait, did you know she's gone?"

The man's face drooped. "I never got to see her, sir, but my cousin lost his job not long before the day Farragut sailed in. Terrible sad thing. Does Mr. Deramus know, sir?"

Mick said, "Yes, he found out just before he had to leave the city with General Lovell and the Confederate soldiers. But the cat survived."

"The cat, sir?"

Looking around, Mick caught sight of the orange tabby sunning himself in a shaft of light in the hallway. "Duckie." At Archie's puzzled look, Mick said, "I know, I know. Frankie saved him from a sinking boat. It's a long story."

Mick reached into his tunic's inner breast pocket and took out a silver flask. He uncapped it and poured an amber liquid into his coffee. He saluted the others with the cup, saying, "Cheers."

Archie's eyes went a little round, but Charles William was looking down.

"By the way, Archie, if you aren't in the army yourself, I wish you'd stop calling me sir."

Archie sat for a second, staring at his host. "I'm sorry, sir—I mean, Mick."

"Good. Now tell me more about your brother."

"You can help me?" Archie said, his face looking surprised and hopeful.

Mick sighed. "I don't know, but I can try. Just tell me everything you do know and what you do not."

Archie proceeded to describe that their family usually got an envelope of money to help them out every couple of weeks from what Quintus earned. After two weeks, no envelope came, then none the week after. "After a month went by, I wrote to him to ask if he was all right, but he never answered. I don't even know if he got my letter."

"So you came to look for him?" Mick asked.

"I got an earful from the landlady at his boarding house about deadbeat soldiers who disappear and don't pay their rent. She wouldn't let me get in another word, but then I finally got through to her, telling her I didn't know where Quintus was and had come to the city to find out. Then she quieted, asked me to sit down, and listened as I asked her questions."

Charles William saw that the young man's cup was empty and got up to take the coffeepot off the fire to pour him more.

"I told her about not hearing from him for over a month. She told me that was about the time he stopped coming to the house."

"You will have to give me the address there."

Archie took a pencil out of his pocket and wrote out the address on a scrap of paper Charles William provided. He went on, "I asked the landlady if she knew any of his friends or anyone who might know where he was or where he might go in the city. I told her I had been to the Customs House to talk to the army. But they told me he was unaccounted for. I don't know if that means he's a straggler who will eventually catch up with his unit or if he's out and out deserted."

Mick sat back in his chair. "What was his duty? I mean, what was his job in the army?"

"They told me he was a guard at the Mint."

Mick put a finger to the underside of his lower lip. "Did you find out who his friends were?"

Archie shook his head. "Seems like he spent a lot of time by himself. That was like him, to spend time alone, but I got the impression the reason he didn't have no friends is that he didn't like how colored were treated by the people of the city."

Charles William made a "hmph" noise. Archie's head swung toward the doorway. Mick looked up and smiled at the woman who stood quietly and politely, not interrupting.

Mick said, "Dominique, this is Septime Archibault. He has asked me to help him find his missing brother."

Dominique came into the kitchen and picked up the coffeepot from the table to return it to the stove. She said, "The Archibaults? From Mound Bayou?"

Archie smiled up at her. "Why, yes. Do you know my family?"

Dominique nodded. "I believe I do." Going around to the kitchen counter, she asked, "Who needs something to eat? I have pastry."

"Do you have any beignets?" Mick asked, smacking his lips. "I'd love a couple of those if you made them."

Dominique took some beignets out of the cupboard and put three on a napkin for Mick and some more in the middle of the table for the other two men.

Archie continued with a beignet in his mouth. "I did find one soldier who seemed to know more about Quintus than most. He said Quintus was boiling mad about something to do with our sister, Madeleine. She's a *placé*, an octoroon woman who is cared for financially by her lover, a wealthy white Creole man. They met at an octaroon ball, and he gave my mother money for Madeleine to come live in a house he bought her. I think he lives somewhere in town, in the fancy part of the city. Her man's name is Adam Brunel."

At the white patron's name, Mick and the two Albrights looked at each other in alarm. Dominique shook her head and went back to get more coffee. Charles William pressed his lips together tightly and Mick frowned. "Brunel," he said. "The man who was shot a few weeks ago."

Archie's young face took on a sick expression. "Oh, *mon dieu.*"

Mick hastened to add, "Do not worry. Brunel's all right. Got hit in the shoulder, but he wouldn't say who shot him. He's terribly fond of that Madeleine and won't say a word against her or hers. I wonder. . ." He left the words unfinished.

Dominique came over to the table, fists planted on her hips. "I heard that Brunel was talking about marrying Madeleine, even though it ain't legal for coloreds to marry whites. She's expecting, you see, and he ain't married yet, so he said he'd take her to Cuba or Jamaica and they'd tie the knot. But that's all I know. I ain't seen Madeleine in a while."

"She keeps to her house," Charles William said. "Brunel's been there ever since he saw a doctor about the gunshot wound. He's staying there while she nurses him."

Mick turned to Archie. "Do you think your brother might have anything to do with the shooting?"

Archie stood, pulled a clean white handkerchief from his trouser pocket, and went to the kitchen window to stare out. "I don't know. I don't think so. But I wonder if. . . He's always protected Madi. Why would he hurt the man she loves and loves her?"

Mick sat tapping his finger on the tabletop, staring at nothing in particular, thinking. He finally said, "Well, I must go talk to them. Do you want to come to your sister's house?"

Archie turned and nodded solemnly.

Mick rubbed the two-day-old whiskers on his chin. He was glad for the coffee for it had decreased his hangover. "I will change out of this dirty uniform," Mick said, "and we can leave shortly."

WALKING DOWN THE RUE, Mick was deep in thought. He suddenly cleared his throat and looked at his companion. "So what do you do for a living in—what did you call—Mound Bayou?"

Clearly startled out of his reveries, Archie said, "Me? I'm a carpenter's apprentice. I should be a full carpenter by fall."

"So you're a *gens de couleur libre?*"

"Oh yes, at least three generations now on my *papan's* side have been free men of color. My *maman's* grandfather was a slave in Haiti, but my *grandpère* was freed by his master way back in the nineties. I was born in 1841."

Mick figured quickly that this made Archie 22 years old, but he looked younger. "Have you got a wife?" he asked.

Archie looked down at the road in front of his feet for a moment. "No, sir. Not found a gal I want to marry yet. "

Mick made a note of this unusual fact. In this time and place, young men were often married or at least living with a girl at 17 or 18, if not younger. But he dismissed his thought, knowing there could be any number of explanations.

Archie asked, "You got a gal back in—wherever you're from?"

"Naw. No girl back in New York. I never married. Moved around too much, I guess. You didn't join the colored guard?"

Archie looked up at him and shook his head. "My *maman* and *papan* needed me at home. I kind of wanted to, though." He cast a glance around at the neighborhood, then asked, "You been in the army long?

"I graduated from the military school in New York, West Point it's called, when I was 21. Went straight into the Mexican War. That's where I got this limp."

Archie must have noticed it but had been too polite to call attention to it. "What happened? You get shot?"

He smiled. "Bayonet."

Archie said. "That's bad. It's lucky you survived."

"Indeed it is. Here we are." They had come to a neat little house. Mick slowed and stepped across the flowing gutter to the wooden banquette sidewalk. Respecting a New Orleans tradition, he did not go to the front door but led them around to the back to the French doors of a parlor. He tapped quietly on the wooden part of one panel.

They could see the basic outlines of three people through the thin lace curtains. One appeared to be a largish man in a dressing gown sitting in a chair with pillows propped around him. The woman fussing over him was likewise in a dressing gown with a pale *tignan* scarf over what looked like auburn hair poking out from under and done up in rag curlers. The third person was another woman, in the garb of a servant. She held a silver serving pot in one hand.

The woman in the dressing gown righted herself from her attentive posture and called, *"Oui, qui est-ce?"*

Archie said, "*C'est moi*, Madi. *Je viens avec le* Captain Michael Murphy."

They heard a quizzical "*Qui est- ce?*" from the man in the chair.

One of the women said, "*C'est mon frère.*"

The man said, "Michael Murphy *était une fois un enquêteur confidentielle ici dans la ville. Est-ce le même homme?*"

Mick wondered if the man was Brunel and how he knew Mick had been a confidential agent.

"*Je ne said pas,*" was the woman's reply. "*Oh mon dieu, Je suis honteux! Je vais robe. Tu leur parles, mon cher.*"

As the panicked woman in the dressing gown fled to an open doorway, the seated man gestured the servant toward the French doors. "*Cécile, s'il vous plaît.*"

Mick exchanged an uncomfortable look with Archie that bespoke their embarrassment at Madi's confusion and her rushing away, assumably to make herself presentable. Mick shrugged and Archie gave him a half-smile.

The servant was a pretty African woman with a dignified expression. She glanced from Mick to Archie, then addressed Mick. "May I help you?" she asked in heavily accented English.

Archie was the one who replied. "I am Madeleine's brother, Septime. Captain Murphy and I are trying to find my brother Quintus. I hear he came to this house before he disappeared."

"Let them come in, Cécile," the man inside the room called out.

Cécile stepped out of the doorway.

The man gestured the two visitors in. "Sit down, *mes amis*. And can my girl get you some refreshment?"

They heard the other woman's voice from another room. "But of course, *mon cher*. Cécile, go fetch some tea and pastries from the kitchen."

The servant started for the kitchen, but Mick said, "No need, Miss. We have only a few minutes."

Archie looked disappointed, but he lowered his knapsack to the floor and sat on a divan, which was decorated with silk with tiny pink and green flowers on a sort of balustrade design. Mick let his eyes roam the room, noticing the lace curtains, the green Persian rug, and the neat but sumptuous furniture, all probably supplied by Monsieur Brunel.

Brunel tried to sit up better in his chair and winced. "Aren't you the Michael Murphy who used to have an office down on Rue Royale?"

Mick smiled. "You have a long memory. That was at least seven or eight years ago. Until the war came and I headed off to rejoin the Union Army."

Brunel looked his uniform up and down. "I see you did. Is it nice to come back to a Union-controlled Crescent City?"

"With General Nathaniel Banks in charge, it isn't so clear the Union *is* in charge. But Archie here, that is, Septime and I, came to talk to you and your lovely lady about her other brother Quintus. I believe he stopped by here before he took off for parts unknown."

Brunel let out a little laugh. "Parts unknown. *Oui,* the man did stop by. We had a brief conversation, he and I and Madeleine, but he was quite drunk and decided to leave."

Just then Madeleine returned to the parlor. She was radiant in a loose, plum-colored taffeta with a rather large emerald hanging on a thin chain around her neck. Her hands were encased in off-white lacy gloves, and as she stepped toward the men, Mick saw she was wearing slippers of the same plum color as her dress. She also wore a simple white silk *tignan* over her hair. She floated into the room and settled on the arm of his chair.

Brunel looked at her lovingly and took her hand.

"Oh, Adam," she whispered and turned her attention to the visitors. "Archie, so good to see you.

Her sweet smile widened as Archie reached into his knapsack. "I brought you a present, Madi."

She put her palms to her cheeks and gave him a delighted look. "*Oh mon cher*, Septime! How thoughtful of you. What is it?"

He handed her a brown paper wrapped box. "Maman's best croissants and some homemade butter."

Madi squealed and looked at her lover, who beamed right back at her. "How simply delicious!" To Mick she said, "I insist you have some with us, monsieur."

This time Mick relented. Cécile came in with a pot of tea in a silver carafe and teacups on saucers. She laid those items on a small table, then took the brown box toward the kitchen.

"Two more cups, then, Cécile," Madi said as Cecile departed.

Mick returned to his line of inquiry. "So you say you had a brief conversation with Quintus?"

Madi cast her eyes down modestly, and Adam replied. "He was, shall we say, unhappy with some information he had gotten."

Mick noticed that Madi put her hand on her somewhat rounded belly when he said this. Mick waited until the man went on.

"He was under the mistaken impression that I was leaving the city for Cuba, and he was afraid I would go without my darling Madi."

Madi broke in, "He thought my beloved Adam was leaving me, well, with child. But he was not."

Mick narrowed his eyes. "Not leaving you? Or not going to Cuba?"

The two lovers took each other's hands and smiled lovingly into each other's eyes. "We are both going to Cuba. We can be married and have our child there," said the man with a clear sense of the gravity of the subject.

"Congratulations on the blessed event!" Mick said as Archie jumped up to kiss his sister on the cheek. Mick knew, and he was sure Archie did, too, that it was rare for a Creole man to wed a quadroon or octoroon *placé*, especially since mixed race marriages were illegal in Louisiana and the rest of the United States—and the Confederate States, for that matter. Mick was also perfectly aware from his many years in New Orleans that such marriages were not unheard of. The heart wants what the heart wants. He thought it unfortunate that a philosophy like that would never apply to two men who were in love.

They continued to talk when the croissants and two more cups arrived, but neither Madi nor Brunel had any idea where Quintus may have fled. But Mick did get the two to admit that before he disappeared, Quintus had pulled his army pistol and shot Brunel.

"It was merely a flesh wound," Brunel said. "The man was so drunk."

Madi put her palms to Brunel's face, "But oh, my darling, I was so afraid he had killed you!"

LATER, WHEN MICK AND Archie arrived in the neighborhood of the Customs House, Mick went on alone and talked to a few of the men of the Corps Afrique about where they thought Quintus might have gone, and for once, he learned something useful.

"Come quickly," he called to Archie as he fetched him from the open air market where he was sipping a cup of coffee. "I have a lead on where Quintus may have gone."

In no time at all, the two were across the city and moving toward the more disreputable area called "The Swamp." Living there was a mix of the refugees from plantations along with the poorer sorts of foreigners and even a few American whites. The neighborhood was right up against the bayou.

"Are we going in there?" Archie asked, clearly hesitant.

"We have to if we want to find the Snake Woman's cabin." Mick led the way along whatever solid ground they could find among the cypress and the heavy Spanish moss. They had to jump to avoid getting their feet wet in the swampy water. Mick wasn't sure the risk of losing a foot to the alligators was worth it, but he kept on going.

Somehow Mick managed to find an old dilapidated cabin festooned in clumps of string-tied herbs and chicken feet and feathers and other unidentifiable items of the voudou trade. "This has to be the Snake Woman's place," he said. His heart beat a little faster, and he took a deep breath to calm his nerves about approaching it.

As they stood, trying to decide how to get into the cabin, a strangely attired black woman came to the open door and snapped, "Well, whatchu wait for? You come to see Madame Marie?"

She ushered them into a dim room with a cluttered table, covered with items they could not identify. She swept the things into a basket already half-full of the arcane tools of her profession. "Sit."

Finding two stools, Mick and Archie sat and waited for her to talk.

"Well?" the woman said sharply.

Mick said, "We want to know if this young man's brother was here sometime in the past couple of weeks."

"Quintus was here, devil take him. Drunk and weeping. He thought he'd kilt a man. I told him, no, he done missed him and the man lives."

Mick stared at her, and when he glanced at Archie, he looked incredulous, too. Madame Marie seemed to know everything. How did she know who they were? Or who Quintus was? Was it her magic? Or did she have informers in the city?

She suddenly got up and rummaged around in a series of baskets and boxes until she found a packet wrapped up in white cotton with a black ribbon. She brought it over to Mick and handed it to him. "You going to need one of dese."

He stared at the object in his palms. It was lumpy, as if it contained a number of small things, but he absolutely did not want to open the parcel. "What is it?" he asked.

She sniffed. "It will help you get over the drink."

Archie spoke up, "But my brother—"

The woman made a shooing gesture toward him. "He dead now. You go find him if you want, but you won't find much."

Mick let out a breath. He saw Archie's face go from inquisitive to crestfallen.

"What do you mean my brother's dead?"

She clearly had no more to say. She wouldn't meet their eyes as she rose and went to the doorway, waiting until the two men got up.

Archie continued to ask questions, but when she didn't say another word, he went through the doorway and Mick followed.

"She didn't have time for us." Mick blushed and felt embarrassed about stating the obvious.

"What is that thing she gave you?" Archie asked.

"Some voudou trash." He threw it into the underbrush.

They wandered about near the cabin for some time as Archie adjusted to the possibility that his brother had died. Mick thought he'd give Archie a few minutes to himself. He strolled off the path and caught sight of what looked like a fallen log near the edge of the pond peered closer.

"Oh, dear lord, no," he said quietly, then called back to Archie. "I think I found your brother, but you don't want to see him. He died badly."

He tried to intercept Archie, but the man pressed forward anyway, and cried out his brother's name when he saw the body. The face was filthy and swollen from lying in the hot swampy water and air, and the damage to his body was shockingly brutal, but enough of Quintus's face remained for Archie to identify him.

"Poor bastard," Mick said mournfully. "Gator must have got him."

He put his arms around a sobbing Archie. The young man cried out his grief for how his brother had died.

Mick pulled Archie away from the grisly scene. "I'll get someone to come and take him back to the undertakers. He will get a proper burial, with a band and mourners and a tomb in the St. Louis Cemetery."

As they walked out of the swamp, Mick took frequent sips from his flask of Irish whiskey. He offered some to Archie but he shook his head. Mick guzzled some more whiskey. He knew he was dealing with the horror of what he'd seen by getting progressively drunk, but that was all he could do to handle his emotions. Archie watched him nervously, but Mick managed to get them both back to the cottage behind the big house. For Mick, it seemed like days had gone by since they'd had coffee and pastries there that morning.

Mick opened the front door of his cottage and directed them both into the bedroom. Without another word, Mick fell onto the narrow bed and passed out.

"MICK, WAKE UP. PLEASE!" came a voice from afar. Mick awoke from a bad dream.

A beautiful naked figure stood by the bed.

His eyesight was fuzzy, but Mick beheld a coffee-colored angelic shape calling out to him. The figure lifted Mick's head gently and put something around his neck.

Mick slowly came out of the haze and realized it was Archie who sat on the edge of the bed. His arms settled down on the pillow on either side of Mick's head, and full lips pressed against his own. He thought for a split second of how his breath must reek but Archie did not seem to mind. Mick opened his mouth and let his tongue be coaxed out into a soul-healing kiss.

His first tendrils of full consciousness brought him to a sudden realization that this in fact was the man he had met yesterday—or was it today?—and taken first to his sister's house and then to the Snake Woman in the bayou. Then he remembered the horrible images from the bayou. He jerked, and Archie pulled away from the kiss.

"Your brother…" Mick breathed hard from fright.

"While you were resting, I took care of him."

"I must have been out for quite some time then."

"Yes," Archie said, his eyes full of ardor. "Now kiss me."

Mick put his arms around Archie's neck. Their lips came together again. Mick allowed himself to dismiss his surprise at the fact that Archie wanted to make love with him. He thought for a moment and realized it had been such a long time since anyone had wanted him. He lost himself in the joy and passion of the young man's attentions and some time later rejoiced to hear Archie's voice call out "Mick, oh Mick!"

They lay together afterward and slept, but Mick awoke more clear-headed than he had in years. From the time of leaving New Orleans—where he had been the object of brutality because of his predilections—and up through the carnage of the war, he realized he'd been bereft of all passion, of all ardor, with no lover to take his mind off his troubles. Now he was whole again, healed. And, to his surprise, he felt no remnants of hangover.

The radiant face of Septime Archibault, angelic Archie, looked up at Mick from where it rested on his bare chest. Mick could not remember when he himself had undressed, but he was lying nude under a sheet, which also covered the miracle worker.

"Archie? What—uh," Mick stammered. "What? How—"

Archie reached up and put a finger to Mick's lips, silencing him. "I wanted you as soon as I saw those angel eyes of yours."

They came together again, and once more Mick rose to the challenge. They lay gasping afterward.

"I don't understand it," Mick said. "I feel completely clear and refreshed."

Archie lifted a cord that was attached to the little bag of voudou looped around Mick's neck. "It might be the work of Papa Legba."

Mick was surprised to see the charm. "Who is Papa Legba?"

"A powerful spirit. One who speaks and knows. The Snake Woman follows his *loa*."

"Where did this come from?"

"When I went back for my brother, I picked it up from the underbrush. Something told me you would need it."

Remembering the Snake Woman's words as she handed him the thing, he realized it must be some witchery to combat his increasing overindulgence in alcohol. "It worked so fast!" he exclaimed.

Archie shook his head. "It's not finished yet. I did what I could to increase its power, but you have a long way to go. And much to do. And I won't be here to help you."

Mick forgot what he was going to say about Archie's part in the voudou magic and said in a sorrowful voice, "You won't?"

Archie shook his head and planted a kiss on Mick's chest. "I have to go home to mourn with my family. And..." He hesitated. "I can't be with you while you drink. It is not how I want to live. But you will be better now. You will find love and healing somewhere else in this magical city, or back in New York, or in Paris, or somewhere else where you go to live."

And Mick had a feeling that the lovely Archie was correct.

THE NEXT DAY, MICK saw Archie off at the train station that would take him and his brother's body down to Mound Bayou where Quintus would be home to lie with his family, generations past, in the cemetery there.

When the train was out of sight, Mick sighed deeply and turned his steps to a nearby cathedral. He went into the nave and over to the confessional. When he said what his sins were, the kindly but admonishing priest gave him absolution and his penance. He came out of the confessional and settled in a pew.

As he sat, he gazed at the figure of Christ on the cross that hung above the altar. He thought about the good and compassionate man he saw in the figure. He knew that this man never condemned anyone, no matter their proclivities. In fact, he doubted Christ would even object to a little voudou magic here and there. He reached into his tunic front and felt the charm tucked inside.

He would heal. With Jesus' and Papa Legba's help, he would heal.

From somewhere in the cathedral he heard the soft sweet voices of the boys' choir. In Latin they were gently singing, *"Oremus: Concede, misericors Deus, fragilitati nostrae praesidium."*

He understood the words. "Let us pray: Grant, O merciful God, to our weak natures Thy protection."

Mick made the sign of the cross on his chest over the charm and silently began to pray.

Stepping Toward Freedom

By
Nann Dunne

*"All I ask of our brethren is that they will take their
feet from off our necks and permit us to stand upright
on the ground which God intended us to occupy."*
~Sarah Moore Grimke, one of the first American Feminists

October-November 1917

IN LAFAYETTE PARK IN Washington, DC, across from where the National Woman's Party was picketing the White House, Anna Morrivale slumped onto a bench, her tour over for the day. For five hours on the picket line, she carried a large wooden sign that read, "Mr. President, How Long Must Women Wait For Liberty?" She had passed the placard along to the next group of picketers and walked into the park to rest a minute.

That morning, she had risen at dawn and grabbed a biscuit with jam to eat on the run. She sneaked out of the house before her father awoke; he didn't approve of the picketing, and she hid her part in it. He thought she went into the city to wander through the stores, which he considered an acceptable way for a well-to-do young woman to pass her time.

As she had reached the corner, a gust of chill wind blew past and she clutched her long coat tighter to her body with one hand and anchored her hat to her head with the other. Her calf-length dress ended just above her high-heeled boots. The weather had turned colder. She gave great credit to the women who picketed all night long in the fall weather.

A streetcar took her near Cameron House on Lafayette Square, headquarters of the National Woman's Party, where the day's picketers assembled and picked up their signs and banners. The picketers walked across Lafayette Park to the White House gates and relieved their sisters, who returned to Cameron House or passed their signs to another person and went home.

Anna had paraded with the heavy sign for what seemed to be forever. Her shoulders felt like she carried the world on them, and in some respects, she did. At least her world. As she rested on the bench, other women passed out literature and talked to the onlookers who had followed them into the park. The NWP members worked hard to persuade new recruits to the cause of women getting the right to vote.

According to newspaper reports Anna had read of previous demonstrations, marchers were hit or spat upon, even arrested. Some were sent to the District Jail, and some had gone to Occoquan prison. They had endured unspeakable conditions in both places. But today was relatively peaceful. Mean-spirited people engaged in name-calling such as "whores" or "traitors" or shouted obscenities and ridiculous statements like "get back in the kitchen where you belong" or "women are too dumb to vote," but no one threw anything or spat on anyone.

Sitting quietly on the bench, Anna tensed when fingers touched her neck and shoulders, but when they began to massage her aching muscles, she relaxed and sighed. After a few minutes of the heavenly ministrations, she said, "Oh, that feels so wonderful. Can I take you home with me?"

A throaty laugh answered her, and a voice said, "That's a tempting offer, but I have to be somewhere else soon."

The massage stopped, and Anna turned to see who the woman was. She recognized the tan skin and piled, wavy, brown hair of the woman whose commanding presence had caught her notice earlier. "Thank you, I enjoyed that." She stretched her neck and shoulders. "In fact, I really needed it." She stood up and held out her hand. The woman was a head taller than she was. "My name's Anna. Anna Morrivale. You have magical fingers."

The woman's eyes twinkled. She took Anna's hand in both of hers and held it. "So I've been told. My name's Jo Perrina. I'm pleased to meet you, Anna."

"And I'm pleased to meet you, too, Jo. Is that short for Josephine?"

"Josephina."

Anna chuckled. "So it's Josephina Perrina."

Jo rolled her eyes. "My parents were poetic Italians. What can I say? Other than I prefer to be called Jo." She slowly brushed her fingers along Anna's palm as she released her hand.

Anna's hand tingled. What a strange reaction. Why did she get the feeling that Jo was flirting with her? A woman flirting with a woman? Granted, she had heard whispers of such happenings, but she'd never experienced it. Her breathing increased.

Jo said, "I really do have to leave. Perhaps I'll see you tomorrow?"

Anna caught herself staring into Jo's warm brown eyes. "I hope so." The possibility excited her.

Jo no sooner left than an older woman, one of the picketers, approached Anna.

"You look like a decent young person," the woman said. "I feel I should warn you about associating with a woman of that sort."

"And what sort is that?" Anna asked.

The woman covered her mouth and whispered, "She has liaisons with other women."

Anna raised her eyebrows in mock innocence. "Doesn't she have the freedom to make that choice? Aren't we all marching for the vote so we can have freedom in other areas of our lives as well?"

The woman sniffed. "Not the freedom of immorality."

Anna stood her ground. "And who decided that having 'liaisons with other women' was immoral?" Was she referring to a woman making love to another woman?

"The Holy Bible tells us that."

"Ma'am, I'm very familiar with the New Testament, but not everyone agrees with everything it says."

"Humph! I can see my warning is wasted on you." She hurried away.

Actually, Anna thought with an inner smile, the Old Testament doesn't mention women loving women, at all. In the Jewish patriarchy, women didn't count for much. But she wanted to count. Just as the pamphlets she had read in the past noted, getting the vote for women would be a big step toward their freedom in other areas. The potential for that lifted her heart. And her hopes.

THE NEXT DAY, WOMEN donned their purple, white, and gold sashes, gathered their signs, and crossed Lafayette Park to replace the nighttime picketers at the White House. Anna saw Jo Perrina and hurried to her. "Hello."

Jo's face lit up. "Hello, there. I'm happy to see you were able to come." She rested her sign on her shoulder, shook Anna's hand, and again let go slowly.

Anna's heart fluttered. "I wouldn't want to miss being here. Marching as one of the 'Silent Sentinels of Liberty' is important to me."

"Me, too. I heard that since it began, well over a thousand women have signed up to take part, in spite of all the arrests."

"Isn't that wonderful!"

"Remarkable. Every year we get more and more women and men on our side. Where's your sign?"

"I'll get one from the night marchers." Anna tilted her head. "What does yours say?"

Jo lifted it off her shoulder and held it so they both could see it. Jo read the words aloud. "President Wilson, How Long Must Women Wait For Liberty?"

They resumed their walk across the park.

"I've been told," Anna said, "that President Wilson used to tip his hat and smile to the picketers. Now he seems to ignore us."

"Yes, but the newspapers have said some nasty things. They've called us 'hecklers' and 'women howlers.'"

Anna laughed. "I guess we really are, but it's in a good cause. Anyway, that's enough shoptalk for now, don't you think?"

As Jo nodded, Anna said, "I haven't seen you around here before. Are you new to this area?"

"No, I've been taking part in marches in different parts of Virginia. After the last one I attended, my feet started complaining. I bought some Scholl Foot-Eazers, which helped a lot, but I thought for a while I'd try the more static approach that the Silent Sentinels use. So here I am."

"I'm glad you are." Anna felt herself blush. "One of the older women warned me about you."

Jo halted one step and then resumed walking. "Warned you? What about?"

"She said you had liaisons with other women."

Jo raised her eyebrows. "I'm open about it, but that sounds like I'm promiscuous and I'm not." She laughed. "I don't have time to be. Does it bother you?"

"No. I told her you were free to make your own choices. After all, we're marching for freedom, in a sense." Anna cleared her throat. "I've never met a woman who chooses women as her romantic partners."

Jo came to a full stop and set the post of her sign on the ground. She bent over, put one hand over her mouth, and started laughing. "You can't be serious," she managed to say.

Anna suddenly felt shy. "Why is that so amusing?"

Jo straightened up and flung her free hand out in a semicircle. "Many women who've pushed this cause from the beginning are believed to practice lesbianism. You'll hear such rumors even about Susan B. Anthony, one of the founders of the suffrage movement. In fact, she wrote the amendment we're trying to get passed. There's talk about Alice Paul and Lucy Burns, the founders of NWP. And other women, too, some of them married."

Anna raised her hand to her cheek and spoke softly. "I had no idea." How unsophisticated she must seem. And ignorant. That's what came of being "protected" from the world as so many men—like her father— claimed women needed to be.

Jo sobered. "Will that deter you from marching with us?"

"No, I'm just embarrassed. You must think me naïve."

Jo threw the sign back up onto her shoulder. "Uninformed, perhaps. Right now, I believe we should take our place with the Silent Sentinels." She strode toward the picketers at the White House gate, and Anna hurried to keep up with her.

"I doubt," Jo said, "that we'll have much opportunity for more talk in this vein, but I'll walk back with you when we finish. Okay?"

"Okay." Anna stopped a woman who was leaving and relieved her of her sign. Jo was five women beyond her, already in line. The woman on Jo's right looked askance at her and moved to a different spot. Anna stepped into the empty place, looked up at Jo, and saw pain in her eyes. The subtle shunning seemed to have hurt her. Anna smiled at her until Jo smiled back.

After their watch was over, Anna and Jo discovered they lived only six blocks apart in Alexandria. They traded addresses, boarded the streetcar, and agreed to ride together to future demonstrations. Anna's heart was singing when they parted. *Jo lives six blocks away,* she kept saying to herself like a mantra. *Jo lives six blocks away.*

THE NEXT MORNING, ANNA noticed a swollen vein edging her father, Gerald Morrivale's, temple like a purple ribbon. His voice rose as he grabbed the newspaper lying on the kitchen table, crumpled it in one hand, and shook it at Anna. "Your picture is on the front page. You've been participating in these vile demonstrations. These women are nothing but prostitutes and manly women, and that's the name that will be put to you, too."

Anna's mother, Sybil, and her younger sister, Deborah, sat silent at the table next to Anna. All three women were of small build with blonde hair and blue eyes. Gerald, tall, but also light-haired and blue-eyed, stood over them, the undisputed head of his household.

Anna scowled. "That's not true, Father. Those women are just like me. They're tired of having to ask a man to take care of everything in their lives. They especially want the right to choose who represents them in our legal system. They've been working for years to make that happen."

Gerald said, "Giving women the right to vote doesn't make sense. Women are of delicate constitutions with little worldly experience. They aren't physically or intellectually the equal of men. You women need a man's protection and guidance."

Anna jutted out her chin. "I think I should have the right to choose whether I want that protection and guidance and from whom it should come." She stood up. "And how am I to get worldly experience if I can't step out into that world without a man dictating my every move?"

Gerald threw the newspaper onto the table and pointed his finger at her. "Don't be worrying about getting worldly experience. The world isn't a friendly place for women to be alone in. You will not take part in those demonstrations, and that's final. In fact, you're not to leave this house without my permission. If you can't abide by that, then find somewhere else to live." He strode from the room and left the house.

Sybil looked up at Anna. "Why must you persist in upsetting your father?"

Stricken by her father's ultimatum, Anna sat back down. "I've educated myself about the struggles women have gone through to get a voting rights amendment as part of the United States Constitution. I wish I had been involved sooner. Did you know that they held a women's rights meeting in 1848 in Seneca Falls, New York? That's 69 years ago! An amendment allowing voting for women was introduced to Congress in 1878, but it didn't pass. We still don't have full rights as citizens. The National Woman's Party is working to change that."

Sybil's and Deborah's eyes were glazing over, and Anna's frustration increased. "You don't care, do you? Well, I care, and I'll continue to be a part of the movement, in spite of Father's orders."

Sybil patted Anna's hand. "He only wants what's best for you."

"No, Mother. He wants what he thinks is best for me. I'm determined to make that decision for myself. Since our country entered the war in April, women have been stepping into the jobs men left behind when they joined the military service. Women are serving in the Navy, the Marines, the Coast Guard, and as nurses and ambulance drivers. Women have proven their worth, and I'm going to keep picketing until we have equal voting rights."

"What picketing is that?" Deborah asked.

Anna tapped her fingers on the table. "The National Woman's Party has been picketing at the White House gates since January."

Sybil said, "I do recall your father getting angry about some women parading in Washington on the day before Mr. Wilson's inauguration, but I didn't pay much attention to it. Are they picketing now?"

"Thousands of women marched that day."

Anna felt she shouldn't fault her mother for her inattention to the suffrage cause. At first, Anna herself had been deficient in that respect. She hadn't even heard about the parade until it was over. "Yes, they are picketing, and I've joined them several times. I intend to keep joining them."

Deborah frowned at her. "Father will get furious if you do."

"I expect so, but the choice is mine."

In most ways, her father was a good man, but he couldn't be budged about how to treat women. The anger Anna had suppressed bubbled up. "I'll move out of this house right now, before that happens."

Sybil gasped. "But where will you go? What will you do?"

"I don't know. I'll find something."

Anna ran upstairs, packed two suitcases with her belongings, said her goodbyes, and left. She would miss her family, but she was determined to fight for the right to vote. All women would benefit from it, whether they understood that or not. But where would she go; what would she do? She had only $2.10 in change from the allowance her father gave her regularly. Maybe someone at Cameron House could advise her. She didn't know where else to turn. Jo came to mind, but she didn't want to impose on her; they'd barely met. She lugged her suitcases onto the streetcar and was on her way to Washington.

WHEN ANNA ARRIVED AT Cameron House, she set her suitcases against a wall and walked into a commotion. "Alice Paul has been arrested again!" she was told by one of the women, Mary.

"Again?" Two weeks ago, Alice Paul, the head of the National Woman's Party, had been arrested while picketing and then released. "What for this time?"

"They're still accusing us of obstructing traffic."

Anna frowned. "But it's not our fault that people crowd around us and clog up the street. We're just standing there out of the way."

"Try convincing the court of that. Fighting for our cause while there's a war going on makes us guilty of treason in their eyes. The arrests are their way of showing us a lesson."

Anna's heart grew heavier. "What will become of Miss Paul?"

"Who knows what they'll do this second time. They've been handing down longer sentences lately. We'll just have to wait and see."

Anna left to join the picketers. She spied Jo and slid into line next to her.

"Hi." Jo flashed a smile that boosted Anna's morale a bit. "I missed you on the streetcar. Is anything wrong?"

Anna made a face. "Family trouble. My father got really angry and told me if I continued to picket I'd have to leave. So I did."

"What are you going to do?"

"I don't know yet. I packed a couple of suitcases and left them at Cameron House. I'm praying someone there can help me figure out what to do."

"I hope so. You missed the excitement. Miss Paul was here this morning, but she and a few other women got arrested. I was just coming across the park when it happened."

"Mary told me about it at Cameron House."

The woman standing on the other side of Anna, Louise Ashburton, heard their talk about Alice Paul's arrest. She told Anna she also had been arrested twice.

"Oh my," Anna said. She turned to Jo. "Louise says she's also been arrested before, twice."

"What was it like?" Jo asked Louise.

"Awful. The first time, I went to the District Jail for ten days. The second time I was sent to the Workhouse for Women at Occoquan, Virginia. Both places were honest-to-goodness"—she put a hand next to her mouth and whispered loudly—"hellholes."

"I heard that the food was pretty terrible," Jo said.

Louise made a quick gesture with her hand. "Spoiled meat, moldy green cornbread, and the grits contained worms, dead flies, and rat droppings. One place was as bad as the other. We all lost weight."

Louise went on to give them detailed descriptions of her stints of imprisonment. The stories made Anna feel sad for the women who had been so poorly treated. But she also felt strengthened by them. Realizing that she could be arrested scared her, but she believed in women's suffrage, and she vowed to put up with whatever was needed to achieve it.

AT THE END OF the day, when Anna and Jo were crossing Lafayette Park, Anna's thoughts turned once again to her own plight. She gave a wry grin. Maybe she should have been arrested. Then she wouldn't have to worry for a while about a roof over her head.

Jo stopped walking, so Anna stopped, too. "Anna..." Jo hesitated. "What would you think about coming home with me? No strings attached. I have an extra bedroom you could stay in."

Anna's heart soared, then it came back to earth. "I don't have any income. I can't offer you anything."

"I've thought about that. I'd like to hire you to keep house for me, if you're willing. I come here for five or six hours each day, plus I work in the shipyard all night. I don't have time to care for my house properly—as you'll see if you accept my offer."

Anna was so relieved, she bit her lower lip to keep from crying. "I'm thrilled to accept. Thank you for being so generous, especially to someone you hardly know."

"I know we get along all right, and we both have a strong interest in the suffrage movement. That's enough for me. Besides, if it doesn't work out, it will give you time to consider other options."

"That's true. But I think it will work out."

They walked a little farther, and Anna said, "I'm curious. Why didn't you say something earlier?"

"I was hesitant to."

"Hesitant? Why?"

Jo took a deep breath. "If you said no, I'd wonder whether my attraction to women had repelled you, and that might end our friendship. I didn't want that to happen. But I know you're in need of a place to stay, and my offer is a purely business one. Like I said, no strings attached."

Anna took hold of Jo's arm and gave it a tug. "No strings attached is good." She hoped she would be forgiven that little lie. Being around Jo excited her in a way she'd never known before.

JO'S HOUSE DID NEED attention, and Anna loved every minute of putting it in order. She had been responsible for most of the housework at home, so she carried out her duties with an experienced hand. She hated that Jo had to work every evening, except the weekends, but she set her own work and sleep cycle to coincide with Jo's. She did all the heavy housecleaning during the time when Jo worked at the shipyards, about 10:30 p.m. to 7:30 a.m. Then, after breakfast, they joined the

Silent Sentinels on Monday through Saturday for five or six hours each day—depending on how long Jo's feet held out.

In the limited free time they had in the evenings after sleeping, they learned more about each other. Anna told Jo about her family—how her father made all the rules and how her mother and sister fell right into those roles without any qualms. Jo had no siblings. Her parents had pushed her out of the house six years earlier when she was nineteen, not because of her women's suffrage movement activities—she hadn't been involved then— but because she loved women.

"How awful," Anna said. "What did you do?" They were sitting on the sofa in the living room.

"Fortunately, I had a job teaching kindergarten in a private school, so I got my own apartment. As soon as I had enough money saved, I bought this house."

"How resourceful of you. Why did you switch jobs?"

"The men have been going off to war, and companies began hiring women. The shipyard pays three times what teaching did. But I do want to go back to teaching eventually. I'm saving money to go to school after the war and be an accredited teacher."

Anna grabbed Jo's hand. "Oh, Jo, my being here cuts into your savings."

"Not too much." Jo turned her hand so it lay palm-to-palm with Anna's and entwined their fingers. "I like having you here. Coming home to an empty house wasn't any fun."

Anna gave a big smile. "I'm glad. I like being here, too."

JO SIGHED. THIS "NO strings attached" promise was harder than she expected it to be. She wanted to pull Anna closer and… She groaned inwardly as Anna stuck the tip of her tongue out and moistened her lips, the lips she so wanted to kiss. But she daren't. She could picture Anna looking shocked, jumping up, and running off to Cameron House again. Anna had confided that she had never had so much as a beau, much to her parents' consternation. Both parents at various times had proposed suitors, but Anna said none had appealed to her. Was that a sign that she'd welcome Jo's advances? It was too soon to tell. She had to give Anna more time. But when she looked deep into those gorgeous blue eyes and thought about that compact but curvaceous body, her hands got sweaty. Like now. She released her hold on Anna's hand and jumped up from the sofa. "Time to get ready for work."

Anna's expression dimmed, leaving Jo feeling a surge of hope. Anna didn't seem to want to let go of her hand. Or was Jo reading more into that than actually existed? She hurried away before she said or did something irreversible that could doom their friendship.

WHEN ALICE PAUL WAS sentenced to seven months in jail, the women of the NWP were startled and appalled. That was the longest sentence for any of them to date. In previous jailings, suffragists had experienced vermin-infested cells, horrible food, and harsh treatment. No one doubted that Alice Paul's treatment would be just as detestable, if not worse.

One cold day, while standing on the picket line, Anna and Jo heard that Paul had been put in a prison psychiatric ward, had promptly gone on a hunger strike, and was being force-fed. "Oh my God," Anna said. "What can she be thinking?"

"She's using a tactic she learned while in Britain," Jo answered. "I read an article in *McClure's Magazine* a few years back by Sylvia Pankhurst, the British activist. She and some other women were arrested because of their actions on behalf of women's suffrage. She went on a hunger strike and they force-fed her. Alice Paul had the same experience when she was arrested over there."

"How were they force-fed?"

"They pried Miss Pankhurst's teeth apart with some kind of metal instrument that made her gums bleed when she tried to prevent what they were doing. Then they stuck a rubber tube down her throat and poured some liquid straight into her stomach. The first time they did it, she threw up as they pulled the tube out. She fought against it each day and vomited off and on until she was too weak to fight anymore."

Anna cringed. "That's gruesome. Then what happened?"

"She demanded that the Home Secretary be petitioned to stop the force-feedings. After four months of this treatment, the Home Secretary had her released. She continued to suffer for a long time afterwards from the abuses she endured."

"I would think so. That had to affect her health. Did it do any good for the movement?"

"It made people a lot more aware. Women there have some local voting rights, but Miss Pankhurst and her group are aiming at full, national rights, just as we are."

"Just think," Anna said, "Miss Paul's going through that same thing right now. She's a brave woman."

"She and all the others."

"A bunch of women are being released today."

"But not her." Jo shuffled her feet and grimaced.

"Are you all right?" Anna asked.

"I forgot to put my Foot-Eazers in this morning, and my feet are really bothering me. I think I'll go sit in the park for a while. Do you mind?"

"Not at all, except for having sympathy for your pain. I'm sure this cold weather isn't helping. Do you want me to come with you?"

"No, I'll be fine. I just need to put my feet up for a while. I'll be back soon."

When Jo left, the cold, dreary day seemed even colder and drearier. Watching Jo limp away, Anna admitted she had fallen for Jo the first time she saw her, even though she herself hadn't realized it. But Jo never made any advances toward her, and Anna supposed that meant Jo didn't find her attractive. Those long, slow handshakes must be an unconscious habit of hers. That possibility was a hard pill to swallow, but Anna was glad she had the chance to be near her. She couldn't imagine what her life would be like without Jo in it.

She looked toward Lafayette Park and blinked in surprise. A single file of women holding banners was making its way toward her. What on earth was going on? She counted at least forty women. Within minutes, they spread out and swelled the ranks of the picketers at the White House gates.

Loud horns interrupted her musings. A police paddy wagon pulled up, and policemen arrived in cars. The women in the picket line moved closer together, but not one of them tried to run away. A policeman grabbed Anna's arm, knocked her sign to the ground, and yanked her toward the wagon. She tried to resist, but he was larger and stronger than she was.

IN SPITE OF THE cold, Jo removed one boot and rubbed her sole. She had her back to Cameron House and was surprised to see a long line of women march past her bearing suffrage banners. More picketers? Curiosity made her want to join them. She put her boot back on and tried to tie it. She peeled off the gloves that hindered her and got the laces tied. By then, she heard a commotion and horns blaring in the direction the picketers had gone. She ran toward the White House, as did others in the park.

Her heart dropped when she saw Anna about to be put into a black van. She hurried to the policeman. "Take me instead," she yelled. "Leave her alone and take me!"

Then the policeman shoved her away and drew his billy club. "Get out of here. These traitors are getting what they deserve."

"Go, Jo," Anna said. "Save yourself."

"But we aren't traitors." Jo plucked at the man's sleeve, and he hit her in the arm with the club.

Anna shouted, "Stop it. Leave her alone. I'll go peacefully."

"Yer girl friend ain't being so peaceful." The man swung the billy forcefully toward Jo, who jumped back to avoid another blow.

"Please, Jo, don't resist." The anguish on Anna's face made Jo back down. As soon as Anna was shoved into the wagon, a policeman closed its doors and the vehicle pulled away. So many women were being arrested that the police had to commandeer cars to transport them. Jo stood helplessly, massaging her bruised arm, and watched the wagon until it was out of sight.

When she looked behind her and saw that other women had filled the picket line in again, she joined them and lifted one of the signs that had been knocked down to the ground by the police. Her heart beat so hard against her chest that it hurt, and she rubbed the spot.

An older woman next to her said, "Hope for the best, dear. Most of the women have been given short sentences. A few days and she'll be back home."

"What about Alice Paul and the women arrested with her?" Jo said. "They got more than a few days."

"Law enforcement wanted to make an example of her because she's our leader. The only way we can stand by her and the others now is to keep picketing."

That made sense. Anna would want her to continue. But as soon as Jo's tour was over, she'd find out what happened.

At Cameron House, Jo learned that the police were giving no information about the prisoners, and no visitors were allowed. The bad news arrived the next day. The arrested women had been sentenced to Occoquan Workhouse.

ANNA STOOD STOIC IN court with the others when they heard their sentences, ranging from six days to six months. Anna got ninety days. She looked up and down the lines of women, thirty-one in number. Lucy Burns, a tall, attractive redhead, caught her eye and winked at her, the only bright happening of the day. Lucy, a co-founder of the National Woman's Party, worked hand in hand with Alice Paul and had been arrested twice before. Anna promised herself she would be just as strong as Lucy.

After the sentencing, the women were herded into a bus and transported to Occoquan. When they arrived, rough hands grabbed them and yanked them out of the vehicle. Anna caught a glimpse of the man who directed guards to "put them in the Punishment Cells." Guards kicked and punched and beat the women who struggled to get past them.

Two men twisted Anna's arms and nearly lifted her off her feet. They dragged her along, not caring that her body banged against tables and chairs, scattering them. One of the men punched her in the side and slapped her five times in the face. Her lips and nose bled down the front of her coat. She was barely conscious when they roughly threw her into a cell with iron-barred doors. She hit the concrete hard, rolled onto her back, and lay there, trying to catch her breath.

The noise outside increased. She grabbed one of the bars and struggled to rise. Guards continued to beat and shove women into the tiny enclosures. One woman had been handcuffed to the bars. Anna saw a flash of red hair and surmised that was Lucy Burns.

She looked away from the turmoil and glanced at her more-immediate surroundings. A straw-filled pallet with one blanket sat on the floor. One corner held an open toilet. Those served as the cell's furnishings.

So this was the notorious Occoquan Workhouse. Never, as a youngster, had she expected to land here, a place rife with thieves, prostitutes, and other prisoners—some with frightening diseases such as syphilis.

Stop thinking about that! She sat on the bed and tore a piece of cloth from her petticoat, glad she had decided to wear one instead of her one-piece undergarment. She gently dabbed at the blood oozing from her nose and lips.

She heard a loud whisper from the adjoining cell to the right. "We're refusing to give up our clothes, and we're doing the hunger strike. Can you hear me?"

Anna hurried to the corner. "Yes, and I'll join in."

"Pass it on."

Anna whispered directions to the next cell and shivered. She wondered when the force-feeding would start.

JO WAS BESIDE HERSELF with fear for Anna. She had been upset at previous arrests of the suffragists, but this time it tore her apart. She finally conceded that she loved Anna. Even if Anna didn't return that love,

Jo ached to hold her in her arms and tell her so. Oh God, she prayed, let me get a chance to do that.

At Cameron House, Jo read newspaper bits and pieces about the imprisoned women, and indeed, they immediately went on a hunger strike. That knowledge seared her soul. She had saved the old copy of *McClure's Magazine* that held Sylvia Pankhurst's story, and she read it over and over until she couldn't bear to look at it anymore.

AFTER SEVEN DAYS OF fasting, Anna felt weak and disoriented. Her skin was dry and peeling, her lips swollen. Nausea and dizziness plagued her.

Then the force-feeding started. Getting through the horrible ordeal took all her strength. She endured it by picturing Alice Paul suffering the same treatment over and over. Anna vomited every time the hard tube was pulled from her mouth. The feeling of not being able to breathe terrified her. What if the tube went down the wrong way? What if she suffocated? Tears streamed down her face. Her lips, mouth, and throat burned. Her stomach hurt. Her whole body ached from being held down as a doctor administered the liquid food.

Some of the female prison staff whispered apologies as they held her, but that didn't keep her from instinctively thrashing about, causing more bruises and chafed skin on her weak body. This happened three times a day, and after a while, the days ran together. Anna's mind wandered. She had trouble sleeping. She lost track of what day it was.

Finally, the force-feeding stopped. Guards herded together the weak, bruised, bedraggled women and transported them to the U.S. Court of Appeals in Alexandria, Virginia. NWP Attorney Matthew O'Brien had secured a hearing for them. Anna tried to look for Jo in the courtroom, but she couldn't hold up her heavy head. After the hearing, the women were sent to the District Jail instead of back to Occoquan.

UNABLE TO FORCE HER way into the packed hearing, Jo gave up and joined a large group outside the building near where the suffragist prisoners would be ushered into the courtroom. The quick glimpse she caught of Anna, her clothing bloody and her head lolling, clutched at Jo's innards. Bruised and battered, all the women needed help to walk.

How, Jo wondered, can our country treat our own women this way?

At the end of the hearing, someone told the crowd the suffragists would be transferred to District Jail. As the first women exited, Jo saw Alice Paul blink her eyes in the sunshine. Too weak to stand, she needed help to get in the conveyance waiting to take the women to the jail.

The boarding of the women happened quickly, but not before Anna's head swung up and her gaze met Jo's. Her expression lightened. Jo waved and yelled, "I'm waiting for you." Anna had no time to respond, but the look on her face cheered Jo.

THREE DAYS LATER, ON November 27, with no explanation, all the suffragist prisoners were set free. At Cameron House, Jo persuaded one of the women, Edna Mae, to use her Pierce-Arrow automobile to pick up Anna. When they arrived at the jail, Jo hurried inside and found her.

Anna clung weakly when Jo encircled her with her arms. "Oh, Jo, how good to see you," she said, her voice cracking.

Jo picked her up, carried her to the car, and sat on the rear seat with Anna in her lap. She rocked back and forth and kissed the top of Anna's head. Edna Mae put the car in gear and sped off. When they reached home, Jo thanked their driver profusely.

She carried Anna into the house, removed her coat and gloves, and sat her on the sofa. "What can I get you?"

"Water, please," Anna said in a faint voice.

"Coming right up." Jo peeled of her coat and gloves, dashed into the kitchen, filled a tumbler, and ran back to Anna. The tumbler seemed too heavy for Anna to hold, so Jo took it and held it to her lips.

Anna sipped at it until she finished the water. "I'm so tired. Just let me lie here for a while, please." Jo helped her get situated on the sofa and held her hand until she went to sleep. Anna's hand jerked spasmodically, and Jo kissed it and held it to her cheek. "I love you, Anna," she whispered. "Thank God, you're back."

Now that Anna was home, Jo was shy about revealing her feelings. Best to let Anna heal first, she told herself.

ANNA SLEPT FOR A day and a half. When she awoke, she called out for Jo, who came running to her. Anna took hold of her hand and smoothed it with her thumb. "I wanted to make sure I wasn't dreaming," she said with a small laugh.

"It's no dream, thank goodness. Can I fix you some food? You must be hungry."

"They fed us at the jail, but I couldn't eat most of it. My stomach hurt. Do you have any soup?"

"Chicken noodle. I'll fix some for you."

"That sounds wonderful."

"Then I'll help you bathe and change your clothes." Jo wrinkled her nose and smiled. "You're pretty rank."

Anna laughed. Jo's offer to help her bathe and change also sounded wonderful. She didn't have the strength to do whatever her mind might conjure up, but that wouldn't stop her from wishful thinking.

FOR THE NEXT WEEK, Jo attended to Anna during the day, slept in the afternoon, and worked at night. Anna's return to normal health would take time, but Jo could already see a change for the better. Anna could eat without discomfort and had shed her weakness as soon as her appetite improved.

When Jo returned home each morning after work, the possibility of a future with Anna swirled through her mind. But, Jo, she told herself, you won't have the future you dream about unless you tell her how you feel. Anna was brave enough to put up with being imprisoned and force-fed. Where's your bravery?

Jo stopped outside Anna's open bedroom door. She was asleep. Blonde hair encircled her sweet face like an angel with a halo. Mesmerized, Jo neared the bed. Her gaze fell onto Anna's lips and tarried there. Longing for Anna surged through her. Could she dare kiss her?

"Yes," Anna said. Jo jumped and her gaze moved to Anna's, which reflected so much desire, Jo's knees grew weak. Anna's arms reached for her. "Please kiss me, Jo."

Jo dropped against the bed into Anna's arms and met the lips she had been yearning for forever. Anna's lips conveyed a love that filled the emptiness in Jo that nothing else had.

Anna pulled her fully onto the bed and rolled so that Jo was on top of her. "Teach me, Jo. Teach me how to make love to you."

Anna was a quick learner.

Epilogue

ON JANUARY 10, 1918, forty years after being introduced into Congress, the "Susan B. Anthony" Amendment passed the House of Representatives, but it fell two votes short in the Senate. The NWP resumed picketing. On June 4, 1919, the Senate passed the amendment, but it had to be ratified by a two-thirds majority of the states.

On August 18, 1920, after receiving a ten-page letter from his elderly mother urging passage of suffrage for women, Tennessee legislator Harry

Burn changed his vote. He cast the deciding one, and Tennessee became the crucial thirty-sixth state to ratify.

On August 26, 1920, the Nineteenth Amendment to the Constitution became the law of the land: *The right of citizens of the United States to vote shall not be denied or abridged by the United States or by any State on account of sex.*

JO CAME THROUGH THE door and threw her arms wide. "We made it! Tennessee reaffirmed its vote and our amendment is finally in effect."

Anna rushed to her and they embraced. "I can hardly believe it. We're free to vote!"

They kissed. The kiss grew heated and hands roamed.

Anna interrupted the kiss and leaned back in Jo's arms. "I love you so much. I wish we were free to marry, too."

"Remember," Jo asked, "how this all started with baby steps, then bigger steps, and then giant steps?"

"Yes."

"We can do the same thing with marriage. Baby steps, sweetheart. Then bigger steps and giant steps. And maybe, someday, a tide of people will support the right for everyone to marry whom they choose."

Anna tilted her head. "You know what? This Nineteenth Amendment could be one of the baby steps in that direction."

"It might prove to be a giant step," Jo said. "Time will tell."

Hijacked Love

By
Ethan Stone

Chapter 1

TALK ABOUT BEING AT the right place at the right time. It was 1971, the day before Thanksgiving and my first day at the Portland FBI office. I was finally meeting my boss, Agent Milton Donaldson. We were shooting the breeze, when Donaldson's secretary dashed into his office.

"Sir, there's been a hijacking!"

Donaldson glanced at me and shrugged. "Looks like you'll be hitting the ground running."

My plans for Turkey day were going to hell. Phil was not going to be happy.

I followed Donaldson down a hallway and into a large conference room where half a dozen men in matching dark suits and ties milled around a table and talked over one another. Donaldson's presence hushed everyone as he strode to the end of the table. I stood off to the side.

"What do we know, gentlemen?"

Everyone began talking at once. Donaldson straightened, crossed his arms, and scowled. This was not a man I ever wanted to anger. The room quieted, and Donaldson pointed at a barrel-chested man with a receding hairline. "Duke."

"Flight"—Duke paused to review some notes—"305. Northwest Orient Airlines flying from Portland to Seattle. Just after takeoff a male passenger gave a note to a stewardess informing her he had a bomb."

"What does he want?" Donaldson asked.

A couple of men started to speak, but Duke drowned them all out. "Two hundred thousand dollars, four parachutes, and a fuel truck standing by in Seattle to refuel the aircraft on arrival."

Donaldson pointed at another agent. "Felder, get on the phone with the

Seattle office. Let's make sure we're working together on this one. I don't want any pissing matches about who's in charge. This is a joint operation."

"Yes, sir."

"The airline's president, Donald Nyrop, has been informed of the situation," Duke continued. "He'll call me back once he's made a decision."

"Good," Donaldson said. "We'll wait for his call. Whether or not he agrees to pay the money determines our next action. I don't want anyone harmed if we can avoid it. Do the passengers know what's going on?"

An agent sporting thick sideburns spoke up. "The pilot has already announced that landing in Seattle is delayed due to minor mechanical difficulty."

"Good. What do we know about our hijacker?"

"Nothing yet," Duke said. While others had taken seats, he had remained standing, and alternated between pacing alongside the table and leaning over it. "I'd like to be on the ground when it lands so I can interview the witnesses."

"I'm fine with that. I'd like you to wait until we get a call from the airline president. You've already talked to him and it'd be better if he spoke to you again."

Duke nodded. He leaned against the wall, crossed his arms, and tapped his foot impatiently. It was easy to tell this was Donaldson's right-hand man. I'd researched most of the agents I'd be working with but the name Duke didn't ring a bell. Then it struck me. Wayne Magruder. Twenty-five-year veteran of the Bureau. He'd worked in offices all across the country and in several different departments. He had a reputation for closing cases as well as for being a hard ass. Magruder didn't work well with others.

Donaldson issued assignments to almost every agent in the room before a phone on the wall rang. Duke grabbed it. "Magruder." He nodded. "Send it through." He put a hand on the speaker and said to Donaldson, "It's the airline president." A moment later, "Hello, Mr. Nyrop. This is Agent Magruder. Have you made a decision?" Pause. "I think you've made the right choice, sir. We'll be in contact soon." He hung up the receiver and turned. "He's paying the money and has instructed his employees to cooperate fully."

"Okay, Duke, get your ass to Seattle. Work with agents there to get the money. When the plane lands, interview anyone released. Let's figure out who this guy is."

"Yes, sir."

Duke dashed past me and was almost out the door when Donaldson glanced at me and blinked as if he'd forgotten I was even there.

"Duke...wait."

He stopped. "Yeah?"

"This is Special Agent Zachary Pomeroy."

Duke looked at me and I extended my hand. He shook it briefly, obviously uninterested.

"Call me Zack," I said.

He didn't reply, instead facing his boss again.

"I want you to take Pomeroy with you."

"Sir, I don't need—"

"It's not a request," Donaldson snapped. "He came with good recommendations after years of dealing with organized crime. I was going to assign you to train him anyway."

Duke inhaled then slowly let out his breath. Without looking at me, he said, "Fine. You better not hold me back."

"No, sir, I..."

He took off down the hallway with long strides..

"He's not joking," Donaldson said. "He will leave without you." He patted my back and pushed me out of the room.

I jogged until I caught up with Magruder. "Do I have time to make a phone call?"

"You got a wife you need to check in with?"

"Uh, no." I did have a partner, but I couldn't exactly tell Duke that.

"Nobody else matters."

Arguing would be pointless so I followed Magruder outside to his car, a cherry red 1966 Mustang. I whistled as I slid into the vehicle. "She's beautiful."

He grinned for a moment. "Thanks."

Moments later we were on our way to Seattle, driving well above the speed limit. After my attempts at conversation were met with monosyllabic responses, I stopped trying. We made it to Seattle in just under two hours. The Seattle office was expecting us, and we were ushered into a conference room and given quick introductions.

"What happened while I was on the road?" Duke demanded, apparently not catching the looks of irritation on the other agents' faces.

"We've gathered the money the hijacker requested," Special Agent in Charge Gary Floyd responded. "Agent Walker has handled all that."

He gestured to a smallish man with slicked brown hair and wire rim glasses. He sat at a table and had a knapsack full of cash in front of him.

I shook Walker's hand and introduced myself. "Call me Zack."

He smiled and held the grip a second longer than normal. "Ernest, but my friends call me Ernie." I couldn't be positive, of course. It's not like FBI agents wore colored hankies in their pockets while on the job, but I was pretty sure Ernie was gay like me.

"Enough with the goddamn small talk," Duke said. "What's going on with the case?"

"Please excuse Duke," I said. "His mama never taught him manners."

Everyone chuckled except Duke, who scowled at me instead.

"I got the money from different banks in the area," Ernie said. "Ten thousand unmarked twenty dollar bills. Most have serial numbers beginning with the letter L. That makes it easier to trace."

"I assume you've got a list of those serial numbers?" Duke asked.

"Yep." Ernie stood and closed the knapsack. "We're good to go, sir."

Floyd nodded and lifted the receiver in front of him. "Let him know his demands have been met."

I glanced at my watch. 5:24 p.m. Phil would be expecting me home any minute. I had no idea when I'd make it back. So much for the job transfer giving me more reliable hours.

Duke said, "Let's get to the airport, Pomeroy. I want to be there when the plane lands." He left the room without a word to anyone else.

"We're on our way, too," Floyd said as he grabbed the bag of money.

I tugged on Ernie's shirt sleeve. "It was nice meeting you. Maybe we'll run into each other again."

He smiled. "I'd like that."

In the car I said, "How have you survived this long in the Bureau without learning you attract more flies with honey than you do with vinegar?"

Duke snorted. "I don't need or want your opinion about how I do my job, Pomeroy."

"Suit yourself."

At the airport we were directed to the room that housed everyone handling the situation. In addition to some Seattle area agents, the airline president, the airline's Seattle operations manager, and an FAA official were present.

The plane landed and the pilot followed all of the hijacker's instructions, which included taxiing to an isolated, brightly lit section of the tarmac. He then had the pilot extinguish the lights in the cabin.

"This guy's no idiot," I murmured. "He's stopping the snipers from taking a shot."

Duke crossed his arms and watched the scene. "You're right, as much as I hate calling a criminal smart."

Al Lee, the operations manager, delivered the knapsack of money and the parachutes to a stewardess via the rear stairs of the plane. A few minutes later passengers slowly exited the plane.

"Get them all isolated immediately," Duke barked as if the other agents had no idea what they were doing.

"Make sure the hijacker isn't hiding among them," I added.

Duke peered at me, his eyebrows raised. "I'm surprised you thought of that."

I shrugged. "I'm not a total moron." I cringed inwardly, hoping he didn't think I was calling *him* a moron. Duke quickly refocused back on the situation, obviously not caring about my opinion.

As the refueling took place and everyone deplaned and was identified—35 passengers and two stewardesses—Duke and I continued to survey the plane. At 7:40, the 727 took off with the hijacker, pilot, copilot, a third stewardess, and a flight engineer still on board.

"Let's go interview our witnesses," Duke said in a commanding voice, and I followed closely behind to the security department.

"We've got the two stewardesses in separate offices," a security officer told us. "Alice Hancock is right here." He gestured to a room just a few steps away. "We put Florence Schaffner down the hallway in the only other available room."

"You take Schaffner," Duke grunted and stalked off.

I gazed at his back and wondered why Duke was such a jerk. And why wouldn't we want to interview each witness together to make sure we didn't overlook anything?

A guard interrupted my thoughts saying, "I'll show you the way." When we were out of Duke's earshot he leaned close and whispered in my ear, "I figured he'd take Hancock, since she was closer. I wanted you to talk to Schaffner. Her story is much more interesting."

"Why me?"

He scrunched his face. "Because that dude is a knucklehead. You're okay, though."

I snorted. "Thanks."

Florence Schaffner was young, I guessed in her mid-twenties, with short dark hair in a simple wedge cut teased to give it height, then liberally slathered with industrial-strength hairspray. Her hands trembled and there were tears in her eyes.

I grabbed a chair and sat in front of her. "I'm Special Agent Pomeroy, Miss Shaffner. Everything's going to be okay. Can you tell me what happened?"

She sucked in a breath, wiped her cheeks, and began to talk. "It started when a guy handed me a note."

"What did the note say?"

"I don't remember exactly, but it was something like 'I have a bomb in my briefcase. I will use it. You are being hijacked.' I know for sure it contained the words 'No Funny Business.'"

"Go on, ma'am."

"When he first gave me the note, I thought it probably contained a lonely guy's phone number so I didn't read it. Just dropped it into my purse. When I walked by again, he stopped me, leaned forward, and said I should look at the note and that he had a bomb. I showed it to Alice, and we went to the pilot."

"Then what happened?"

"When I went back to him he had put on dark sunglasses and moved to the window seat. I sat next to him and asked if I could see the bomb."

"Did he let you?"

"Yes." She paused. "He opened the briefcase quickly but I saw a large battery and eight red cylinders coated with red insulation."

"You noticed all that in just a few seconds?"

She shrugged. "I knew it would be important."

"I'm amazed you kept your head about you."

A single tear dripped down her face. "I was terrified, but I was also concerned about my passengers."

"Then what happened?"

"He took back the note and had me tell the pilot to circle until his demands were met."

"He wanted two hundred thousand and four parachutes, right?"

"He was more specific," she answered. "He said the money had to be in negotiable American currency and all twenties. The parachutes were to be two primary and two reserve. I thought he was going to take a prisoner, maybe me."

"Wow, that must have been very frightening." I reached across the table and gave her shoulder a squeeze. She managed a tearful half-smile. "You're okay though, and you did a nice job handling this man." I sat back in my chair and leaned my elbows on the table. "So, Miss Shaffner, he actually said the words *negotiable American currency?*"

"Yes, I remember because it struck me as odd."

She was right. It was a weird choice of words. Most people, Americans at least, wouldn't say it that way unless they were in a different country.

"So you got a good look at him?"

"Yes, I've already talked to a sketch artist. He was white, middle-aged, and didn't have an accent."

"Was he wearing gloves?"

She nodded.

"Do you know his name?"

"His ticket said Dan Cooper. "Tell me what else you noticed."

"He wore a dark suit and tie, kind of like yours. He was calm and polite. Nothing like the crazy guys who've hijacked planes in the past."

"He wasn't angry at all?"

Florence shook her head. "He was well-spoken and never rude or mean. He even ordered a bourbon and water, paid his drink tab and insisted I keep the change."

"The hijacker gave you a tip?" I frowned.

"Yes, I was astonished, too. This guy's stealing two hundred grand, and he insisted I have a dollar tip."

The man was nothing like any other criminal I'd dealt with or heard of. I continued to talk to Florence Shaffner, but didn't find out anything further.

After twenty-five minutes, Duke interrupted our conversation. "You got anything? I didn't get much."

I raised a finger to Duke, asking him to wait, and returned to my witness. "It was a pleasure speaking to you, Miss. If you think of anything more, please call me." I handed her my business card.

"Thank you, Agent Pomeroy."

I stood and left the room "You're not going to believe what I got from her."

He fumed as I filled him in, but said nothing, though I was sure he wanted to vent and rant. I didn't boast or remind him of what I'd said earlier. I didn't need to; he knew he had no one to blame but himself.

We located the sketch artist and got a look at the drawing. White male, mid-forties, between five-ten and six-foot tall. Around 170 to 180 pounds. Dark hair, eyes possibly brown. Heavy smoker. There was nothing extraordinary about the man. No scars or birthmarks. Nothing special except that he'd just hijacked a plane and got away with a couple hundred grand.

A few minutes later we were ordered to join Special Agent Gary Floyd and the other local agents in the situation room at the airport.

Floyd recapped what they had learned. "While the plane was being refueled, Cooper told the crew he wanted to go to Mexico City via a southeast course. The plane was to fly at the lowest possible airspeed. The landing gear was to remain down and the cabin stay unpressurized. He was also specific about what degree the wind flaps should be lowered. The pilot informed Cooper that a second refueling would be necessary before entering Mexico, and they agreed on landing in Reno, Nevada.

"After takeoff, Cooper ordered stewardess Tina Mucklow to go to the cockpit and stay there. Around 20:00 hours a warning light went on in the cockpit indicating the rear stairs had been activated. According to the pilot, at 20:15 hours there was a quick and unexpected upward shift in the aircraft's tail section."

"What does that mean?" I asked. "Most likely that Cooper jumped, but we can't be sure. The crew has been instructed to remain in the cockpit, just in case. We don't want to anger Cooper or risk anyone's lives." "So what are we going to do now?"

Floyd said, "Let's continue with the plan to land in Reno. We'll find out then if Cooper's still there."

I glanced at my watch—8:30 p.m. "What's the ETA?"

"Between 22:00 and 22:30 hours," Floyd said.

That meant waiting around for two hours. I turned to Duke. "I hope you aren't planning on driving to Reno."

"I wish." He shot me an annoyed glance. "We wouldn't be there in time."

"Besides," I said, "if Cooper did jump, we'd be better off trying to find where he landed."

Duke snapped his fingers and pointed at me. "You're not as dumb as you look. We can use the time to do just that."

We returned to the Seattle office and he instantly ordered someone to get him maps of Oregon and Washington.

Ten minutes later, Duke and I had maps spread out on a table to mark off an area where Cooper could've landed.

I said, "The wind makes it nearly impossible to narrow the search down to a smaller area. We'll just have to get as many crews out there as possible to check basically everywhere."

"The woods are going to make it difficult. That's a lot of forest land. It'd be easy to miss him. The forest canopy adds to the difficulty."

I sat down on a small couch and leaned my head back. I was exhausted but afraid to fall asleep.

"Go ahead and take a catnap, Pomeroy," Duke said. "I'll wake you up."

I eyed him suspiciously. "You wouldn't just take off and leave me behind?"

"Nah. You got some good ideas. I thought I was going to have to train you. But you're not a doofus like other newbies."

I gave him a thumbs up. "Thanks." I scooted down so my head rested on the back of the couch and within a few seconds I was out.

I FELT LIKE I'D only slept a couple minutes when Duke shook me awake, but it had been more than an hour.

"The plane's fifteen minutes out of Reno, he said. Everybody's gathering in the conference room."

"Give me a minute to wake up and I'll join you. Save me a seat."

He grinned and left the room. I sat up, stretched, yawned and scratched my balls just like I did at home. Damn, Phil had to be worried about me. Or furious. Most likely both. When I stood, my bladder reminded me I'd drunk numerous cups of coffee and it was time to let it out.

I located the bathroom, walked up to the piss trough, pulled out my cock, and let it go. The door opened and Ernie walked in, strode up next to me and whipped it out. I was almost certain he was queer now. Straight guys normally tried to make a space between you and them and attempted not to make their privates visible. Ernie wasn't shy in the slightest. I kept my eyes forward at first, but felt his gaze on me. I glanced over and we made eye contact before he peered down at my cock and smiled. Fair play called for me to do the same, so I did. He had a thick one, rather impressive, in fact.

The different head took over, and I desperately wished I could drop to my knees. What stopped me wasn't my boyfriend at home—we'd always had an open relationship—but we were at work.

"Damn, different time and place," Ernie murmured.

I knew exactly what he meant. "Yeah."

He leaned in close. "If you ever have free time in Seattle, there's a bar called The Double Header. Great drinks and private enough to be out without worry."

I winked, shook off my prick and put it away. "Thanks for the tip." I washed my hands and splashed some water on my face before going into the conference room. Duke sat near Floyd and had indeed saved me a chair, even though I'd been joking earlier.

"Anything new?" I asked Duke after I sat.

He shook his head. "We may not know anything right away. Depends how long the crew there wait before going into the cabin."

"Got it." I stretched my legs and interlocked my fingers behind my head.

"So, Pomeroy, you got a girlfriend?" Duke asked.

My eyes went wide and I froze for a second. "Uh, no I don't."

"A single man. That's good, makes it easier. My wife was never able to handle the strange hours."

"You're married?" He wasn't wearing a ring.

"Divorced," he said. "Five years now."

"Any kids?"

Duke nodded. "She's sixteen. They live in Kansas. I don't see her often. The job makes it hard."

As much as I wanted a career, I never wanted to sacrifice my personal life to such an extent that I was alone forever. I loved Phil; we'd been together since high school. He'd moved with me to New York after I finished at the FBI Academy and knew the score about having to keep our relationship a secret.

My being gone for months at a time was one of the reasons we'd agreed to an open relationship. We both accepted that there was a risk of falling in love with someone else, but we'd managed to stick it out. Together we had even invited a third into our bed. It didn't work for everyone, but it had for us. So far, anyway.

At 10:15 p.m. the phone rang and Floyd answered it.

"Floyd here." He made an affirmative sound, pressed a button, and put the receiver down. "Agent Wells, you're on speakerphone."

"The plane has landed, and so far we've heard nothing from the hijacker. The back stairs are still open. The team has surrounded the plane and they're preparing to board. Hold on, they're going in."

There was a collective hush in the room as if everyone was holding their breath.

"More officers are entering the plane," Wells added.

A minute felt like an hour as we waited.

"Okay, they're coming out. There are a couple people who appear to be the flight staff. I don't see…wait. Okay, I just got a signal saying that Cooper is not on the plane. Repeat, the hijacker isn't on the aircraft. Holy shit, he actually jumped. In the dark."

Wells continued nattering for a few minutes before ending the call.

Floyd wiped his forehead. "Okay, gentlemen, I don't have to tell you how important this is. We have to find this man and get the money back. We will be working with the Portland FBI Office and every other law enforcement agency in both states."

Duke stood. "Pomeroy and I have a good idea where he might have landed. We're thinking around Mount St. Helens, southeast of Ariel and near Lake Merwin."

I rose to stand next to Duke. "I'd say focus on Clark and Cowlitz Counties."

"Okay then, sit down. This is how we're going to do it." Duke and I plopped down in our chairs, and Floyd leaned forward, putting his palms on the table. He outlined the search plan, which included agents and officers on foot and in helicopters, and separated us into teams. Duke and I were assigned together and were to meet up with other Portland officers. He asked Duke to be the liaison between the two offices, but Duke turned it down.

"Pomeroy would be a better choice. He's a bit easier to get along with."

Several agents snickered and someone murmured, "A recently castrated bull is easier to get along with than you."

Duke scowled but bit his lip and relaxed in his chair.

"Can you handle the job, Pomeroy?" Floyd asked.

"Yes, sir."

DOZENS OF SEARCH PARTIES assembled with four to eight men in each group. They spent thousands of man-hours looking for any sign of Dan Cooper, who, thanks to a mistake on the part of a reporter, was now being called D.B. Cooper.

Duke and I, along with Agents Childress, Jurgens, and Oliphant, went door-to-door, talking to people, searching houses, farmhouses, outhouses, and even an illegal whorehouse.

The powers that be went so far as to have patrol boats on Lake Merwin and Yale Lake.

And nothing was found. Absolutely nothing. No parachute, no money, no Cooper.

Donaldson ordered us back to Portland Saturday evening. After a brief relay of information he told us to go home, get some rest and return on Monday, ready to work our asses off again.

"You did good, Pomeroy," Duke said as we walked to the parking lot. By the time I turned around to thank him, he was in his car and revving the engine. I waved and I know he saw me, but I got nothing in response.

I STUMBLED INTO OUR three-bedroom house, wanting nothing more than to take a shower and sleep. Phil must have heard the door open. He dashed from the living room, wearing only a pair of shorts. He was still as hot as he'd been in high school. He was a few inches shorter than me, with a flat stomach and almost hairless body. He wasn't out of shape, but as an accountant he spent most of his time at a desk poring over paperwork and using a typewriter.

"Hi," I whispered.

"You look exhausted."

"I am."

He stepped forward, pulled me into his arms, and embraced me tightly. It felt damn good and I fought back tears. The adrenaline and lack of sleep were hitting me in a major way.

"I love you so much, Phillip Smalley." I buried my face in his neck and inhaled his scent.

"I love you, too, Zachary Pomeroy."

"I'm so sorry. I would've called but—"

"Shush, we can discuss it later." He sniffed my hair and made a gagging sound. "You need a shower, hon. You are ripe."

He took my hand, and led me to the bathroom, stripped me, turned on the water, and guided me under the stream before slipping out of his shorts and joining me. Phil rinsed me down then shampooed and washed my hair. It felt so good not to have to think and to have my man take care of me.

Chapter 2

"SO HIS NAME *WASN'T* D.B. Cooper?" Phil asked as we ate lunch naked in bed. I'd awakened to his mouth on me and we'd made love first in bed and then again in the shower. Then I filled him in on the case as much as I could.

"I'm sure neither was his real name, but he claimed his name was

Dan Cooper." I took a bite of the peanut butter and jelly sandwich.

"Why does that sound familiar?"

I was about to ask for clarification when it hit me that I *did* recognize the name. As a kid I collected comic books. I wasn't an avid buyer but I still had a small collection of a couple hundred.

Jumping to my feet, I brushed the crumbs from my body and asked, "Do you know where my comics are?"

Phil scrunched his eyebrows, "The closet in the extra bedroom. Why?"

Without answering, I tore from one room to the other, slid open the wood panel doors and pulled out the box. My collection was eclectic because I tended to buy whatever caught my attention. Several issues each of Spider-Man, Batman, and Superman. Marvel Super-Heroes number 18 with some group called the Guardians of the Galaxy. Ah, there it was. "Holy shit, Phil, check this out." I showed him a comic book with the title Dan Cooper. It showed a man in a jet giving a thumbs up.

He grabbed it from my hands and flipped through the pages. "Where did you get this?"

"Dad brought it back from a business trip in Canada." I continued searching through my collection and found two other Dan Cooper comics, one of which showed the hero jumping out of an airplane.

"What do you think it means?"

I set the Cooper issues aside and lay down on the bed. "I'm not sure. I need to think about it."

He grinned and crawled up my body, kissing everywhere as he did so. "Do you realize we haven't christened this room yet?"

"Is that so?" I shot him a mischievous grin. The extra bedroom was, technically, Phil's room. As far as everyone else was concerned, he and I were roommates. We had a few personal things of his in there to help with the charade. I wasn't happy with the deception. I loved Phil and wanted to shout it from the rooftops, but the climate we lived in didn't make it possible.

"Whatcha thinking?" Phil asked between kisses.

"How much I truly love you," I said honestly. "I hope you know that, even when I don't call, I'm thinking about you all the time."

He curled up next to me, and I wrapped my arm around his shoulder. "Yeah, babe, I know you love me. I never doubt that. I get angry when I don't hear from you. Then I get sad. But I will never question how you feel for me, or how I feel about you."

"So you've forgiven me for not calling?" I cocked an eyebrow and glanced down at him.

Phil chewed on his bottom lip for a moment before nodding. "For the most part. I would appreciate a ring if you're going to disappear for more than a few days."

"I couldn't figure out how to do that this time. I'll find a way."

"Good." He went up on an elbow so we were eye-to-eye. "One more stipulation."

"Yes?"

"Every homecoming has to be like this one, okay?"

I pulled him close to me and rolled on top of him. "You mean having lots of sex?"

He nodded and beamed.

My love for Phil was different now. More emotional. Not any less carnal though. I desired him so much it consumed me. I hadn't experienced that with any other man.

"You're beautiful, Phil. So goddamn gorgeous. I can't believe you're mine."

"Well, I am. All yours."

"I want you to be *all* mine," I said before I'd thought it out. I mean, it'd been on my mind, but I'd been scared of bringing it up. I instantly regretted saying it and wished I could turn back time just a few seconds.

"You *don't* want an open relationship anymore? Is that what you're saying, Zack?"

"Maybe this isn't the best time."

We were lying in bed, basking in the afterglow of our passion. I hoped I hadn't spoiled it.

"Tell me what you're thinking." His voice was taut but softened when he added, "Please?"

"Yes, fine. I don't want you to be with other guys. But I know it was what we agreed to years ago. Because I'm gone all the time and you never knew when I'd be back. It's been working so we should just leave it as is. If it ain't broke, don't fix it."

He playfully slapped my face. "Stop babbling, Zack, and look at me."

I focused on his eyes and noticed the smile stretching from ear to ear.

"I want that, too. Just you and me. No one else. It was fine before and it probably kept us together. But now... I don't think we need to be open. Maybe a threesome here and there, but only with both of us there. I've been meaning to bring it up but wasn't sure what your reaction would be."

"Really? You don't want to be screwing around with anyone else?"

He shook his head. "You good with that?"

"Definitely, babe, definitely."

Chapter 3

I ARRIVED AT WORK Monday morning with three comic books. Duke was at his desk so I went to him and tossed the comics at him.

"What the hell are these?"

"Look at the title."

He picked one up and examined it. His face lit up and he cocked an eyebrow. "Dan Cooper."

"Yeah, just like our suspect."

"It's interesting, Pomeroy, but I'm not sure how it could help."

I leaned against the corner of his desk as he shifted back in his chair. Pointing at the comics, I said, "These are from Canada. There hasn't been an American distribution. I think our suspect got his fake name from them. He may have even gotten the idea of jumping out of a plane from them."

"What's your point?"

"What if he's from Canada? It's not likely he would've seen these any other place."

"*You* have them, don't you? And you ain't from Canada?"

I waved a hand. "That's different. I just happened to have these in my collection. For him to pick his name from them he would've had to have more than a passing interest."

Duke tapped his chin. "Okay, yeah, that makes sense."

"There's something else that makes me believe that he's at least not from the U.S.."

"Go ahead."

"He specified the money be in negotiable American currency. Why would he do that unless he wasn't from here?"

"Okay, so let's say he is from Canada," Duke mused, "now what?"

I stood and paced a few steps. "I'm not sure, but it may help us narrow down any suspects we get. If we *ever* get any."

Duke rolled his eyes. "Are you kidding? The damn phone's been ringing off the hook with people claiming they've seen him or know him. He's their crazy uncle, or missing father. One old dude in his eighties claimed to *be* him."

"Should've known this would bring out the crackpots," I said. "But we have to look at them all, don't we? Can't miss the one that could be the real thing."

"That's on the list for today. We've got the most likely leads and we'll be driving around following up."

I sighed. "Wish I'd brought a Thermos of coffee."

Duke grinned and pulled one out of his desk drawer. "We'll stop at a great diner a few blocks from here. Their java is a helluva lot better than the swill the office has."

DUKE AND I SPENT ten hours a day for three weeks talking to dozens of people, and every lead went nowhere. That was the bad news; the good news was that Duke and I were actually getting along. We talked about our personal lives, which meant lying about my relationship with Phil. I told Duke he was a high school buddy who'd happened to need a roommate when I returned from being undercover.

On a Friday night, Phil and I were looking forward to a quiet evening reading and making love. We were going to hit an outdoor market the following day, buy fresh vegetables, fruits, and maybe even honey and some flowers, then make dinner for friends.

We were in the living room in nothing but our boxers when the doorbell rang.

"You expecting anyone?" I asked.

Phil shook his head without setting his book down. I got up and just about screamed when I looked through the peephole and saw Duke. I dashed back to the living room and yanked the book from Phil's hands.

"What the hell, Zack? You lost my place."

"It's Duke," I whispered. "My partner."

"Oh, hell."

We scrambled to the bedroom and quickly pulled on sweats and T-shirts.

"Should I answer the door with you?" Phil asked.

"No! That'll look suspicious. Just go sit on the recliner with your book."

He ran off while I jogged to the door just as Duke rang the doorbell again. I inhaled and opened the door.

"You *are* here," he said. "I was about to give up."

"Sorry. I was in my bedroom and my roommate is reading a book.

He gets so sucked in, a twister could come through and he wouldn't notice."

Duke cocked an eyebrow. "Am I interrupting anything?"

"Oh, no, of course not. Come in." He followed me to the living room where Phil had done as instructed and did his best to act surprised that we had a guest. He got up and said, "Hi, I'm Phil Smalley."

Duke introduced himself curtly and they shook hands. He viewed Phil for a second before turning to me. "Can we talk in private, Pomeroy?"

"Sure." I led him through the kitchen and to the small dining room where we had a card table set up. "Do you want to sit? Can I get you a cup of coffee?"

He shook his head. "I'm sorry about bothering you. I just had a thought about that last lady we interviewed."

"Sadie Craig?" She'd originally called insisting her former friend had to be D.B. Cooper. However, by the time we interviewed her, she'd changed her story.

"I'm sure she's hiding something. I want to interview her again."

"On Monday?" I asked hopefully.

He shook his head. "I'd like to surprise her tomorrow morning. That might spook her enough to be honest. I could do it by myself, but I figured it'd be better if it was both of us."

There went my plans for the outdoor market and time with Phil. "Sure. I didn't have any plans tomorrow morning. You think we'd be done by noon? I have a dinner party in the evening. Just a couple of friends."

He pursed his lips. "Yeah, we should be done by then. I'll write the report so you don't have to worry about it."

"Sounds like a good deal to me."

After a solid handshake, Duke glanced at me and asked, "I gotta take a piss. You mind if I use your bathroom?"

"Of course not." I led him back to the living room and pointed down the hallway. Second door on the right."

I watched as he went past the bathroom, instead opening the third door—the extra bedroom.

"Oh, you did say the second door, didn't you?" He blushed, found the right room and entered.

I dared to peer at Phil, who was staring at me, wide-eyed.

"What's going on?" he mouthed.

I shrugged.

Duke was in the bathroom only a few minutes but it felt more like an hour. Him being in my personal space definitely made me nervous. Finally, he emerged, said he'd pick me up at nine a.m. and left.

I breathed a huge sigh of relief when I watched him pull out of my driveway.

"Sorry about the plans for tomorrow." I dropped to my knees in front of Phil and laid my head in his lap.

"Don't worry, I understand." He massaged my scalp as he ran his fingers through my short hair. "That man is intimidating. He scared the hell out of me."

"Welcome to my world."

I WAS DRESSED AND ready way before nine Saturday morning, not wanting to give Duke any reason to come inside again. When I spotted him pulling up, I was out the door in a flash.

He gave me a nod of recognition as I climbed into the car, but he ndidn't speak. It wasn't totally unlike him to be quiet, but we'd been building a rapport and I'd gotten used to conversation.

He had a Thermos of coffee and I reached for it, but he stopped me. "Sorry, didn't bring an extra cup."

"Oh, okay. No problem. I'll survive."

After several minutes of silence he cleared his throat and spoke. "There's a reason I don't get to know the people I work with. I don't want to know about their personal lives or what they do when they're not on the job. I wish I hadn't come by your place because now I know something I really, really wish I didn't."

My chest tightened and it took effort to breathe. Was he talking about what I thought he was? This was my worst fear. Being found out. Being exposed. The damage it could do to my career.

"I liked you, Pomeroy. I did. Thought you had good instincts. But this…" He shook his head.

I had to try to convince him he was wrong, even if he was spot on. "I'm not sure what you're talking about, Duke."

He scowled at me and I instantly stopped talking. The man was not happy.

"Don't think I'm stupid, Pomeroy. I'm many things but a moron isn't one of them." He gripped the steering wheel so hard his knuckles turned white. "You and your… roommate…were acting nervous when I showed up. Thought maybe a girl was there and you were having a two-fer or something. Fuck, I wish that's what it was."

"Duke, listen—"

Another glare cut me off.

"I peeked into that bedroom for a reason," he said. "It was obvious no one sleeps in there."

"Phil's a clean freak."

"The closet doors were open. There were no clothes."

I rubbed my left temple; I had a headache coming on.

"The bathroom, which I assume is the one Phil should be using, didn't have any toiletries. No toothbrush or comb or deodorant. Nothing. Stuff like that might fool your family, but not an FBI agent, especially not one who has been on the job as long as I have."

Shit, I hadn't thought about any of those things. Of course, we didn't have much straight company. Any friends who came over were either gay or knew Phil and I were a couple. Phil didn't talk to his family and my dad was too sick to visit.

"You're a pansy, ain't ya, Pomeroy? A fucking cocksucking faggot." There was no doubt about his feelings now.

"Yes, I'm gay, but I don't see how it matters."

He snapped his head around to face me. "You think it doesn't matter? That's like saying I just found out my partner likes to bugger dogs or little girls but it shouldn't matter."

"There's a big difference between going after kids or animals and being queer."

He shook his head. "I don't agree. Not at all."

There was obviously no talking him out of his beliefs. His mind was set. All I could do was deal with the fallout.

"What're you going to do? If you tell Donaldson, my career is dead."

"I don't give a fuck about your career. But I do care about my job. I don't want your stink rubbing off on me. If I spill the beans about you there'll be splashback. Everyone will think I knew about it or was one of your butt buddies."

Well, that was somewhat good news. An ounce of relief washed through me, but it wasn't going to be great working beside a man who hated my lifestyle.

Duke said, "I have to work with you, right now, but as soon as I can I'll cut ties. While we're together we should work separately as much as possible. I don't want you touching me or anything of mine, you got it?"

"Yes, sir."

"Don't talk to me unless you have to. And so help me God,

Pomeroy, if you ever hit on me I will split your head open."

Why did so many straight guys think we queers wanted them? Duke was definitely not my type. Not even close. Someone into Daddies might like him, but that wasn't me. That was another argument I wouldn't win so I assented to every rule he came up with.

My career wasn't dead, but it was teetering on the precipice. I had to tread carefully or I'd end up filing papers in some dark basement.

Our visit with Sadie went well despite my new anti-partnership with Duke. She admitted she thought her friend, David Campbell, could be D.B. Cooper. He had been a civilian employee on an airbase loading cargo onto planes. That fit with the knowledge the hijacker had possessed regarding how planes worked. We would have to investigate further.

Duke dropped me off at 11:30 and didn't say a word when I said good-bye.

This was not going to be easy. Not at all.

PHIL AND I HAD four friends over that night: Willie and his boyfriend Terry; along with Bobby; and Maureen, the requisite fag hag.

Willie had been one year ahead of us in high school and had gotten us into bars and adult stores with the help of fake IDs. He'd been with Terry now for about three years. Bobby was several years older than the rest of us. Phil and I had slept with him a couple times, and though we'd stopped sleeping together, we remained good friends. Maureen had been Phil's friend in high school, as well as his girlfriend for a short time.

After dinner, we sat around the living room shooting the shit.

"I heard about this D.B. Cooper case," Maureen said. "Are you involved, Zack?"

"I can neither confirm nor deny," I said. "But I have been following it in the papers."

Bobby finished off another glass of scotch. "I read something in the paper about some sort of connection to the Dan Cooper comics."

I tried to keep my expression neutral.

"What about the Dapper Dan books?" Bobby asked. Raising an eyebrow, I shot him a questioning glance.

He poured himself more scotch and took a sip. "You know who Dapper Dan is, don't you?"

"Never heard of him," I said.

"He's one of those gay pulp action heroes, a takeoff of Dan Cooper.

Dapper Dan is a spy who always gets his man, if you know what I mean."
He winked.

Gay pulp novels were cheaply made books with homosexual characters.
Most had explicit scenes and were more pornography than anything else,
but some had actual plots. Some were good, some were decent, and some
were nothing more than masturbation material.

"Are you saying you've actually read these books, Bobby?" Willie
asked.

"Hey, now I ain't a total moron," Bobby complained. "I didn't do the
reading, but this guy I screwed a couple times read them to me between—""

"Whoa," Maureen moaned. "I don't want to hear about your sex life."

Bobby waved a hand in her direction. "Jealous?"

I asked, "Do you know where they're sold?"

He shrugged. "Probably at Club Baths down in Vaseline Alley."

VASELINE ALLEY CONSISTED OF several blocks of gay bars and
gay-owned businesses, all anchored by the bathhouse, a triangle-shaped
building wedged between Stark and Burnside. I'd been to that area of town,
of course, but that particular bathhouse hadn't been in use when I'd lived
here before.

I wasn't exactly relaxed when I entered the building and headed toward
the shelves of books. There were dozens of them with titles like *Mid-Town
Queen, My Purple Winter, Song of the Loon,* and *Train Station Sex.* Most
of the covers featured images of half-naked men. I searched the shelf and
didn't find a single Dapper Dan. Reluctantly, I approached the man at the
counter.

"Can I help you?"

"I'm looking for a specific book," I said softly. "Dapper Dan."

"There weren't any on the shelf?"

I shook my head.

"Then you're outta luck."

I turned to leave, when he spoke again.

"Wait a minute, buddy. I forgot I just got two boxes of books. Let me
go check."

I leaned against the counter and waited, taking a little enjoyment in
watching the men walking around. Some were completely nude while
others had towels wrapped around their waists. Most were good looking,
but Phil was still the only man I wanted.

When the guy returned he had three books in his hand. "It's your lucky
day, fella."

He handed me the novels and I examined them: *Dapper Dan and the Surprised Stiff; Dapper Dan meets Horatio the Hornblower; Dapper Dan Behind Bars.*

"I'll take them." I handed over the money and was out of there as quickly as possible.

"DID YOU FIND THE books?" Phil asked when I returned home.

I went into the living room. "Three of them. Not sure how many there are."

Phil stood behind me as I scanned *The Surprised Stiff.* I found a sex scene on page four and it was very erotic. I got hard and I was sure Phil had too, judging by the way he ran his hands through my hair.

In my perusal, I noticed Dapper Dan often used the term "No Funny Business." The stewardess, Florence Shaffner, had reported that Cooper used that exact phrase while on the plane. Not that the saying wasn't popular, but it was another correlation. Dapper Dan also used the hanky code and always had a blue one in his right rear pocket, indicating he was a bottom. Boy, was he! In the novel, he took a man with a twelve incher and didn't flinch.

When I'd gone to bars looking to meet a guy, I always wore a blue hanky on the left to show I was a top. When Phil and I had gone out together looking for a third we would wear gold ones on the left to indicate we were a couple and wanted someone to join us for some naked fun.

Phil and I pored through the books and didn't go to bed until almost three a.m. We were both exhausted but had sex before going to sleep.

I WOKE EARLY THE next morning and couldn't get back to sleep so I read another of the books. Despite my gut telling me there was a connection, I couldn't draw a logical conclusion. The author was listed as Novae DeNiron, obviously a fake name. If Cooper was a fan of these novels, he was most likely queer. Would Duke even consider looking into these leads? Or would he blow me off?

Chapter 4

I WAS IMPATIENT TO talk to Duke when I arrived Monday morning, but I wanted to follow up on a hunch before approaching him.

I didn't have a desk yet because once the Cooper case was over, Donaldson wasn't sure where he was going to assign me. Mostly I sat at whichever empty desk was near Duke's. However, now I wanted privacy so I went to the basement where the records were kept and found an available desk and phone.

After looking up a number, I dialed and hoped she would answer.

"Hello?"

"Is this Tina Mucklow?" Tina was the stewardess who'd stayed on the plane after Cooper released everyone else. Unfortunately I hadn't been the one to interview her.

"Yes. Who is this?"

"Special Agent Zachary Pomeroy with the FBI. I have a few questions."

"Of course. How can I help?"

"Can you confirm for me that the hijacker used the term 'No Funny Business' once or twice?"

"Yes, he said it many times. I'd say at least seven or eight."

My heart started to race. I asked, "Once the hijacking started, you were the only one who saw him standing, is that correct?"

"Yes, when I was heading to the cockpit, I saw him putting on the parachute."

"By chance, did he have a hanky in his back pocket?"

"I'm not sure. No… wait. He did. I only saw it briefly."

"Do you remember the color or which back pocket?"

She paused. "Blue. Right side."

Bingo!

"Thank you so much, Tina." I hung up and examined my notes.

Was it just coincidence Cooper used a gay character's signature phrase *and* wore a blue hanky in his right rear pocket? I could see there being one coincidence, but two? No way. And who should I inform? It was critical that we have a complete profile on the hijacker including his sexuality. We wouldn't be looking for a wife and kids, but a boyfriend or lovers. We should be looking at gay bars and bathhouses and other such establishments.

I sucked in a deep breath and slowly exhaled. I doubted Duke would take me seriously, but I had to try. If he rejected my theory, I'd go over his head and talk to Donaldson. Then I would wait for the shit to hit the fan.

Back upstairs I located Duke and leaned against the corner of his desk. When he looked up at me he scooted the chair back a foot, giving himself space to avoid the gay cooties, I guess.

I said, "I have some information that might be helpful."

He crossed his arms. "Go ahead."

I laid out my findings regarding the Dapper Dan books, the use of the term 'No Funny Business,' and the hanky.

"What the hell is a hanky code? Never mind. I don't want to know."

"If I'm right and Cooper is gay, then this could be an important part of his profile."

Duke rose but still kept his distance. He flexed his fists like he was itching to punch me. "Just because you're queer, Pomeroy," he whispered so no one around us would hear him, "doesn't mean everyone else is."

I sighed. "I'm not saying *everyone* else is, just him."

"When you're a hammer everything looks like a nail."

"What does that mean?" I glared at him.

"Just something my pops always said. I think that 'cuz you're a fag, you want to find other fags so you don't feel alone. Birds of a feather and all that. It don't matter how many other perverts you find, it don't make what you do right."

"This is about our case, not my life choices."

"Drop it, Pomeroy." He started to walk away.

"No!"

He froze, then turned to face me again. "What did you say?"

"I said no. I'm not going to drop it. I want to show Donaldson what I've found."

Duke lifted an eyebrow. "Is that so?"

I nodded and prepared for further argument. Instead, Duke shrugged. "Okay, let's go."

I followed him to Donaldson's office and tried to get my nerves under control. He knocked, then entered.

"How can I help you?" Donaldson asked.

"Pomeroy here has a theory about Cooper." Duke flopped down in a chair in front of Donaldson's desk but I remained standing. "I don't agree with him, but I wanted you to make the final decision."

Donaldson pursed his lips and peered at me. "Very well. Go ahead, Agent Pomeroy."

I cleared my throat. "We've already discussed the theory that the hijacker was a fan of the Dan Cooper comics. I think he also read a series of novels that were a take-off of those comics. They're called Dapper Dan, and the character is also an action hero. He uses the term 'No Funny Business' just like Cooper did."

"I've never heard of these novels," Donaldson said.

Duke snorted. "Good thing, too."

My boss examined Duke for a moment before turning his attention back to me. "Who writes these Dapper Dan books?"

"The author is someone named Novae DeNiron. Phenix Publishing out of San Diego."

"Why haven't I heard of these books?" Donaldson asked.

"They're written for a…select audience." I paused. "They're gay pulp novels. Written for gay men, with explicit sex scenes."

Donaldson's face blanched. He recoiled as if he'd been slapped. "Books for fags? What the hell? How did you find these books?"

Duke looked at me with a smirk.

"I have a gay friend. He'd heard about the Dan Cooper comics and told me about the books."

"You spend time with a *queer*?" He gave me a sideways glance as if having a gay buddy made you gay as well.

"He's an old friend," I said. "I don't see him often." I hated lying, but revealing my private life to Donaldson wouldn't do anybody any good. Especially me.

"I don't see how any of this matters," Donaldson said.

"Sir, I believe Cooper is gay. I think it's a significant part of the profile."

Donaldson scratched his neck. "You think he's a fag strictly based on these…disgusting books?"

"There's one more thing. One of the witnesses said he wore a blue hanky in his right back pocket."

"Is that supposed to mean something?"

"Yes, sir." I paused and wiped the beads of sweat from my forehead. "In the gay community there's such a thing as the hanky code. At bars and such they wear different colored handkerchiefs so other men know what they like to do."

Donaldson looked really confused. "What they like to do? You mean sexually? How many different things are there?"

"Well, according to my friend, Dapper Dan wore a blue hanky on the right side and that, uh, means…that he's submissive."

"I don't understand."

"He likes to get fucked," I blurted out.

My boss put a hand to his mouth like he was going to puke. Duke, meanwhile, looked like the cat who ate the canary.

"Your theory is…ridiculous," Donaldson finally said. He

reached behind him and pulled out a handkerchief. "I carry a yellow one for allergies. Is that supposed to mean I want a guy to suck my dick?"

I shook my head and stifled a laugh. I wasn't about to tell him if he showed up at a gay bar with a yellow hanky he'd end up being the recipient of golden showers.

Duke beamed with arrogance. "I told him his idea was worthless."

"Worthless and disgusting," Donaldson added.

I stood tall and clasped my hands behind my back. "If Cooper is gay, there are different leads we can follow."

Donaldson came around the desk and stopped just inches from my face. "There is no way in hell this hijacker was queer. No nelly would have the balls to pull this off."

Donaldson seemed to realize how close he was to me and backed away saying, "Any homo would be too worried about his panties riding up his ass. He wouldn't have asked for money—he would've asked for boys to sodomize."

"Sir, please—"

"No, I won't even consider the thought. Cooper was a real man, a smart man. Not some disgusting pansy. Homosexuals simply aren't intelligent enough to pull this off." He glanced at Duke.

"I tried to tell him," Duke said.

I shot him an icy glare, and Duke just smirked in return.

"I don't think Pomeroy is ready for such a big case," Duke said. "Maybe his time in organized crime messed him up."

Backstabber! I couldn't believe what I was hearing. "I'm sorry, sir," I said. "I'll drop this angle and focus on other aspects of the case."

Donaldson paced and shook his head. "No, I think Duke is right. I expected too much from you. Besides, it's good to learn other aspects of the Bureau."

I started to argue but Donaldson raised a hand to stop me.

"I'm going to move you to the Evidence Department. Agent Nelson has been asking for help."

Chapter 5

THREE YEARS LATER, DONALDSON was gone, and I was back in the field after proving myself quite handily in the Evidence Department. Phil and I were doing well, and I'd even arranged a few days off to go to

Seattle. We went to Seattle and did the touristy things like Pike's Market and the Space Needle. On the second day of our trip, I remembered the bar Ernie Walker had recommended so long ago—The Double Header. Phil was up for it, so around nine p.m. we grabbed a cab and went to the club.

The Double Header was a decent place with low lights and music soft enough you could talk and loud enough to dance to. It was a busy night and it was nice to relax and be myself. Phil loosened up enough for me to drag him onto the dance floor.

"This is nice," I whispered in his ear as we swayed to the music.

"It's turning me on."

I pressed my hips closer to show him I was feeling the same way.

"There's a private back room where guys get frisky," he said. "I want you to take me back there."

"Hell, yeah."

With my hand in his, he pulled me toward the door that led to the dark room. I halted when I spotted a face I recognized.

"Hold on, Phil," I said.

He sighed but followed me to the table.

"Ernie?" He glanced up and I saw that it was indeed my old pal from the Cooper investigation. "Hey, man," I said, "long time no see."

Ernie looked startled when he recognized me.

"Agent Pomeroy, what are you doing here?" He bounded to his feet and looked around, as if someone was going to bust him.

"My boyfriend and I wanted to check this place out, since you recommended it." I pulled Phil close to me and wrapped an arm around his shoulder. "Phil Smalley, this is Agent Ernie Walker."

They shook hands, but Ernie couldn't seem to meet my eyes. Why was he so skittish?

Phil squeezed my hand. He was in a hurry to get in the back room. I gave him my "Be patient" look and asked Ernie, "How have things been?"

He shrugged. "Oh, you know. Same old, same old."

"Heard you worked the bank robbery case a few weeks back and cracked it within a day."

This time he raised a single shoulder. "Yeah. Yeah, I did." The front door opened, and a scruffy man came in. Ernie's eyes widened, then his shoulders slumped as if he was a teen caught jacking off by his mom. The guy gazed around the room, spotted Ernie, and came right toward us.

"Hey, babe." He gave Ernie a kiss on the cheek then turned to check us out. "Are these friends of yours?"

"Yes," Ernie said. "This is Agent Zack Pomeroy and his boyfriend, Phil. You should remember me talking about Zack. We worked on the D.B. Cooper case together."

They exchanged a glance. I wondered what it meant.

"It's nice to meet you," I said and extended my hand.

"Oh, sorry, I forgot my manners. I'm Donavon Fields."

Donavon was muscular with thick biceps and pecs. He'd pulled his messy, long hair into a ponytail. He also had a mustache and a long beard. He looked strangely familiar.

"Have we met before?" I asked.

He and Ernie exchanged another look. "I don't think so. I've only lived in Seattle a couple years. Before that I was in Kansas."

Scratching my neck I said, "There's something about your face." In my time in organized crime I'd known people from all over the country, including the sunflower state. He didn't have a hint of a Kansas accent. In fact, there was almost a hint of Canadian in his voice. Ernie laughed but it seemed forced. "Well, we need to get going. We're meeting friends."

"Yes," Phil interjected. "We have plans of our own." He began pulling me away before I could object.

"Nice seeing you again, Ernie." I waved at the couple. "And it was a pleasure meeting you, Donavon."

Chapter 6

JUST OVER A YEAR later I heard that Ernie Walker had been killed in a shoot-out with a kidnapper. He'd managed to protect the victim, a young boy, but had taken a bullet to the brain. I arranged for time off so I could attend the funeral.

A dozen agents and FBI personnel showed up, which didn't seem like very many. I'd been to other funerals where practically everyone in the whole office had attended. I thought Ernie would have been well liked in the Bureau, but maybe not.

The only family in attendance was a brother and sister-in-law. I wondered if that was all his family or if he had been rejected by the others.

The brother was delivering the eulogy when I glanced off to the side and saw Donavon Fields. He was standing next to a column in the church, clearly doing his best to hear the words without being seen.

When the funeral was over I approached Donavon.

"Why were you hiding?" I asked.

He hung his head. "No one knew about me. Why would they? No one knew Ernie was gay. I didn't want anyone asking how I knew him or risk having my emotions making people wonder. There's no need for me to damage his reputation."

Made sense, but it still sucked. I couldn't imagine Phil having to conceal himself at my funeral.

"How're you doing?"

He snorted. "How do you think? I just lost the love of my life, and I can't properly mourn him."

I patted his shoulder but didn't know what to say. "Can I buy you a beer later? I didn't know Ernie well, but you can talk to me about him. It might help."

He shook his head. "Thanks, but I'm not in the mood to socialize."

"Please reconsider, Donavon. I think you need someone to talk to."

His shoulders slumped. "Okay, yeah, I'd like that. I'll meet you at The Double Header in a couple hours."

"Sounds good. See you then."

I waited an hour and a half before going to the bar. When he hadn't arrived an hour later I knew he wasn't going to show. Maybe he'd figured out my desire to chat with him wasn't entirely based on Ernie's death. I still had a nagging feeling I knew him from somewhere and had hoped to figure it out.

I grabbed a napkin and did a quick sketch of him so I wouldn't forget what he looked like. Later, I packed it carefully in my suitcase and returned to Portland.

Chapter 7

OVER THE YEARS THERE were few new findings in the D.B. Cooper case. Several people claimed to be the hijacker or insisted some relative was. There were some possibilities, but nothing could be proven.

The biggest event happened in 1980 when Brian Ingram, an eight-year-old boy, found three packets of what were thought to be the ransom cash. Ultimately, the discovery didn't answer any questions. Every theory contradicted another one. And, once again, nothing could be proven. Just one more enigma in the case I was sure would never be solved.

Chances were the hijacker hadn't survived. Most of the money had never been found, despite serial numbers being available. If the funds had been spent in the US, they would've been flagged somewhere. It didn't make sense for the man to have lived but not spent a dime.

I retired in 2003, at age sixty, after a career full of both successes and failures. Despite the hundreds of other cases I worked, the D.B. Cooper case remained the one I fixated on the most. Phil didn't mind my obsession and often gifted me with Dan Cooper comics or Dapper Dan novels. One of those presents were what finally brought everything together.

I'd been searching for a copy of *Dapper Dan and the Case of the Burglarized Billionaire* to complete my collection for years. Dapper Dan was called in to investigate a break-in at a mansion belonging to a wealthy man named Ward Finley. Of course the rich guy was queer, and he and Dan screwed on the satin sheets of his four-poster bed. The only thing stolen was cash from Finley's safe—over a million dollars.

Finley's assistant, who Dan also screwed, had kept meticulous records of the serial numbers, and everyone was sure that would lead to the thieves. But it didn't. Months later, after numerous sex scenes, the cash still hadn't been located. Dan solved the case by figuring out the assistant had used fake serial numbers on the accounting record and he, in fact, was the thief. Dan took him to jail, but not before some more screwing.

The idea of fake serial numbers stuck in my head as an interesting prospect, one I hadn't seen in a story before. After putting the book down, I picked up that day's newspaper and worked on the word jumble, one of my favorite things.

I wrote down the possible words on a separate sheet of paper but my mind traveled back to Ernie and his boyfriend, Donavon. I scribbled down their names as well and noticed the word *nova* could be made out of Donavon's name. I glanced at the front of the Dapper Dan novel to check out the author's name—Novae DeNiron.

Following a hunch, I crossed the letters N-O-V-A out of Donavon's name. Then an E from Ernie. That made Novae. A D from Donavon and the second E from Ernie for De left Niron, which the remaining letters in the two names finished off. Novae DeNiron was an anagram of their names. What an incredibly huge coincidence.

Was it possible that Ernie and Donavon had written the Dapper Dan novels? And if they did, why did it matter? My brain wasn't in the best shape of its life, but I was far from senile. It had to mean something, but what?

I literally palmed my forehead when it hit me. The goddamn serial numbers. In the novel the assistant had provided incorrect numbers so the money could be spent without worry. And Ernie Walker had handled the ransom money during the hijacking. He'd collected it from the banks and recorded the serial numbers. He could've written down incorrect numbers. He must have. Hell, he'd spelled out his plan in the book.

I jumped to my feet, almost spilling my coffee in the process. "Phil, where's that folder of mine?"

He rolled his eyes and set his book down. "Could you be more specific? You have hundreds of folders, though I don't know why. You're supposed to be retired."

I rubbed my forehead. "When Ernie Walker died, I went to his funeral and talked to his boyfriend."

"Oh, yeah, Dominic, right?"

"Donavon Foster. No, Fields. Donavon Fields. I sketched a picture of him, remember?"

"No, but these days I forget where I put my keys."

Trying not to be too exasperated by my husband's memory loss, I dashed to my office and tore open one of the four-drawer filing cabinets. I scrambled through file after file until I found what I was looking for—the sketch of Donavon. I scanned it into my computer and opened it with Photoshop. I wasn't a whiz at the program but I'd found it useful more than once.

I erased the hair on Donavon's head and face then trimmed his cheeks to see what he would've looked like skinnier. Holy shit! That's why I recognized him. On the Net, I found the drawing of D.B. Cooper and examined it side-by-side with mine of Donavon. They were almost identical. Any differences in features could be attributed to my lack of skills. But I knew I was right.

Donavon Fields was D.B. Cooper, and Ernie Walker had been his accomplice. I had no doubt, but there was no way I could prove it. I couldn't go to anyone in the FBI; I'd be a laughingstock, if not to my face, at least behind my back. Being gay was no longer a big deal, and I'd come out in 1990, but I was certain that my sketch of Donavon wouldn't be taken seriously.

My resolve to prove my theory didn't diminish. I searched for Donavon Fields but found nothing. That wasn't surprising. He'd probably changed his name. So I put out searches for the names Ernie, Walker, Donavon, Fields, Dan, Cooper, and any possible combination thereof.

And last week there was a hit. A man in a Montreal nursing home by the name of Dan Walker. I couldn't be sure it was Donavon, but a look at his records made it very likely. The file only went back a decade, as if he hadn't existed before then. The picture at the nursing home was of an old, wrinkled man with little hair. The photo wouldn't have helped anyone else identify him, except that I recognized those close-set, piercing brown eyes. I had no doubt that Dan Walker was Donavon Fields, and Donavon Fields had been Dan "D.B." Cooper.

After all these years, I had my man.

ON MY FLIGHT TO Montreal, I read Dan Walker's medical file. He was a dying man. His heart was failing, and he was likely to pass within six months.

The nursing home, called Maison Amaryllis, was neat and quiet, but it smelled a little rank, like so many old folks homes did. The receptionist sent me back to room 32A, and I felt so much excitement that I almost wanted to run.

I found 32A and didn't even bother to knock. "How are you, Mr. Walker?" I asked as I strolled to his bedside. "Or should I call you D.B. Cooper?"

He was quiet for a second, then grinned a toothless smile. "Took you long enough to find me."

I shrugged. "What can I say? You were pretty smart."

"Not smart enough, apparently."

I grabbed a stool and sat near his bed. "I'm nothing but an old retired fool. Who would take me seriously?"

He took deep breaths, which turned into a coughing fit. When it subsided he said, "I figured if anybody was gonna catch me, it would be you. Takes a queer to think like a queer, right?"

"In 1971," I said, "no one thought a homosexual could pull off a hijacking. You'd think the story of Sonny Wortzik would've made them re-think that idea, but I guess not." Sonny Wortzik had attempted to rob a bank so his male lover could have gender reassignment surgery. The story was made into a movie—*Dog Day Afternoon* starring Al Pacino.

"How'd you figure it out?"

I gave him the brief version, ending with reading the final Dapper Dan story and how I had pieced everything together. "Did I get everything right?" I asked when I was done.

He nodded. "Yup. You nailed it, Agent Pomeroy."

"Please, Donavon, call me Zack."

The ends of his closed lips turned up slightly. "Feels nice to hear my name again." He extended a hand and I gripped it. "Thank you."

"For what?"

"I'm actually grateful someone knows. I wouldn't want my secret to die with me." He paused to get his breath. "Are you going to arrest me?"

I snorted and squeezed his hand. "What would be the purpose?"

"It would make you famous. You solved the case of D.B. Cooper."

Shaking my head, I said, "I have no desire to be famous. I just want to spend my final years with the man I love. Anything else would take me away from him."

Donavon sighed. "I envy you that, being able to grow old with the love of your life. I miss Ernie every day."

"Why'd you do it? Did you need the money?"

"Nah. Ernie was frustrated with the Bureau at the time. He didn't feel they took him seriously, and he wanted to screw them over. For me, it was the thrill. But over time, being on the run ended up not being as much fun."

"I understand."

"I ran because of you."

I frowned. "Me?"

"After seeing you at Ernie's funeral, I was sure you would figure it out if I spent any time with you. I left Seattle and haven't been back since."

"What did you do with the money?"

He sighed and his face drooped. "Ernie and I were saving it to travel when he retired. He was going to quit, but he got promoted to field agent, which was what he'd always wanted. After he died, I spent the dough here and there just to live on. Now it's paying for me to live here. There's still a lot left. I'm donating it to a children's charity when I go."

I didn't know what to say. He'd gotten away with the crime of the century, but he had nothing to show for it. He'd lost the man he loved and spent decades on the run, always looking over his shoulder. That was no way to live.

"Will you come back tomorrow?" Donavon asked. "I'm about to doze off. I'd like to see you again."

"Sure." I nodded. "I'll be back."

On my way out, I gave my cell number to the nurse with instructions to call if anything happened. I rented a cheap hotel room and called

Phil to let him know I was staying the night.

Just past midnight, my cell rang, waking me from a deep sleep. I didn't know the number, but it was Canadian.

"Yes?" I mumbled.

"Is this Agent Pomeroy?"

"Yes, who is this?"

"I'm Georgette Irwin. I'm a nurse at Maison Amaryllis. You left instructions to call regarding Dan Walker."

"Did something happen?" My first guess was that he'd passed.

"Mr. Walker is gone."

"He's dead?"

"No. He's gone. As in he left and no one knows where he is."

"How the hell do you lose a ninety-year-old man on his death bed?"

"He left an envelope with your name on it."

"I'll be right there."

At the nursing home I got the story from Nurse Irwin. There are bed checks every two hours, but she was late to check on Donavon because another patient needed help. By the time she got to his room, he and all his belongings, were gone.

She handed me a sealed envelope with *Agent Pomeroy* scribbled on it. I opened it in private and read it.

> *Zack, thanks for coming. It was nice seeing someone from my past, especially someone who knew and liked Ernie. He liked you too, spoke of you often. Always said the four of us could've been friends if it weren't for, well you know.*
>
> *The story of D.B. Cooper is a national legend. I like it that way. The legend can live on, even if I don't.*
>
> *The final choice is yours, of course. You choose how it ends.*
>
> *Your friend, Donavon Fields aka D.B. Cooper.*

I put the note back in the envelope, stuck it in my back pocket and strode out the front door of Maison Amaryllis without a glance back. I returned to the hotel, got my stuff, checked out and flew home.

Phil didn't ask about what I'd learned. He was in the beginning stages of Alzheimer's and didn't even remember what the purpose of my trip had been.

I could've found Donavon. A dying man couldn't have gone far. But he wanted to die alone, so I would allow him his final wish. No one would ever know what actually happened to D.B. Cooper, not even me.

And I was fine with that.

My personal story was going to be different though. Phil would most likely precede me in death, so I'd probably die alone, but the difference between Donavon and me was that I'd lived a full life. I spent decades with the love of my life. I still had time with him and was going to enjoy every second of it.

And the legend of D.B. Cooper would live on.

ABOUT THE EDITORS

LORI L. LAKE has edited several anthologies including the Lambda Literary Award Finalist, *The Milk of Human Kindness: Lesbian Authors Write About Mothers and Daughters*; the Goldie Award Finalist, *Romance for Life*; and the Rainbow and Goldie Award-winning *Lesbians on the Loose: Crime Writers on the Lam*. She is the author of two collections of her own stories, *Stepping Out* and *Shimmer.* Lori has edited a great many novels and stories for various small presses. She teaches writing, runs an indie press, and enjoys coaching aspiring writers. She and her partner, Luca, (the chief cook and bottle washer) run writing retreats at Rockaway Beach on the Oregon coast. Lori was born in Oregon, spent 26 years in the snowy Twin Cities, and since 2009 lives in Portland, Oregon.

CHRISTOPHER HAWTHORNE MOSS is a long-time historical researcher and writer, author of several novels including 2014's *Beloved Pilgrim* and 2016's *A Fine Bromance*. A first book, *Loving the Goddess Within: Sex Magick for Women* was published in 1992, and a 25th anniversary edition will be issued in 2017. Christopher has edited and written for many history websites over the years. Under the previous name of Nan Hawthorne, he's researched, written, and edited hundreds of articles published on diverse topics such as disabilities, employment, GLBTQ history, small business, arts and crafts, nonprofit management, and transgender issues. Hawthorne is legally blind but says he "cannot sit still long enough to let that slow me down." With his long-time spouse and their doted-upon cats, he lives in the Pacific Northwest and spends time writing novels, researching early medieval England, and supporting authors in the indie book publishing industry. Christopher came up with the idea to collaborate with Lori to assemble this collection, and this is his first foray into editing an anthology.

CONTRIBUTORS' BIOGRAPHIES AND SELECT BIBLIOGRAPHIES
(Often augmented by the editors
because the contributors are far too humble)

Victor J. Banis

Victor J. Banis was born in Pennsylvania, reared in Ohio, and lived most of his adult life in California. He now resides in the shadow of the beautiful Blue Ridge Mountains in West Virginia. Long associated with the West Coast's first wave of gay publishing, his writing career began with the short story "Broken Record" in *Der Kreis* in 1963. His subsequent works span more than half a century, during which time he has published numerous short stories and poems and in excess of 200 books under various pseudonyms and in many genres: mystery, supernatural tales, gothic thrillers, romance, erotica, westerns, "campy" comedies, and memoir. In the introduction to the novel, *Longhorns,* Michael Bronski calls Victor's 1960s gay pulp novels "foundational" to gay literature. Publishers' Weekly has called him "a master storyteller," and many of his works have been critically acclaimed, including his memoir, *Spine Intact, Some Creases.* Recent works include The Deadly Mysteries Series from MLR Press, *Lola Dances* from Rocky Ridge Books, and *Longhorns*, excerpted here, which was published by The Avalon Publishing Group. A great number of the books listed below in his bibliography are now available in print and/or ebook under the name Victor J. Banis. Please visit Victor at his website: http://www.vjbanis.com.

Selected Bibliography
(All books by Victor J. Banis unless otherwise noted as a pseudonym)

The Affairs of Gloria (1964) by Victor Jay
The Why Not (1966)
The Man from C.A.M.P. (1966) by Don Holliday.
Color Him Gay (1966) by Don Holliday
The Watercress File (1966) by Don Holliday
The Son Goes Down (1966) by Don Holliday
Gothic Gaye (1966) by Don Holliday
Good-bye My Lover (1966) by J. X. Williams
Rally Round the Fag (1967) by Don Holliday
The Gay Dogs (1967) by Don Holliday

Holiday Gay (1967) by Don Holliday
Stranger at the Door (1967) by Don Holliday
Three on a Broomstick (1967) by Don Holliday
Sex and the Single Gay (1967) by Don Holliday
Blow the Man Down (1968) by Don Holliday
Brandon's Boy (1968) by Jay Vickery
Man into Boy (1968) by Jay Vickery
Gay Treason (1968) by J. X. Williams
Homo Farm (1968) by Victor Jay
Friar Peck and His Tale (1969), published anonymously
The Gay Haunt (1970) by Victor Jay
The Sword and the Rose (1975)
The Moonsong Chronicles (1981) by Jessica Stuart
A Westward Love (1981) by Elizabeth Monterey
San Antone (1985)
Spine Intact, Some Creases: Remembrances of a Paperback Writer (2004), edited with an introduction by Fabio Cleto
That Man from C.A.M.P.: Rebel Without a Pause (2004), edited with an introduction and an interview by Fabio Cleto
Tales from Camp: Jackie's Back (2006) by Victor J. Banis, with an interview and checklist by Drewey Wayne Gunn
Avalon (2007) by V. J. Banis
Longhorns (2007), with a foreword by Michael Bronski
Come This Way (2007), edited by Lori L. Lake with a Foreword by Drewey Wayne Gunn
Life and Other Passing Moments (2007), edited by Robert Reginald
Drag Thing; or, The Strange Case of Jackle and Hyde: A Novel of Horror (2007)
Lola Dances (2008)
Angel Land (2008)
Deadly Nightshade: Deadly Mystery #1 (2009)
Deadly Wrong: Deadly Mystery #2 (2009)
Deadly Dreams: Deadly Mystery #3 (2009)
Deadly Slumber: Deadly Mystery 4 (2009)
Deadly Silence: Deadly Mystery #5 (2010)
Dead of Night: Deadly Mystery #6 (2011)
A Prayer for the Dead: Deadly Mystery #7 (2016)
Color Him Gay: The Further Adventures of The Man from C.A.M.P. (2016)

228

Jane Cuthbertson

A longtime student of history, Jane Cuthbertson retired from U.S. Government service several years ago, and now takes full advantage of her free time to travel whenever she can. She has visited monuments, battlefields, churches, ghost towns, and many other places with interesting stories to tell, including Independence Rock and its still-vibrant connection to the Oregon Trail. On the rare occasions she is at home, her mind wanders off into worlds only it can find, and she tries to write it all down. This is her first published story. Please visit Jane at her website: http:///www.janecuthbertson.com.

Nann Dunne

A professional editor for more than thirty-five years, Nann Dunne began writing fiction twenty years ago and has published five novels, a short story collection, and a nonfiction book, as well as short stories in a number of anthologies. As of June 2015, she got her rights back for three novels and republished them under her own imprint, Golden Keys Publishing, while continuing to write new works. Nann's nonfiction book, *Dunne With Editing: A Last Look At Your Manuscript* (a must-have book for all authors), is available via her website and at Amazon.com. Nann edits for a variety of presses, and she's also available for freelance editing. An important election was looming in the United States when Nann wrote "Stepping Toward Freedom." Many young women showed no enthusiasm for voting, and Nann felt they needed to be informed about the suffrage movement of the past, where women were met for years with derogatory insults, physically demanding marches, and actual life-threatening incidents before they were able to procure the vote. She hopes her story conveys that and has some impact on future elections. Nann is just finishing up the final volume in her historical Hearts, Minds, Souls trilogy. Please visit Nann at her website: http://www.nanndunnebooks.com.

Selected Bibliography
True Colors: Book 1 of the TJ & Mare Series [with Karen Surtees] (2000)
Staying in the Game (2001)
Many Roads to Travel: Book 2 of the TJ & Mare Series
        [with Karen Surtees] (2002)

The War Between the Hearts: Book 1 in the Hearts, Minds,
    Souls Series (2005)
The Clash Between the Minds: Book 2 in the Hearts, Minds,
    Souls Series (2009)
Dunne With Editing: A Last Look at Your Manuscript (2010)
Door Shaker and Other Stories (2012)
The Peace Between the Souls: Book 3 in the Hearts, Minds,
    Souls Series (2017)

Jess Faraday

An amazing writing stylist who regularly writes across genres, Jess Faraday specializes in historical fiction and moonlights as the mystery editor for Elm Books. She's garnered some serious recognition for her work. Her novel *Fool's Gold* won a Rainbow Award for Best Gay Historical, and she was shortlisted for a Lambda Literary Award for *The Affair of the Porcelain Dog*. She has edited several award-winning short story collections including *Death and a Cup of Tea* (one of Foreword Review's top Indie mysteries of 2015), *Undeath and the Detective* (finalist for a Silver Falchion Award for Best Multi-Author Anthology), and *Fae Love*, which won an Aspen Gold Reader's Choice Award. When not staring at a computer, Jess enjoys martial arts, the outdoors, and quilting. She lives in California with her family and a small zoo. Please visit Jess at her website: https://jessfaraday.com.

Selected Bibliography
The Affair of the Porcelain Dog: Ira Adler Mystery #1 (2011)
The Left Hand of Justice (2013)
Turnbull House: Ira Adler Mystery #2 (2014)
Fool's Gold: Ira Adler Mystery #3 (2015)
The Strange Case of the Big Sur Benefactor (2015)
The Kissing Gate, a novella in an anthology entitled
    Blades of Justice (2017)

Sue Hardesty

Sue Hardesty was born and raised on the Arizona desert where she was either following her prospecting mom around to watch her pick-axe rocks, or riding horses with her dad to help him trail cattle. After college she moved to the Phoenix area and taught English and Communications. Retirement took her out of the desert heat, and she moved to the beautiful Oregon Coast where she and her partner of forty-plus years run their dog on the beach every morning and where she even takes time to write a little. In a long and varied career, Sue has been a bookstore owner, a book reviewer, a builder of houses, a proprietor of two bed-and-breakfast hotels, and a quiet force in the fight for LGBTQ equality and human rights. Please visit Sue at her website: http://suehardestybooks.com.

Selected Bibliography
The Butch Cook Book, edited with Nel Ward and Lee Lynch (2008)
*The Truck Comes on Thursday: A Loni Wagner Western Mystery
     Book One* (2011)
Panic: A Young Adult Novel of Desert Survival (2013)
*Bus Stop at The Last Chance: A Loni Wagner Western Mystery
     Book Two* (2014)
Taking The Low Road: A Loni Wagner Western Mystery Book Three (2017)

Judy M. Kerr

"Stamped Unnatural" is Judy Kerr's first published work. She lives in Minneapolis and is plugging away on a crime fiction novel, which will be the first in a series spotlighting a female U.S. Postal Inspector as the protagonist. Do you detect a theme in her writing? Judy retired from the U.S. Postal Service at the end of 2016 after 37+ years of service and has chosen USPS-related storylines and characters in honor of a venerable organization that has been such a huge part of her life. Please visit Judy at her website: http://www.judymkerr.com.

E.J. Kindred

E.J. Kindred is an Oregon attorney who would rather write fiction than contracts. She has been a transaction attorney in the computer industry for over twenty years and doesn't mind saying that wrestling with the finer points of intellectual property infringement indemnification isn't nearly as fun as it sounds. She's always loved to write, and in her youth spent more hours than she'll admit writing Star Trek scripts. Other than her first place entry in a short story contest long, long ago in a state far, far away, "The Other Marie" is E.J.'s first published work. Marie Equi was one of Oregon's first women doctors, a crusader for humane working conditions, an anti-war activist who spent time in San Quentin for sedition, and an unabashed lesbian at the turn of the 20th century. She is one of countless women whose stories have been all but lost, and E.J. was compelled to bring her back to life. In addition to writing, E.J. makes quilts, some of which she donates to local cat rescue groups for fundraising. When she's not sewing or writing or wrestling with contract terms, she spends time with friends and takes care of her cats, who take care of her in return. She is currently working on a mystery novel set in rural Oregon. Please visit E.J. at her website: http://www.ejkindred.com.

Lori L. Lake

Lori L. Lake is the author of twelve novels, two short story collections, and the editor of four anthologies. She she has won four Goldies, three Rainbow Awards, and the Alice B. Readers Award. She's known for her enjoyment of teaching and for sharing writing resources with both aspiring and published writers. Lori is co-publisher at Launch Point Press, has judged many small press and mainstream writing contests, and is a founding mother of the Golden Crown Literary Society. Long a supporter of human rights, women's rights, and civil rights, Lori was motivated to write the story in this collection because of her admiration for some of the unsung heroes of the 1960s civil rights struggle. Bayard Rustin was a major player in supporting the movement headed by Rev. Dr. Martin Luther King, and yet it's almost as if he's been lost to history. Lori lives in Portland, Oregon, to which she returned in 2009 after 26 years in snowy Minnesota. When she's not writing, you can find her teaching writing classes and running retreats or curled up in a chair reading at the home she now shares with her sweetie. She's currently working on a book about creativity for writers called *Sparking Creativity: Words of Wisdom for Your Writing Inspiration* and has discovered that being consistently creative is more difficult than expected. Please visit Lori at her website: http://www.lorillake.com.

Selected Bibliography
Gun Shy: Book 1 in The Gun Series (2001)
Ricochet in Time (2001)
Under the Gun: Book 2 in The Gun Series (2002)
Different Dress (2003)
Stepping Out: Short Stories (2004)
*The Milk of Human Kindness: Lesbian Authors Write about
        Mothers & Daughters* (2004)
Have Gun We'll Travel: Book 3 in The Gun Series (2005)
Romance For Life (2006)
Snow Moon Rising (2006)
Shimmer & Other Stories (2007)
Like Lovers Do (2011)
Buyer's Remorse: Book 1 in The Public Eye Series (2011)
A Very Public Eye: Book 2 in The Public Eye Series (2012)
Jump The Gun: Book 4 in The Gun Series (2013)
Eight Dates: A Romance (2014)
Lesbians on the Loose: Crime Writers on the Lam (2015)
*Time's Rainbow: Writing Ourselves Back Into American History
        - Volume I* (2016)
Adventures Unlimited (2017)
Gunpoint: Book 5 in The Gun Series (2017)
*Sparking Creativity: Words of Wisdom to Inspire Your Writing Craft
        —Book One in The Writer's Odyssey Series* (2018)
*Time's Rainbow: Writing Ourselves Back Into World History -
        Volume II* (2018)

Lee Lynch

Lee Lynch is considered a national treasure by many people who have been inspired by her long writing journey and the dogged determination she's displayed over the years. As a young woman in the 1960s, she wrote for *The Ladder,* the first nationally-distributed lesbian publication in the United

States which ran from 1956-1972. Over the years she has consistently published novels, essays, and stories for her lesbian audience, even when she earned very little compensation for her work. She has been writing the nationally syndicated column, "The Amazon Trail," since 1986, and a collection of these columns is available in *An American Queer: The Amazon Trail* as well as in the older book, *The Amazon Trail*. Lee is the namesake and first recipient of the Golden Crown Literary Society's Lee Lynch Classic Award for her stunning and pioneering novel, *The Swashbuckler*. A three-time Lammy finalist, other honors include the James Duggins Mid-Career Award, induction to the Saints and Sinners Literary Hall of Fame, and the Alice B. Readers Award. Originally from New York City, Lee lives in the Pacific Northwest with her wife Elaine Mulligan Lynch. The main character of the story in this anthology, Frenchy Tonneau, is from Lee's award-winning novel, *The Swashbuckler*. Frenchy pops up here and there in Lee's other books and stories. The other main character is Terri LoPresto, from Lee's first published story, which was released in the lesbian multicultural literary and art journal, "Sinister Wisdom." Now retired from her "day job," Lee focuses on writing, reflecting, inspiring a new generation of writers, and spending time with her wife. Please visit Lee at her website: http://leelynch6.tripod.com.

Selected Bibliography
Toothpick House (1983)
Old Dyke Tales (1984)
The Swashbuckler (1985)
Home In Your Hands (1986)
Dusty's Queen of Hearts Diner: Book 1 of the Morton River Valley Trilogy (1987)
The Amazon Trail (1988)
Sue Slate, Private Eye (1989)
That Old Studebaker (1991)
Morton River Valley: Book 2 of the Morton River Valley Trilogy (1992)
Cactus Love (1994)
Off the Rag (1996), edited by Lee Lynch and Akia Woods
Rafferty Street: Book 3 of the Morton River Valley Trilogy (1998)
Sweet Creek (2006)
The Butch Cook Book, edited with Sue Hardesty, and Nel Ward (2008)
Beggar of Love (2009)
The Raid (2012)
An American Queer: The Amazon Trail (2014)
Rainbow Gap (2016)

Kate McLachlan

Kate McLachlan is an award-winning author of lesbian fiction. Two of her inventive Rip Van Dyke time-travel novels have won Goldie Awards, and she was a finalist for a Lambda Literary Award in 2015 for her romantic novella, *Christmas Crush.* Her historical mystery, *Murder and the Hurdy Gurdy Girl,* was a finalist for a Goldie Award and a Rainbow Award. Her most recent novel, *Alias Mrs. Jones,* is a historical mystery set in Eastern Washington in 1902. After teaching in the public schools for well over a decade, Kate developed a case of temporary insanity and entered law school. All she really wanted to do was write stories but, despite the common misperception, legal briefs are not fiction. She now works as an Administrative Law Judge. In her spare time she writes fiction for the satisfaction it brings her and for the joy she hopes to bring to her readers. Kate lives in the Pacific Northwest with her wife, Tonie Chacon, who is also a writer. They have two dogs and two cats, but no parrot (yet). Please visit Kate at her website: http://www.katemclachlan.com.

Selected Bibliography
Rip Van Dyke: Book 1 in The Rip Van Dyke Time Travel Series (2010)
Rescue At Inspiration Point: Book 2 in The Rip Van Dyke
      Time Travel Series (2011)
Hearts, Dead and Alive (2012)
Murder and the Hurdy Gurdy Girl (2013)
Return of an Impetuous Pilot: Book 3 in The Rip Van Dyke
      Time Travel Series (2014)
Christmas Crush (2014)
Ten Little Lesbians (2015)
Alias Mrs. Jones (2016)

Jon Michaelsen

Jon Michaelsen is a writer of mystery, suspense, and thriller fiction where the main character or characters are gay. He discovered his love for mysteries early in life with The Hardy Boys and Nancy Drew mysteries. Through the years he discovered many diverse writers who have influenced his style of writing. Among them are mainstream authors David Baldacci, John Grisham, and Michael

Crichton and groundbreaking LGBTQ novelists such as Patricia Nell Warren, Michael Nava, and Felice Picano. A true southerner at heart, Jon was born near the banks of the Chattahoochee River in Columbus, Georgia. He has spent most of his life in Atlanta, where he remains today. He majored in English and Journalism at Gainesville College in north Georgia before finishing out his studies at Valdosta State College in Valdosta, Georgia. Jon's first novel, *Pretty Boy Dead,* in the Kendall Parker Mystery series, was published in late 2013 and selected as a Lambda Literary Award Finalist in Gay Mystery. The novel has been recently re-released by Lethe Press, which will also publish the second novel, *The Deadwood Murders,* in 2017. Jon lives with his husband of 30 years and four monstrous terriers. His interests include reading, binge-watching HGTV on the weekends, and long drives through the Blue Ridge Mountains. Jon loves to hear from his readers and always responds personally. Please visit Jon at his website: http://www.jonmichaelsen.net.

Selected Bibliography
Men: An Anthology of Erotica, (2008)
False Evidence (2012)
Authors Off the Shelf: An Anthology (2013)
Switch Hitter, written with Alex Morgan (2013)
Pretty Boy Dead: Book One in the Kendall Parker Mystery Series (2013)
Prince of the Sea (2015)
The Deadwood Murders: Book Two in the Kendall
      Parker Mystery Series (2017)

Christopher Hawthorne Moss

Christopher "Kit" Moss is passionate about historical fiction as a means for queer people to find their places in the human story. He has been a history freak for as long as he can remember, playing Robin Hood for hours as a child. Becoming an author of historical fiction has changed only one thing: he now regards each new book as a chance to know "a new group of friends." Kit wrote the early stories found in his first novel, *An Involuntary King,* with a friend at the tender age of 11. He has filled his imagination with kings and queens, bards, crusaders, riverboat gamblers, soldiers, and more. Now living in Seattle, Washington, with his long-time partner Jim and their two doted-upon cats, he involves himself as a voracious reader, writer of book reviews, and author of novels. He writes primarily for Dreamspinner Press and Harmony Ink Press, but is thrilled for any opportunity to share his stories. Severely visually impaired, he uses items of high technology to make him as prolific as any author. Please visit Christopher at his website: http:// authorchristophermoss.blogspot.com.

Selected Bibliography
An Involuntary King: A Tale of Anglo Saxon England,
      written as Nan Hawthorne (2008)
Where My Love Lies Dreaming (2013)
Beloved Pilgrim (2014)
Angel Eyes: A Gay Romance of the Mexican War (2015)
A Fine Bromance (2016)
Loving the Goddess Within: Sex Magick for Women,
      published in 1991 as Nan Hawthorne and re-edited and updated
      by Christopher Hawthorne Moss in the 25th anniversary
      edition (2017)

Patty Schramm

Patty Schramm is the Golden Crown Literary Award-winning co-editor (with Verda Foster) of *Blue Collar Lesbian Erotica.* Her first novel, *Souls' Rescue,* written under the pseudonym Pat Cronin, was a finalist for the GCLS Ann Bannon Popular Choice Award. Patty and Verda Foster have also co-edited *Women in Uniform: Medics and Soldiers and Cops, Oh My!* and, most recently, *Women in Sports: Sweaty, Sexy and Hot, Oh My!* After a 22-year career as a paramedic and firefighter, Patty retired due to injuries sustained on the job. Now, in addition to writing, editing, and working in IT to pay the bills, she's the Editor-In-Chief for Regal Crest Enterprises. Patty lives in the Netherlands with her wife, Sandra, and their much beloved furry-footed felines. Please visit Patty at her website: http://www.patcroninauthor.com.

Selected Bibliography
Blue Collar Lesbian Erotica (2008)
Souls' Rescue (2010)
Women In Uniform: Medics and Soldiers and Cops, Oh My! (2010)
Better Together (2014)
Reflections of Fate (2015)
Women In Sports: Sweaty, Sexy and Hot, Oh My! (2016)
Finding Gracie's Glory (2016)
Because of Katie (2017)

Ethan Stone

Ethan Stone's tagline is "Romance on the Edge." He doesn't write your typical Boy Meets Boy stories. Using a combination of love and suspense, he makes his characters work hard for their Happily Ever Afters. If they can survive what he puts them through, then they can survive anything. Ethan has been reading mysteries and thrillers since he was young. He's had a thing for guys in uniform for just as long. That may have influenced the stories he writes. He's a native Oregonian with two kids, one of whom has made him a grandfather three times over; even though Ethan is way too young for that. Please visit Ethan at his website: http://www.ethanjstone.com.

Selected Bibliography
In the Flesh: Flesh Series (2010)
Flesh & Blood: Flesh Series (2011)
Blood & Tears: Flesh Series (2011)
Wolf Moon (2011)
Transparency, written with Sara York (2013)
Zombie Boyz: Surviving Sin City, written with Daniel Kaine (2013)
Compromised: Uniformity Series (2013)
Damaged: Uniformity Series (2014)
Recruited: Uniformity Series (2014)
Subject 13 (2014)
Bartender, PI (2014)
Dirty (2014)
Tales of a Prison Bitch (2014)
The Beginning of the End (2014)
Vegas Hustle: Adam & Javi Series (2014)
Closing Ranks: Flesh Series (2015)

Small Claims (2015)
Past Tense (2015)
Muse: Love Vegas Style Series (2015)
Lies & Diamonds & Bears: Love Vegas Style Series (2015)
One More Time: Love Vegas Style Series (2016)
Hiding in Plain Sight: Adam & Javi Series (2016)
Being Taught (2016)
Starting Over (2016)
Confessions: Reno, PD Series (2016)
Wild Retaliation: Seaside Shifters Series (2016)
Wild Instincts: Seaside Shifters Series (2017)
Hacked Up (2017)
Hijacked Love: The Novel (2017)

PERMISSIONS

Made in the USA
Columbia, SC
02 July 2017